LaRose

ALSO BY LOUISE ERDRICH

NOVELS

Love Medicine

The Beet Queen

Tracks

The Bingo Palace

Tales of Burning Love

The Antelope Wife (1997;
revised editions, 2012, 2014)

Antelope Woman (2016)

The Last Report on the
Miracles at Little No Horse

The Master Butchers
Singing Club

Four Souls

The Painted Drum

The Plague of Doves

Shadow Tag

The Round House

STORIES

The Red Convertible:
New and Selected Stories,
1978–2008

POETRY

Jacklight

Baptism of Desire

Original Fire

FOR CHILDREN

Grandmother's Pigeon

The Birchbark House

The Range Eternal

The Game of Silence

The Porcupine Year

Chickadee

Makoons

NONFICTION

The Blue Jay's Dance

Books and Islands in Ojibwe Country

LaRose

Louise Erdrich

HARPER LUXE

An Imprint of HarperCollinsPublishers

Grateful acknowledgement is made to the editors of *The New Yorker,* where portions of this novel were published in slightly different form as "The Flower."

Nothing in this book is true of anyone alive or dead.

HarperCollins books may be purchased for educational, business, or sales promotional use. For information please e-mail the Special Markets Department at SPsales@harpercollins.com.

FIRST HARPERLUXE EDITION

ISBN: 978-0-06-246676-1

HarperLuxe™ is a trademark of HarperCollins Publishers.

Library of Congress Cataloging-in-Publication Data is available upon request.

16 17 18 19 20 ID/RRD 10 9 8 7 6 5 4 3

For Persia
and for every LaRose

For Persia

and for every LaRose

Contents

Contents

Two Houses
1999–2000

The Door

Where the reservation boundary invisibly bisected a stand of deep brush—chokecherry, popple, stunted oak—Landreaux waited. He said he was not drinking, and there was no sign later. Landreaux was a devout Catholic who also followed traditional ways, a man who would kill a deer, thank one god in English, and put down tobacco for another god in Ojibwe. He was married to a woman even more devout than he, and had five children, all of whom he tried to feed and keep decent. His neighbor, Peter Ravich, had a big farm cobbled together out of what used to be Indian allotments; he tilled the corn, soy, and hay fields on the western edge. He and Landreaux and their wives, who were half sisters, traded: eggs for ammo, rides to town, kids' clothing, potatoes for flour—that sort of thing.

Their children played together although they went to different schools. This was 1999 and Ravich had been talking about the millennium, how he was setting up alternate power sources, buying special software for his computer, stocking up on the basics; he had even filled an old gasoline tank buried by his utility shed. Ravich thought that something would happen, but not what did happen.

Landreaux had kept track of the buck all summer, waiting to take it, fat, until just after the corn was harvested. As always, he'd give a portion to Ravich. The buck had regular habits and had grown comfortable on its path. It would wait and watch through midafternoon. Then would venture out before dusk, crossing the reservation line to browse the margins of Ravich's fields. Now it came, stepping down the path, pausing to take scent. Landreaux was downwind. The buck turned to peer out at Ravich's cornfield, giving Landreaux a perfect shot. He was extremely adept, had started hunting small game with his grandfather at the age of seven. Landreaux took the shot with fluid confidence. When the buck popped away he realized he'd hit something else—there had been a blur the moment he squeezed the trigger. Only when he walked forward to investigate and looked down did he understand that he had killed his neighbor's son.

Landreaux didn't touch the boy's body. He dropped his rifle and ran through the woods to the door of the Ravich house, a tan ranch with a picture window and a deck. When Nola opened the door and saw Landreaux trying to utter her son's name, she went down on her knees and pointed upstairs, where he was—but wasn't. She had just checked, found him gone, and was coming out to search for him when she heard the shot. She tried to stay on her hands and knees. Then she heard Landreaux on the phone, telling the dispatcher what had happened. He dropped the phone when she tried to bolt out the door. Landreaux got his arms around her. She lashed and clawed to get free and was still struggling when the tribal police and the emergency team arrived. She didn't make it out the door, but soon she saw the paramedics sprinting across the field. The ambulance lurching slowly after, down the grassy tractor path to the woods.

She screamed some terrible things at Landreaux, things she could not remember. The tribal police were there. She knew them. Execute him! Execute the son of a bitch! she shouted. Once Peter arrived and talked to her, she understood—the medics had tried but it was over. Peter explained. His lips moved but she couldn't hear the words. He was too calm, she thought, her mind ferocious, too calm. She wanted her husband to bludgeon Landreaux to death. She saw it clearly. Though she was a small, closed-up woman who had never done harm in her life, she wanted blood everlasting. Her ten-year-old daughter had been ill that morning, stayed home from school. Still feverish, she came down the stairs and crept into the room. Her mother disliked it when she and her brother made a mess, threw his toys in heaps, dumped them all out of the toy box. Quietly, the daughter took the toys out of the box and laid them here and there. Her mother saw them and knelt down suddenly, put the toys away. She spoke harshly to her daughter. Can you *not* make a mess? Is it in you to *not* make a mess? When the toys were back in she started screaming again. The daughter took the toys out. The mother slammed them into the toy box. Every time her mother crouched down and picked up the toys, the grown-ups looked away and talked loudly to cover her words.

The girl's name was Maggie, after her great-aunt Maggie Peace. The girl had pale luminous skin and her hair was chestnut brown—it lay on her shoulders in a sly wave. Dusty's hair had been a scorched blond, the same color as the deer. He'd been wearing a tan T-shirt and it was hunting season, although that wouldn't have mattered on the side of the boundary where Landreaux had shot at the deer.

The acting tribal police chief, Zack Peace, and the county coroner, an eighty-two-year-old retired nurse named Georgie Mighty, were already overwhelmed. The day before, there had been a frontal collision at 2:30 a.m., just after the bars closed—none of the dead in either car were wearing seat belts. The state coroner was traveling in the area, and stopped at the reservation to expedite the paperwork. Zack had been struggling with this side of things when the call about Dusty came in. He paused to put his head on the desk before he called Georgie, who would persuade the coroner to stay a few more hours and examine the child so that the family could have an immediate funeral. Now Zack had to call Emmaline. As cousins, they'd grown up together. He was trying to hold his tears back. He was too young for his job, and anyway too good-hearted to be a tribal cop. He'd come over later on, he said. So Emmaline knew about it while her children were still at school. She'd come home to meet them.

Emmaline stepped to the door and watched her older children get off the bus. They walked toward the house with their heads down, hands flapping at the grasses as they crossed the ditch, and she knew they had also heard. Hollis, who'd lived with them since he was little, Snow, Josette, Willard. Nobody on the reservation gets a name like Willard and doesn't pick up a nickname. So Willard was Coochy. Now her youngest boy was stumbling down to meet them, LaRose. He was the same age as Nola's boy. They'd been pregnant at the same time, but Emmaline had gone to the Indian Health Service hospital. Three months had passed before she'd met Nola's baby. But the two boys, cousins, had played together. Emmaline put out sandwiches, heated the meat soup.

What happens now? said Snow, quietly watching her.

Emmaline's face was filling again with tears. Her forehead was raw. When she'd knelt to pray she'd found herself beating her head against the floor—and now fear was leaking out of her in every direction.

I don't know, she said. I'm going down to tribal police and sit with your dad. It was such . . .

Emmaline was going to say a terrible accident but she clapped her hands over her mouth and tears spurted down, wetting her collar, for what was there to say about what had happened—an unsayable thing—and Emmaline did not know how she or Landreaux or anyone, especially Nola, was going to go on living.

Minute by minute, a day passed, two. Zack came over, sat on the couch, running his hand over his brushy hair.

Watch him, he said. You gotta watch him, Emmaline.

At the time she thought he meant Landreaux was suicidal. She shook her head. Landreaux was devoted to his family and cared to the point of obsession about his clients. He was a physical therapy assistant, in training as a dialysis technician. He was also a personal care assistant trained and trusted by the Indian Health Service hospital. Emmaline phoned Landreaux's clients. There were Ottie and his wife, Bap. When she called the sweet old man named Awan, a terminal patient, and told his daughter that Landreaux would not be coming, the daughter said she'd take off work and care for her dad until Landreaux was back. Her father loved playing cards with Landreaux. Yet there was in the daughter's tone a note of tired unsurprise. Maybe Emmaline was paranoid—her nerves were buzzing— but she thought Awan's daughter hesitated and then nearly said the same thing as Zack. You gotta watch him. Emmaline told herself it was because they loved Landreaux, but later on she knew that was only part of it.

There was the short investigation, the sleepless nights before Landreaux was released. Zack took the key from Emmaline and put the rifle in the trunk of the car. After Landreaux walked out of the tribal police headquarters, Emmaline went with him, straight to the priest.

Father Travis Wozniak held their hands and prayed. He didn't think he would find the words, but they came. Of course words came. *Incomprehensible, His judgments. Unsearchable, His ways.* He'd had years of too much practice even before he became a priest. Father Travis had been a Marine. Or still was. BLT 1/8, 24th May. He had survived the barracks bombing in 1983, Beirut, Lebanon. The thick scars roping up his neck, twisting down in random loops, marked him on the outside and ran inside of him, too.

He closed his eyes, gripped their hands tighter. Went dizzy. He was sick of praying over the car accident victims, sick of adding *buckle your seat belts* to the end of every sermon, sick of so many other early deaths, ready himself to fall down on the floor. He wondered, as he did every day, how he could go on pretending to the people he loved. He tried to calm his heart. *Weep with those who weep.* Tears scored Emmaline's cheeks. The two kept pushing tears impatiently off their faces as they talked. They needed towels. Father Travis had both tissues and a roll of paper towels. He tore off squares. Two days before, he had done the same for Peter, though not Nola, whose eyes had been dry with hate.

What should we do? Emmaline asked now. How can things go on?

Landreaux began muttering the rosary, eyes shut. Emmaline glanced at him, but took a rosary from Father Travis and kept going. Father Travis did not weep, but his redhead's eyes were delicately pink, his lids lavender. The beads dangled in his grip. His hands were strong and callused because he moved rocks, hacked out brush, did general grounds work—it calmed him. There was a big woodpile behind the church now. He was forty-six—stuck—powerful, deeper, sadder. He taught martial arts, did Marine workouts with the God Squad teens. Or by himself. There were free weights behind the desk in a neatly graduated stack, and a bench behind the choirboy curtain. Landreaux sat silent after they finished. Father Travis had been through everything with Landreaux—the years sorting out boarding school, Kuwait, then wild years, through the drinking and after, straightening out through traditional healing, now this. In his life on the reservation, Father Travis had seen how some people would try their best but the worst would still happen. Landreaux reached over and gripped the priest's arm. Emmaline held Landreaux. They murmured another round of Hail Marys together; the repetition quieted them again. In the pause before they left, Father Travis had the feeling that there was something they wanted to ask him.

Landreaux and Emmaline Iron came to the funeral, sat in the back pew, melted out the side door before the small white casket was carried down the aisle.

Emmaline was a branchy woman, lovely in her angularity. She was all sticks and elbows, knobby knees. She had a slightly crooked nose and striking, murky green, wolfish eyes. Her daughter Josette had her eyes; Snow, Coochy, and LaRose had their father's, warm and brown. Emmaline's hair and skin were light but she tanned instantly. Her husband, darker, gave her babies a richly toasted color. She was a passionate mother. Landreaux understood after the babies were born he would come second, but that, if he hung tough, one day he would again be first in her heart. Driving home after they saw the priest, she kept her hand on his leg, gripping him hard when he shook. In the driveway, he put the car in park but kept it idling. The shadowy light cut their faces.

I can't go home yet, he said.

She cast her disturbing gaze on him. Landreaux thought of her at eighteen, Emmaline Peace, how in the beginning of their years that look of hers, if she grinned, meant they were going to go crazy together. He was six years older. They did some wild stuff then. It was confessed but not done with. They had this streak together, had to sober up in tandem. So she knew right now what was pulling him.

I can't make you come inside the house, she said. I can't keep you from what you're going to do.

But she leaned over, took his face in her hands, and placed her forehead on his forehead. They closed their eyes as if their thoughts could be one thought. Then she got out of the car.

Landreaux drove off the reservation to Hoopdance, turned in at the drive-up liquor store window. He put the bagged bottle on the passenger's seat. Drove the back roads until he saw no lights, pulled over, and cut the engine. He sat for about an hour with the bottle beside him, then he grabbed the bottle and walked into the icy field. The wind rattled around his head. He lay down. He tried to send the image of Dusty up into the heavens. He made fierce attempts to send himself back in time and die before he went into the woods. But each time he closed his eyes the boy was still ruined in the leaves. The earth was dry, the stars bursting up there. Planes and satellites winked over. The moon came up, burning whitely, and at last clouds moved in, covering everything.

After a few hours, he got up and drove home. A light shone dimly from their bedroom window. Emmaline was still awake, staring at the ceiling. When she heard the car crunch on dry gravel she closed her eyes, slept, woke before the children. She went outside and found him in the sweat lodge curled in tarps, the bottle still in its bag. He blinked at her.

Oh boy, she said, a handle of Old Crow. You were really going to blast off.

She put the bottle in the corner of the lodge, went in and got the children to the bus. Then she dressed LaRose and herself in warm clothing, took a sleeping bag out for her husband. As he warmed up, she and LaRose built a fire, threw tobacco from a special pouch into it, put grandfather rocks in it, made it hotter, hotter. They brought out the copper bucket and ladle, the other blankets and medicines, everything they needed. LaRose helped with all of this—he knew how to do things. He was Landreaux's little man, his favorite child, though Landreaux was careful never to let anyone know about that. As LaRose squatted so seriously on his strong, skinny bowlegs, carefully lining up his parents' pipes and his own little medicine bundle, Landreaux's big face began slowly to collapse. He looked down, away, anywhere, struck heavily by what had befallen his thoughts. When Emmaline saw him looking that way, she got the bottle and poured it out on the ground between them. As the liquor spilled into the earth she sang an old song about a wolverine, Kwiingwa'aage, helping spirit of the desperately soused. When the bottle was empty, she looked up at Landreaux. She held his gaze, strange and vacant. Right about then, she had her own thoughts. She understood his thoughts. She stopped, stared sickly at the fire, at the earth. She whispered no. She tried to leave, but could not, and her face as she set back to work streaked over wetly.

THEY MADE the fire hot, rolled in eight, four, eight rocks. It took them extra long to keep heating the rocks in the fire and also keep opening and shutting the flaps, the doors, and bringing in the rocks. But it was all they had to do. All they could do, anyway. Unless they got drunk, which they weren't going to do now. They were past that, for the time being.

Emmaline had songs for bringing in the medicines, for inviting in the manidoog, aadizookaanag, the spirits. Landreaux had songs for the animals and winds who sat in each direction. When the air grew thick with steamy heat LaRose rolled away, lifted the edge of the tarp, and breathed cool air. He slept. The songs became his dreams. His parents sang to the beings they had invited to help them, and they sang to their ancestors—the ones so far back their names were lost. As for the ones whose names they remembered, the names that ended with iban for passed on, or in the spirit world, those were more complicated. Those were the reason both Landreaux and Emmaline were holding hands tightly, throwing their medicines onto the glowing rocks, then crying out with gulping cries.

No, said Emmaline. She growled and showed her teeth. I'll kill you first. No.

He calmed her, talked to her, praying with her. Reassuring her. They had sundanced together. They talked about what they had heard when they fell into a trance. What they had seen while they fasted on a rock cliff. Their son had come out of the clouds asking why he had to wear another boy's clothing. They had seen LaRose floating above the earth. He had put his hand upon their hearts and whispered, *You will live.* They knew what to make of these images now.

Gradually, Emmaline collapsed. The breath went out of her. She curled toward her son. They had resisted using the name LaRose until their last child was born. It was a name both innocent and powerful, and had belonged to the family's healers. They had decided not to use it, but it was as though LaRose had come into the world with that name.

There had been a LaRose in each generation of Emmaline's family for over a hundred years. Somewhere in that time their two families had diverged. Emmaline's mother and grandmother were named LaRose. So the LaRoses of the generations were related to them both. They both knew the stories, the histories.

OUTSIDE AN isolated Ojibwe country trading post in the year 1839, Mink continued the incessant racket. She wanted trader's milk, rum, a mixture of raw distilled spirits, red pepper, and tobacco. She had bawled and screeched her way to possession of a keg before. The noise pared at the trader's nerves, but Mackinnon wouldn't beat her into silence. Mink was from a mysterious and violent family who were also powerful healers. She had been the beautiful daughter of Shingobii, a supplier of rich furs. She had also been the beautiful wife of Mashkiig, until he destroyed her face and stabbed her younger brothers to death. Their young daughter huddled with her in the greasy blanket, trying to hide herself. Inside the post, Mackinnon's clerk, Wolfred Roberts, had swathed his head in a fox pelt to muffle the sound. He had fastened the desiccated paws beneath his chin. He wrote an elegant, sloping hand, three items between lines. Out there in the bush, they were always afraid of running out of paper.

Wolfred had left his family behind in Portsmouth, New Hampshire, because he was the youngest of four brothers and there was no room for him in the family business—a bakery. His mother was the daughter of a schoolteacher, and she had educated him. He missed her and he missed the books—he had taken only two with him when he was sent to clerk with Mackinnon: a pocket dictionary and Xenophon's *Anabasis*, which had belonged to his grandfather, and which his mother hadn't known contained lewd descriptions. He was just seventeen.

Even with the fox on his head, the screeching rattled him. He tried to clean up around the fireplace, and threw a pile of scraps out for the dogs. As soon as he walked back inside, there was pandemonium. Mink and her daughter were fighting the dogs off. The noise was hideous.

Don't go out there. I forbid you, said Mackinnon. If the dogs kill and eat them, there will be less trouble.

The humans eventually won the fight, but the noise continued into darkness.

Mink started hollering again before sunup. Her high-pitched wailing screech was even louder now. The men were scratchy-eyed and tired. Mackinnon viciously kicked her, or kicked one of them, as he passed. She went hoarse that afternoon, which only made her voice more irritating. Something in it had changed, Wolfred thought. He didn't understand the language very well.

The rough old bitch wants to sell me her daughter, said Mackinnon.

Mink's voice was horrid—intimate with filth—as she described the things the girl could do if Mackinnon would only give over the milk. She was directing the full force of her shrieks at the closed door. Part of Wolfred's job was to catch and clean fish if Mackinnon asked. Wolfred walked out, heading down to the river, where he kept a hole open in the ice. He could tell how bad it was and crossed himself. Although of course he wasn't Catholic, the gesture had cachet where Jesuits had been. When he returned, Mink was gone and the girl was inside the post, slumped in the corner underneath a new blanket, head down, so still she seemed dead.

I couldn't stand it another minute, Mackinnon said.

✢

THAT NIGHT, LaRose slept between his mother and his father. He remembered that night. He remembered the next night. He did not remember what happened in between.

They burned the rifle, buried the ammunition. The next day, they decided to take the same path the deer had taken. The land between the two houses was dense with wild raspberry in an area cleared by the fire of lightning that had struck an oak. The heat had moved beneath the bark of the tree, flowing from the twigs and branches down into the roots, until the tree could not contain it all and burst. The fire in the roots had killed the smaller trees in a circle but the rain had contained the fire after that. About a mile outside the mark of that tree, Emmaline's mother had been raised. In the old time, people had protected the land by pulling up survey stakes. A surveying man had even gone missing. Although the lake at the center, deep and silent, had been dragged and searched, his body was never found. Many tribal descendants had inherited bits of land, but no one person had enough to put up a house. So the land stayed wild and fractionated, except for

160 acres, an original allotment owned by Emmaline's mother, who had signed it over intact to her daughter. The woods were still considered uncanny. Few people besides Landreaux and Peter hunted there.

The trees were vivid, the sumac scarlet, the birch bright yellow. Sometimes Landreaux carried his son, sometimes he handed LaRose over to Emmaline. They didn't speak or answer LaRose with words. They held him close, stroked his hair, kissed him with dry, trembling lips.

Nola saw them cross the yard with the boy.

What are they doing here, what, what, why are they, why are they bringing . . .

She ran from the kitchen and shoved Peter in the chest. It had been a calm morning. But that was over now. She told him to make them get the hell off their property and he told her that he would. He stroked her shoulder. She pulled violently away. The black crack between them seemed to reach down forever now. He had not found the bottom yet. He was afraid of what was happening to her, but it wasn't in him to be angry when he answered the door—anger was too small— besides, he and Landreaux were friends, better friends than the two half sisters, and the instinct of that friendship was still with him. Landreaux and Emmaline had their boy with them, completely unlike but like Dusty because of the way a five-year-old is—that inquisitiveness, that confidence, that trust.

Landreaux slowly set the boy down and asked if they could come in.

Don't, said Nola.

But Peter opened the door. Immediately LaRose looked up at Peter, then peered eagerly into the front room.

Where's Dusty?

Peter's face was swollen, charged with exhaustion, but he managed to answer, Dusty's not here anymore.

LaRose turned aside in disappointment, then he pointed to the toy box shoved into a corner and said, Can I play?

Nola had no words in her. She sat heavily and watched, first dull, then in fascination, as LaRose took out one toy after the next and played hard with it, serious, garbled, original, funny, obsessively involved with each object.

From up the stairs, forgotten, Maggie watched everything. Both boys had been born in early fall. Both mothers had kept them home, feeling they were too young for school. When the boys played together, Maggie had bossed them, made them play servant if she was a king or dogs if she was queen of the beasts. Now she didn't know what to do. Not just in playing but in her regular life. They didn't want her back in school yet. If she cried, her mother cried louder. If she didn't cry, her mother said she was a coldhearted little animal. So she just watched LaRose from the carpeted steps while he played with Dusty's toys.

As Maggie watched, her stare hardened. She gripped the spindles like jail bars. Dusty was not there to defend his toys, to share them only if he wanted, to be in charge of the pink-orange dinosaur, the favored flame-black Hot Wheels, the miniature monster trucks. She wanted to storm down and throw stuff everywhere. Kick LaRose. But she was already in trouble for teacher sassing and supposed to be locked in her room.

Landreaux and Emmaline Iron were still standing in the doorway. Nobody had asked them in.

What do you want? said Peter.

He always would have asked how he could help a visitor, but only Nola caught that this rudeness was how he expressed the jolts of electric sorrow and unlikeness of how he was feeling.

What do you want?

They answered simply.

Our son will be your son now.

Landreaux put the small suitcase on the floor. Emmaline was shredding apart. She put the other bag down in the entry and looked away.

They had to tell him what they meant, *Our son will be your son*, and tell him again.

Peter's jaw fell, gaping and stricken.

No, he said, I've never heard of such a thing.

It's the old way, said Landreaux. He said it very quickly, got the words out yet again. There was a lot more to their decision, but he could no longer speak.

Emmaline glanced at her half sister, whom she disliked. She stuffed back any sound, glanced up and saw Maggie crouched on the stairs. The girl's angry doll face punched at her. I have to get out of here, she thought. She stepped forward with an abrupt jerk, placed her hand on her child's head, kissed him. LaRose patted her face, deep in play.

Later, Mom, he said, copying his older brothers.

No, said Peter again, gesturing, no. This can't be. Take . . .

Then he looked at Nola and saw that her face had broken open. All the softness was flowing out. And the greed, too, a desperate grasping that leaned her windingly toward the child.

The Gate

Along toward evening Nola made soup, laid out dinner on the table, all with great concentration. After each step in the routine, she went blank, had to call back her thoughts, find the bowls, butter, cut the bread. LaRose spooned up the soup with slow care. He buttered his own bread clumsily. He had good table manners, thought Nola. His presence was both comforting and unnerving. He was Dusty and the opposite of Dusty. Roils of confusion struck Peter. The shock, he thought. I'm still in shock. The boy drew him with his quiet self-possession, his curiosity, but when Peter felt himself responding he was pierced with a sense of disloyalty. He told himself Dusty wouldn't care, couldn't care. He also realized that Nola was allowing herself to be helped somehow, but whether it was that she accepted this unspeakable gift as beauty, or whether she believed the child's absence over time would leak the lifeblood from Landreaux's heart, he couldn't tell.

You take him to the bathroom, Nola said.

Then . . .

I know.

They looked at each other, searching. Both decided they couldn't put him to sleep in Dusty's bed. Besides that, twice LaRose had asked about his mother and accepted their explanations. The third time, however, he'd hung his head and cried, gasping. He'd never been away from his mother. There was his rending bewilderment. Maggie stroked his hair, gave him toys, distracted him. It seemed Maggie could soothe him. She slept in Grandma's old carved double bed. Plenty of room. I can't deal with her right now, said Nola. So Peter brought the suitcase and canvas bag of stuffed animals and toys into Maggie's room. He told Maggie that she was having a sleepover. Peter helped LaRose brush his tiny milk teeth. The boy undressed himself and put on his pajamas. He was thinner than Dusty, tensile. His hair flopped down in a forelock, just a shade darker than Maggie's. Peter helped him into bed. Maggie stood uncertainly. Her long white flannel nightgown hung like a bell around her ankles. She pulled back the blankets and got in. Peter kissed them both, murmured, turned out the lights. Closing the door, he felt like he was going crazy, but the grief was different. The grief was all mixed up.

LaRose squeezed the soft creaturelike doll he played with the way his older brother played with plastic superhero action figures. Emmaline had made the creature for him. The grubby fur was rubbed away in spots. One button eye had popped off. She'd pushed cattail fluff through the butt when it split and stitched it back together. Its red felt tongue was worn to a ribbon. At first, the shivers LaRose had been holding back were so delicate they hardly made it from his body. But soon he shook in wide, rolling waves, and tears came too. Maggie lay next to him in the bed, feeling his misery, which made her own misery stop her heart.

She rolled over and shoved LaRose off the edge of the mattress. He tumbled, dragging the bedspread with him. Maggie tugged it back and LaRose hiccuped on the floor.

What are you crying for, baby? she said.

LaRose began to sob, low and profound. Maggie felt blackness surge up in her.

You want Mom-mee? Mom-mee? She's gone. She and your daddy left you here to be my brother like Dusty was. But I don't want you.

As she said this Maggie felt the blackness turn to water. She crawled down to find LaRose. He was curled in a ball, in the corner, with his scroungy stuffed creature, silent. She touched his back. He was cold and stiff. She dragged out her camping bag and slipped it over them both. She curled around him, warming him.

I do want you, she whispered in fear.

Some years later this night became a memory for LaRose. He recalled it, cherished it, as the first night he spent with Maggie. He remembered the warm flannel and her body curled around his. He believed they became brother and sister with each other as they slept. He forgot she'd kicked him out of bed, forgot she'd spoken those words.

WOLFRED STARED at the blanketed lump of girl. Mackinnon had always been honest, for a trader. Fair, for a trader, and showed no signs of moral corruption beyond the usual—selling rum to Indians was outlawed. Wolfred could not take in what had happened, so again he went fishing. When he came back with another stringer of whitefish, his mind was clear. He decided Mackinnon was a rescuer. He had saved the girl from Mink, and a slave's fate elsewhere. Wolfred chopped some kindling and built a small cooking fire beside the post. He roasted the fish whole and Mackinnon ate them with last week's tough bread. Tomorrow, Wolfred would bake. When he went back into the cabin the girl was exactly where she'd been before. She didn't move or flinch. It appeared that Mackinnon hadn't touched her.

Wolfred put a plate of bread and fish on the dirt floor where she could reach it. She devoured both and gasped for breath. He set a tankard of water near. She gulped it all down, her throat clucking like a baby's as she drained the cup.

After Mackinnon had eaten, he crawled into his slat-and-bearskin bed, where his habit was to drink himself to sleep. Wolfred cleaned up the cabin. Then he heated a pail of water and crouched near the girl. He wet a rag and dabbed at her face. As the caked dirt came off, he discovered her features, one by one, and saw that they were very fine. Her lips were small and full. Her eyes hauntingly sweet. Her eyebrows perfectly flared. When her face was uncovered he stared at her in dismay. She was exquisite. Did Mackinnon know? And did he know that his kick had chipped one of the girl's sharp teeth, left a blackening bruise on her flower-petal cheek?

Giimiikawaadiz, whispered Wolfred. He knew the words for how she looked.

Carefully, reaching into the corner of the cabin for what he needed, he mixed mud. He held her chin and with tender care dabbed the muck back into her face, blotting over the startling line of her brows, the perfect symmetry of eyes and nose, the devastating curve of her lips. She was a graceful child of eleven years.

THEY SLEPT on the floor last night, said Nola. I told Maggie it had to stop. If you want the ground, I'll ground you. She sassed me. Okay, I said. You're grounded to your room. You won't be going outside. He's crying again. I don't know what to do.

She flapped her fingers. Her face was pinched and gray, her body frail. She'd done well all week, but now it was the weekend, and Maggie home all day.

Let her out, said Peter.

Ohhh, she's out already, wouldn't mind me, said Nola, angry. She's eating breakfast.

Why don't you let them play together? They'll be happy.

Peter and Nola had resolved always to uphold each other's decisions where the children were concerned. But things were breaking down, thought Peter. A few minutes later, he caught Nola pushing Maggie's head, almost into her bowl of oatmeal. Maggie resisted. When Nola saw Peter, she took her hand off Maggie's neck as if nothing had happened.

Breathing hard, Maggie stared at the oatmeal. It was congealed and her mother didn't let her have raisins or brown sugar because she might get a cavity. She looked up at her father. He sat down and while Nola's back was turned he scooped most of her oatmeal into his bowl. He mimed eating. She lifted her spoon. He dipped his in first and put the oatmeal in his mouth, made a sad clown face. Maggie did the same. They rolled their eyes at Nola like anxious dogs. So did LaRose, though he didn't know what was going on. Without turning around, Nola said to Peter, *Stop that shit.*

Peter gripped his spoon and stared hard at her back.

Peter thought his wife would begin to heal once this was resolved. He thought it was time to take LaRose home. But he wanted Nola to say so. Instead, she invented plans.

I'm going to make him a cake, she said, eyes blurring. With candles on it like a birthday cake. I'll put them in over and over, and let him blow them out. He can have a hundred wishes.

She turned away. The doctor had given her a few Klonopin. She would drug herself on Christmas. I'll make LaRose a cake every day, she thought, if he'll only stop crying, if he'll cling to me like Dusty did, if he'll only be my son, the only son I will ever have. Some stubborn long-standing resentment had kept Nola from telling Peter that her periods had stopped shortly after Dusty, and the doctor couldn't tell her why. Peter hadn't noticed the change, but then, she had always been secretive about her body. Emmaline was the only person she had told. How breathtaking that she had entrusted that secret to Emmaline! Her heart clenched. It was, thought Nola, the reason LaRose was brought to her. Emmaline understood.

Because her half sister understood her so well, Nola would turn from her, afraid of her, and harden herself against Emmaline.

PETER FINALLY went over to find Landreaux. He could have walked, it was just a half mile. West, there was Hoopdance. East and north, reservation and reservation town. South, the dying little community of

Pluto, which still had a school. That's where Maggie went and where they would send LaRose if this situation lasted. Pulling into the Irons' empty driveway, Peter cut the engine. The little gray house was completely dark. A half-constructed plywood and buffalo-board platform sagged off the side. The tarps were pulled away from the bent poles of the sweat lodge out back. There was a bird feeder made from a milk jug, a full box of canning jars in the driveway, and a few toys scattered in the yard. The dog that hung around was gone. The Irons had probably gone to visit relatives in Canada, or to the local guy, a medicine man, Randall, for a family ceremony. He knew from his friendship with Landreaux that their people would put them through religious rituals. What they were called, he could not remember. Peter was only vaguely interested in the traditional things Landreaux did. They'd fished and hunted together. Peter knew how careful Landreaux was and it seemed impossible that he could have made such an error. Peter left his car in the driveway and walked out behind Landreaux's house, into the woods.

He followed a path that would take him to the spot where Dusty had died. On the way there, he saw that dog—short-haired with a rusty tinge to its coat. It was still, as if waiting for him. The head was sensitive, a lighter buff. Its ears flared up as it came out of the brush. The dog studied him. Peter stopped, startled at its composure and how it measured him. The dog vanished when he took a step. There was no sound, as if the woods had lightly absorbed the animal.

An overnight blast of wind, a short quick rain, had taken down most of the leaves. They lay brilliant on the ground, layer on layer of shattering color. The morning light struck the white birch to near incandescence. As he passed through a stand of bur oak, the air darkened. At last he stood where Landreaux had stood, straight across from where the buck must have stopped. Directly between them was the climbing tree Maggie had told him about. Peter had no idea his children had been playing so deep in the woods and so far from the house. But the tree with its low crotch and curved limbs was irresistible. One limb was blasted. He walked up and ran his hand along the shafted needle-sharp spikes of wood. Then the patch of ground below the tree limb knocked him to his knees. He put his hand on the place. All around, the ground was trampled and torn. Peter lay on his back. Looking up, he worked it out that just before he died Dusty had climbed the tree—he had been sitting on a limb. He'd seen the great buck. Startled, he'd fallen just as Landreaux shot. Peter had read Landreaux's statement and everything he said matched.

Now he lay down on the place where Dusty's life had flowed into the earth, closed his eyes, listened to the sound of the woods around him. He heard a chickadee, a faraway nuthatch, a crow ragged in the distance. He heard his own voice, crying out. Then the hum and tick of twigs, leaves. Rush of pine needles. The scent of sweetgrass, tobacco, kinnikinnick, offerings. Landreaux had been there, too.

❦

LANDREAUX WAS at present doing what he did every couple of weeks. He was helping Emmaline's mother. Before she was his mother-in-law, she had been his favorite teacher. In fact, she had saved him the way she always saved people. She was not on his client list, but he helped her anyway. He arrived at her apartment in the Elders Lodge, a rangy brick building shaped like a thunderbird—you could see the shape looking down from an airplane. Emmaline's mother lived in the tail. Nobody called her grandma, kookum, or auntie. Her first name was LaRose, but nobody called her that either. They called her by her teacher name, Mrs. Peace.

Generations of students had loved her as a teacher and were aware of no vice, yet Mrs. Peace claimed that she wasn't entirely wholesome. She had a checkered past, she liked to say, though she had at last remained faithful to the memory of Emmaline's father, Billy Peace. It was reverently said that she had tried to throw herself into his grave. He had actually been cremated, but no one remembered. Billy Peace was also Nola's father. Nobody really knew how many wives had married Billy, or what had gone on in that cultish compound of his decades ago. Billy's children and now grandchildren kept turning up and were usually added to the tribal rolls.

Mrs. Peace had been a sad-looking, pretty woman with long flossy brown hair. She had long flossy white hair now and was still pretty but looked happy. She didn't cut and curl her hair like most of her friends, but wore it in a thin braid, sometimes a bun. Every day she wore a different pair of beaded earrings. She made up the patterns herself—today sky blue with orange centers. She had taken up this hobby, and the smoking of cigarillos, after she left off teaching and moved back to the reservation. She rarely smoked a cigarillo now. She said beading had helped her quit. Her stand-up magnifying glass was placed just so on the table, for her vision was poor. When she looked up at Landreaux, her thick eyeglasses gave her a bewildered otherworldliness, adding to her aura.

Landreaux entered as she nodded him in, hugged him. They stood wordlessly in the embrace, then stepped back. Mrs. Peace held out her hands, palms up.

He took his boots off by the door. She was boiling water for tea. Landreaux waved the stethoscope and blood pressure cuff at her, but she told him to put that stuff away. She felt fine. The lodge owned a carpet-shampooing machine, and half her apartment, covered deeply in an ash-blond fiber, needed Landreaux's care. For the moment, he left the machine and jug of soap parked outside the door. Though she still had an occasional attack, LaRose's enigmatic pain had nearly vanished after the death of Billy Peace. Neuralgia, full-body migraine, osteoporosis, spinal problems, lupus, sciatica, bone cancer, phantom limb syndrome though she had her limbs—these diagnoses had come and gone. Her medical file was a foot high. She knew, of course, why the pains had left her at that time, rarely returning. Billy had been cruel, self-loving, and clever. His love had been a burden no different from hate. Sometimes his ironies still sneaked at her from the spirit world. People thought she had been faithful to his memory because she had abjectly adored Billy Peace. She let them say what they wanted. Actually, he had taught her what she needed to know about men. She needed no further instruction.

Landreaux, who as a man believed the tragic lovelorn-teacher story, was solicitous, convinced that she presented a brave face to the world. Today he saw with concern that her face was crashed out, blank, and she was trying to make herself comfortable in her reclining chair. Perhaps she was having an episode because of what he had done.

Don't even worry about me, she said. This will take a long time to work out, eh? You're a good boy to come over here and help me at a time like this.

I can't just sit around, he said, and tried to coax her into an opiate or two.

It makes me loopy.

She peered at him through her bottle-glass-thick lenses, her eyes swimming.

Are you looking forward to having your carpet shampooed? he asked, hearing what he said as ridiculous or maybe pathetic. But she made his awkwardness okay.

It's amazing what a kick I get out of that, she answered. You go ahead.

He drank the tea and brought in the machine.

Landreaux moved the reclining chair, magazine rack, television, and television stand off the carpet. He put water into the tank, mixed the soap into the water, and began. The machine made purring, bubbling sounds.

He moved it back and forth. The sound was low and mesmerizing. Sure enough, Mrs. Peace closed her eyes, beatific, smiling. When he was done, her eyes flipped open and she got up to bustle around the edges of the wet carpet. He put the machine away and sat down to eat the Juneberry coffee cake she'd put out for him. Then she answered a phone call and said that she had to help Elka with her eyedrops. Her slippered feet slapped away down the hall.

When the door shut, Landreaux went into the bathroom. He checked her medicine cabinet as he always did, to make sure that her medications were filled and up-to-date. She was almost out of two, so Landreaux put the bottles on the table. When she came back, he said that he'd go down to the hospital pharmacy and refill them.

Before you go, she said, here. Take a look.

LaRose opened her closet. She had certificates, brittle school reports, clippings of poems, stacks of ancient letters in there, seeking after the first LaRose. Emmaline called her the historical society. At least her photographs were all in albums now, organized by Snow. Mrs. Peace took a big, black, battered round tin from a low shelf. The top was painted with three faded roses. People gave her things with roses on them because of her name, and perhaps the same had been true of her mother, because this tin was quite old. Mrs. Peace kept odd-sized papers in this tin—aphorisms, and newspapers, pictures, stories of dogs, papers in her own writing. The sight of her penmanship, the swirls of her name, filled Landreaux with memories of Emmaline as a girl.

Look at what? he said.

She handed him the poem—a copy of the poem "Invictus." Generations of her students had memorized it.

Keep it, she said.

I still know it by heart. This is the foul clutch of circumstance, all right, he said.

Fell clutch, she said.

He looked at a piece of grainy Big Chief tablet paper. It was filled with his writing but he did not remember having written it. *I will not run away* was written on it over and over.

I made you write ten pages just like it, but I only kept this one, she said.

She put her fine-boned little hand on his shoulder. Warmth spread instantly from her fingers.

I will not run away, he said. They sat together holding hands on the couch.

Before he left, Landreaux gave Mrs. Peace the two plastic bottles, and she read the numbers off into the pharmacy telephone line. She gave Landreaux the bottles to put back in the medicine cabinet. These weren't the ones he cared about, she knew. It was true, also, that he hadn't taken any of those other ones for a while. Unlike many of her friends, she kept careful count of the pills in her bottles. Old people were such an easy source.

Landreaux needed the pickup to haul tipi poles, hay bales. He needed it for dump runs or just to be a man. But he made Emmaline drive the pickup to work because it was safer, and he took the magic Corolla—the car that would not die. They had inherited the Corolla when Emmaline's mother moved into the nursing home. Beyond the suggested upkeep, which Landreaux himself could do, the car never broke down. Compared with the other cars he'd had in his life, this car seemed mystically dependable. It was a drab gray color and the seats were worn, the padding crushed. Landreaux couldn't push the driver's seat back far enough to accommodate his long legs, but he liked driving it. Especially after the first snowfall, when he put on the snow tires, he took pleasure in growling around on the back roads to visit his clients.

Ottie Plume, a foot lost to diabetes, lived with his wife, Baptiste, a few miles out of town on a coveted section of the lake. Bap didn't want her husband in the rehab, so Landreaux came over there to do physical therapy, shower, toilet, count pills, give shots, feed, trim nose and ear hair, clip nails, massage Ottie, and swap bits of gossip with the two. He also drove Ottie to dialysis and stayed with him while he got recirculated.

Bap opened the door when Landreaux tapped.

I didn' know if you'd show up, she said.

Life stops for nothing, even what I done, said Landreaux, and his saying it like that, taking it on, calmed Bap. She called into the other room.

He showed up, Ottie!

She stayed, though she'd ordinarily have left to do her own things while Landreaux worked with Ottie. Landreaux knew they'd been discussing him and that Bap was staying so she could tell her relatives how Landreaux behaved. What signs he showed. Emmaline said it would be tough going back to work. The story would be around him for the rest of his life. He would live in the story. He couldn't change it. Even LaRose won't change it, she said.

But Landreaux knew that wasn't exactly true. LaRose had already changed the story.

Oh, I'm glad you're here, said Ottie. His brown-gold cherub face, round and worn by suffering, brightened. Once a powerful wrestler, Ottie hadn't quite softened.

His pounds went on sleek, like seal fat. Most people in his family had died more quickly of diabetes' complications.

I was saying to Bap, life don't quit.

It don't quit until it does, said Ottie. I managed a shit on my own the other day. Nearly fell off the fucken stool.

Jeez, Ottie, said Bap.

Let's get it done, said Landreaux, wheeling Ottie down the short hall.

The tribe had sprung for a disability bathroom and Ottie had a shower chair. After Landreaux helped Ottie into the chair, he scrubbed Ottie's back and hosed him off. The door opened a crack. Bap's arm came through with a set of clean clothes. When they came out to the kitchen, there were blueberry pancakes with fake maple syrup, cooked up with powdered commodity eggs. Landreaux could taste the familiar flat chemically dry eggish quality and the aspartame over the maple. It was good.

So how's everybody dealing? Bap sat back from the table. She was a small, husky woman who still kept up the fiction that she was jealous as hell of other women, had to keep them from pursuing Ottie. She wore makeup all the time for Ottie. Eye shadow a different color for each day of the week. It was Purple Tuesday.

She pulled her hair back in a scrunchie and sprayed her bangs in a massive pout over her plucked-skinny eyebrows. Her nails were lacquered an innocent pink. One finger tapped her lips.

Maybe I shouldn't say nothing. Keep my trap shut?

Nah, said Landreaux.

Emmaline was her cousin.

You're family, he said.

Emmaline's real strong, said Bap.

Real strong, said Landreaux. His head began to buzz. I wanna establish a fund, you know? When they get better, when our families get more healed.

Bap and Ottie nodded warily, as if they might be asked to contribute.

Everybody makes a fund up now, said Bap.

Me, said Ottie, I know this is a sad time. But when I go, I want my fund to be a high-heels fund for reservation ladies. I sure like it when Bappy dresses up for me and does her thing. I'd like to see a few more ladies make that click sound when they walk. Drives me fucken wild.

Bap took Ottie's hand in hers.

You don't need no fund, babydoll. You ain't gonna die.

Except piece by piece, said Ottie.

Hate diabetes, said Landreaux.

We gotta get him ready for his appointment, said Bap. You gotta test his sugar.

Already done, said Ottie.

Landreaux didn't say he'd tested Ottie's sugar when he smelled the pancakes, knowing the carbs would spike Ottie's blood up no matter how much fake sweetener Bap threw at the problem. They were liable to hallucinate on that aspartame shit, he sometimes thought. He and Ottie were in the car, wheelchair folded in the trunk, before Landreaux realized he'd escaped without really answering Bap's question about how they were dealing. Ottie had deflected that line of inquiry with his high-heels death fund.

Thanks, he said to Ottie.

For what?

I didn't know what to say to Bap. How we're doing. We're still in that phase where we wake up, remember, wanna go back to sleep.

I spose you won't never hunt no more.

Burnt my gun. Well, what much of it that would burn.

That don't do nobody no good, said Ottie. Now who is gonna get your children the protein they need to grow big and strong?

We'll set snares, said Landreaux. Fry some waboose.

That would be on my diet, said Ottie. I'll trade you some a them pills you like.

Landreaux didn't answer.

But I'll miss your deer meat, Ottie went on. I guess it ain't something you get over, though. You keep on going through it.

Over and over, said Landreaux. Maybe trade you later. I don't need that stuff.

But he did, ever so bad.

THE HOT BAR at Whitey's gas station sold deep-fried wings, gizzards, drummies, pizza, and Hot Pockets. Romeo Puyat saw Landreaux drive by the gas station and park out back in the weeds. Romeo was a skinny man with close-set, piercing eyes and a wounded, hunching walk. His right arm was always held close to his body because it had been broken in so many places that it was pinned together. His right leg too. Still, he could move quickly. Thinking that Landreaux would stay inside and eat his lunch, Romeo grabbed the siphon hose and his bright-red fire-code-approved plastic container. He lurched, crooked but efficient, over to Landreaux's car and set up his equipment. Romeo was adept from frequent practice and soon had the gasoline flowing from Landreaux's gas tank, through the rubber tubing, into his container.

Landreaux walked out of the store carrying a small grease-proof cardboard box. His eyes flicked when he saw Romeo, but he did not acknowledge his old classmate. The reasons for hating each other went back to their childhood's brutal end. The two had stopped talking back in boarding school. And then there was the time Romeo had tried to murder Landreaux in his sleep. That was in their early twenties, and it just happened that Landreaux had been in possession of a lot of money that one night. As the money was the main corrupting influence, Romeo was hurt that Landreaux still mistrusted him over the botched knifing. These days, at least, Romeo wasn't after his old schoolmate's life.

Romeo had accepted, at least in theory, how Landreaux had stolen his first love, Emmaline, who maybe hadn't liked Romeo anyway. Romeo was grudgingly okay with how Landreaux and Emmaline had unquestioningly taken in, and admirably looked after, his surprise son, Hollis. Romeo told himself that they got a good deal in that boy, because Hollis was A-number-one. Still, he had to admit there was a lot of upkeep involved there. These days, anyway, the main thing was that Romeo just wanted Landreaux to share and share alike. As a personal caregiver well-known at the hospital, surely Landreaux had lots of access to prescription painkillers. Why not make his old friend a little happier? Take away his agonies? Yes, Romeo had his own prescription, but it just was not OxyContin and sometimes he had to sell his lesser stuff to pay for the really good stuff. Like Fentanyl. He had been trying to buy a patch somewhere.

Landreaux walked over to his car.

Well, well, well, said Romeo, glancing down at the gas flowing through the tubing. Long time no see.

Landreaux was touched, in a sad way, to find his old schoolmate stealing his gas. He had long ago decided that whatever Romeo or anyone else did to him resulting from his hell days he had coming. So he said nothing, except I gotta go. My mozzarella sticks are getting cold.

Mozzarella sticks, said Romeo, with a look of distaste.

For the kids, said Landreaux.

Oooooh, said Romeo, as if he'd heard something wise and surprising. He jerked back his head, frowned in concentration, and gently removed the tubing.

Got something for me, old niiji? He fussily tapped the tubing against the inside of the tank. Then he screwed the pressure-lock lid back on the red plastic jug and replaced the gas cap on Landreaux's car. He smacked the cover closed.

No, said Landreaux.

Well, my work here is done, said Romeo.

Picking up the red gas can, he gave a jaunty, irritating hand salute and stepped into the road that would take him back to his car and empty tank.

Give my regards to Emmaline, he yelled over his shoulder.

Landreaux gave him a sharp sidelong glance, put the mozzarella sticks on the hood of his car. As he got in, the way Romeo had saluted started him remembering. There was plenty to recall, but the knife Romeo had stuck in his forearm, then his bicep, left a visible scar. Amazing that in his sleep Landreaux had rolled over and reached up to scratch his nose as Romeo struck. Wandering back in thought, Landreaux forgot the carton on top of his car and drove by Romeo, who was filling his tank with the siphoned gas. As Landreaux rounded the corner, the mozzarella sticks flew off the roof at such an angle that they slid onto the hood of Romeo's car. When his tank was no longer empty, Romeo reached for the box, took out a mozzarella stick. He took only one bite—they had gone cool and rubbery already. He drove to the Hot Bar and complained.

I'll heat them up for you, said the girl behind the counter.

I'd rather get my money back, said Romeo.

⁂

AFTER THE first weeks, LaRose tried to stop crying, around Nola at least. Maggie told him the facts again, why he was there. His parents had told him, but he still didn't get it. He had to hear it again and again.

You don't even know what dead means, said Maggie.

You don't move, said LaRose.

You don't breathe, said Maggie.

Breathing's moving!

Here, said Maggie, let's go outside and I'll kill something to show you.

What would you kill?

They looked out the window.

That dog, said Maggie, pointing.

It was at the edge of the yard, just lazing in the sun. It was the dog LaRose's family fed. He didn't say that he recognized it, but he did say, You must be mean. Nobody just goes and kills a dog for nothing.

Your dad went and killed my brother for nothing, said Maggie.

On accident.

Same difference, said Maggie.

LaRose got tears in his eyes and then Maggie did too. She was overcome by a restless wretchedness. Dusty had come to her in a dream and showed her a stuffed dog that looked, she now remembered, just like that orange dog out there. She turned back to check on the dog, but it was gone. She had a thought. She could get something from LaRose. Get him to help her.

Okay, little dork.

Don't call me that.

I won't call you dork if you change my mom from evil, like she is now, into nice. If you can do that? I think they would make a TV show about you.

What should I do?

To make her nice?

LaRose nodded. Maggie told him to ask if she needed a foot rub, but LaRose looked confused.

Do anything she tells you to do, Maggie directed. And eat her cakes. Also, hugs.

LaRose waited for Nola to tell him to do something. Later on that day, Nola said that LaRose should call her, Nola, mother.

Okay, Mother.

Give me a hug?

He did that too.

Nola smoothed back his hair, looked into his eyes, and her face ballooned up and went red, like she might roar.

What's your favorite food? she asked.

Cake?

She said she would make him lots of cakes. When LaRose put his arms around her neck he could feel her bones jutting up under her skin.

You're boney, he said to Nola.

You can feel my skeleton, Nola said.

Are you a Halloween lady? he asked carefully.

No, she said, I'm not. My mother was a witch. I don't want to be my mother.

LaRose laid his head on her chest to make sure her heart was beating. Her collarbone jutted against his temple.

Boney, he thought. She's boney. He'd heard his father tease his mother. *You're getting boney!* He'd heard his grandmother say this about his sister Snow. *You don't want to be so boney, like your mother.*

He'd landed in a world of boney women. Even Maggie was boney with her gangly legs. He hadn't said it, though. Nor had he said that Maggie called her mother evil. Something stopped him. He didn't know why he just didn't say everything in his mind anymore.

It was like his mouth had a little strainer that only let through pleasant words.

✦

LAROSE SAW his real mother in the grocery store. He ran to Emmaline and they melted together. Romeo happened to witness this incident. He stood in the meat-case radiance, swaying, clasped his basket to his chest. Across his face there passed an expression that did not belong to the dangerous scumbag he considered himself now. Romeo caught himself, narrowed his eyes, and pretended to examine the tubes of cheap hamburger.

It was good that LaRose was with Peter, who didn't interfere. For a while Emmaline held on to her child, smelling his hair. She looked at Peter, and when he nodded she let LaRose hang on to the cart for a ride. She walked the store with him, talking. It was like being heart-dead and then heart-alive, but she couldn't shop forever. Peter helped her carry groceries out and then she brought LaRose to the Ravich car. LaRose got in without crying, buckled himself into the backseat. His wordless bravery choked her. As they drove away, he waved at Emmaline. He seemed to float from her on a raft of frail sticks. Or was that a dream? Every morning, she floated to consciousness on that same dis-integrating raft. Many times each day, she questioned what they had done.

After seeing LaRose, she couldn't go home. She thought that she might see her mother, but instead found that she was drawn to the church. She then thought that she might pray there, for peace. But in-stead she walked around back of the church. She thought that she might find Father Travis, but he wasn't in any of the church offices or at the rectory—a simple boxy house. She started to feel uncomfortable, tracking him down this way. Then she saw him at a distance, working a little Bobcat by the lake, building a walkway. He was wearing a droopy brown stocking hat pulled down behind his ears. The hat made his ears stick out. It should have made him look ridicu-lous. But it was hard to make Father Travis look ridic-ulous. He had wind-toughened skin, lightly freckled, the classic red-blond's sun-shy complexion. His cheekbones were planar, almost brutal, and he had a chiseled movie-star chin. Just as his looks had begun to grate on people, he'd gotten older, which made him easier to bear. Also, scars flamed down his throat. Father Travis's eyes could be warm if he smiled, the lines around them starred pleasantly outward. His eyes could also go the other way—somber, colorless, maybe dangerous—but of course he was no longer an earthly soldier.

He shut the Cat down when he saw Emmaline and got off. She was used to seeing him in a cassock. Father Travis wore cassocks most of the time because he liked the convenience. He could put them on over T-shirts and work pants. The old people liked to see him in one, and after *The Matrix* the young people liked it too. But right now he wore old jeans, plaid flannel shirt, a brown canvas jacket.

Emmaline smiled at him, surprised.

He glanced around the yards, checking to see if anybody was watching. It was that—the checking—he thought later, that gave it all away. His heart was hidden from his thoughts for days, until he remembered glancing over Emmaline's shoulder to make sure no one was watching.

They shoved their hands in their pockets and walked the fitness trail that he was making through the woods. They passed the push-up rail, the chin-up bar, before she could say anything.

I didn't want to give LaRose to them, she said.

Why did you?

The sun glowing in green lake water on a bright day—her eyes were that color.

It seemed the only way, she said. She's my sister, after all. I thought she would let me see him, spend time. But no. So I want him back. I just saw him. He's going to think that I don't love him.

Father Travis was still surprised by what they had done. He thought back to their visit just after Landreaux was released—they had wanted to tell him something. He had heard of these types of adoptions in years past, when disease or killings broke some families, left others whole. It was an old form of justice. It was a story, and stories got to him. A story was the reason he had become a priest, and a story was why he'd not yet walked off the job. In the evenings, between action movies, Father Travis parsed out the New Testament.

Mary gave her child to the world, he almost said, looking at Emmaline. It all made sense for she was wearing a sky blue parka. The hood was missing the fur band, so it capped her head in a way that reminded him of pictures of the Blessed Virgin. Her hair, parted in the middle, flowed back under the blue material in smooth wings.

You tried to do a good thing, said Father Travis. LaRose will understand that. He will come back to you.

Emmaline stopped and looked closely at him.

You sure?

I'm sure, he said, then couldn't help himself. *Neither life, nor angels, nor principalities nor things present, nor things to come, nor powers, not height, nor depth, nor any other creature will separate you.*

Emmaline looked at him like he was crazy.

It's a Bible quote.

He looked down at the scraped path. Quoting Romans like a pompous ass . . .

LaRose is young, she said, her hungry eyes blurring. They forget if you're not with them every day.

Nobody could forget you, thought Father Travis. The blurted thought unnerved him; he made himself speak sensibly.

Look, you can retrieve LaRose at any time. Just say you want him back. Peter and Nola have to listen. If not, you can go to Social Services. You are his mother.

Social Services, she said. Huh. Ever heard of rez omerta?

Father Travis abruptly laughed.

Besides, I am Social Services. The crisis school is all a social service. I'd have to get in touch with myself.

What's wrong with that? said Father Travis.

She shook her head, looked away as she spoke.

You mean I didn't see it coming? Didn't know it would be this difficult? Can't understand why this is unbearable when there is history and tradition, all that, behind what we did?

She rubbed her face with her hands as if to erase something else.

Yes, I wasn't exactly in touch with myself. Also, there's Nola. She gets mad at Maggie, I think. What if she treats LaRose that way?

Father Travis was silent. He still heard individual confessions and knew about Nola's temper.

As they walked back to her car, a sensation he didn't recognize kept him from offering the usual offhand comment, to seal things off. He stayed silent because he didn't want to ruin the confiding way she had spoken to him. Emmaline got in the car. Then she pulled her hood back and rolled down her window. She looked up into his face. Her longing for her son was so naked that he seemed to feel it pressing into him. He closed his eyes.

When his eyes were shut, Emmaline saw, he was an ordinary man with weather-raked skin and chapped lips.

She looked away and started up the car. Her tragic thoughts shifted as she drove off, and she remembered laughing until her stomach cramped as Josette and Snow discussed the priest.

He can't help his eyes, one of them said.

His sex-toy-robot eyes.

Josette and Snow had a thing about male robot/ cyborg movie characters. They had an ancient Radio Shack VCR-TV in their room, and picked up old movies for it at yard sales and discount bins. Their collection included *Westworld*, *RoboCop*, *The Black Hole*. They rifled through video sale bins hoping for their favorite, *Blade Runner*. They'd made drawings of robots and cyborgs—smooth, perfect, doomed for feeling something, maybe like Father Travis.

He's got replicant eyes!

No shit, Father Travis could be a replicant. Batty!

I've seen things you people wouldn't believe, they intoned together. *Attack ships off the shoulder of Orion. I watched C-beams glitter in the dark near the Tannhauser Gate.*

Their voices dropped to exhausted rasps.

All those moments will be lost in time. Like tears in rain. Time to die.

They lolled their heads over and Emmaline had cried out, Quit this! She frowned now. Like any mother, it made her uneasy to see her children feign death.

The Iron girls. Snow, Josette. The Iron Maidens. They were junior high volleyball queens, sister BFFs, heart-soul confidantes to each other and advice givers to their brothers. They were tight with their mom, loose with their dad. With their grandma they got bead-happy and could sew for hours. Snow was going to be the tall, intense one who had trouble concentrating on her schoolwork and whom boys only liked as a friend. She was in eighth grade. Josette was going to be the smart one who despaired about her weight but magnetized clumsy desire among boys whom she liked only as friends. She was in grade seven.

Landreaux dropped his daughters in Hoopdance to shop and drove back to take Ottie to dialysis. The girls went straight to the one drugstore. They walked in with a puff of snowy cold. A store clerk with flat dyed red hair and glasses on a chain asked if she could help them.

No thanks, said Josette, and you don't need to follow us around either. We have money and we're not going to steal.

The woman pulled her chin down into her neck and kept this odd posture as she turned away and walked to the cash register.

You didn't have to say that, said Snow.

Maybe I'm too defensive, said Josette, fake-meek. Attached to the drugstore was a gift shop full of decorative flowers and knickknacks, which their mother did not like. But they did. They went through and admired all the ceramic snow babies, the glitter fronds, the stones cut with words. Dream. Love. Live.

Why not Throw? said Josette. How come they don't have one that just says, Throw?

You don't get inspiration, do you, said Snow.

That's not inspiration, that's mawkish.

Ooooo! Snow licked her finger and made a mark in the air. Vocab word.

They went back to the other section. There was a small selection of windshield scrapers and emergency flashlights, maybe for their dad.

Better things at the hardware store, said Josette.

Let's test perfumes for Mom.

No, lotion.

You get that. I'll get perfume.

All of the good perfumes were locked up under the glass counter with the eyeglass lady's hands resting on it.

Shit, now we'll have to deal with her, said Josette.

I'm the good one, said Snow. I'll do the talking.

Josette rolled her eyes and made an oops face.

Snow walked up to the clerk and smiled. How are you today? Snow used a bright inflection. We're looking for a really nice Christmas present for our mother. Our mom is so special. Snow sighed. She works so hard! What do you suggest?

The woman's stabbing glare bounced off Josette, who was bent over the glass, scanning. The woman's hand hovered among the jewel-bright boxes, spray bottles, and plucked up a tester of Jean Naté.

Too white-bread, said Josette.

Snow pointed at Jovan Musk.

That doesn't smell like Mom. She's more, I don't know, clear.

Maybe Charlie, or Blue Jeans?

So casual, though.

They meditated, frowning, on the array.

I wanna get something special. I have my job money, said Snow to the counter lady. Maybe something from a designer or movie star.

The woman displayed a box. White Diamonds. Elizabeth Taylor.

America's number one fragrance, said the woman, reverent.

Who's Elizabeth Taylor? asked Josette.

Duh, Cleopatra?

They'd both pondered the cover of the VHS at the video rental.

Plus friends with Michael Jackson?

Oh yeah. Josette sniffed the spray nozzle. Fancy. I like this.

Enjoli, in a hot-pink box, decorated with an embossed golden flower.

But Mom's not this spicy. I mean, she smells good.

It would clash with Dad's Old Spice.

So would the Wild Musk?

Maybe Wind Song.

Grandma wears that.

The woman behind the counter brought out an elegant box hiding behind the others. It was a lavendery pinkish box, one of those expensive indeterminate colors. A blackish gray band. The bottle fit firmly in hand, a band of embossed diamond shapes, neatly swirled glass. Eau Sauvage. The woman sprayed a little on a Kleenex, waved the tissue in front of their noses. Waited. The smell was green and dry. Faintly licorice. Maybe a hint of cloud. A trace of fresh-cut wood? Crushed grass. A rare herb in a rare forest. Nothing dark, nothing hungry. Something else, too.

Most people think this one smells too plain, the lady said. It's not like any other perfume. Nobody buys it. We only have this one bottle.

Snow watched Josette, her eyes wide. Josette breathed the scent in again.

I wish things could be that way, said Snow.

So pure, said Josette, putting down the bottle. Must be pricey.

It's a bit expensive, yes, said the woman. She seemed embarrassed by the amount. I just work here. It's not my store, she said.

Yeah, said Snow. It's kinda too much. I was saving. But, well.

It can be for a man or a woman. Eww Savage.

Eau Sauvage, said Josette, with an exaggerated French accent. We gotta have it. She turned to Snow, eyes sparking.

Smell!

This is it, said Snow.

Josette had an old-lady-type money pouch hidden deep in her purse. She took it out. Snow hugged her passionately.

Then right there, in front of the counterwoman, they began to cry because they both knew: the trace was there. The cologne also smelled like LaRose's clean hair on a cold autumn day when he came in and Emmaline would bend over him.

Oh, you smell good, she used to say. You smell like outside.

Leaving the drugstore, Josette and Snow talked about the outside smell and decided they were psychic with each other like in a witch coven.

Or maybe our people had these powers before the whiteman came.

Yeah, said Snow, and we lived five hundred years.

I actually heard someone say that.

Me too. And we could change the weather.

I believe that one.

Great, said Snow. Let's do it now.

I shoulda been named Summer, said Josette. All you can do is make it snow.

It was blustery. They were walking toward the place they would meet their father. He had agreed to pick them up after he got Ottie settled back home. They were going to sit in the Subway, maybe split a twelve-inch turkey with American cheese, on whole wheat, for their complexions, with lettuce, tomatoes, pickles, and sweet onion sauce dressing. For sure they would. They were hungrier than usual and had enough money left for the turkey sub if they just drank water.

It's better for us, said Josette, who loved Sprite.

They showed us in health class, said Snow mournfully. Just a can a day you get diabetes.

Landreaux never bought soda because he didn't want his kids to lose their feet. When he put it like that, they'd squint as if in pain, Yeah, Dad. They drank forbidden pop at Whitey's. Now, waiting for their father, they stared down at their sub sandwich wrappers and looked amazed.

I ate that so fast.

How'd that happen? Josette burped.

Gross. Now what?

We're broke so we sip our healthful waters.

And wait for Dad.

They met each other's eyes. Nobody at school had been very mean. Everybody in their school had something awful happen someplace in their family. Everybody just got sad for everybody, usually, or said tough shit, or if you were a girl maybe you gave a card. There were no cards for what had happened. But one of her girlfriends had beaded Snow a pair of earrings and she knew it was to say what there were no words to say. There were no words to say to their father, either. At least no words they wanted to say. In the car, maybe they'd be silent. Maybe they'd ask about Ottie or Awan or another client. Maybe they'd say something general about schoolwork. They'd avoid true feelings because it could go real deep real sudden with their father. He would get into that seriously real mode like when he did a ceremony. Where you let thoughts and feelings buried inside you come out into the circle so other people could pray and sing to help you. But, the girls agreed, they weren't into having that kind of energy leak out of their dad when things were going on like normal. So when he drove up in the Corolla they eye-spoke. Josette would ride shotgun because she was good at keeping him on topics like haircuts, car batteries, winterizing the windows of the house with Saran wrap. And if it seemed like he might veer south, she could always ask him to tell her again what was wrong with drinking pop.

⚓

Y2K KEPT Peter occupied now and when he was preparing he could think of something other than Dusty. On the way to Fleet Farm, he berated himself for not having bought live chickens last spring. He'd been planning on turning one of the old outbuildings into a chicken coop. Nola had even agreed although she was generally against having animals. He'd never gotten organized about the chickens, although the dog, he'd fed the dog he had seen in the woods. Maybe part cattle dog. It would have guarded the house, Peter thought. It would have saved Dusty, maybe. He knew that was irrational, but he bought dog food anyway. Peter also purchased seven bags of parched corn and a windup flashlight. He drove home and brought his new purchases down to the room in the basement where he'd already stored six sealed ten-gallon drums of whole wheat flour, powdered milk, oil, dried lentils, beans, jerky. He'd bought and stocked a freezer, which he'd hooked up to a generator. He'd bought a backup generator. He bought a wood-burning stove and every day he chopped wood for an hour after work. That kept his mind focused, just like the priest. He and Father Travis were chopping themselves calm, miles apart, stacking heartache. Peter had a water filter, but to make sure, he bought another water filter. Last year, he'd had a new well put in, hooked to yet another backup generator. He had prebought shoes enough for two years of growing children's sizes. Dried apples, pears, apricots, prunes, cranberries. More water in five-gallon plastic jugs. Extra blankets. And then the guns—a gun case and locks. He kept his guns loaded because otherwise he saw no point. Twice he'd shot coyotes off the porch. Once a deer. He'd missed a cougar. The key was taped to the top of the seven-foot case. He was obsessive about testing that the case was locked. Boxes of ammunition. A trunk of flares. Cake mixes, sugar, cigarettes, whiskey, vodka, rum. He could trade it for things they would need—surely there was something he'd forgotten.

Actually, he'd forgotten what high interest his credit card charged. He was working extra hours now just to pay the minimum. Every time he found himself putting another sack of pancake mix or a shovel on the credit card, he told himself that after Y2K the credit card companies would be so messed up by confusing

2000 with 1900 that chances were his statements would get lost. The credit card companies would vanish, the banking system, crippled, would go back to swapping gold bricks. There would be no telephones, televisions, energy companies, no automobiles except old beaters without computerized engines, no gas pumps, no air traffic, no satellites. He would communicate by radio. He'd had an amateur's license for years. Already, at night all December, he had tense conversations with his contacts all around the world. Every morning, he woke and jotted down another item on his list. On the weekends, he took Maggie and LaRose with him to purchase a ream of paper, a case of envelopes. Pencils and pens. Stamps. Would there be an old-fashioned ground mail system? Probably, his contacts said. The storage room was jammed. Nola didn't notice because she was busy cooking those damn cakes.

Those chickens could have lived for months on the stale cakes, Peter thought. Nola smoothed rich frosting over sheet cakes, layer cakes, Bundt cakes, then carefully decorated each with LaRose's or Maggie's name. Even the children had now stopped eating them. He'd rescued the cakes and stored them in the unheated garage. When the local high school was renovated, he'd salvaged things he could use. It almost made him smile to look at the row of tin lockers and realize that behind each numbered door, on the narrow top shelf, there rested a pastel cake.

THE PARENTS didn't want it, but Christmas came for both families. Nola woke a week before the twenty-fifth, picturing her heart as a lump of lead. It lay so heavy in her chest that she could feel it, feebly thumping, reasonlessly going when she wasn't interested in its efforts. But Christmas. She turned over in bed and nudged Peter—she resented that he could sleep at all.

A tree, she said. Today's the day. We have to decorate a Christmas tree.

Peter opened his eyes, his bright, dear, blue eyes that never would belong to another child. The boy had come out true to both of them, the best of each of their features, mixed, they had marveled. The framed photographs were still arranged across the top of the dresser. Dusty still ran in the sun, posed as Spider-Man, played in a wading pool with Maggie, stood with them all in front of last year's Christmas tree. Nola found comfort in the pictures but closed her eyes now so that she would not see the likeness in Peter. To distract herself, she started humming, switched thoughts to her daughter. The thought of Maggie was complicated, sometimes alive with love. Sometimes heart-thumping fury. Maggie looked like her tough, impervious Polish grandmother or like her wild and devious Chippewa auntie. Those slant gold eyes that went black in her head when she was angry. That kind little startling crooked grin.

Nola's gentle humming was encouraging to Peter. It was a thing she used to do. He reached out and stroked her fingers. Maybe?

I can't, she said. Still, he kept asking either outright or with a touch.

I'll take the kids out.

He had a chain saw, he had three chain saws. They were all big brute chain saws overqualified for cutting Christmas trees. All he needed was a handsaw.

In fact, he said, sitting up in the chilly room, the handsaw with the red handle. We'll each take turns sawing down the perfect tree. He pictured it and he was surprised that it was even possible. But it was possible for him to get out of bed and do this thing that he'd done last year with a boy who had worn Maggie's hot-pink Disney Princess parka because his parka was in the wash. Dusty'd had so much confidence. When Maggie mocked him by calling him her little sister, he struck a Gaston pose and made Maggie laugh. She used to have a laugh like little bells.

It had changed, Peter thought. Her laugh had become a jeer, a bark, a series of angry shouts, an outburst. She laughed now when things were sad, not funny.

OUT IN the woods, in the scant snow and from a distance, Landreaux saw the three examining small spruce trees. He retreated. He had been checking snares, not looking for a tree. But when he saw them he remembered.

Well, said Emmaline, yes. We should.

I want a tree with white lights, said Snow.

Let's get out the colored lights, said Josette. White's too blah.

I like uniformity, said Snow. Everything else in this house is mixed up.

Hey, said Emmaline.

No offense, Mom, but a tree with solid white lights. It would be pretty.

Let's cut two trees then, said Emmaline.

Really? You mean really?

Little ones.

By the end of the day two small trees were set up in a corner of the living room, one decorated by each sister. For the first time, Emmaline didn't make the slightest effort—the sisters were competitive. They made ornaments from sequins, ribbons, powwow regalia bling, and LaRose's Play-Doh. They had never wrapped presents in wrapping paper. They used magazines, colored newspaper, shopping bags. At some point, though, everything stopped and the girls started crying. Coochy rolled his eyes and glared, then stalked out. Hollis made a strategic exit to the boys' room. Landreaux went to work early, and Emmaline was left stirring a pot of stew. Because of LaRose.

This exact thing had happened every week or so since Landreaux and Emmaline had explained to the other children what they had done.

In the boys' bedroom, Hollis plugged in his blow-up air mattress and turned the dial to inflate. For a minute or two, the high-pitched whine blocked out their voices. When the mattress was plump and comfortable, he lay back and shut his eyes.

Nothing. There was silence.

Hollis knew that his own dad, Romeo, had dropped him off with Emmaline and Landreaux sometime around Christmas. He'd been five, maybe six, like LaRose. He'd slept in one of the bunks for a while, but liked the blow-up better. He also knew that he'd been born in some sort of house, not a hospital. His memories of his first years were a jumble of sleeping under tables with people's feet, or better, in a dog bed with a dog, or with some other kids one winter, all wearing their parkas in the bed. There was a salty skin-dirt smell, overlaid with sour weed and clumped hair, that still closed his throat. The smell was on some people, some kids, and he'd back away from it. He took a shower now every day. He washed his clothes. Liked the smell of ironing. The girls teased him, but they liked it too. Being clean wasn't something he took for granted, or having his own bed. So, no, he didn't get involved with this LaRose issue. For safety, he just eased away. But they started up again. He could hear them.

So will you give me away if you kill somebody, Mom?

That was Josette shouting.

Snow stepped forward and slapped Josette, who slapped her back. Emmaline dropped the spoon and slapped them both—she had never slapped her child, or any child, before that moment. It happened so quickly—like a scene choreographed by the Three Stooges, which was what saved it. Emmaline started crying, Josette started crying, then Snow. The three of them clung together.

I want to cut off my hand, wept Emmaline. I never slapped you girls before.

We should each cut our hands off, wailed Snow.

Then making frybread two of us will have to stand together, you know, like each use our remaining hand, pat, pat. Josette and Snow demonstrated.

Pat, pat, how pitiful, cry-laughed Emmaline.

Slowly, one by one, they came back to the stew pot that Emmaline kept on sadly stirring. Hollis had dozed off, a short nap. Coochy had wrapped small things that he had stolen months ago from each of his sisters in order to give them something on Christmas. He placed the packages in the branches. Landreaux came home with two black Hefty bags full of mittens and hats, boots, jackets, all new. Father Travis had picked them out from the mission store before anybody else had been through the donations. Hollis came out of the bedroom and helped haul the bags to the house and sort the gifts. He tried to be jovial but couldn't. It was in his blood to give off feelings of holiday suspicion, instead of cheer, but that gave the girls reason to pick on him.

Quit making booda, the girls said to Hollis. Get your Christmas game face on and don't tell LaRose there's no Santa Claus.

If you see him, said Josette.

Snow slumped.

I'll find him, said Hollis. He didn't want to get involved but the words came out. I'll tell him that Santa's coming.

Hollis was not exactly handsome. His nose was big. Yet he was bitter and moody, so maybe more attractive than someone truly handsome. His hair was cut so it swept too neatly across his forehead.

He smoothed his hair to the side with the palm of his hand.

Rock it old school, said Josette when she caught him smoothing his hair that way.

She gave him her raised eyebrow, an accidental gesture that made him stare at her in fascination as she turned away.

The girls had decided to bring out the Eau Sauvage for their mom last. They did not trust Hollis or Willard, or even their dad, not to shatter the bottle with their feet. It was like that to live with guys. They just stepped on things, even gifts. Ojibwe girls, traditionally and now throwback traditionally, were taught from a young age not to step over things, especially boy things. Grandma's friend Ignatia Thunder, their traditional go-to elder, had told them all that their power might short out the boys' power. It was sexist, Josette said, another way to control the female. Snow semi-agreed. Emmaline went poker-faced. Maybe the Iron women weren't a hundred percent with the rule, but they still couldn't get themselves to forget about it.

The girls had bought weird gadgets for their brothers and dad. For the first time ever, Josette and Snow had bought colored tissue. They carefully arranged the boxes wrapped in transparent red paper. They put the box for their mother on a shelf. The glossy bow they'd bought for it shed red glitter on their hands.

What do we do with the presents for LaRose? said Snow.

They pushed aside the stuff on the big table—their beading, the jar lids of screws, the newspapers, schoolbooks—and began to eat their bowls of stew. Josette wanted to go over to the Ravich house and give the presents to LaRose. Snow said she couldn't stand Aunt Nola because she was picky. Coochy just hung his head down and ate. Hollis looked at him and ducked his head down too. Emmaline watched them until they turned to her.

Did you make LaRose his moccasins? Coochy asked. He had been the youngest until LaRose. There was a note in his voice of something like panic, and his eyes were glossy with tears.

Every year Emmaline made each of them new moccasins out of smoked moosehide, lined with blanket scraps; sometimes the ankles were trimmed with rabbit fur. She did this while visiting her mother, or at home, while watching her favorite TV shows or sitting with her children at the table to make certain they finished their homework. She was very good at it and people bought special orders from her. Her moccasins sometimes fetched two or three hundred dollars. The family was proud of her work and only wore their moccasins inside the house. Even Hollis wore them—his feet cute with beadwork, not cool. They each had a box of moccasins—one pair for every year.

I made them, said Emmaline.

⚜

SHE MADE LaRose his moccasins, Landreaux told his friend Randall, who ran sweat lodges and taught Ojibwe culture, history, and deer skinning in the tribal high school. Randall had been given ceremonies by elders he'd sought out and studied with—medicine people. Landreaux had demons, he said. Demons did not scare Randall, but he respected them.

It must have been something that happened to me when I was a kid but I can't remember, Landreaux said.

That's what everybody thinks, said Randall. Like if you suddenly remember what happened, you kill the demon. But it's a whole hell of a lot more complicated.

Going up against demons was Randall's work. Loss, dislocation, disease, addiction, and just feeling like the tattered remnants of a people with a complex history. What was in that history? What sort of knowledge? Who had they been? What were they now? Why so much fucked-upness wherever you turned?

They had heated up and carried in the rocks and now the two were sitting in the lodge wearing only baggy surfer shorts. Landreaux got the tarp down and sealed them inside. Randall dropped pinches of tobacco, sage, cedar, and powdered bear root on the livid stones. When the air was sharp with fragrance, he splashed on four ladles of water and the hot steam poured painfully into their lungs. After they prayed, Randall opened the lodge door, got the pitchfork, and brought in ten more rocks.

Okay, we're gonna go for broke, he said. Get your towel up so you don't blister. He closed the door and Landreaux lost track of the number of ladles Randall poured. He went dizzy and put the towel across his face, then dizzier, and lay down. Randall said a long invocation to the spirits in Anishinaabemowin, which Landreaux vaguely understood. Then Randall said, Ginitam, because Landreaux was supposed to speak. But all Landreaux could think of to say was, My family hates me for giving away LaRose.

Randall thought on this.

You did right, he said at last. They'll come to know. You remember what all the elders said? They knew the history. Who killed the mother of the first one, Mink, and what she could do. Then her daughter, her granddaughter, the next one, and Emmaline's mom. Evil tried to catch them all. They fought demons, outwitted them, flew. Randall talked about how people think what medicine people did in the past is magic. But it was not magic. Beyond ordinary understanding now, but not magic.

LaRose can do these things too, said Randall. He has it in him. He's stronger than you think. Remember you thought they said he was a mirage?

Gave him the name, Mirage. I know.

That's right.

Mirage knew how to dream the whereabouts of animals, how to leave his body during a trance and visit distant relatives. A trader named George Nelson had known others who could do this and had written about it back in the eighteenth century.

Landreaux spoke haltingly. What if the elders are just a bunch of regular old people no smarter than any of us, what if . . .

They are regular old people, said Randall. But they're people who learned off their old people, right?

Like here, we had the starvation year when most of our old people gave up their food. That generation died for us, eh? So we go north. Accept their words if they feel right.

But maybe they don't know?

Quit asking dumb questions. You'll bust your brain if you think like that. Let me ask you something. What was that boy Dusty like anyway?

Don't ask me that.

He ain't a footnote to your agony, bro. What was he like? Who knew that boy the best, of your family?

Landreaux finally answered.

LaRose.

So what did LaRose know about him?

Funny kid. Played adventures. The two of them had a pack of toys they made into cartoon characters. They were hilarious if you listened in on what they made up. Dusty . . .

Yeah, say his name, but use the spirit world marker. Use iban.

Dusty-iban liked to draw. He was good at drawing. We got some drawings he made for us.

Of what?

Horse. Dog. Spider-Man.

Landreaux was crying steadily in gulping sobs. Randall let that go on for a while.

Don't you cry no more. Unless it's for that kid. Don't you cry no more for your own pain. You put that cry energy into your family. Into doing good for Dusty-iban's family. When I hear you cry, I hear you cry for what you did, but you quit that now. Were you high when you shot him?

The medicine crackled. No.

Were you high?

No.

Were you high?

No.

We let our people get away with shit. We shouldn't. That's why I ask. Randall was quiet for a long time.

You're a good hunter. You take your shot careful, said Randall. Everybody knows you are careful and every year you bring down your supply. So I hadda ask.

Okay, said Landreaux.

I ain't totally convinced.

Okay, said Landreaux.

You off the booze?

Yes, said Landreaux.

Pills?

Yeah.

Okay. You gotta take on faith you did right with LaRose.

What about Emmaline, though? said Landreaux.

Nola is her sister.

Half sister, said Landreaux.

There are no half sisters, said Randall.

Emmaline doesn't like her sister.

She say that?

I can tell. And Nola can't stand Emmaline. So we don't get to see LaRose. Guess we assumed she'd bring him over; the boys used to play and all that.

Give them time to work it out, said Randall. Door! Oh, I forgot we ain't got no doorman. Door! I'm calling myself. Randall threw the tarp aside. Then he brought in more rocks and dropped them off the end of his pitchfork.

So many? Landreaux was already melted.

Haha, said Randall. Let's party. I'm gonna boil you alive.

Still, even after being poached like a frog by Randall, there was no peace. Landreaux felt worse and worse. He mourned LaRose's stringy arms hugging him, blamed himself for making LaRose his secret, favorite child. He began taking Coochy places, everywhere, keeping the one son close. Coochy was earnest, a cloudy boy, and he took things hard. Inside, he was deeply jolted. But he was so quiet nobody knew that.

Why so quiet? Landreaux asked, once.

Why talk when Josette's always talking?

He had a point.

Emmaline still thought about what Father Travis had said. If she wanted to, yes, she could take her son back. She wouldn't go through the system. With social work files, always sprouting forms in triplicate, anything could happen. But always, instead of taking that step, pushing things that far, Emmaline thought of Nola's loss, her husband's responsibility for Dusty's death, and she did something else. In the last few months she'd scraped bits of money for LaRose into a savings account. At other times she stitched her love into a quilt that she brought to the Ravich house. Emmaline gave the quilt to Nola, who thanked her at the door, folded up the blanket, and put it on the highest shelf of a closet. Also, every couple of weeks, Emmaline couldn't help herself from making the special soup and frybread that her son favored. She put it on Nola's doorstep or even into Nola's hands, hoping that LaRose would taste her love in it. Nola tossed it out. Just before Christmas, Emmaline came back with the moccasins. Left them wrapped with LaRose's name on them. Nola put the moccasins in a plastic box. Stuffed into that container they waited, and

Nola feared them, for their woodsmoke scent held the power of creation.

On those occasions she brought offerings, Emmaline saw that her half sister knew who was in charge. When Nola opened the door, her smile was pasted on lopsided. Sometimes before accepting the food, Nola's hands clasped and unclasped in distress. Nola's scrupulous thank-you covered a desperation that made Emmaline turn away. In the car, she put her hand in her pocket and touched a slip of paper upon which she had written *You can take him back.*

One day, just before Christmas without LaRose, after dropping off the food, she couldn't leave. Emmaline got out of the pickup and went back to the house. Maybe talk to Nola? Glimpse LaRose? She knocked, but Nola didn't answer. Emmaline knocked harder, then so hard her knuckles stung. She knew that Nola was somewhere in the house with her son, pretending that the knocks were not Emmaline.

Inside the house, LaRose heard his mother's voice and knew the smell of that soup which he wouldn't taste. Nola just kept reading *Where the Wild Things Are* over and over, until the knocking went away. Nola's voice was hoarse and thin.

And it was still hot, Nola said, and closed the book. Shall I read it again?

Okay, said LaRose in a tiny voice. A fuzzy wash of draining sadness covered him. He closed his eyes and fell asleep.

Is there a bitch gene? said Emmaline, walking in the door after standing outside the Ravich house, knocking.

Snow gave Josette a look and Josette said, Did my mother really say that?

Because if there is, Emmaline went on, my sister got it from her mother, who was renowned as a prime bitch.

The girls stared at Emmaline, frowning in an effort to reject their mother's talking this way.

Marn was her name. She killed her husband and got away with it. Of course, he was the leader of a cult.

Whoa.

The girls put their hands up.

Crazy talk, Mom, said Josette.

It's true, though, said Emmaline.

Okay, Mom, but may we remind you that you're talking about our grandfather? Josette and Snow nodded vigorously.

What you're saying, Mom, is way too weird. I mean a bitch is one thing, but killing your husband is out of whack. We don't want that.

So you don't want truth. What do you want? said Emmaline.

We want our life to get normal, duh, said Josette.

Uneventful, except for good things, said Snow.

Melodrama? That detracts.

Vocabulary words!

The girls smacked hands.

Fine, said Emmaline. I acquiesce.

⚜

MACKINNON SPOKE to the girl in her language, and she hid her muddy face.

All I did was ask her name, he said, throwing up his hands. She refuses to tell me her name. Give her some work to do, Roberts. I can't stand that lump in the corner.

Wolfred made her help him chop wood. But her movements displayed the fluid grace of her limbs. He showed her how to bake bread. But the firelight reflected up into her face and the heat melted away some of the mud. He reapplied it and tried to teach her to write. She formed the letters easily. But writing displayed her hand, marvelously formed. Finally—she suggested it herself—the girl went off to set snares. She made herself well enough understood. She planned to buy herself back from Mackinnon by selling the furs. He hadn't paid that much for her. It would not take long, she said.

All this time, because she understood exactly why Wolfred had replaced the grime on her face, she slouched and grimaced, tousled her hair and smeared her features. And she picked up another written letter every day, then words, phrases. She began to sprinkle them in her talk.

For a wild savage, she was certainly intelligent, thought Wolfred. Pretty soon she's going to take my job. Haha. There was nobody to joke with but himself.

FATHER TRAVIS answered the telephone, tipped back his chair. When he heard the name of the new bishop of the diocese, he said nothing.

No surprise.

The new bishop, Florian Soreno, would take a hard-line stance toward all the hot-button issues—this was a red state. Father Travis worked in a blue zone.

Reservations were blue dots or blots, voting Democrat. The only Republican he could think of, beside himself, was Romeo Puyat. With a new bishop, Father Travis might get a Dominican with a liberation-theology bent because this bishop might want to punish such a priest by sending him to a reservation. Or perhaps a new order would take over entirely—there were so many fundamentalist orders springing up. He rather liked SSPX. Society of Saint Pius the Tenth. He missed Latin Mass and they were big on keeping the Tridentine Mass going. However, the other issues, abortion for instance, left him cold. His father had taught him that women's business is women's business. There was yet another possibility—church authorities still played the shell game with their pederast priests.

Getting rid of the last one had been difficult.

He himself might be reassigned, or he might suddenly have a priest here with more authority and seniority to whom he must answer. He might get a swamper for a housemate—a sick priest in the slump of a long depression. Or a whole sack of nuns might be assigned to the convent suddenly, where now it was run by an oblate group of laypersons and used as a retreat and conference center.

Or, sometimes, nothing happened. He could always hope. He looked up at the cracked plaster ceiling of his office. There was a pale-blue line on the ceiling, scraped of carpenter's chalk. That color. It was as if she had opened a blue door in his mind.

Father Travis pulled on his coat and walked into the brilliant, dry snow. It was the time of hallowed peace. He loved Christmas and Midnight Mass. The glow of candles spiritualized the features of people who drove him nuts. *Let us lay aside the works of darkness and put on the armor of light,* he would say in his sermon. And then there was that blue door. There was no shame in it, no sense that he was violating his or Landreaux's or her vows or anything else. He could be happy in his thoughts, couldn't he? In spite of Matthew? Not his favorite gospel. White wings rustled. He glanced around, filled with an odd joy. Brightness falls from the air.

NOLA MADE their Christmas lavish, but it didn't help. The lead sinker in her chest was leaking molten lead into her veins, slowly stopping her circulation. Her feet and hands were bone cold. She shivered in layers of fleece, sat next to the woodstove, and drank hot tea all day. Getting out of bed, out of a chair, changing her position, was like moving furniture. She could loosen her limbs only by holding LaRose in her lap every afternoon until he slept. He napped hard and sweetness flowed into Nola. She didn't move except to rock him back to sleep if he stirred. When he woke, she was reluctant to let him go. Then she pushed herself along and pretended around the children that she was really there instead of in the ground. She could not pretend so well with Peter, but he was obsessed the week after Christmas with what would happen on New Year's Eve. He'd planned it all out. When the night came, he put his plan into action.

December 31, 1999. Peter stuffed enough wood into the living room bins to keep the stove going all night—he was certain that their computer-regulated electric power would fail. He filled jugs for drinking water, and pails for flushing the toilets, then turned off the water just in case the pipes froze. He made beds downstairs in the living room, where the woodstove would give off a comfortable heat. He'd bought high-loft sub-zero sleeping bags, thinking that they might have to use them all winter. In hope, he'd bought a double bag for himself and Nola. And he'd bought thick foam pads. He spread all of this attractive bedding out on the floor, and the children brought down their pillows. LaRose cradled his action creature. There was food, the battery-powered radio, the computer to watch go crazy at midnight, and card games. Nola made popcorn and she laughed at everything LaRose did. She seemed delighted, and she was, because if the world did end this would all be over. She would not have to keep pretending to get better. Any chaos that happened wouldn't be her fault. Peter and Maggie played Go Fish, Crazy Eights, Hearts, and in a hushed, excited voice, Nola read book after book to LaRose.

Eventually, the children wormed into their puffy silken sleeping bags and fell asleep. Peter lighted candles, brought out a bottle of sparkling wine, built up the fire. He poured the amber froth slowly down the side of Nola's champagne flute, then his own. They raised their glasses in silence. Nola pushed her hair, the slack blond curls, off her face. As they drank they looked into each other's eyes and saw the strangers who now inhabited the bodies that had together made their son.

I wonder who you are now, Nola said.

It's just me, said Peter, the same old me.

No it's not. We'll never be the same.

All right. Peter drank deeply. We'll never be the same. That doesn't mean we change, you know, how we are with each other. I still love you.

His words hung out there in the stillness.

I still love you, too, she said at last, forcing conviction into her voice, sipping at her wine, then suddenly draining it. More! Nola held out her glass, laughing. After all, what does it matter if we're the same or not? It's the end of the world! Let's toast the end of the world.

Her face was bright and hot. She flashed her pretty, good-luck, crookedy smile. Her teeth were small and pearly. He'd always said her smile blasted happiness into a room—and it was true that when she got excited she was infectious, as cool people are when they suddenly let go. They carry others by the force of surprise. Peter filled her glass and then motioned up the stairs. She rose exalted from the sleeping bag, tousled, barefooted. They climbed the stairs together, and in their bedroom locked the door. They made love with an urgency sweet at first. But as they twined deeper they jolted down into a mean-walled, sour place.

She seemed to be trying to choke him. Her thumbs were at the base of his throat, pressing. He swiped away her arms but her hands sneaked back as claws and clenched his ass. That hurt, but so what because she slammed him into her and he drove himself until he stopped thinking. She slid out from under his chest. He let her get on top of him but then remembered— she looked frail but she could slap like a motherfucker. She knocked tears into his eyes. He caught her arms at the wrist, turned her over, forced her to kneel. When he started again, she said, Wait, you're hurting me.

He let her go and she rolled out a foot, heel first. Tried to end things with a dirty kick, but missed. The next day there'd be a hot bruise on his thigh. Maybe he was too rough after that, except the whole time as she fought him she was coming, and coming, furiously mute, then weeping as he slowed down and finally left her.

I shouldn't have done that, Peter whispered after a while. Are you okay? he asked when she didn't answer. The black silence fizzed in the room. Aw, he said, okay, I'm sorry it got like that but not sorry because you were there, too, I felt it. I love you so much and maybe it could happen, we could have another baby, Nola, we haven't talked about that and it wouldn't replace Dusty and it wouldn't replace LaRose and I love him too, it wouldn't change what happened but a baby might make you feel, something, something that might help, even happy.

I'm cold, said Nola. I hate your guts.

He said nothing. After a while she dropped her head on his chest and soon her breath came, slow and even. He left her upstairs once she fell asleep. Downstairs, he pulled the covers tenderly up the throats of the sleeping children. Something made him look up. The rusty dog was on the porch watching through the sliding glass doors. To let the dog in was so simple—on this night of nights. He opened the door. The dog entered, quivering with attention. His rosy upright ears drooped slightly, but strained to undertake the meaning of his admittance.

You . . . said Peter. He couldn't talk to this dog like a regular dog.

You aren't a regular dog, are you. You must be hungry. We had chicken, but no bones for you.

He looked down at the dog, who sat expectantly, as if he were trained.

The bones splinter, said Peter to the dog, who cocked its head, an alarming gesture of understanding.

You could choke, said Peter.

The dog's brown eyes were riveted on Peter's hands as he pulled meat from the chicken carcass. When Peter put down the pan of scraps, the dog lunged forward moaning with joy and bolted the food in three heavy gulps. After, the dog went straight to the children. He stood over Maggie, then LaRose, utterly still, except that his nose worked, obtaining what would seem to us a supernatural knowledge of all the children had done, eaten, touched, in past weeks. Satisfied, tail beating the air, the dog toured restlessly all around the room and sniffed every object as though to memorize its essence. When he was finished with his inventory, the dog trod out a bed for himself at the children's feet. It was made of all kinds of other dogs—a tawny head, delicate paws, a roan coat, dark patches where eyebrows would be on a person. Peter scratched its back. The dog beamed, then made a sound that conveyed great pleasure, an unusual clucking sound, and fell asleep, stinking gently in the luscious warmth. Peter adjusted the children's sleeping bags again and turned away. Then, like a hungry man who has waited for his meal, he poured himself a glass of whiskey and sat down before the computer. It was almost midnight. He sat through midnight. For hours afterward he kept meandering about in cyberspace. A few digital clocks in France read 1900. Circuits in a few places faltered and flickered. There was no panic. At some point, he put his head down and must have passed out. Dawn was sad, calm, and brimming with debt.

The Passage

The daughter of Mink brooded on the endlessly shifting snow. *I will make a fire myself, as the stinking chimookoman won't let me near his fire at night. Then I can pick the lice from my dress and blanket. His lice will crawl on me again if he does the old stinking chimookoman thing he does.* She saw herself lifting the knife from his belt and slipping it between his ribs.

The other one, the young one, was kind but had no power. He didn't understand what the crafty old chimookoman was doing. Her struggles only seemed to give the drooling dog strength and he knew exactly how to pin her quickly, make her helpless.

The birds were silent. Snow was falling off the trees that day. She had scrubbed her body red with snow.

She threw off everything and lay naked in the snow asking to be dead. She tried not to move, but the cold stabbed ice into her heart and she began to suffer intensely. A person from the other world came. The being was pale blue without definite form. It took care of her, dressed her, tied on her makazinan, blew the lice off, and wrapped her in a new blanket, saying, *Call upon me when this happens and you shall live.*

⸎

THIS DOG reeks, said Nola.

I'm going to wash him some more, said Peter. He's kind of got a natural smell.

The dog eyed Nola adoringly, bowed to her twice, then stretched its nose tentatively toward her knee.

Don't, said Nola to the dog. She glared into its questing eyes, and the dog sat back on its haunches, struck with wonder.

You stink, said Nola again.

The dog pantingly grinned, alive to her every word.

It had wandered outside and fought. Peter had heard other dogs yapping and howling in the woods. Some years in winter the dogs from the reservation formed packs, chased and slow-killed deer. He'd shot them down on his own land. This dog had come back with a nick in its nose, a torn tail, and an injured eye.

That one eye is going to be permanently bloodred, she pointed out.

This dog loves life, he said. I'm going to tie him up, though. Keep him in the yard.

Going to neuter him?

Peter didn't answer.

He might have eaten a lit firecracker, see? One whole side of his lip is swollen up!

Well, he's got a story. He's come from somewhere, said Peter, rubbing the dog all over so it grunted with pleasure. The dog's eyes shut in bliss; its torn lip showed sharp teeth. Peter laughed. This dog will snarl forever but his eyes are joyous, he said. Even the red one.

We're not keeping him, Nola said.

We have to, said Peter.

Nola stiffened and left the room. The dog's eyes followed, weak with loss.

Rolfing the dog's ears and neck, Peter whispered, Hey, you know something! I know you know something. What you gonna tell me?

As he rubbed the dog, Peter's thoughts drifted. His mind relaxed, and so he wasn't upset by the words that formed in the flow of ease.

I saw Dusty that day, said the dog in Peter's mind. I carry a piece of his soul in me.

Peter put his big windburned forehead on the dog's forehead.

I'm not crazy, am I?

No, said the dog. These are things a normal man might think.

IN THE middle of February a south wind blew through and thawed down the snow, warmly rattled the doors and windows. Landreaux was out in his shirtsleeves pumping gas into the Corolla and didn't notice that Peter was pulled up to Whitey's store. When Peter came out carrying a couple of dripping cold six-packs—there they were. Landreaux turned away, frowned at the quickly rising numbers on the readout.

I know. Peter was suddenly next to him. It cost me thirty to fill the tank.

The two hadn't spoken since Landreaux brought his son to the Ravich house. Landreaux nodded and said something neutral.

Nola took the kids to Minot, said Peter. They're staying over. I'm batching it tonight.

He asked if Landreaux wanted to drop by.

Sure, said Landreaux, not thinking of the beer but then thinking of it as he drove the ten miles to the edge of the reservation and past, to the Ravich house. He still thought of getting drunk every day, but he'd gotten used to the thought and stood outside of it. The tires crackled in the Ravich driveway. Snow thinly frosted the clipped evergreens planted at the foundation of the house. At the sight of the still windows a choking panic grabbed Landreaux, and he almost drove away. But there was Peter in the doorway, gesturing.

Landreaux slowly got out of the car and Peter waved him through the door. The dog that their family had been feeding was standing behind Peter. It recognized Landreaux and turned away after a resonant glance. Even with the dog living there now, the house smelled of nothing. Nola would light a scentless scent-sucking candle if she whiffed an odor. Her house never smelled of people's habits. It never smelled of stale clothing, old food, or even what she was freshly cooking because she ran a hood fan that sucked the smells right up through the roof. But nothing has a smell too, and Landreaux remembered.

He left his shoes at the door, walked across the carpeted living room, sat with Peter among the polished antiques. The living room was set off from the kitchen by a long island-type counter. Without remembering, or maybe remembering too well, Peter went into the kitchen and opened the refrigerator. He cracked a cold beer. Sitting at the table now, he invited Landreaux to do the same. He did. Landreaux didn't see himself from the outside the way he normally witnessed his thoughts. Somehow he'd slipped around his thoughts in that moment, and as he sat down he also took a drink. When he did that, his porous brain sponged up the action, and then at a cellular level, the substance.

Thanks, said Peter, looking at the table.

Thanks, said Landreaux, looking at the can.

They allowed a swell of emotion to envelop them. Started talking about things in general, about the people Landreaux worked for and the crisis boarding school where Emmaline was the sort of director who also ended up teaching classes, about the farm and Peter's jobs selling lumber and at Cenex, extra jobs that Peter had taken to clear up bills, but would probably keep in order to afford to farm. They finished one beer and started on another. Four or five and Landreaux would start to feel the slide; there would be no going back. He tried to sip this one calmly but the non-present presence of his son was balling up inside him, ringing in his head. The first swell of emotion had been an ache of fellow feeling. That was quickly sliding away with the second beer. Landreaux put his broad hand up, touched his cheek. His face was pitted not with old acne scars but from a case of chicken pox that had nearly blinded him as a child. He tried to veer from what was developing between them.

Have to make sure he gets that new vaccination covers chicken pox, said Landreaux. That's what did this.

Peter's gaze was fixed on Landreaux's face. Nola's periodic furies damped down his anger. He defused her with his calm. Any irritation of his would ignite her bleak fury. So the sudden, tremendous pain below his ribs was confusing. He didn't recognize it or want to recognize it.

Chicken pox, huh?

Yeah.

Thought you'd been sprayed in the face with buckshot, you know, by some asshole with a shotgun.

Peter was surprised to hear what came out of his mouth. Unnerved, he jumped up, let the dog out, and ripped another beer from the plastic rings. He decided he was glad he had spoken. Why not. How would Landreaux take it?

With a deep, blue dive. Taking the words down with him. Holding his breath as he went. Landreaux shut his eyes. Held his hand out. Peter slapped a can into his palm. He stood there leaking aggression. Landreaux's eyes flew open. He jumped up and swiftly brought the can to Peter's temple—not much of a weapon—but

Peter wasn't there. He'd dropped and hit Landreaux in a tackle, tried to pin him, but Landreaux got his knees up and Peter had to lean in to throw a punch, which gave Landreaux a chance to put a headlock on him, roll him, so it went. They smashed the table over, stood up on either side of it, mouths hanging open, eyes locked in shame, panting.

Okay, said Peter, forget the beer.

Outside, the dog was barking.

You know about me, Landreaux said.

Yeah, said Peter, righting the table. Fuck it.

Landreaux pulled a chair around and sat down, put his head in his hands.

Go ahead. Beat the fuck out of me, he said.

I wish.

The pain was still balled up in Peter but now more familiar. I could make you into a dirty drunk. I could ambush and blow you away. I could get you somehow but it wouldn't do the thing I want. Dusty. I dream about him every night.

Even with LaRose here?

I do, and I feel guilty, I mean, I love your boy.

Landreaux relaxed at that *your boy*. He looked at Peter.

I'd give my life to get Dusty back for you, said Landreaux. LaRose is my life. I did the best that I could do.

They righted the chair, the table, and sat again, nodding, but they didn't drink another beer. Peter put his hand across his face, tipped his chair back, then came back down and looked straight at Landreaux.

As far as that goes, he said carefully, some questions need to be asked.

Let's ask the questions later, said Landreaux.

He dropped his gaze, pushing slowly away. He was disoriented, suddenly heavy with despair. He'd been waiting for something legal. Legal adoption. He got up and walked out the door. He needed to wait some more.

☙

MRS. PEACE smiled at the rug. The carpet still smelled like a sweet chemical bouquet. Floating in her gray velveteen recliner, with flowers blooming at her feet. She held the tin on her lap. Almost half a year had gone by without an attack, but her enemy had sneaked in. Billy inhabited her like a wave. She fought him off. The Fentanyl was at its strongest now. Agony that had squeezed her worn old body from heart to gut was releasing her, reluctantly. It didn't like to let her go. But there, free. Her body blossomed with each easier breath. From her clear paneled doors, Mrs. Peace could see across the snow-swept yard, past a gnarled apple tree and tangled fence line, down the long swoop of field, to the cemetery.

People had started putting sun-powered lawn ornaments alongside the other mementos they left on loved ones' graves. She and Emmaline had staked quite a few lanterns into the ground in August. A daughter who at birth had almost killed her was down there. Her mother was down there. There was a white stone, fadingly scratched. There were so many relatives and friends down the long hill, people she loved. In an hour the homes of the dead would begin glowing milkily beneath the snow.

Pain relinquished her to dreamy ease. Her mother came to visit, walking up the hill in that old fatally thin coat. She didn't have to knock on the door, she just came through and sat down, kicking off her galoshes, very nice galoshes trimmed with plush. Curling up on the couch with the peppermint pink afghan, she said, All is calm, all is bright.

I know, said Mrs. Peace. But that yarn was supposed to be a duller and more soothing shade of pink. I misjudged the effect.

At Fort Totten boarding school, I had a dress this color in a white and blue calico print. Well, it wasn't the dress, which was gray like all the dresses. Just the sash. We sometimes got to wear a sash or a scrap of color in our hair. Special occasions only. After all, it was military. From a military post to an industrial military school.

I still think of you every day, said Mrs. Peace. I just have these few pictures, but I memorized your pictures. I looked at you a lot.

Her mother shivered in the afghan.

Can you turn up the heat?

Here, just watch!

LaRose had a can-snatcher, an elongated grasping tool. She used it to turn the dial on the wall. Her mother cried out with pleasure.

Pretty soon that's going to feel so good!

I'll make you tea.

They don't let us have tea. We had milk. Porridge and blue milk. What's left when all the cream is skimmed off, eh? We drank that. The bell rang. It was always the bells. All we did was to the bells. Pretty soon you started hearing them all the time.

I still hear them.

Bang around in your head, eh?

Like a feast day.

Goodness, my girl. I feel that heat coming on. The cold sinks into my bones down there, like always. That first year, they took away my blanket, my little warm rabbit blanket. They took away my fur-lined makazinan. My traditional dress and all. My little shell earrings, necklace. My doll. She's still down there in that souvenir case, eh? They sold things our family sent along with us for souvenirs. Traded them. You wonder.

What they did!

I know! With all the braids they cut off, boys' and girls', across the years.

There was hundreds of children from all over as far as Fort Berthold, so hundreds and hundreds of braids those first years. Where did the braids go?

Into our mattresses? We slept on our hair, you think?

Or if they burned our hair you would remember the smell.

But with our hair off, we lost our power and we died.

Look at this picture, said Mrs. Peace. Rows and rows of children in stiff clothing glowered before a large brick building.

Look at those little children. Those children sacrificed for the rest of us, my view. Tamed in itchy clothes.

These kind of pictures are famous. They used them to show we could become human.

The government? They were going for extermination then. That *Wizard of Oz* man, yes? You have his clipping.

LaRose drew out bits and scraps of paper, newsprint.

Here.

THE ABERDEEN SATURDAY PIONEER, 1888

BY FRANK BAUM

. . . the nobility of the Redskin is extinguished, and what few are left are a pack of whining curs who lick the hand that smites them. The Whites by law of conquest, by justice of civilization, are Masters of the American continent, and the best safety of the frontier settlements will be secured by the total annihilation of the few remaining Indians. Why not annihilation? Their glory has fled, their spirit is broken, their manhood effaced, better that they die than live as the miserable wretches they are.

1891

BY FRANK BAUM

. . . our only safety depends upon the total extermination of the Indians. Having wronged them for centuries we had better, in order to protect our civilization, follow it up by one more wrong and wipe these untamed and untameable creatures from the face of the earth.

Oh well, said Mrs. Peace, here we are. It's a wonder.

This ain't Oz, said her mother.

Looks like Oz down in your graveyard. All those green glowy lights.

No poppies there in winter.

I've got better stuff in here.

Mrs. Peace rummaged around. Under all of the papers and mementos in the rose tin, she kept her Fentanyl patches—white with green lettering, in translucent pouches. She was extremely careful with their use. She was supposed to keep ahead of the pain, but she didn't like to get too cloudy. She let the pain crank her up until she could think of nothing else. Her patches gave the medicine out in a slowly timed release. The amount she took now would have killed her years ago.

Exterminate or educate.

Just take the pain away, she said.

It was good we became teachers so we could love those kids.

There was good teachers, there was bad teachers. Can't solve that loneliness.

It sets deep in a person.

Goes down the generations, they say. Takes four generations.

Maybe finally worked itself out with the boy.

LaRose.

Could be he's finally okay.

It's possible.

The recliner went plushier. The air dripped with sound. Watery streams of soft noise rushed along her sides. She put out her arms. Her mother took her hands. They drifted. This is how she visited with her mother, who had died of tuberculosis like her mother and grandmother. It was a disease of infinite cruelty that made a mother pass it to her children before she died. Mrs. Peace had not died of her mother's tuberculosis. She had been in the sanitarium in 1952, the year isoniazid and its various iterations astonishingly cured the incurable.

I was sure that I would die like you. So I tried not to get attached to anything or anyone. You are numb for years, she said to her mother, then you begin to feel. At first it is a sickening thing. To feel seems like having a disease. But you get used to sensations over time.

You were saved for a reason, eh?

Those kids, said Mrs. Peace. To knit with them, make them powwow clothes, bring them up dancing. Have our little tea parties where I put just a little coffee in their mugs of milk.

Do you ever see them now?

From time to time, the ones that lived. Landreaux, of course. And that Romeo comes around. I hear about lots of others. Successful. Not.

The two bobbed in space, still holding hands, and her mother cried out, Even I want to give you all the love I never could! I hated to die and leave you. How good that we can be together now!

✦

NOLA DRAGGED Maggie to Holy Mass. While kneeling, Maggie slumped, resting her buttocks impudently on the edge of the pew. Her mother elbowed her, and Maggie slid out of reach. The sly movement triggered Nola and she struck out. In one motion, she backhanded Maggie and clawed her back into place. She'd moved with such swift assurance that Maggie gaped and plunked down. Nobody else around them seemed to notice, though Father Travis's eye flicked as he walked up to the pulpit.

Father Travis had long ago stopped giving sermons. He just told stories. Today he told how Saint Francis preached to the birds, the fish, the faithful rabbit, and then was called in to rescue an Italian village from a ravenous wolf.

Father Travis walked out into the middle of the aisle and acted out the meeting between Saint Francis and the wolf. He described the Wolf of Gubbio, monstrous large and enthusiastic about eating people. When Saint Francis arrived at the village, he followed the wolf's tracks into the woods and then confronted the wolf. This wolf had never been challenged, and was surprised that Saint Francis was not afraid. The wolf listened to Saint Francis and agreed to stop marauding the village. The wolf sealed its promise by placing its paw in St. Francis's hand.

When a person speaks calmly and exudes peace, even a wolf may listen, said Father Travis.

Maggie thought, Yeah, but sometimes you have to bite.

Saint Francis brought the wolf back to the people of Gubbio and extracted mutual promises. They would feed the wolf. Every day it could make the rounds of the houses and receive a handout. In return, it would stop attacking people. Again, the wolf put its paw in Saint Francis's hand, this time in front of the villagers. The wolf swore an oath by rolling over on its back and then bounding up on its hind legs and howling. So there was peace. The wolf died of old age. The people of Gubbio buried it beneath a tombstone and mourned its passing.

Maggie held her fury back because she wanted to hear the story, but when Father Travis finished, she moved away again, this time safely out of her mother's reach.

People only listened to the wolf because it ate them. Maggie was certain.

＊

EVERYONE KNEW the stray rez dog who'd lived in the woods was Peter's dog now. But the dog slipped off his dog run and made a polite visit to Landreaux's place one afternoon. So when Landreaux had to go take his shift at the housing complex, where Awan waited for attention, he coaxed the dog into the back of his car, intending to drop him off at the Ravich house.

Landreaux meant to leave the dog at the door, that's all. But Peter answered, and after he took the dog back he abruptly spoke.

We should finish that conversation.

I'm late, said Landreaux.

Won't take long, said Peter. Can you come in? Five minutes?

Landreaux hunched his shoulders, made to kick off his boots at the door.

Nah, don't worry, said Peter.

Landreaux sat down at the table, touched the edge. He didn't want to speak, to bring up the thing he dreaded. He could feel the tension bubbling up inside, the quickened pump of his heart.

The agreement, whatever we call it, Peter started.

Landreaux just nodded, staring at his fingers.

The question is, said Peter.

Landreaux's heart just quit.

The question is, said Peter. What's it doing to him?

Landreaux's heart started beating again.

What's it doing to him, he weakly said.

He's sad, said Peter. Missing his family. Can't understand. You're right there down the road. I catch his face in the rearview when we pass. He's so quiet, just looking at his old house.

This was all Peter could stand to tell. About the muffled crying, nothing. About LaRose beating his head with his hands, nothing. About his secret questions whispered only to Peter, *Where is my real mom?*, he couldn't tell.

Landreaux took in what Peter did say, then spoke. Feel like I used him to take it off me. Traditional ways. Fuck. This isn't the old days. But then again there was reason in it. I wanted to . . .

Landreaux trailed off. Help, thought Peter.

I think it does. I know it does. Help. As long as we're with LaRose we're thinking about him, and we love him. He's a decent boy, Landreaux, you've raised him right. Him being with us helps Nola. Helps Maggie. It does help . . . but what's it doing to him? I mean, he's holding Nola together. Big job. Meanwhile this is probably tearing Emmaline apart.

Oh, said Landreaux, she hides it.

Nola doesn't hide it, said Peter. You can see it everywhere. He gestured, jerky with anxiety, around the area—living, dining, kitchen. Both men dropped into their own thoughts. An itchy claustrophobic feeling had been gathering in Landreaux. This feeling was stirred up whenever he entered a house or building that was aggressively neat. He had already felt that here—life consumed by order. Also in Landreaux's past there were the buzzers, bed checks, whistles, bells, divided trays, measured days of boarding school. There was the unspeakable neatness of military preparation for violence.

I can't move anything, said Peter. She puts it back. She's got a mental tape measure. She can tell when anything is changed in the slightest. Believe me, she knew we tipped the table over.

Landreaux nodded.

I'd like to . . . switch that off in her, said Peter.

Then felt disloyal. After all, Nola had moved into the Ravich house, fairly new, but also filled with things that his parents and grandparents had owned. Her meticulous care of these objects comforted him.

I mean if she could just let go sometimes, he added.

You'd like her to be happy again, said Landreaux.

Happy? Peter said the word because it was an odd, archaic word. She gets mad at Maggie, that's the worst, but really, she's done nothing but try. She's a good mother. At first I tried to bring LaRose back to you guys. I thought what you did was all wrong, thought she would get better without him. Then I realized if I brought him back, that would kill her.

Landreaux thought of Emmaline wretchedly bent over in the sweat lodge.

Still, it's LaRose, said Peter. His breath rasped. His heart sounded in his ears. He knew what he was going to say would make Nola cry in that shrill animal keening way she went out to the barn to do, after the kids were sleeping, hoping she could not be heard. It's LaRose, said Peter. We have to think of him. We should share him. We should, you know, make things easier between us all.

Oh, said Landreaux.

As if the lid had lifted off his brain he blazed with shock and light. He couldn't speak. Weakness assailed him and he put his head down on the table. Peter looked down on his parted hair, the long tail of it, the loose power of Landreaux's folded arms. A sinuous contempt gripped him and he thought of the rapture he would feel for an hour, maybe two hours, after he brought down his ax on Landreaux's head. Indeed, he'd named his woodpile for his friend, and the mental image was the cause of its growing size. If not for LaRose, he thought, if not for LaRose. Then the picture of the boy's grief covered his thinking.

After Landreaux had left, Peter lay on the living room carpet, staring at the ceiling fan. Hands on his forehead, stomach whirling with the blades. He wasn't a man to make friends, and it was hard, this thing with Landreaux. Peter was six foot two, powerful because he worked the farm, but weak, too, in the ankles, in the knees, in the wrists and neck. Wherever one part of his body met up with another part, it hurt. Still, it was his method to suck it up. High school coaches had taught him that. This was his family's farm before the family died off, except for one now Floridian brother he'd bought out. Peter's family were Russian-German immigrants, there long enough to have picked buffalo bones off the land.

When he is feeling well, Peter throws LaRose and Maggie in the air. Falling, they catch the smile on his cool, Slavic face. He rises at 5:00 a.m. and goes to bed at midnight. He works those other jobs, plus the farm, yet there is so much left over. Nola, he met in Fargo. They both went to NDSU and it was a surprise they'd never run into each other in small-town Pluto—a raw little place with a few old buildings, a struggling grocery, some gift shops, a Cenex, and a new Bank of the West. Peter's family had farmed outside of town and Nola's mother, Marn, had lived there as a child—they sometimes visited the land she had leased out. Once things became too difficult after Billy Peace died, she had moved with the kids to Fargo. Made them go by their second names because of certain people.

From the beginning, Peter was crazy about Nola. She was tensile and finely made. Her hair was dirty blond, though she bleached it brighter. It turned brownish in the winter if she let it go, exactly his shade. Her face was cheerleader-cute and dainty, but her eyes were slant and calculating. She was elusive, sliding away into her thoughts. No matter how much energy he expended he couldn't catch her. He couldn't even find her when she was right in front of him. Sometimes her merciless dark eyes gave nothing back. Her face shut. She was a blank wall, fresh painted. He groped to find a secret hinge. It sprung sometimes in bed and she was alive to him with radiant warmth, her face rosy and gentle, her eyes merry with affection. That was real, wasn't it? He couldn't tell anymore.

How would he give her the news? The plan that he and Landreaux had agreed upon. Sharing the upbringing of LaRose—a casual arrangement month by month that the men would set up, it being too loaded otherwise. He would tell her carefully. He would tell her in the barn. Then Nola could react however. Peter had become adept at maintaining an inner equilibrium during the screaming, shouting, foul shouting, rage, sorrow, misery, fury, whimper-weeping, fear, frothing, foaming, singing, praying, and then the ordinary harrowing peace that followed.

Sometimes now in the ordinary peace they made love. It wasn't mean like the first time. He was not forgiven, but he was accepted. As an asshole, maybe, but one who would not hurt her again. Okay, slug me, he had told her every time she was on top. No thanks, she always said, it will make us even. Their love was quiet, maybe tender, maybe odd or maybe fake. She hummed while she sucked his cock. But now she hummed actual tunes. The next day he'd remember the melody as sly and mocking, though he couldn't name the words. Her glow of sweet responsive warmth sank into him like radiation. Sometimes it strengthened him. Sometimes he felt it poisoning his bones.

After he and Landreaux spoke of raising LaRose together, it was as if she knew. Nola came to Peter deliciously needy. Afterward, she nestled against him, pushing him around to get comfortable. No way he was going to tell her then. Maybe in the morning, he thought. After Maggie went to school.

You dove, he said. He stroked her shoulder all one way, like feathers.

A mean dove. Who will peck out your heart, she said.

That would hurt.

I can't help myself. Will you stay with me, she said, suddenly, if I go crazy?

There was desolation in her voice, so he tried to joke.

Well, you already are crazy.

He felt tears on his chest. Oh, he'd gone too far.

In a good way. I love your crazy!

How come you're not crazy?

I am, inside.

No, you're not. You're not crazy. How can you not go crazy? We lost him. How can you not go crazy? Don't you fucking care?

Her voice rose sharper, louder.

You don't fucking care! You cold bitch, you Nazi. You don't care!

Hey, he said, holding her. Both of us can't go crazy. At the same time, anyway. Let's take turns.

She went silent, then abruptly laughed.

Bitch. Nazi.

She laughed harder. Her laughing slipped a bolt in Peter, and then they were both laughing in a sick way, both unhinged again with the same first anguish, both weeping into each other's hair, snot dripping in the sheets.

You're still my dove, he said, later on. I'll never stop loving you.

But she terrified him, freezing his love, and he could hear the death of certainty in what he said. The worst kind of loneliness gripped him. The kind you feel alongside another person.

Later still, waking in the dark, he put his hand on her skin, sleepily wishing his strange old wish, that he could dissolve into her, be her, that they could be one creature rocking in the dark.

Yes, wearily, as he drifted again toward sleep. All this and he still had to give her the news tomorrow. Not in the house where LaRose could hear, but out in the barn. It might drive her dangerously past crazy, at first, to share LaRose, but it had to be. He couldn't bear the weird indecency of what he felt they were doing to the child.

Nola was fine when he told her and fine for days after. She'd expected it. She was all right, until she saw the mouse, not that she was afraid of it. But when you saw one, that meant ten thousand had already invaded. It was in the entryway to the garage. She cornered and tried to stomp it, but the mouse popped from under her shoe. That steamed her up. She was not alone at the house that day but Maggie and LaRose were out in the yard. She had just made sure. They were not allowed to leave the yard and knew she would check on them every fifteen minutes. Nola stood in the little mudroom between the house and the garage. She rarely went into the garage—it was Peter's place, his workshop. She hardly drove anywhere, but when she did he moved the car out for her. Since he'd taken the extra jobs, he did not spend much time out in the garage.

She entered and was hit immediately, loathsomely, with the sour fug of mice. She backed out, stood in the entry gulping fresh air, then swallowed a giant breath, flipped the lights on, and walked back in. There was a swirling sound, a sense of invisible motion. Tiny black mouseshit seeds covered Peter's workbench. The bucket of rags. She ran back out to the entryway, breathed, saved another deep breath, and walked in again. Maybe there was grain in the bottom of the bucket. Something had drawn them. Maybe he'd left some of his prep food unsealed. But everything looked fairly neat because he wasn't a man to make a mess, thank god, even in his own space. She opened the first of the bank of lockers that he used to stash his tall tools—the long-handled clippers, his ax, spades, and the small shovels. What she saw made her forget she was holding her breath.

On the locker's top shelf, there was a cardboard gilt cake plate, lots of mouseshit, and birthday candles, nibbled. Same thing in the next locker, the next and next, except in one there was her good yellow Tupperware container. She had missed that container. The mice hadn't gotten to the cake inside, although a few squares that Peter had eaten out of duty were missing. She'd lightly tinted the frosting yellow, like the container, and made some flowers out of purple icing. It wasn't a complicated cake. It had the children's names on it. She pulled it out and held it for a while. Then she lifted out a light, dry piece, touched her tongue to it, and took a bite. It tasted of nothing. She stood cradling the yellow container on the curve of her left arm, and ate the rest of the cake, the flowers, the names, even the black-tipped candles that discouraged the mice. She licked her finger and pressed up the crumbs. When the yellow container was entirely clean, she walked back into the kitchen and washed it in hot, soapy water. The sugar would jangle her nerves, she thought, but it didn't. It slowed her heart. A dopey, fuzzy wash of pleasure covered her and she nearly blanked out before she made it to the couch.

Maggie and LaRose came inside an hour later, hungry, wondering why she hadn't checked on them, and found her lying on her back, looking severe, like she was dead. Her mouth was slightly open. Maggie put her fingers near to check for breath.

Maggie made a funny skulking gesture, and LaRose ducked his head and tiptoed away. They removed two spoons from the cutlery drawer. Then Maggie pulled the door of the freezer open and silently removed a carton of strawberry Blue Bunny. They eased out the door and ran to their hideout in the barn—a warm corner where they could flick on Peter's space heater. There they ate the ice cream. Afterward, they buried the box, the spoons too, out back in the fresh snow. They were passionate about ice cream.

ROMEO PUYAT entered the Dead Custer and saw the priest sitting on a barstool. Father Travis was the only priest in reservation history who actively went out and trawled the dive bars. He seemed to enjoy performing as an actual fisher of men. He'd sit next to a gasping walleye and even buy him or her a beer to set the hook. He liked to catch real fish, too. His tactics there were the same. You got to catch them in the weeds, he said. *To the weak I became weak, that I might gain the weak. I became all things to all men, that I might save all.* If Father Travis had a tattoo it would be the words of the apostle Paul. He had nearly become a drunk to catch the drunks, too, but that was over. He now ran fierce AA meetings in the church basement.

Although Father Travis had never quite submerged into heavy drinking, ten years ago he'd seen where things were going—that lonely beer turning to a six-pack and soon the addition of whiskey shots to render him unconscious. He was surprised at how hard it was to quit, so he had some sympathy, but he hid it and was ruthless with his drunks. Even ruthlessly prayerful. If someone fell off the wagon or got unruly in the Dead Custer, he would take that person outside to pray. Romeo Puyat had prayed twice, hard, face against the wall where Father Travis had slammed him, before they'd become friends. Father Travis had already spotted him and said hello.

There was coffee. Virgil served in the morning, but besides the coffee no hard liquor, only beer. Romeo sourly accepted a sour cup of the weak, lukewarm stuff.

MAKADE MASHKIKI WAABOO, a scrawled sign on the pump carafe.

Black medicine water, said Romeo. Howah. So you watch the news last night? He and Father Travis were both CNN junkies. Father Travis was stirring into his own cup a long stream of hazelnut cream powder from a cardboard carton.

What brings you down here? Father Travis took a careful sip as if the coffee were actually hot.

I heard McCain on Leap Day, said Romeo. He told the televangelists to fuck a dead sheep, uh, not in so many words. Then what he said about pandering to the agents of intolerance? Falwell? Robertson? My man, said Romeo, punching air.

Romeo had a caved, tubercular-looking chest, scrawny arms, a vulturine head, and perpetually stoked-up eyes. His hair had started falling out and his ponytail was a limp string. He flipped the string behind him with the flat of his hand, as though it were a lush rope. The day was bright. He had hoped to start the morning with beer to dim the sunshine, but of course he couldn't do that in front of his sponsor.

I've been following that story, said Father Travis. Waiting for our maverick to make his move.

So what are you up to?

I'm on my way to work, said Romeo.

That's a new one, said Father Travis.

Romeo glanced over at Virgil, who was wiping down the other end of the bar, not watching. Another customer, on the other side of Father Travis, asked the priest a question. While his back was turned, Romeo rummaged in the Styrofoam cup that customers paid into for the coffee. It was labeled 25 cents. The cup was over halfway full of change, mainly quarters. Romeo took a dollar from his pocket as if to change it. He then transferred all the change in handfuls from the cup into his pocket. He put the dollar in the cup and set it on the counter. Father Travis turned back to Romeo and said, I never see you at Mass.

Exhaustion, said Romeo.

Oh? Where you working now?

Same place. Here and there. Substitute sanitation engineering. Maintenance, you know.

Maintenance could mean anything. He could be maintaining a healthy supply of substance. Father Travis took the long view with Romeo. He was working on him, dropping tiny stones into the pond.

Romeo was wearing a lurid purple mock turtleneck and a black zip hoodie printed with tiny skulls that matched the tiny skulls tattooed around his neck.

Like the work?

There's a glass bottom to it, said Romeo, shaking his head. I can see the fish down there eating the shit. They're the bottom-feeders. You know me, right? Romeo smiled. His tiny brown teeth ached but he poured some sugar into the coffee and watched the oily stuff swirl around a red plastic stirring stick.

Yeah, I know you, said Father Travis.

Then you know I don't travel with the top of the food chain. I don't eat top shelf. Bottom-feeder, like I said. I can't talk to the high-class Indians around here. Like Landreaux. He twirls the pipe and all, thinks he's a medicine man like Randall. That's how they get the women. With that old Indian medicine. Emmaline's witched, you know. He gave his usual two-finger salute as he got up to leave, and asked.

Did you hear what Landreaux said about you?

Don't try that alkie trick on me, said Father Travis, laughing.

If you don't want to know . . . Romeo playacted hurt. Never mind.

Romeo lunged out the door, pocket sagging from the weight of the change. He crossed the street to Whitey's Hot Bar, and emptied his pocket of the coffee change. He came out four dollars ahead.

Slice a sausage pizza, donut, Mountain Dew, he said to Snow behind the counter. How's your dad?

THE ONE psychologist for a hundred miles around was so besieged that she lived on Xanax and knocked herself out every night with vodka shots. Her calendar was full for a year. People who couldn't get on it went to Mass instead, and afterward visited Father Travis in the parish office.

I'm scared, said Nola, picking at her pale rose nail polish.

Father Travis had a Pre-Cana class in half an hour. His desk was heavy oak, from the old parochial school. His legs were stretched out long underneath. Instead of a desk chair, he sat in a fold-out camping chair with a mesh cup holder—it held his insulated thermos coffee cup; it used to be just right for a beer. Sunlight filled the south windows. The papers on his desk were dazzling. The light reflected up; his pale eyes shimmered.

Mrs. Ravich, said Father Travis gently, don't be afraid. The worst has happened. And now you've been given two children to cherish. LaRose and Maggie.

We are sharing him now. I mean LaRose. If they take him back I'm scared, scared of what I'll do.

Do?

To myself, said Nola softly. She looked up in appeal, mistily. There was something disturbing in her doll-sweet prettiness.

Father Travis shifted slightly back in his chair. The snake of the livid purple scar slid up his neck.

He was careful with Nola. Kept her on the other side of his desk. Kept the door open. Pretended he didn't quite understand that she gave off the wrong vibe.

Or if he noticed, as he noticed, a detail that might stab his sleep. Like the shadow of her black bra lurking underneath the thin cotton of her shirt.

Are you planning to harm yourself? Father Travis asked, blunt but kind, trying to stay neutral.

She backpedaled, pouted out her lips, manufactured a startled look. Her gaze flickered away as she realized the priest might call Peter.

That's not what I meant?

Father Travis took a drink of coffee. He stared at her from under his brows. He couldn't tell how much of what she said was bullshit. Suicide to him seemed an affront to his friends who had died in Beirut. They had wanted to live, made the most of their lives, died for nothing—except he hadn't. So maybe he was still on this earth to honor 241 lost destinies. This thought hardened his emotions. His fist clenched and unclenched.

Let's talk about Maggie.

What about her?

Father Travis frowned steadily and Nola dropped her eyes like a sullen girl.

She seems to be adjusting. They all are. I am the only one not adjusting. I came to talk about myself.

Okay, let's talk about you as the mother of Maggie. If you in any way are self-destructive, you'll take her down with you, Nola. Do you get that?

Nola cocked her head. She looked ready to stick out her tongue. This was going horribly, horribly, the priest treating her like an appendage to her family. Like a nothing. Not listening.

I don't really want to talk about her, Father Travis!

Why?

She's oppositional. Nola's face worked. Suddenly she began to cry, groping for a tissue. Father Travis pushed the roll of towels at her. She choked on her tears; they became too real. It could be that Maggie was the key to her unhappiness, her inability to process the grief. She's a little bitch, Nola whispered into the paper towel.

Father Travis heard.

Nola shook the tears from her eyes and cleared her face. I'm sorry, Father. Maybe things should feel normal. Maybe I should be doing normal things. I should get used to the way things are. Accept and accept. Stop thinking about Dusty.

Father Travis got up and walked around the desk.

It's normal to think about Dusty, he said.

He stood behind her and spoke at the fluffy top of her head. It was perhaps here that he should have held back, waited. But Nola's fake flirtatiousness felt like mockery.

It's not normal to do what you did at Mass, he said. You struck Maggie.

She turned hotly. I did not!

Father Travis stared her down, but it was difficult. Her prettiness was a deflecting foil. She was tougher than his AA crowd.

If Peter comes to me about your treatment of Maggie, if Maggie comes herself, if anybody from the Iron family, or a teacher, anyone, comes to me about it? I'll go to Social Services.

You really would do that?

Nola spoke sobbingly, but her face tightened in rage. She bolted up with such a slick, sudden movement that her breast bobbed into Father Travis's fingers. He flinched as if scorched.

Nola stepped backward, her wide eyes marveling.

I don't think you meant what you just said, about Social Services, Father Travis. I'm going to pretend you didn't touch my bosom. Nola dimpled, eyes hard.

He looked at her and did something he was later ashamed of. He laughed. Bosom? He shooed her out, breaking into guffaws.

Hey Stan! he yelled into the hallway. The church janitor turned, broom in hand. Listen! Mrs. Ravich is going to pretend I tried to cop a feel.

Yeah, okay, Stan said, and kept sweeping.

You're not the first who tried that, said Father Travis when she turned to him, furious, injured. You should know I don't touch anybody like that. I am not one of those kinds of priests.

She began to weep for real, then tottered away from him bowlegged in her high heels.

🙣

LANDREAUX AND Emmaline's house contained the original cabin from 1846, built in desperation as snow fell on their ancestors. It satisfied them both to know that if the layers of drywall and plaster were torn away from the walls, they would find the interior pole and mud walls. The entire first family—babies, mothers, uncles, children, aunts, grandparents—had passed around tuberculosis, diphtheria, sorrow, endless tea, hilarious and sacred, dirty, magical stories. They had lived and died in what was now the living room, and there had always been a LaRose.

After a time, an extension had been built onto the original cabin. Those log huts had become one house during the 1920s, when Emmaline's grandfather had bought board lumber, sided the house, then shingled it under one roof. During the fifties a lean-to built alongside the house was insulated and became a set of bedrooms. Up until the 1970s, they had used an outhouse, hauled water, washed with a wringer washer, tubs, a washboard. The bathroom and a tiny laundry room completed the house.

During the next ten years, Emmaline had lived there with her mother. When there were too many children and Emmaline had her degree, Mrs. Peace had moved into the Elders Lodge. From her small bedroom, where Emmaline and Landreaux now slept, a door led into the bathroom. Josette and Snow took long baths there and did their complex beauty routines, sending their brothers to the old outhouse when they banged on the door.

The kitchen and living room, the oldest parts of the house, still bore the fifties wallpaper. It rippled under layers of paint—first dark green, then light green, then a blue-gray color chosen by Snow. It was never approved of by Josette, so she got her way with the bargain wallpaper in their shared bedroom—bouquets of lavender flowers tied up with floating white ribbons. Nobody had ever thought about the paint in the boys' room—it was ancient red papered over with ripped posters of Ninja Turtles, Sitting Bull, Batman, Tupac, Chief Little Shell, Destiny's Child, and *The Sixth Sense*.

Back during the eighties the entire house had levitated. Jacked up, set on top of a cinder-block foundation, it was freed of creeping rot and damp. It became a real house then, with a narrow crawl space under. When Emmaline married Landreaux, he built a small deck to formalize the front entrance—a landing big enough for two lawn chairs and a flowerpot that sprouted grass. Once this was accomplished, the house looked suddenly like many houses and Landreaux imagined the two of them getting old there, sitting on that deck, watching the occasional car pass through a rift in the trees beside the road, waiting for their children, then their grandchildren, to exit the school bus and climb toward the house through the grassy wildflowered ditch, across the strip of beat-down weeds, or now, in winter, up the plowed frozen gravel.

It will be all right. We will get old here together after all.

This was Landreaux's thought the first time Peter dropped off LaRose. They would be together through spring and summer into the dog days, when the house heated through, and the old logs deep inside gave off the earthen scent of loam.

Landreaux opened the door and LaRose ran straight past him, clutching his stuffed creature, shouting for his mom. Landreaux turned back to wave good-bye, but Peter had quickly swung back out onto the road. Landreaux closed the aluminum storm door and then pushed the wooden door shut behind it. To see LaRose and Emmaline fly together would hurt, so he bent over by the mud rug and took a long time pairing up the scattered shoes and setting them in lines. When he finally came to them, his long arms dangling, they were talking about how to use the potato peeler.

LaRose sat down at the table by the window, in feeble winter sunlight. The edges of the storm window were thick with frost. Steam had frozen in gray fuzz upon the sides and sills. He peeled the potato skin away from himself, bit by skimpy bit, onto a plastic plate. Emmaline shook chunks of meat in a bag with flour, then pinched up each chunk and dropped it carefully into hot grease. The cast-iron skillet was smooth and light from fifty years of hard use. Her mother had left it.

Landreaux sat across the table and opened out the rest of the newspaper. The rustling it made caused him to notice his hands were lightly trembling.

Snow and Josette pushed through the door first. Willard and Hollis were hauling all of the gym bags. Everything scattered into piles at the door. The girls ran to LaRose and grabbed him, knelt by the kitchen chair dramatically weeping. The older boys slapped LaRose's palm.

We saved your bunk for you, man, said Hollis.

Yeah, I tried to sleep there and he slammed me off onto the floor, said Coochy. It's all yours now.

He's sleeping here! Here in his own house! Josette moaned.

You knew that, said Snow.

LaRose smoothed their hair as they competition-wept. Mii'iw, said Landreaux.

The sisters sniffed and looked redeemed, like a light had been restored inside of them. They were so happy

they didn't know how to show it without seeming fake.
The girls sat down to do the carrots.

You're cutting too fat.

No, I'm not. Look at the potatoes.

Proportion, Josette.

Don't be oblique.

They had acquired a list of SAT words from a
teacher who liked them both. Most teachers liked them
because they studied. They were relieved to finish out
their volleyball season. The games were an hour, two
hours away. They took all night. So did Hollis's and
Willard's basketball games. Landreaux and Emmaline
took turns driving them because the bus added on the
hours. Besides, they made their children study in the
car in the backseat with a flashlight. How did they know
to do this? They had learned from Emmaline's mother.
This sort of devotion was not from Landreaux's side.
His parents had been alcoholics with short lives.

❧

ROMEO PUYAT really did have a job—in fact, several
jobs. His intermittent sub-assistant maintenance position at the tribal college kept his bottom-feeder jobs
viable. He did a lot of reading at the tribal college between carpet shampoos and window polishes. He was

hoping to move to another venue, like the tribal hospital, but people kept those jobs forever. Anyway, his official job fed his second jobs the way a big fish feeds a school of little fish—with waste and wasted food.

Romeo's second jobs, though unofficial, maybe even volunteer, were lucrative and multi-aspected. For one thing, he picked up and disposed of the hazardous waste usually contained in medication bottles and prescribed by the Indian Health Service doctors. Nobody had hired or invited him to do this—but it had become a part of his way of life. When cleaning at his venue, he went to great lengths to hang around each classroom as long as possible in order to check for medications that might have mistakenly been left in handbags. On a volunteer basis, he even removed the hazardous waste that accumulated outside the other buildings, especially when he visited the hospital. To the casual eye it might look as if he was trawling for cigarette butts. But although it was a fact that he could rely on finding a lightly smoked cigarette outside certain doorways (tossed out in haste from the smoke-free environment), his mission was more far-reaching. Part of his job was, in fact, more in the line of clandestine work. Someone at the bar, maybe it was the priest, had even referred to Romeo once as the reservation's information specialist. He thought that true. He was a spy, but a freelancer.

Nobody ran him, he ran his one-man operation for his own benefit.

He had his methods. He came by lots of important information by busying himself around the tribal college coffeepot, or by standing outside the doors of teacher coffee rooms, or just sitting in the social areas acting invisible. On a rare occasion or two, he had been ignored as he weeded the grassy scarp in the shadow of the on-call ambulance crew. They knew everything about every catastrophe that happened, things that never made it out into the public. Romeo had heard about deaths where a suicide was covered up so the corpse could be blessed and buried by the church. He'd found out about botched abortions and suspicious deaths of newborns that looked almost like SIDS. He knew how people overdosed, on what, and how hard the crew fought to bring them back. When it was time to let them go. All this information kicked around in his head. It was good to know these things. In fact, Romeo had decided that information, long of reach, devastating, and, as a side benefit, a substance with no serious legal repercussions, was superior to any other form of power. So there was that.

Also, Romeo went through trash. Pharmacy trash was his specialty. The trash was usually shredded and the Dumpsters locked, but Romeo had a certain pharmacy employee who "belonged" to him as the result of information. Every few days he could spirit away a couple of bags and stuff them into the trunk of his car.

Romeo occupied a condemned disability apartment in the condemned tribal housing complex nicknamed Green Acres—built unfortunately over toxic landfill that leaked green gas. Romeo was immune to the noxious air that seeped up between the cracks in the linoleum. Mold, also, black or red, never bothered him. If smells got strong, he would lift new car fresheners from Whitey's—mango was his favorite. His apartment decor was centered around a fake year-round Christmas tree. The foil tree was decorated with the mango car fresheners. His walls displayed photographs tacked into the softened drywall. There was a television, a mini-fridge, a boom box, a mattress, two grubby polyester sleeping bags, and a beautiful handmade diamond willow lamp with a broken shade like a tipped hat.

In the light from his lamp, on a captain's chair torn from a wrecked van, Romeo went through the contents of the bags. All he could wish for was there on paper—discarded printouts, labels, prescription script, pharmacist's notes—that his information-bought informant had failed to shred. Within these piles, he found what drugs everybody in the entire community was on and which, for their mighty highs, could be pilfered by close relatives. It was there that Romeo found out who was going to die and who would live, who was crazier than he was, or by omission, sane and blessed with health. He kept track of his calculations on a scratch pad— drug, dosage, refill dates, how the patient should take the medicine. Though never in any case in Romeo's file did the doctor recommend that a patient crush to powder and inhale a single medication, that was often his preferred method of delivery.

Tonight, the words *palliative care* appeared again. He kept anything with those words in a special paper-clipped pile. Also discarded in the bag was a bonus feature. His favorite section—the tribal newspaper's obituary page. He matched several enticing prescriptions to one of the names, then noted the funeral would be tomorrow.

At 9:45 the next morning, Romeo stopped at the grocery, invested in a pound of stew meat, and then drove to church. He parked at the edge of the lot next to a pickup with a gas cap that could be easily pried up with a screwdriver. He sat in his car until everyone had entered the church, then quickly siphoned into his own car more than enough gas to carry him to the home of the deceased and back again. It was six miles out, and he got there within fifteen minutes.

Romeo pulled up next to the house, went right up to the front door, knocked. The big outside dogs were barking wildly, but he threw down a few bits of meat for them to argue over. The little inside dogs barked in the house entry. Nobody else answered and it was a cheap key lockset from Walmart. He pried the worn bolt gently from the frame with his flat-head screwdriver, entered, threw down a few more pieces of stew meat. The dogs wagged their tails and followed him straight to the bedroom. The TV tray table beside the bed held a few amber plastic bottles, which he examined. He took one. There was a bedside table with a half-open drawer. Bingo. Three more bottles, one entirely full. In the bathroom, he went carefully through the medicine cabinet, examining each medication with a frown. He smiled at one and shook it, pocketed three more. No need to be greedy. It was 10:30 now. He fixed the lock so it wouldn't fall off and left. And there was still half a pound of meat in his pocket.

Back at the funeral by 10:55, he rolled the prescriptions in a plastic bag and stashed them under the backseat. The meat too. He took a small dose of Darvocet and entered the church silently. Everyone was focused up front, on the gathered pallbearers. As they carried out the body, he put his hand on his heart. To save gas, he hitched a ride to the cemetery.

After the sad burial, everybody cried in relief. Romeo rode back to the church and followed the mourners downstairs to the funeral lunch. There, he ate his fill. He drank weak coffee and talked to his relatives and their relatives. He stayed to the end of things, drank more coffee, ate sheet cake, took home leftovers stacked precariously on paper plates. He accepted with a sad little nod the program featuring the picture of a man who was smiling into the camera and holding an engraved plaque that must have honored him. Once back in his apartment, Romeo used the stiff paper to neaten and fix his first two lines.

Where to, my man? he said to the universe.

Romeo sniffed up the lines and fell back in the captain's chair. Away he traveled safe in the backseat, comfy in the shaved gray plush. His companions, the photographs on his wall, smiled into the faces of lost photographers. Some were school photos, one was of Emmaline and her mother, his beloved teacher, Mrs. Peace. There was Landreaux and two other boys—both dead now. A smudged picture of Star hoisting a beer. Hollis, several photographs from grade school, one from high school, one of the two of them together. Romeo and Hollis. Much cherished. There was a long ago clipped yellowed newspaper wedding picture of Emmaline and someone with Landreaux's body and a scratched-out face. Also, there were people whose names he'd forgotten. Romeo now lifted off. Floated up through the popcorn ceiling and the black mold. Up through the asphalt shingles flapping on the roof. On the other side of the reservation town his fellow traveler, Mrs. Peace, passed him in space. She laid her hand on his shoulder, the way she'd done to boys in school. He ducked, though she had never struck him. He always ducked when someone gestured too quickly. Reflex.

Hello, beauty

Nola came to weekday Mass and sat down in Father Travis's office afterward, waiting for him. He was often detained in the hallway. Sure enough, Nola heard someone talking now. Father Travis was listening, dropping in an occasional question. The two voices were figuring out some repair detail on the basement wall. Or maybe the windows. Cold was threading in, then spring would bring seepage, mud, snakes. There had always been snakes around and sometimes inside the church. Several places in the area and on the Plains, into Manitoba, were like that. The snakes had ancient nests deep in the rocks where they massed every spring and could not be driven out.

Nola had never been afraid of snakes. She drew them to her. Here was one now—a gentle garter snake striped yellow with a red line at the mouth. Hello, beauty. The snake curved soundlessly under a shelf of books and pamphlets, then stopped, tasting the air. I might as well talk to you, thought Nola. He's not coming and I don't think he wants to see me. Thinks I'm weak. I'm alone with this, anyway. I don't like where my thoughts go but I can't argue them down all of the time, can I? Maggie will be all right, after, she'll just flourish away. LaRose will be so relieved. Peter is becoming love-hate for me, you know? He's getting on my last nerve. I know I shouldn't sleep so much. Who would notice an old green chair? Snakes notice. You, or the one in my iris bed when I was putting them to sleep, the irises. When you're thinking of not being here, everything becomes so fevered, fervent? And the sun comes in. Strikes in. To be alive for that, just to see it striking through a window in the afternoon. A warm light falling on my shoes. And the steam comes on, hissing in the pipes. That sound's a comfort. Maybe I'm not seeing properly. No, there is not a snake underneath that shelf, it's just a piece of dark nylon rope.

Nola!

I'm just waiting here. I thought you'd maybe have time.

Father Travis stood in the doorway. It was disturbing that she'd showed up after she'd tried to blackmail him, he thought. You'd think she'd have better sense. Meaning she might be serious about suicide. He should stop comparing normal people to lost Marines. And he should never have laughed.

I'm leaving the door open, see? Don't pop your breast at me again, okay?

I won't, Nola said.

How are you?

Better, not better.

Father Travis sighed and tore off a piece of paper toweling, slid it across the top of his desk. Nola reached out, caught it up, and put it to her face.

I don't like where my thoughts go, she sorrowed.

I've heard everything, said Father Travis.

I thought that piece of rope underneath your shelf was a snake.

They both looked; there was nothing.

Probably there was a snake, said Father Travis. They like the steam pipes.

Of course they do. She smiled. I don't know why I thought it was a rope.

Father Travis waited for her to say more. The steam pipes clanged and hissed.

A rope, he said. Why?

I have no idea.

Because you have a plan?

She nodded, mutely.

A plan to hang yourself?

She froze, then babbled. Don't tell, please. They'll take him away. Maggie already hates me. I don't blame her but I hate myself worse. I am a very, very bad mother. I let Dusty go outside, didn't watch him. I sent him up to bed because he was naughty, fingerprints on everything. He climbed up, got a candy bar. He loves, loved, chocolate. Maggie put him up to it. She was sick that day, or anyway she was pretending. And she put him up to being naughty and I sent him up to bed. But he sneaked out.

Do you blame Maggie?

No.

You sure?

Maybe I did at first, when I was crazier. But no. I am a bad mother, yes, but if I permanently blamed her that would be, I don't know, that would be a disaster, right?

Yes.

Nola studied the palms of her hands, open on her lap.

To blame yourself, that would also be disaster.

Her head swirled and yellow spots blazed in space. She lay her forehead carefully on the desk.

I yelled, Father Travis. I yelled at him so loud he cried.

After Nola left, Father Travis stared at the desk phone. She had a plan, but telling about Dusty's last day had seemed to lift a burden. She seemed reasonable, denying the possibility that she might hurt herself now. Begged him not to tell Peter, not to add this to his burden. He'd crack, she said. Father Travis didn't doubt that. But there would be no piecing him together if his wife killed herself. He lifted the receiver out of the cradle. But then he put it back. Such an air of relief surrounded her as she walked away— she was wearing white runners. Her step was springy. She had promised to talk to him if these thoughts came over her again.

<hr>

WOLFRED HACKED off a piece of weasel-gnawed moose. He carried it into the cabin, put it in a pot heaped with snow. He built up the fire just right and hung the pot to boil. He had learned from the girl to harvest red-gold berries, withered a bit in winter, which gave meat a slightly skunky but pleasant flavor.

She had taught him how to make tea from leathery swamp leaves. She had shown him rock lichen, edible but bland. The day was half gone.

Mashkiig, the girl's father, walked in, lean and fearsome, with two slinking minions. He glanced at the girl, then looked away. He traded his furs for rum and guns. Mackinnon told him to get drunk far from the trading post. The day he'd killed the girl's uncles, Mashkiig had stabbed everyone else in his vicinity. He'd slit Mink's nose and ears. Now he tried to claim the girl, then to buy her, but Mackinnon wouldn't take back any of the guns.

After Mashkiig left, Mackinnon and Wolfred each took a piss, hauled some wood in, then locked the inside shutters, and loaded their weapons. About a week later, they heard that he'd killed Mink. The girl put her head down and wept.

Wolfred was a clerk of greater value than he knew. He cooked well and could make bread from practically nothing. He'd kept his father's yeast going halfway across North America, and he was always seeking new sources of provender. He was using up the milled flour that Mackinnon had brought to trade. The Indians hadn't got a taste for it yet. Wolfred had ground wild rice to powder and added it to the stuff they had.

Last summer he had mounded up clay and hollowed it out into an earthen oven. That's where he baked his weekly loaves. As the loaves were browning, Mackinnon came outside. The scent of the bread so moved him, there in the dark of winter, that he opened a keg of wine. They'd had six kegs and were down to five. Mackinnon had packed the good wine in himself, over innumerable portages. Ordinarily, he partook of the undiluted stuff the bois de brule humped in to supply and resupply the Indians. Now he and Wolfred drank together, sitting on two stumps by the heated oven and a leaping fire.

Outside the circle of warmth, the snow squeaked and the stars pulsed in the impenetrable heavens. The girl sat between them, not drinking. She thought her own burdensome thoughts. From time to time, both of the men looked at her profile in the firelight. Her dirty face was brushed with raw gold. As the wine was drunk, the bread was baked. Reverently, they removed the loaves and put them, hot, inside their coats. The girl opened her blanket to accept a loaf from Wolfred. As he gave it to her, he realized that her dress was torn down the middle. He looked into her eyes and her eyes slid to Mackinnon. Then she ducked her head and held the dress together with her elbow while she accepted the loaf.

Inside, they sat on small stumps, around a bigger stump, to eat. The cabin had been built many years ago, around the large stump so that it could serve as a table.

Wolfred looked so searchingly at Mackinnon that the trader finally said, What?

Mackinnon had a flaccid bladder belly, crab legs, a snoose-stained beard, pig-mad red eyes, red sprouts of dandered hair, wormish lips, pitchy teeth, breath that knocked you sideways, and nose hairs that dripped snot on and spoiled Wolfred's perfectly inked numbers. Mackinnon was also a dead shot, and hell with his claw hammer. Wolfred had seen him use it on one of the very minions who'd shadowed Mashkiig that day. He was dangerous. Yet. Wolfred chewed and stared. He was seized with sharp emotion. For the first time in his life, Wolfred began to see the things of which he was capable.

The Crossbeams

June. Between the two houses, maybe six billion wood ticks hatched and began their sticky, hopeful, doomed search. In that patch of woods, there was perhaps a wood tick for every human being on earth. Josette said this to Snow because she knew her sister was deeply repulsed by wood ticks. No matter how meticulously Snow checked, washed, shook out her clothing, and avoided the woods, she would get wood ticks. She drew them worse than anyone. Because of the ticks, she said she couldn't wait to live in some big tickless city.

You'd miss your little friends, said Josette. Her jeans were too tight and it was hot. She snapped open the waist and flapped her arms.

They were going over to fetch LaRose. The first heat brought ticks swarming out of their hatch nests. They filled the grass and flung themselves off leaves and twigs toward the supersensory scent of mammals. Walking the path, Snow felt one in her hair and snatched it out.

I'm going back, she said. I'll take the road even if Mom sees me.

That's just a baby tick, Josette scoffed. Hey, I'm not taking that dust-ball road. It's twice as long. If you leave me to get LaRose by myself, dude, you can't have my turn with the walkman.

The Sony Walkman was their joy, their baby—a sleek metallic CD player for the few CDs they owned: the soundtrack to *Romeo + Juliet*, Ricky Martin, Dr. Dre, Black Lodge Singers. They had to share it and were strict about scheduling their days and hours. Josette had been sent to bring LaRose back to their house. She didn't want to go alone and had bribed Snow with all of tomorrow's hours.

Okay. Snow bent like a dark birch, took off her long-sleeved shirt, and draped it over her head, huddled underneath.

I should have worn my hoodie.

It's so weird to see you not wearing your hoodie. I mean, Shane's hoodie.

It was his wrestling team hoodie, which he'd given to Snow in order to show how serious he was about her. But then.

I'm just off him today, Snow said.

Josette knew that Snow's boyfriend had found a different girlfriend, but she didn't say so. It made her furious. She wanted to punch Shane in the liver. But when she said things like that to Snow it upset her. Snow said violence gagged her.

I just hate having to work there now, said Snow.

They both worked more regularly now at Whitey's. They were the youngest, but Old Whitey and his stepdaughter, London, ran it and they liked how the girls gave their all to the job. Every time Snow worked, handsome Shane came in and bought Gatorade and microwave burritos.

See why we like robot guys? Always so much better than real guys. If Shane was only a mech. He'd do my bidding.

Haha, what would you command him?

Just be nice, you know?

I know. Don't worry. I'll bust his ass.

Snow must have been deeply upset because she said thanks in Ojibwe, miigwech, which sort of meant this is a real thank-you. Josette was moved.

There was the house. They paused in the brush and regarded the angry neatness of its yard. There were planted flowers, bunched and glowing. A small hedge fiercely trimmed.

La vida loca, said Josette.

I know, it's so sad.

She tries so hard to be okay, said Josette. I kind of get it. And I like her flowers.

Me too. But she scares me.

You go first.

No, you.

Okay, but you talk to her.

No, I can't. I'll bust out.

Nola had developed an unnerving force field. The vibrational aura flowed with her to the door and pulsed toward the girls when she opened it—not wide, just a crack—and said, *Oh, it's you.* Vibrations flowed out when she spoke, and sealed the door like plastic wrap when Nola closed it softly in the girls' faces. When she opened the door again, she did it so slowly that the ions were only slightly disarranged. With his backpack on, LaRose popped through. The aura was sucked back in and the three of them ran across the lawn.

After the first time, Nola had stopped herself from watching out the window. She grabbed her headphones and walked straight through the house, out the sliding double glass doors, out onto the deck and down its four steps, across the yard to the shed with its crossbeams that worried Peter. She opened the doors, topped up the tank of the riding lawn mower, then got on and adjusted the walkman clipped to her belt. Peter had given her some very strange music for Christmas. It was soothing and yet disturbing, pipes and echoey voices chanting, ethereal soprano solos, wordless and mysterious voices, melodies that swirled, collapsed, revived in some ruthless disorienting key. She could listen to this music indefinitely as she cut the grass over and over on the riding lawn mower.

Eventually she parked, got off, and went into the house. She went up to her room, leaned on the closet door, stared into the clothing. Except for her one purple dress, she had four of everything, in neutral colors, and she wore only these things. Four jackets, four pants, four skirts, four jeans, four shirts, four panty hose. Four of everything for dress-up, and four for everyday. But she had lots of pretty underwear that she bought from a catalog.

At first, she was only going to change her underwear. Her belly was tight. A push-up bra of scratchy maroon lace. A tiny white bikini. Then she stood there and laid out the eggshell white shirt, the whiter pants, upon the bed. She took the brown heels out of their box. Laid the gray jacket, tailored, with no collar, around the eggshell shirt. The whole outfit was assembled there as though by an undertaker. Too businessy to be dead in, she thought, and took away the white pants and replaced them with a short, flaring skirt. I'll have to think again, she decided. She tapped her lips and opened the closet.

WILD THINGS

The two girls and LaRose between them walked back through the woods. Snow did not forget about the ticks but just gave up, she was so happy. They had their little brother back for a few days now and the light was pure green, cool, the sun hot only outside the trees, on the road. Halfway there, LaRose stopped and said to them, Can we go? They knew he meant to the tree. Nobody knew how he knew about the tree, but he did know and often he insisted on going there when the girls came to get him. They didn't mind so much. They never told their parents. It was easy to get to and in a moment they stood before Dusty's climbing tree, the branch, and the space of ground beneath, where dead flowers, tobacco ties, loose sage, and two small rain-beaten stuffed animals—a monkey and a lion—were arranged. LaRose put his backpack down and took out *Where the Wild Things Are.* He gave it to Josette and said, Read it. She read it out loud. After her voice stopped, they stood in the resounding sweetness of birdcall.

What was that about? said Josette.

LaRose took back the book. He turned it to his pack with a little frown.

I think it was his favorite, said LaRose. Because she reads it to me all the time.

Snow and Josette put their hands over their hearts and mouthed the words *for sad, for sweet.* They each took LaRose by a hand and kept walking.

I am so over that book, LaRose said loudly.

The girls batted their eyes at each other to keep their laughs inside.

Maybe you should leave that book for him, said Snow.

Put it with his stuffed monkey and stuff.

I can't, said LaRose. She would search.

Well, said Josette, okay, but she wouldn't find it. So she'd give up, right?

No, said LaRose. She would never give up. She might go out to the barn and scream like a banshee.

Ooo, said Snow. What's a banshee?

It's a boney old woman with long teeth that crawls around graves and screams when someone dies.

Holeee, said Josette.

Creep me out! said Snow. Where'd you get that?

Maggie told me. She's got a collection of pictures from books and things that she keeps underneath her bed. All scary.

She keeps scary junk underneath her bed?

Josette and Snow looked at each other.

Whoa, for badass.

Where's she get that crazy shit?

Don't say that to LaRose.

She rips pages out of library books at school, said LaRose.

Little man, said Josette. Don't let her bother you.

I'm used to her, said LaRose. I'm used to everything now.

The girls just held his hands and didn't talk after that.

Before they took LaRose to the Ravich house last fall, Landreaux and Emmaline had spoken his name. It was the name given to each LaRose. Mirage. Omban-itemagad. The original name of Mink's daughter. That name would protect him from the unknown, from what had been let loose with the accident. Sometimes energy of this nature, chaos, ill luck, goes out in the world and begets and begets. Bad luck rarely stops with one occurrence. All Indians know that. To stop it quickly takes great effort, which is why LaRose was sent.

☩

EMMALINE PEACE. A+ English student. Thought she'd like to teach literature. Got her teacher's certificate, taught high school, and only got high on weekends. She decided she was better with little kids than teenagers because the teenagers were too much like her, and she was right. Any authority she had literally went up in smoke the night she was enjoying skunky fine weed at a party and a couple of her students entered the room.

After the momentously drunk days with Landreaux, she received an offer. Funding for a degree in administration because the tribe was taking control of the school system from the top down. Emmaline went back to graduate school, grew up. Returning with her expedited degree, she got excited about a newly funded pilot program—an on-reservation boarding school for crisis kids.

People didn't want to think about boarding schools—the era of forced assimilation was supposed to be over.

But then again, kids from chaotic families didn't get to school, or get sleep, or real food, or homework help. And they'd never get out of the chaos—whatever brand of chaos, from addictions to depression to failing health—unless they got to school. To succeed in school, kids had to attend regularly, eat regularly, sleep regularly, and study regularly. Maybe the boarding schools of the earliest days had stripped away culture from the vulnerable, had left adults with little understanding of how to give love or parent, but what now? Kids needed some intervention, but not the wrenching away of foster families and outside adoptions. A crisis intervention, giving parents time to get on track. The radical part was that, unlike historical boarding schools, this one would be located on the reservation. Pre-K through grade 4. After that, kids could board but go to regular school. This new/old sort of boarding school, equipped to pick up the parenting roles for families that went through cycles of failure and recovery, became Emmaline's mission.

Two double-wide trailers for classrooms. Renovated BIA family group housing with houseparents, teachers, teacher's aides, all supposedly trained in child psychology or working on their own teaching licenses. At first she was the assistant director, which meant she helped collect data, strategize, order supplies, lead meetings, organize funding, construct endless progress reports, plans, plus a host of functions that weren't in her job description. Heartbreak mitigation. That was not described. Her heartbreak. Kids' heartbreak. Parents' heartbreak. Also: mop puke, replace paper towels, lock and unlock doors, rock sobbing hurt little boys until their fury slept, play Crazy Eights with little girls while they told how their mom had stabbed their dad, or vice versa, make muffins with the moms who were getting straight, raise hell with the moms who weren't. She didn't deal with the dads. Left that to the director. Then she became the director.

She tried not to bring the day home, but it did come. In her zeal for stability and calm, it came home. In her need for dependable household structure, it came home. In her frequent failure to hold structure, her episodes of neatness and relapse, her struggle to find balance, it came home. In her need for privacy, when she made her own sweat lodge and just sat inside, steaming the sorrow out, it came home. In her coping strategies—smudge the dysfunction off with burning sage, surround the bed with eagle feathers, drink, once a week, two glasses of the best wine she could afford, alone—it came home. In her attempts to rebuild what she had so carefully constructed before—the Irons as a strong family, as good people— it came home. She had understood that the only way was through LaRose, but she could not bear it.

Now, knowing that she'd see him, that again there was a place for her as a mother, she swept through her days in an excited bubbling way nobody ever saw with her. Her jerky, angular movements eased into grace. Her eyes rested on her paperwork without comprehension or worry. Even the ends of her hair hung slack, relaxed, not skinned back into a tail or poked up in a beaded clip.

Emmaline left her back-of-the-trailer office and drove home carefully. She hadn't picked LaRose up from Nola because Peter had asked Landreaux not to send her, or for him to go either. He knew Nola would have a hard time with either parent. Peter had heart pangs when he remembered how LaRose had run to his mother at the grocery, electrified by the sight of her, dropping everything to gallop at her headlong. That's why the sisters or the brothers were dispatched. Now Josette and Snow were in their room, door locked, checking each other for ticks. Snow continually whimpered and sometimes danced around screaming. On the living room floor, LaRose was wrestling with Hollis. He had him down and was holding his fist in Hollis's face demanding he give up.

Hollis beat his arm on the floor.

He's got you by the balls, said Coochy, sitting back on the couch. He was eating a cold piece of bannock.

Don't say that to him!

Wanna take me on? said LaRose, swaggering.

Hollis was laughing. He destroyed my ass.

Don't say that to him, Josette said, coming out of the bedroom.

How many?

Like, twenty. She freaked. She'll be taking one of her forever showers now.

Emmaline drove up and LaRose heard her car. He slammed out of the house and ran across the cindery yard. Emmaline got out just in time to catch LaRose as he jumped into her arms. He was still small enough to ride her hips, her arms hugging his waist. He molded to her, then leaned back and told her all about the secret fort in the lilac bush, a new action figure, the church preschool where Nola took him. But not Maggie. He didn't talk about Maggie. He felt in some vague way that he should not have told his sisters about the banshee. There was always something like that, something not okay, and he always tried to avoid it. But sometimes he wouldn't know what it was until he said it, like with the long-toothed boney thing that screamed for the dead.

Other things that Maggie told him in their lilac-bush hideout he knew right away not to tell because she said so. She said: *Never tell I told you this*—your dad was really aiming for my little brother, your dad's a killer, your dad murdered my little brother, I'll show you the place, my brother's blood soaked into the ground, the worms came up, the buzzards landed, you could go crazy if you stood there, at night his ghost would choke you, nothing grows there now or will ever grow there, though just that afternoon LaRose had seen to his relief that things were growing all over.

BIINDIGEG!

Here's my boy!

The apartment was filled with the friends of Mrs. Peace, all excited to see LaRose. He was a favorite.

Here's the boy who likes us, said Sam Eagleboy. The boy who wants the stories. You raised this boy good, Emmaline.

Sam was a thin man with beautiful upswept lines around his eyes and mouth, as if he was smiling even when he was serious. There was nothing wrong with him except he was old. He wore a brown checkered shirt, neatly tucked. An agate bolo tie, jeans held up by a belt of cracked amber leather. On his slim feet, running shoes. Sam put in miles walking the halls and grounds. Malvern Sangrait, a mean little washtub of a woman, glowered from her permanently squinted left eye and gave a suspicious little huff. She leaned forward on her walker. She was wearing eyeliner and Meow Girl red lipstick.

So you got your boy back, she said to Emmaline. Her hair was pulled to one side with a purple plastic barrette. He's skinny, ooh. They didn't feed him good.

He's just growing, said Emmaline. And she smiled. She was smiling all the time.

Mrs. Peace passed around paper plates and napkins, then frybread and chokecherry jelly. There was coffee. Powdered orange drink for LaRose. Everybody ate except Sam Eagleboy, who did not eat the whiteman's food. Though he did drink coffee.

You could use some whiteman food, said Malvern. You're all boney.

Boney where it counts, said Ignatia Thunder, who wheeled an oxygen tank nonchalantly around with her. She laughed so hard she had to dial up her nozzle.

So they say, said Malvern. I ain't seen it.

Her face was sly.

Yet, said Ignatia. Turn on your bedside lamp. You never know.

Hey, said Emmaline. She nicked her head at LaRose.

Malvern touched her barrette and twitched her pouting red lips from side to side, glancing at Ignatia. She raised her thatchy gray eyebrows. They didn't match her blue-black hair. She ate some bread in tiny bites, drank some coffee. Sam spoke to LaRose in Ojibwe. He was teaching him words for the plates and dishes. He told how to make a spirit dish and how the spirits appreciated when a person noticed them. How the spirits were there in things, all things, and would talk with the Ojibwe. How they came in dreams, and also in the ordinary world, and how LaRose should tell his mom when he encountered them. He pursed his lips toward Emmaline.

Malvern jutted her lower lip out and stared at Sam, then shook her head and popped her eyes at Ignatia.

Oh, he talks a good one, she said, sure enough. Then he goes on his night prowls. Tapping on the ladies' doors.

Let him be, laughed Ignatia. He can't do no harm where we can watch him. Let him talk to this here gwiiwisens. This boy should get teachings. He wants to learn. He wants the story. Besides that, we know Sam's only got an eye for you.

Pah, said Malvern. You think?

FATHER TRAVIS could not exhaust himself, although he drove his body with unrelenting ardor along the outdoor fitness trail. The push-up station, poles bolted between the short logs, was unsatisfactory. He'd left the popple bark on the poles because it helped him grip. That wasn't it. The irritating fact was the ground was uneven or the pieces of log weren't exactly the same size—though he'd carefully measured. It was impossible to do a push-up correctly. He finally compromised by switching sides twice to work both arms the same. The instructions he'd lettered neatly on a board gave no hint of this solution.

He jogged the short distance to the next station, and had done two hundred sit-ups on the heavy rubber mat when he noticed that he was surrounded by used condoms. They drooped among the leaves and lay shriveling into the weeds or mowed to shreds. Kids. They'd gum up the mowing machine! He did a hundred more sit-ups, fed by outrage, and when he calmed down felt ridiculous. No, condoms wouldn't gum up a lawn mower. He proceeded to the chin-up bar. After the chin-up bar there was the step-up, which he did until his legs wobbled. He didn't just stagger on, though, but did lunges until the madness of the jump-rope spot. He'd brought his rope so he could whirl in place, switching up, backwards, forward, until his lungs burned and then burned some more. How nice if he could sink an old-fashioned well pump right here! The sulphur-laden rez water containing all the minerals and iron a body needs. That water would be cold, and he'd find it sweet.

He loved it here. He loved his people. They were his people, weren't they? They drove him nuts, but he was inspired by their generosity. And they laughed so much. He hadn't known funny before. So with or without his savior, or his sanity, he wanted to stay. He had made another sit-up station, for reverse sit-ups, again with a decomposing rubber mat, but not decorated by a single condom. Well, it was too far into the bush. After the horror movies these kids watched they were all scared of the woods—Indians. Millennial Indians. Nobody had vandalized his outdoor heavy bag 'cause that was too far into the woods as well. He beat the wood ticks off the bag with a host of vicious side kicks. It had taken a world of groin pain to free that adhered scar tissue. But he could now lift his leg as high as his brain. Haha, God, he said when he walked with God. You saved me for a reason—so that I could develop my crazy showgirl kick.

Sometimes he didn't feel the shift occur; he was just back there sliding from his sleeping bag, then flying. The sentries guarding the former office building where the Marines were barracked had been expecting a water truck. Instead a yellow Mercedes stake-bed truck sped straight past and the bomb it carried detonated in the lobby. The building went up into the air in pieces and then the pieces, with Marines in them, rearranged as they came down. Father Travis felt the dream flying, the down slamming, but not the slashing and tearing of his body. The black whirling energy became black crushing silence. Then the screaming started. It wasn't until he tried to get to the others that he realized he couldn't move. That's when he started screaming too, not for help, but *Get off me*, because he understood that he was the meat in a steel and concrete sandwich and could feel the rubble shifting. Dust in. Dust out. Scream the dust out. Take a breath of dust. Scream again. Then voices. *We got one. Get off that slab. He's in there. We need a crane.*

A skinny, shirtless, tattooed Marine slipped in next to Travis and then somehow he lifted things—the beam—and pushed—the slab—and bore him out to other arms. Father Travis knew exactly who that man was. He'd spoken to him on the phone. Vast strength had entered the slim man as he was rescuing his friends, the way it did with mothers rescuing their babies. They'd talked about that. They kept in touch, but he didn't get together with the other guys and the families of the dead. He didn't go to Camp Lejeune or the memorial reunions. He feared the black energy and how he could not control his breathing once the shift occurred.

Father Travis switched the jump rope along his thighs, then started it whirling. He was living out Newton's Third Law—for every action there is an equal and opposite reaction. Time was the variable. Getting blown up happened in an instant; getting put together took the rest of your life. Or was it the other way around? He thought of Emmaline.

THE GREEN chair had rested in the barn for two months and nobody noticed that it was gone from the kitchen. Nola was ready to say that she was going to restore it, if Peter asked. But it was just a green wooden chair, and who cared? Yet this painted chair was key. It would be the last solid thing her feet touched. She'd push off and kick the backrest down. But the part where she strangled, not good, she was not ready, she was afraid of that when she put her hands around her neck and squeezed. The feeling made her gag and she went wooden and cold until she thought maybe she would get the release she needed if she killed Landreaux instead of herself. Sure, she might go to jail. Maybe for a long time even. She'd plead guilty, but who would not understand? Even Maggie would understand, perhaps even approve. Peter would understand—part of him would envy her, in fact. Only LaRose wouldn't get it. He'd lose out. She saw his face, devastated, crumpling, pasted over Dusty's face, devastated, crumpling.

Boxed in, she thought.

Then she had another thought—their tradition worked. Dazzling act. How could she or Peter harm the father of the son they'd been given? She closed her eyes and felt the heavy warmth of LaRose as she rocked him to sleep, legs dangling over her legs, breath steaming a passage to the crater of her heart.

ROMEO HELD on to his first love, but generally did not like women, especially when they got older and turned into scabby vultures. They could tear a man to pieces with their biting talk. Always, he tried to placate them. Always, he tried to bring them gifts. In his work, Romeo often came across pockets of reservation conference swag—extra T-shirts, mouse pads, soft-foam-grip hand exercisers, mini-flashlights, pens and pencils, water bottles, even pristine fleece throws embossed with acronyms and symbols. His special stash of these objects was contained in his giant wheelchair-accessible bathroom.

He had been sunk in dire depression since Super Tuesday. George Bush had nailed the door shut on his man. McCain was out. Romeo had bad feelings about the race now. At the last AA meeting he'd confided to the group that Bush reminded him of all the things he hated worst about himself: weasel eyes, greed, self-pity, fake machismo. In this nation of self-haters, Bush could win. Everyone looked blank except Father Travis, who'd hung his arm for half a second around Romeo's shoulders, bro-like, afterward. Romeo was moved. The priest was not a hugger. Still, he walked away and decided to put into action a plan for getting regularly wasted until the election was over.

Today he picked out several gift ideas from a large black garbage bag he'd cleaned up with after a tribal college conference. There were the flexy-turtle hand exercisers—but those ladies' claws were strong enough already, he decided. He threw back some bookmarks, gimme hats, cheap eco bags already fraying apart. The leftover T-shirts were always small and he had XL ladies to appease. Except for dear old Mrs. Peace. She was better than the others, tiny, not so mean. He took one small 5K Diabetes Walk T-shirt, yellow, for her. He found a couple of fleece throws. He examined, but rejected, frog-shaped zipper pulls. Nobody wanted them because they looked too real. He rolled up a fleece throw and left for the lodge.

Not that he always got into their rooms. Not everyone let him in their door. Some people were suspicious of him at the Elders Lodge, like Mrs. Peace. She'd even had a chain put on her door because he'd once foolishly insisted on entry when she wasn't in favor of it. Romeo drove up to the lodge. As he walked into the main hallway, he saw Mrs. Peace. As soon as she saw him, she slippered along in her quick and mouselike way, large eyes peeping at him as she made a swift turn into her apartment and clicked the door emphatically shut.

And she used to be my favorite teacher, thought Romeo, sad. She was everybody's favorite teacher. She took me home. She fed me from her table.

No longer. And she rarely accepted his gifts. But there was always his aunt, or mother, or foster mother, Star. He was bringing Star the prize—the purple fleece throw that said Sobriety Powwow 1999 in one corner. Nice throws had been left over at the giveaway because of relapse behavior. Romeo knocked on Star's door, re-

membering the prescriptions she had for severe arthri-
tis. She opened the door, her little smile glinting.

It's peckerhead! she yelled to her other visitors.

Oh, him, said Malvern Sangrait to Mrs. Webid.
Let's have a look at him. Skinny, but you never know.

For me? Star took the purple fleece. Very cozy.

The women sat at the kitchen table, looking avidly
at Romeo. Their eyes were bright and roved over him,
but stopped so pointedly that he glanced down, a reflex.
Sure enough.

Twenty cows got out the barn door, Mrs. Webid
shrieked.

Romeo tugged. His zipper stuck.

The old ladies began to count out loud. They reached
thirty before he managed to violently wrest it all the
way shut. Watch out! Weweni! Be careful!

Way-weeny, cackled Malvern.

Be careful so its head don't get stuck! Ow! It's trying
to peek at us!

The women pretended to shield their eyes.

There was a little tap and his schoolteacher entered.
Mrs. Peace's feet slapped gently to another chair and
she joined the three other women and Romeo at the
table. Her coffee cup was still sitting where she'd left it.

Aren't you asking Romeo to sit himself down?

Sit down, sit down!

Why do you look confused?

His brains are down there, in his ass. Maybe he doesn't want to crush his thoughts.

Star poured a cup of coffee out for him and pushed a Ball jar full of sugar his way.

There he goes. He's going to sit. He had to tie his pecker in a knot first, said Mrs. Webid. His thing was trying to get out.

Oh my, gasped Mrs. Peace. She didn't join in their lewd talk, but her eyes pooled with delight. The ladies stared harder now at Romeo.

He was a puny boy, said Star, he's just got a little pinkie-doodle in his pants. It was something else he had in his pocket this time.

Perhaps some other little "gift" he scrounged up, said Malvern. Maybe one of his free Maglites—with the dead batteries.

Dead batteries! Mrs. Webid's face crinkled up. Her cheeks puffed mightily, but she couldn't contain herself and started to wheeze with happiness.

Have you charged up your batteries lately?

Juiced 'em up?

Mrs. Peace suddenly broke into a startling musical chortle, and Romeo excused himself.

Take your time, take your time, Malvern said. Give those batteries a good hard crank!

Ah, they screamed with merriment.

Romeo closed the door and locked it, turned on the water, pissed, and flushed. In the noisy rush from the faucet he eased open the medicine cabinet. Disappointing. He took one bottle even though the label said, Insert into rectum. There was another painkilling item that did not break down when crushed, but could only be swallowed. It was full, though, and there was a duplicate bottle. Hardly be missed. He combed his watery hands through his hair, retied his skinny ponytail, made sure his zipper was shut, and came out.

It was so nice to see you, my boy, Star said immediately. Nice you visit your old auntie. Please close my door carefully on your way out, eh?

He did shut the door as he quickly left, which caused a burst of hilarity. It should have roused his suspicions, maybe, but they were always like that.

That night, at home, he decided to sell the rectals in a different bottle, but took a triple dose of the pills that didn't crush. He took them with a full glass of water, as recommended, and waited. Nothing happened so he took one more. Perhaps half an hour passed. He looked at the date on the bottle, then peered closer and held the bottle in the light of the cockeyed lamp. One label had been carefully pasted over another

label. He couldn't scratch the second label off though
he tried with his longest fingernail, tried with a razor
blade, and then realized with a twisting rush of his
guts that the contents of the bottle were effective in
the place the old ladies said his brains were located.

God! The pain was sickening. He loped, slung over
his stomach, to the door of the disability bathroom.
Crashed through. The toilet still had a decent flush and
that night he gave it hard use. The cramps were nails
driven deep into his lower abdomen. Those ladies must
have rocks in their bowels, he thought. How could they
stand it? Even a fraction of a dose would have done the
trick. He didn't sleep. Dawn found him raving, exhausted, dehydrated, famished, gutted, unable to go to
work. But no, it wasn't over. Other feelings surfaced.
His skin began to prickle and burn. His nose grew
giant and his feet seemed far away. There was an ab-
normally disgusting taste in his mouth, then his penis
turned rock hard and would not go down even if he
thought of frog-shaped zipper pulls.

All day, blankets nailed over windows, Romeo lay
in his pile of sleeping bags experiencing bouts of sickness, disorientation, and sexual excitement simultane-
ous with explosive gas. CNN wavered and sparked.
Ann Kellan, one of his favorite reporters, was doing
a comforting story about the language of elephants.

When you hear these calls, you know there's going to be a mating event, said Ann. Male bull elephants trumpeted. The competition was on. Trunks blared. Romeo's penis throbbed. He flicked off the volume. He lay still underneath his sleeping bag. He didn't dare move for fear of disrupting the weak equilibrium he'd gained below the waist.

Maybe the old ladies were right—his brains were in his ass and now it was cleared out—for he found himself thinking with uncommon clarity. Thinking with strange focus. Considering where he'd sell and how much he'd reap for the pills he'd stashed, even counting it all up in his head and deciding what he would do with the money. He thought of his aunt, who'd raised him at the edge of her household, Aunt Star. In spite of her evil trick, he would buy groceries for her. Clean her place up so it didn't stink. He thought of ordinary and extraordinary things. Should he live this way? He asked himself that. Should he be subject to the cruel pecking of the buzzards at the Elders Lodge? How could he rise? How could he gain respect? Should he run for office? Which office? If he was on the tribal council he would immediately declare it against tribal law to store psychotropic laxative erection pills in a painkilling drug container. He spent the most time, though, reviewing bits, sorting words, scanning possibilities. Information. What certain knowledge might get him. He considered all aspects of what gossip gave him what sorts of power. He made up his mind to go deeper, investigate, maybe put up a bulletin board of clues like his *Law & Order* hero, Lennie Briscoe. He'd put everything together.

WOLFRED SORTED through the options: they could run away, but Mackinnon would not only pursue but pay Mashkiig to get them first. They could stick together at all times so Wolfred could watch over her, but that would make it obvious that Wolfred knew and they would lose the element of surprise. Xenophon had lain awake in the night, asking himself this question: What age am I waiting for to come to myself? This age, Wolfred thought. Because they had to kill Mackinnon of course. Really, it was the first thing Wolfred thought of doing, and the only way. To feel better about it, however, he had examined the options.

How to do it?

Shooting him was out. There might be justice. Killing him by ax, hatchet, knife, or rock, or tying him up and stuffing him under the ice, was also risky that way. As he lay in the faltering dark imagining each scenario,

Wolfred remembered how he'd walked the woods with her. She knew everything there was to eat in the woods. She probably knew everything there was not to eat as well. She probably knew poisons.

Alone with her the next day, he saw she'd managed to sew her dress together with a length of sinew. He pointed to the dress, pointed in the general direction of Mackinnon, then proceeded to mime out picking something, cooking it, Mackinnon eating it, holding his belly and pitching over dead. It made her laugh behind her hand. He convinced her that it was not a joke and she began to wash her hands in the air, biting her lip, darting glances all around, as though even the needles on the pines knew what they were planning. Then she signaled him to follow.

She searched the woods until she found scraggly stalks that drooped with black shriveled berries. She put a bit of cloth on her hand, picked the berries, and tied them in the cloth. Then she searched out a stand of oaks, again covered her hand, and plunged it into the snow near a cracked-off stump rotted down to almost nothing. Eventually, from beneath the snow, she pulled out some dark-gray strands that might once have been mushrooms.

That night Wolfred used the breast meat of six partridges, the tenders of three rabbits, a shriveled potato, and the girl's offering to make a highly salted and strongly flavored stew. He unplugged a keg of high wine, and made sure Mackinnon drained it well down before he ate. The stew did not seem to affect him. They all went to their corners, and Mackinnon kept on drinking the way he usually did until the fire burned out.

In the middle of the night, his thrashing, grunting, and squeals of pain woke them. Wolfred lighted a lantern. Mackinnon's entire head had turned purple and swollen to a grotesque size. His eyes had vanished in the bloated flesh. His tongue, a mottled fish, bulged from what must have been his mouth. He seemed to be trying to throw himself out of his body. He cast himself violently at the log walls, into the fireplace, upon the mounds of furs and blankets, rattling guns off their wooden hooks. Ammunition, ribbons, and hawks' bells rained off their shelves. His belly popped from his vest, round and hard as a boulder. His hands and feet filled like bladders. Wolfred had never witnessed anything remotely as terrifying, but had the presence of mind not to club Mackinnon or in any way molest his monstrous presence. As for the girl, she seemed pleased at his condition, though she did not smile.

Trying to disregard the chaotic death occurring to his left, now to his right, now underfoot, Wolfred prepared to leave. He grabbed snowshoes and two packs, moving clumsily. In the packs he put his books, two fire steels, ammunition, bannock he had made in advance. He doubled up two blankets, another to cut for leggings, and outfitted himself and the girl with four knives apiece. He took two guns, wadding, and a large flask of gunpowder. He took salt, tobacco, Mackinnon's precious coffee, and dried meat. He did not take overmuch coin, though he knew which hollowed log hid the trader's tiny stash, a gold watch, and a wedding ring, which Mackinnon rarely wore.

Mackinnon's puffed mitts of hands fretted at his clothing and the threads burst. As Wolfred and the girl slipped out, they could hear him fighting the poison, his breath coming in sonorous gasps. He could barely draw air past his swelled tongue into his gigantic purpled head. Yet he managed to call feebly out to them.

My children! Why are you leaving me?

From the other side of the door they could hear his legs drumming on the packed earth floor. They could hear his fat paws wildly pattering for water on the empty wooden bucket.

Almond Joy

September again. Over the course of the day it became oppressively hot. Not a leaf stirred. It was the first day of school and by the time the class let out, Maggie and LaRose were drooping. When they got on the bus, trees started whipping around. Hot grit flew through the air. By the time they jumped off at their stop, big fat drops were smacking down. Nola and the dog met them with a flimsy red umbrella that nearly flew out of her fist. They struggled inside and just as they shut the door lightning pulsed around the edges of the yard and half a second later there were slams of thunder.

Inside, before the dog could shake himself, Nola rubbed him hard with an old towel she kept by the door. The dog trembled with excitement, but was unafraid. He fixed Nola with a calculating gaze, then jumped onto the couch, trying his luck. She had taught him the rules for everything—no begging, no jumping on people, no chewing anything but chew toys, no shitting in the yard, only at the edge of the yard, no puking or drooling in the house, if he could help it. She even taught him not to eat until she said eat. The only thing she was inconsistent about was the couch. Sometimes she ordered him off, sometimes she allowed him on. Sometimes she even let him get close to her. He had to read her mood to find out if he would be allowed onto the hallowed green poly-filled pillows. Now the signs were good. He curled silently between Nola and Maggie, and allowed his weight incrementally to sink against them. Gradually, his brows unknit. Moving by centimeters, he managed to rest his head near Nola's thigh.

Rain surged down in sheets and waves, pounding on the roof like people trying to get in. This scared Maggie but not LaRose. His father had put an eagle feather up in the lodge for him and talked to the Animikiig; he had explained to the thunder beings where LaRose lived so that they wouldn't shoot lightning and hit him or anyone else in that house.

Nothing's gonna happen, LaRose said to Maggie. He put his hand on her cheek. Maggie stopped jittering when LaRose touched her cheek. LaRose knew she loved when he was fearless. It was a burden for her always to be the fearless one. Because of what Maggie had said about his father killing Dusty, he didn't tell her why they were safe.

Maggie clung to him while Nola made their sandwiches and poured their milk. LaRose watched the rain ripple back and forth.

Let's eat back here, Nola said, nodding at the couch.

The dog raised his head at the proximity of food to cloth but tried to conceal his shock.

They sat with their food and looked out the window from against an inner wall. Sometimes the house vibrated with sound. Maggie quailed deeper into the cushions and pressed against the dog. When LaRose looked up at Nola, she made a funny face, a confusing face, a face LaRose hadn't seen before. Nola's eyes went shiny as she looked back at the streaming glass doors. She seemed mesmerized by the branches violently whipping. The face she'd made at him had been a smile.

At school, in LaRose's combined K–1 class, there was a bigger, older first grader named Dougie Veddar. He throttled kids and gave them what he called the Dutch Rub—grinding his knuckles into their skulls.

Twisting their ears. He turned his attention to hating LaRose. Tripped him, pushed him, called him Rosy Red Ass.

Can I borrow your pencil? Dougie asked LaRose during class. When LaRose gave him the pencil, Dougie snapped off the end and handed it back. LaRose sharpened the pencil.

Can I borrow your pencil? Dougie asked when LaRose sat down.

No, said LaRose.

Dougie made a sad face and raised his hand.

Mrs. Heaper, Mrs. Heaper! LaRose won't let me borrow his pencil!

You have your own pencil, Douglas, said Mrs. Heaper.

Dougie grabbed LaRose's sharpened pencil when Mrs. Heaper wasn't looking, and drove it into LaRose's arm so hard the tip broke off under the skin. Dougie laughed and said he'd given LaRose a shot. That night, LaRose showed his shoulder to Maggie, the pencil tip driven deep.

Her face swelled up. Her lips tightened. Her golden eyes went black.

When she was six years old, her teachers started calling Maggie "a piece of work." But after her brother died, her work came together. She revved up the other kids by picking friends, rejecting those who displeased her, pitting them against each other for her favor. Although she didn't exactly talk back to the teachers, there was sarcasm in the elaborate politeness she showed.

Yes, Miss Behring, she would say, and in a whisper only the other children heard, Yes, Miss Boring.

She rolled her eyes, made spasmodic faces, behind her teachers' backs. They never caught her when she periodically dropped a BB from her jeans pocket and it rolled around and around on the unlevel floor. It made a high, thin, zinging sound that kept everyone in suspense. She kept it up, flicking a BB out every few days until Miss Behring searched everyone's pockets. Maggie's were empty like the others. She told nobody what she'd done so that nobody could rat her out. She was a disciplined piece of work.

Maggie had a list.

Dougie Veddar was now on it.

Recess came. He ran thumpingly around thinking he was safe, with his blond crew cut and rabbity teeth. Maggie was friends with an older girl, Sareah, who was fast and tough. The two girls closed casually in on Dougie and herded him away from the other boys.

Wanna share?

Maggie waved a candy bar from her lunch. He came around the playground tree. Sareah stepped behind him and pinned back his arms. Maggie had worn her hard-soled shoes for this. She reared back and kicked him between the legs. Then as he doubled over she stuffed back his shriek with the candy bar.

Don't touch my brother, she said in that scary-nice way she had, her eyes turning gold with satisfaction. Please?

Sareah dropped Dougie and they ambled off, talking. I mean, what's he gonna do? Go whine? Two girls dropped me. Kicked my nuts off. He's gonna lay there, maybe puke. I dunno. They puke in movies when you kick their nuts off. Let's go see if there's chocolate milk left.

They paused to watch the action before they ducked into the lunchroom.

Maggie had made sure LaRose was on the other side of the tree, that he saw what happened. But she told him to be running past and just watch out of the corner of his eye. He should disappear immediately to the other side of the playground. LaRose saw it as he ran past them and then pulled himself high into the monkey bars. He sat on top, pretending to pay attention to the children around him, but watching as the girls sauntered slowly back inside.

There was a stir of energy. The teachers ran past. They were running toward Dougie; some kid said in

awe, *He's blue, he's blue.* The teacher hefted Dougie.
Heimliched Dougie. Two teachers held him upside
down by the legs and shook him. Finally, a scream
from Dougie, *Whoa, whoa, whoa.* Relief and cynicism
settled once more over the teachers as they threw playground sand on a puddle of Almond Joy.

Maggie now slept in Dusty's old room, and LaRose
had a bunk bed, new. It was red metal and the bottom was a double. Just right for sleepovers, said Nola.
When she said that, LaRose looked away from her.
He knew that she meant other kids from school while
his first thought was sisters and brothers. Anyway,
some nights Maggie would come sleep with him. She'd
sneak away before morning because her mother had
made a rule about them not sleeping in the same bed
anymore.

Dougie won't bother you now, Maggie said. Lemme
see your arm.

Maggie put on LaRose's bedside lamp and studied
the arm.

Does it hurt? She touched the spot.

Not no more.

Not anymore, LaRose. You have to say not anymore.

LaRose didn't say it. Maggie looked at his arm from
many angles.

I think it looks cool, she decided. It's a tattoo. I want one.

She went over to LaRose's backpack, took out his pencil bag. There was a sharpener on top of his dresser. Maggie sharpened a pencil with great care.

Okay, you're gonna stick me like Veddar stuck you. Same place. It will be like we're getting engaged or something.

LaRose was almost six.

I'm only almost six, he said.

Age doesn't matter.

I mean, I'm scared to stab you.

You mean you'd cry. Maggie studied him sharply.

LaRose nodded.

Okay, watch.

Maggie gripped the needle-sharp pencil like an ice pick. She peered at LaRose's tattoo and licked her lips. She made a light mark on her arm the same place as his. Then she lifted her hand, drove the pencil into her arm. The tip came off. She threw the pencil across the room and fell onto the bed, kicking, holding her arm, biting the pillow to smother her noises.

After a while she sat up. There was some blood on her hand but the graphite tip stuck in her arm blocked most of it.

That hurt more than I thought it would, she said, wide-eyed, looking into LaRose's eyes. Now I'm glad Veddar almost died.

Huh?

He choked on that candy bar. I smashed it down his throat. It went down the wrong pipe. He turned blue as a dead person. Even maybe he *was* dead until Mr. Oberjerk lifted him up by the ankles and shook out Veddar's puke. You saw it all, right?

LaRose nodded.

So now you know what revenge looks like.

Maggie was apt to say things like that, not only from reading her mother's discarded gothic romance novels. Peter worried about her when she asked—she still asked—exactly what had happened to Dusty. Specifically, his body. Was he bones? Was he jelly? Was he dust? Air? Was she breathing him into her lungs? Was she eating something grown from his hair? Were his molecules in everything? And why do you still have your guns? she asked. I hate them. You should get rid of them. I'll never touch one. That, at least, made sense.

Peter worried about her when she kept checking out a book from the library called *Dark Creatures*. He was relieved when she stopped checking it out. Disturbed when the librarian called to tell him it was mutilated. He worried over how Maggie snatched snakes from the woodpile and let them twine up her arms, how she tamed spiders then casually smashed them. How she opened a neighbor's brooding chicken egg before it hatched to see how the thing inside was coming along. How she took the dead chick home to bury and dug it up every day to see how the world digested it. There were days when the dog ignored Maggie, even walked away from her, as if he didn't trust her. These things worried Peter.

Nola, however, was reassured by her daughter's compulsion to tear aside the plastic wrap that divides the universes. It was only natural, thought Nola, to live in both. When you could see one world from the other world, the world for instance of the living from the world of the dead, there was a certain comfort. It relaxed Nola to imagine herself in a casket. She dreamed variations on her look much the way, during high school, she'd mentally put together the perfect outfit. The jeans, the tailed shirt, the funny socks, the shoes, heart necklace, hair sprayed up or falling loose. Of course, she couldn't wear *those* clothes, so out-of-date, when dead. Or maybe yes . . . what a hoot! When all the steps leading to Nola's death were assembled, her anxiety faded. On the other hand, a blue buzz took hold of her when she went past her death and imagined everyone, everything, going on as before, only without Nola. All of this made her feel so guilty, though. She rarely allowed herself. It was like when she ate the whole stale cake and the sugar put her straight to sleep.

After she ate the cake that time, everything went still. The evening was deep and pure. The lights went out and Peter wrapped a soft woolen blanket around her. In darkness, she wound herself into the blanket still more tightly. She was swaddled, confined, protected from herself—as in a very exclusive privately run mental hospital devoted solely to the care of one person: Nola. She fell asleep bothered only by the nagging thought that she would have to start all over in the morning. Existence whined in her head like a mosquito. Then she swatted it. Rode the tide of her comfort down into the earth.

ON SNOWSHOES of ash wood and sinew, Wolfred and the girl made their way south. They would be easy to follow. Wolfred's story was that they'd decided to travel toward Grand Portage, for help. They had left Mackinnon ill in the cabin with plenty of supplies. If they got lost, wandered, found themselves even farther south, chances were nobody would know or care who Mackinnon was. And so they trekked, making good time, and made their camp at night. The girl tested the currents of the air with her face and hands, then showed Wolfred where to build a lean-to, how to place it just so, how to find dry wood in snow, snapping dead branches out of trees, and where to pile it so that they could easily keep the fire going all night and direct its heat their way. They slept peacefully, curled in their separate blankets, and woke to the wintertime scolding of chickadees.

The girl tuned up the fire, they ate, and were back on the way south when suddenly they heard the awful gasping voice of Mackinnon behind them. He was blundering toward them, cracking twigs, calling out for them, Wait, my children, wait a moment, do not abandon me!

They started forward in terror and loped through the snow. A dog drew near them, one of the trading post's pathetic curs; it ran alongside them, bounding effortfully through the snow. They thought at first that Mackinnon had sent it to find them, but then the girl stopped and looked hard at the dog. It whined to her. She nodded and pointed the way through the trees to a frozen river, where they would move along more quickly. On the river ice they slid along with a dream-like velocity. The girl gave the dog a piece of bannock from her pocket, and that night, when they made camp, she set her snares out all around them. She built their fire and the lean-to so that they had to pass through a narrow space between two trees. Here, too, she set a snare. Its loop was large enough for a man's head, even a horribly swollen one. They fed themselves and the dog, and slept with their knives out, packs and snow-shoes close by.

Near morning, when the fire was down to coals, Wolfred woke. He heard Mackinnon's rasping breath very close. The dog barked. The girl got up and sig-naled that Wolfred should fasten on his snowshoes and gather their packs and blankets. As the light came up, Wolfred saw that the sinew snare set for Mackinnon was jigging, pulled tight. The dog worried and tore at some invisible shape. The girl showed Wolfred how to climb over the lean-to another way, and made him un-derstand that he should check the snares she'd set, fetch anything they'd caught, and not forget to remove the sinews so she could reset them at their next camp.

Mackinnon's breathing resounded through the clear-ing around the fire. As Wolfred left, he saw that the girl was preparing a stick with pine pitch and birchbark. She set it alight. He saw her thrust the flaring stick at the air again, and again. There were muffled grunts of pain. Wolfred was so frightened that he had trouble finding all the snares, and he had to cut the sinew that had choked a frozen rabbit. The girl finished the job and they slid back down to the river with the dog. Behind them, unearthly caterwauls began. Quickly they sped off. To Wolfred's relief, the girl smiled and skimmed forward, calm, full of confidence. Yet she was still a child.

⚓

MISS BEHRING heard.

Maggie, please come to the front of the class, she said.

Maggie had poked her head into her desk for a straw sip of apple juice. She had a little box of it for emergencies. She stuck it under her shirt, in her waistband. Humbly, with shy obedience, Maggie walked down the row of desks, dragging her feet for drama.

Right now!

Yes, Miss Behring.

Or is it Miss Boring? asked Miss Behring.

What, Miss Behring?

Maggie! You will walk to the corner and stand there with your face to the wall.

The children tittered with excitement. Maggie turned and smiled, too nice. They stopped. She walked to the corner and stood there, next to the watercooler, with her face to the wall.

Now you will see what boredom is really like! exclaimed her teacher, who was right behind her.

This time the children really did laugh. Maggie tried to turn around again, but Miss Behring was still there. The teacher held her head with flat patty-cake hands at either temple. Maggie's stomach boiled. She had told LaRose that when someone made her stomach boil she always got them. Miss Behring took her hands away from Maggie's head and began a lesson on fractions. Maggie stood there, thinking. After a time, she asked.

Please, Miss Behring, can I go to the bathroom?

You went at recess, said Miss Behring, and smoothly continued with ⅛ + ⅘.

Maggie jiggled.

Miss Behring, Miss Behring! I need to go anyway.

No, Miss Behring said.

Maggie allowed the lesson to continue. But silently she plucked a paper cup from the stack next to the watercooler. She waited.

Miss Behring, please, she said at last. Her voice was strained. I had to go so bad I peed in a cup.

What?

Maggie turned around and held out the cup of apple juice.

May I please empty this?

Miss Behring shut her mouth. Her eyes darted around like trapped flies. She pointed at the door. Then she sat down at her desk staring at some papers.

Maggie carefully bore the brimming cup down the aisle, every eye in the classroom on her. Miss Behring put her head in her hands. Maggie turned and made sure her teacher wasn't watching. She grinned at her classmates. Then she drained the cup, and slammed out the door. She paused outside a moment to enjoy the shrieking gabble and Miss Behring's storm of useless threats. When she came back, she sat down as though nothing had happened. Miss Behring didn't send her back to the corner. She seemed to be making notes. Maggie had been hoping she would cry.

Making people cry was one of Maggie's specialties, so she would have enjoyed her teacher's distress. As for herself, she could luxuriate in tears, she could almost command them into her eyes. She was training herself.

☙

ONE SUNDAY when Nola was at Mass, it occurred to Peter that he might go over to Landreaux's house. He took Maggie along. It wasn't that he missed LaRose. It was the friendship—it was all he had. His brother down in Florida was someone to visit maybe, someday. Landreaux and Emmaline's family were his closest people.

What are we doing? asked Maggie as they drove up.

Just visiting, he said.

Landreaux had already come to the door, and they went in.

LaRose was sitting on top of Coochy pretend-punching. He looked up in surprise. Peter looked down in surprise. LaRose never roughhoused or fake-punched at their home.

Is it time? LaRose asked.

No, said Peter, I'm not coming to get you. Me and Maggie were just rattling around at home, so we thought we'd visit you guys.

Hey! Landreaux's big face went wider and his soft smile came out. He shook Peter's hand, whirling with apprehension, but maybe pleasure. I just made coffee.

They sat down at the kitchen table, and Maggie went straight to Snow and Josette's bedroom. She could smell the nail polish.

Maggie! C'mere. Snow was painting each of her nails with a white undercoat and painting black spirals

alternating with black checkerboards. Josette was ap-
plying a set of stick-on nails with toxic glue. She sat
waiting for them to dry, moving only her face, blink-
ing and rolling her eyes to the music plugged into her
head.

Can you do mine?

What you want, Maggie?

Purple? And white skulls on them.

Geez, I can't make skulls. Snow laughed. Something
easy. She took from her plastic case a tiny jar of purple
polish and shook it, rattling the bead. Maggie loved the
sound of that.

Maybe just dots?

I can do that.

They became absorbed in the intricacy of the under-
coats, the first color, clear coat, second color, clear top
coat. They held their breaths as Snow filed and then
painted Maggie's fingernails. While each coat dried
Snow and Maggie talked.

How come you guys are visiting? You never visit.

I think my dad was lonesome. Mom's at Mass.

It's good, better that you guys came over. We used
to play! Makes it less weird, huh?

Yeah, I mean, sometimes I think . . . Maggie
frowned, then brightened. There could be a whole re-

venge plot going between our families. But now I don't think there ever will.

Snow was startled.

'Cause why . . . 'cause we guys all love LaRose?

Huh-huh. Me and him, we stabbed ourselves to be brother and sister.

Holeee, what?

With pencils. To give a blue dot. Maggie pulled her sweater down.

Can I see? Oooo. Look, Josette. Right on her arm. LaRose and Maggie tattooed themselves to be a family.

LaRose got stabbed by a kid at school. I took care of the kid. Then I stabbed myself so we could be engaged, at first. But I didn't know what engagement meant.

Yeah, gross. He's your brother, so . . .

Keep your fingers still now, said Snow. Put them back on the newspaper.

I like this, said Maggie, almost shy with delight. She stretched her hand out for her purple polka-dotted fingernails to catch the light.

What do you mean you took care of it? said Josette. You beat that kid up?

He had to be revived, said Maggie in a modest way.

For real?

Did you get in trouble?

Not that time. If I do get in trouble, I can handle it.

Josette nodded at Snow. She can do the time, ayyyy. She's looking out for our baby brother, no shit, she's for real.

If we were all a family it would be much better, Maggie said. You guys could sleep over.

Noooo, Josette smiled. Just that we're too old.

We could have the same tattoos then, Maggie said. I know how to give them.

Whoa, hold on! The girls collapsed, laughing.

I just sharpen up a pencil real fine, then pow. She made a quick stabbing motion with a pen.

Assassin! said Snow.

Coochy stuck his head in the door and made a girly face. Your dad says it's time to go.

The girls held their arms out for hugs.

Kiss, kiss, one on each cheek, like we're in the mafia.

✣

WOLFRED ASKED the girl to tell him her name. He asked in words, he asked in signs, but she wouldn't speak. Each time they stopped, he asked. But though she smiled at him, and understood exactly what he wanted, she wouldn't tell her name. She looked into the distance. Near morning, after they had soundly slept, she knelt near the fire to blow it back to life. All of a sudden, she went still and stared into the trees. She jutted her chin forward, then pulled back her hair and narrowed her eyes. Wolfred followed her gaze and saw it, too. Mackinnon's head, rolling laboriously over the snow, its hair on fire, brightly twitching, flames cheerfully flickering. Sometimes it banged into a tree and whimpered. Sometimes it propelled itself along with its tongue, its slight stump of neck, or its comically paddling ears. Sometimes it whizzed along for a few feet, then quit, sobbing in frustration at its awkward, interminable progress.

The Pain Chart

Mrs. Peace pointed to the sweating, crying grimace face on the illustrated list the nurse put in front of her. It was a pain chart.

Real bad, huh?

I have a lot of pain, Mrs. Peace said, a lot of pain. And I was doing so good with no attacks! Now I don't even remember where I put my patches. I thought they were right here, in the bottom of my papers. In my tin.

Where does it hurt? asked the nurse on duty that afternoon.

Here, here, and here. And my head.

This will help you.

That's a shot?

And your usual, your patch. Remember, you have to guard these things. We can keep them locked up in the safe, at the desk.

I'll just keep one, for emergency.

Good, okay. But remember not to let anybody else take them, use them. They are a hundred times stronger than morphine, right? Morphine.

That's what it takes.

Now you'll sleep.

I'd rather stay here, in my recliner. She'll come and visit me.

Who?

My mother.

Oh, I see.

You're smiling. I see your smile. But it is true, she will come. After all these years, they finally let her visit me.

I wrote our name everywhere, said LaRose to her mother. LaRose and LaRose and LaRose going on forever. I was proud of my penmanship, and careful with every letter. I wrote my name in hidden places they would never see. I wrote my name for all of us. I made my name perfect, the letters curved in Palmer A+. Once, I carved my name in wood so that it could never be erased. Even if they painted over the letters you could still read it. LaRose.

Faintly, in the girls' dormitory at Fort Totten. On the top of a wooden door, the underside of chairs, on the shelves of the basement storage room where I was locked up once for sassing. Number 2 lead government-issue BIA pencil, in a notebook, stored now in the National Archives in Kansas City. On a mopboard, inside a cupboard, on top of a closet door in Stephan. Underneath a desk at Marty, and a chalkboard rail. Scratched into a brick grown over with grass at the old powerhouse in Wahpeton. Chamberlain. Flandreau. Fort Totten and Fort Totten. We left our name in those schools and others, all the way back to the first school, Carlisle. For the history of LaRose is tied up in those schools. Yes, we wrote our name in places it would never be found until the building itself was torn down or burned so that all the sorrows and strivings those walls held went up in flames, and the smoke drifted home.

DOUGIE VEDDAR had an older brother, and his brother had friends. They weren't in the same K–6 school but in the junior high, which was connected to the high school. Tyler Veddar, Curtains Peace, Brad Morrissey, and Jason "Buggy" Wildstrand tried to call themselves the Fearsome Four. Until later, it never caught on, except as a joke. At present, they were skinny, soft, and hadn't got their growth. Mainly they played video games and fooled around with Curtains's guitars, left to him by his brother. They had a songbook but didn't know what the markings meant or how to tune their instruments. Their noise was good, they thought. Dougie told his brother how Maggie had tried murder on him. Tyler told his friends and they kept their eyes out for the right chance to get her. Nothing happened. After school, she always took the bus. And then because she got a part as a singing mushroom in the play and stayed after, she had to be picked up.

One day they lucked out because her mother was late.

Maggie was walking in a circle, fuming, kicking up leaves. It was cold, clammy, wet outside. She didn't like it. Tyler came by and said in a nice voice, You okay? He was that much older she didn't recognize him.

No, said Maggie. My mom's late.

We live over there. He pointed at the garage where they hung out. Me and my bros. You wanna come hang out until your mom gets here? You can see from the side window.

I dunno, Maggie said.

My mom's there.

Okay.

She followed him to the garage and they went inside. There were Tyler's friends. They stood around awkwardly, then Tyler said, Wanna sit on the couch? As soon as Maggie sat down, she knew this was bad. They jammed in beside her, pinning her, and Tyler said, You tried to kill Dougie. Then he and the other boys started putting their hands all over her. Their fingers went straight to her non-breasts and poked into her Tuesday panties. They dog-piled her, their grubby paws pinching, prodding, prying her apart. She had a fainting feeling, like she was weak and drained of all her strength. A floating grief came over her like a soft veil. Her head buzzed. But the fingers moved still harder and a hot burn hit her gut. She shrieked. When Tyler tried to cover her mouth, she bit down on his finger until she tasted blood. Buggy pushed her back in the cushions and she screamed louder, slammed her knees into his crotch so hard he yipped and howled like a puppy. Curtains tried to keep a hold but her thumbs went out and jabbed his eyeballs. He fell back, yelling he was blinded, and she jumped toward a guitar, swung it up against Brad's face. She knocked him against the wall. He curled his arms around his head.

Buggy was curled in a corner, bawling. Brad was wheezing. They were all in trauma.

Boys? Boys? You hungry? The mother out the back door.

Naaah! called Tyler.

The boys, except for Buggy, still curled on the floor, stood panting, staring at one another, in a circle.

Finally Tyler said, Fuck, that was amazing. Hey, Maggie, we need a front man. We need a girl. Wanna join our band?

Join? Maggie tossed her hair, inching backward. Straightened her clothes. Adrenaline was wearing off and common fright was telling her to find the door.

We'll tell if you don't join, said Tyler.

She stepped to the door, opened it. Rage whirled around her like a burning hula hoop.

Tell? Tell? Go ahead. You know Landreaux who killed my brother? Well, he's my stepfather now. He'll hunt every one of you down. He'll shoot your heads off. Bye.

Maggie ran back to the corner where she was supposed to meet her mother. The car was pulling up.

Sorry I was late, honey. Did you get bored?

Shut up, said Maggie.

Shut up? Shut up? Is that any way . . .

Shut up! Shut up! Shut up! Maggie shrieked.

She ran straight into the house, into her room. Slammed the door. After a while she sneaked out to go to the bathroom. Then in the hallway LaRose came up behind her.

Quit following me around, brat, Maggie said.

Her head felt funny, like what those boys did sucked her brains out. Their touching hands were gross and left germs of stupidness. She wanted to wash and wash.

Little asshole. She nearly slapped LaRose.

But she couldn't hold on to the bitchiness. LaRose was so frustrating, melting her with nothing particular except he never hurt *anything*. It got dark early, so Maggie and LaRose went downstairs to see if there was food. They ate some ice cream.

Maggie poured a can of Dad's beer into the dog's water bowl. He walked over and sniffed it suspiciously, but the smell was good. He lapped it up. She poured him another. He liked that one too. Then he got a smashed look on his face, walked head-on into the closed glass doors, and fell over. LaRose slid open the doors and helped the dog outside.

Poor stupid dog, said Maggie.

The dog walked in circles and fell off the deck. LaRose sat down in the cold grass with him and cradled its head in his lap. The dog was panting, his eyes were glassy, but his snarl could have been a smile. Maggie sat shivering on a deck chair looking down at them.

The dog whimpered, a drunk dog whimper.

You need coffee, said LaRose. The dog didn't move; slobber dripped until the dog's breath bubbled all over LaRose's hands and legs.

Maggie watched, admiring LaRose because of the way he let the dog slobber on him. And he was always like that. There was the way he always captured spiders, never squashed them, calmed hens before they had to be killed, saved bats, observed but never drowned hills of ants, brought stunned birds to life.

Nola said her Catholic grace before dinner. A thought nagged at Maggie. She looked at LaRose, who was studying his food. He was like that monk in the brown robe, Francis. The animals came to LaRose and laid themselves down at his feet. They were drawn to him, knowing they would be saved.

This thought was erased by the way her mother chewed. Actually, it was everything about the way her mother ate. She was already furious with her mother for being late. For putting her life in danger from those maggots. Maggie tried to turn away, to pretend her mother did not exist. But she couldn't help watch. Nola poked her fork into one green bean, then raised it to her mouth. Sometimes Nola would look around the table to see if anyone else in the family was eating a green bean at the exact same time. At this moment, she was alone with her bean. Nola caught her daughter's look of contempt. Surprised, she opened her mouth, bared her lips, and snatched the green bean off the fork with her teeth.

Maggie whipped her head back. How could she? How on this fucking earth? The teeth, the teeth, scraping the fork. The metal-on-enamel click. Maggie felt a sodden roar rising. She stared down at her plate, at the green beans, and tried to counsel her hatred to get behind her, like Satan, as hunky old Father Travis had suggested when Nola dragged her to confession that one time.

She took a deep breath. She picked up one green bean with her fingers. Nobody noticed. It took six hand-plucked green beans, a casual, *Hey, hey Mom!* Then a provocative mad flare of her eyes as she chomped green beans off her fingers, then the freakish grin that always got a rise.

Nola sat back, her fork half raised. She emitted a blistering wave of force.

This is how you eat a bean, Maggie, she said. Then she lifted the fork, bared her lips, scraped the bean off the fork with her teeth.

Maggie looked straight at her and mouthed words that only Nola, only her mother, could see: *You are disgusting.*

What's happening? cried Peter, feeling the soundless screech, missing the lip sync.

The dog dry-heaved in the corner.

LaRose took the bowl and scooped the last of the green beans onto his plate. He ate them fast. He glanced over, worried, but the dog had quietly passed out.

Nola's face darkened. She was panting hard now, with the *shut ups* adding to the *you are disgusting.* Maggie leaned her chair back, satisfied. She excused herself and sauntered up the stairs. Nola's eyes followed her daughter, sour death rays. She had raised a monster whom she hated with all the black oils of her heart but whom she also loved with a deadly confused despair. Quietly, sinking back into her chair, she experimentally ate a green bean off the end of her fork. Neither Peter nor LaRose seemed to notice. So it wasn't her? She was not disgusting? A tear dropped on her plate.

Peter saw another tear plunk. Are you okay?

Somebody told me today? said LaRose.

Peter put his arm around Nola, just held her. He was getting good at that.

Told you what?

They said, Your mother's beautiful.

Nola smiled a wan, bewildered smile.

Before he'd spoken, LaRose had made sure Maggie was shut in her room. This was so awkward for him always to be caught between the two—he had confided in Josette. She had told him it was awkward. She told him that for one thing, Maggie had some kind of grief disorder, probably, that made her act out. It's us who should adopt her, said Snow. We love her, but she's hard. Also there were communication problems at her house. Josette said it was very common at her age, the mother-daughter thing. She and Snow and their mom were lucky because Emmaline had given birth young and also she was kind of a ding like the two of them and not trying to be so goody-goody and above them. Whatever works, do it, Josette said, but I feel sorry for you because it is awkward.

Maggie slipped into his room that night. She had been lying in her room—cooling off after another hot, hot shower. She had started to cry, alone. It was okay alone. But she still cut off the crying as quickly as she could, to toughen herself. She was a wolf, a

wounded wolf. She'd sink her teeth in those boys'
throats. Her thoughts returned to how the animals
were drawn to LaRose. She would trust her paw to
his boy hand.

Move over, she whispered, and popped under his
quilt.

Her hot feet on his shins.

I gotta ask you something. Her nose was still plugged
by the unwilled crying. Her face was swollen. But his
skin cooled the soles of her feet.

Please, LaRose. Don't laugh. I'm gonna ask you
something serious.

Okay.

What would you do if boys jumped me, if they
touched me and stuff, all over, in a bad way.

I would make them die, said LaRose.

Do you think you could?

I would figure it out.

Could a saint kill for love?

Saints have superpowers, said LaRose.

Do you think you're a saint?

No.

I think you are, said Maggie.

She rolled over, stared at the crack of dim light underneath the door. It was a cool night. The warmth of
him suffused the bed. The itchy, dirty, cooty-fingered

film on her skin dispersed. The roiling craziness her mother caused with her chewing habits dissipated. Everything bad was drawn into the gentle magnetism of the bedsheets. She began to drift.

LaRose stroked the ends of her hair on the pillow beside him.

I am a broken animal, she whispered.

⚓

IT WAS going to snow, first snow of the season, Romeo could smell it. He could always smell that gritty freshness before it happened, before the weatherpeople turned the snow to drama on his television. He plunged outside, across the lumps of torn earth, and took the road to town. Sure enough, as he rollingly walked, flakes began and he had the impression, maybe it was the drug he'd taken, that he was all of a sudden stuck. He was in a globe, frozen on a tiny treadmill in a little scene of a man walking to the Dead Custer, forever, through falling bits of white paper or maybe some snowlike chemical that would sift down over and over as a child turned his world upside down in its hands. He liked this idea so well that he had to remind himself it wasn't true. The mo-

tionless motion was so transfixing, and his thoughts—
his thoughts were centered.

Landreaux happened to drive through this tableau,
oblivious as always, but the snow swirled in his wake
and got Romeo's thoughts back on his old favorite, revenge. Landreaux believed he was outside of Romeo's
reach and interest. But no, he wasn't. Landreaux was
so full of himself, so high on himself that even now he
did not remember those old days of theirs. Far back
when they were young boys hardly older than LaRose.
That's how far back and deep it went, invisible most
times like a splinter to the bone. Then surfacing or
piercing Romeo from the inside like those terrible fake
pills the old vultures had tricked down him.

Bits of snow melted in Romeo's filmy hair. It was
just a fluke, maybe, but he'd got himself put on to a
substitute maintenance list at the hospital. Be still my
heart! So many prescription bottles, so little time. Because his habits had already become invisible to the
ambulance crew, he overheard a sentence that he'd
copied out on scratch paper. *Never touched the carotid.*
He'd palmed a box of colored tacks and fixed the paper
to the wall. Working out connections. It would be the
first of many clues to what had really happened on the
day Landreaux killed Dusty.

Lennie Briscoe, the weary hound, and Romeo, his weasel sidekick, would assemble the truth.

In the clarity of thinking that he enjoyed after Landreaux's car passed, Romeo thought about how people with information spoke quietly, in code. He was learning to decipher what they said. Sometimes he had to make an educated guess. But he knew they were possessed of crucial knowledge.

To get the truth, I must become truth. Or at least appear truth-worthy, he decided.

Therefore, Romeo cleaned himself up. He applied for a real full-time at the hospital. Slim chance. And the paperwork always made him sweat. But there, at the hospital, he thought maybe he could be important again. The other people on maintenance were respected community members. Some of them even drove the ambulance, and all of them were trusted. Sterling Chance really was, for instance, sterling. As head of maintenance, he listened to Romeo answer interview questions with a calm and perceptive gaze.

Self-contained, thought Romeo. He admired Sterling Chance. For the first time since, well, since Mrs. Peace was his teacher, Romeo truly wanted something other than reliable pathways to oblivion. He wanted this job. Not just a measly part-time intermittent job, but a full-time job. True, his motives were sketchy.

Drugs and vengeance. But why quibble with a budding work ethic? There was no question that this job would make his old drug sources look pathetic. Never again would he have to suffer the indignation of crisscrossing side effects. And information? If he did get information on this job, it would be information he would keep until he really needed it—sad information. But information so rare and shocking that maybe, perhaps, you could use it to blackmail a person for life. Which was a satisfying thought when you'd previously failed to kill that person.

FIGHTING OFF, outwitting, burning, even leaving food behind for the head to gobble, just to slow it down, the girl, Wolfred, and the dog traveled. They wore out their snowshoes. The girl repaired them. Their moccasins shredded. She layered the bottoms with skin and stuffed them inside with rabbit fur. Every time they tried to rest, the head would appear, bawling at night, fiery at dawn. So they moved on and on, until, at last, starved and frozen, they gave out.

The small bark hut took most of a day to bind together. As they prepared to sleep, Wolfred arranged a log on the fire and then fell back as if struck. The simple action had dizzied him. His strength had flowed right out through his fingers into the fire. The fire now sank quickly from his sight, over some invisible cliff. He began to shiver, hard, and then a black wall fell. He was confined in a temple of branching halls. All that night he groped his way through narrow passages, along doorless walls. He crept around corners, stayed low. Standing was impossible even in his dreams. When he opened his eyes at first light, he saw the vague dome of the hut was spinning so savagely that it blurred and sickened him. He did not dare open his eyes again that day, but lay as still as possible, only lifting his head, eyes shut, to sip water the girl dripped between his lips from a piece of folded bark.

He told her to leave him behind. She pretended not to understand him.

All day she cared for him, hauling wood, boiling broth, keeping him warm. That night the dog growled ferociously at the door, and Wolfred opened one eye briefly to see infinitely duplicated images of the girl winding her hand in a strip of blanket to grip the handle of the ax, then heating its edge red hot. He felt her slip out the door, and then there began a great babble of howling, cursing, shrieking, desperate groaning and thumping, as if trees were being felled. Every so often, silence, then the mad cacophony again. This went on all night. At first light, he sensed that she'd crept inside. He felt the warmth and weight of her curled against his back, smelled the singed fur of the dog, or maybe her hair. Hours into the day, she woke and he heard her tuning a drum in the warmth of the fire. Very much surprised, he asked her, in Ojibwe, how she'd got the drum.

It flew to me, she told him. This drum belonged to my mother. With this drum, she brought people to life.

He must have heard wrong. Drums cannot fly. He was not dead. Or was he? The world behind his closed eyes was ever stranger. From the many-roomed black temple, he had stepped into a universe of fractured patterns. There was no relief from their implacable mathematics. Designs formed and re-formed. Hard-edged triangles joined and split in an endless geometry. If this was death, it was visually exhausting. Only when she started drumming did the patterns gradually lose intensity. Their movement diminished as she sang in an off-key, high-pitched, nasal whine that rose and fell in calming repetition until, at last, the concatenations ebbed to a mere throb of color. The drum corrected some interior rhythm; a delicious relaxation painted his thoughts, and he slept.

Again, that night, he heard the battle outside. Again, at first light, he felt her curl against him and smelled the scorched dog. Again, once she woke, she tuned and beat the drum. The same song transported him. He put his hand to his head. She'd cut up her blanket, crowned him with a warm woolen turban. Toward night, he opened his eyes and saw the world rock to a halt. Joyously, he whispered, I am back. I have returned.

You shall go on one more journey with me, she said, smiling, and began to sing.

Her song lulled and relaxed him so that when he stepped out of his body, grasping her hand, he was not afraid to lift off the ground. They traveled into vast air. Over the dense woods, they flew so fast no cold could reach them. Below, fires burned, a village only two days' walk from their hut. Satisfied, she turned them back and Wolfred drifted down into the body he was not to leave again until he had completed half a century of hard, bone-break, work.

Two days later, they entered from deep wilderness a town. Ojibwe bark houses, a hundred or more, were set up along the bends of a river. Along a street of beaten snow several wooden houses were neatly rooted in a dreamlike row. They were so like the houses Wolfred had left behind out east, that, for a disoriented moment, he believed they had traversed the Great Lakes. He thought he was in home country, and walked up to the door of the largest house. His knock was answered, but not until he explained himself in English did the young woman who answered recognize him as a whiteman.

She and her family, missionaries, brought the pair into a warm kitchen. They were given water and rags to wash with, and then a tasteless porridge of boiled wild rice. They were allowed to sleep with blankets, on the floor behind the woodstove. The dog, left outside, sniffed the missionaries' dog and followed it to the barn, where the two coupled in the steam of the cow's great body. The next morning, speaking earnestly to the girl, whose clean face was too beautiful to look at, Wolfred asked if she would marry him.

When you grow up, he said.

She smiled and nodded.

He asked her name.

She laughed, not wanting him to own her, and drew a flower.

The missionary was sending a few young Ojibwe to a Presbyterian boarding school that had recently been established for Indians only. It was located out in territory that had become the state of Michigan, and the girl could travel there, too, if she wanted to become educated. Only, as she had no family, she would become indentured to the place. Although she did not understand what that meant, she agreed to it.

At the school, everything was taken from her. Losing her mother's drum was like losing Mink all over again. At night, she asked the drum to fly back to her. But it never did. She soon learned how to fall asleep. Or let the part of myself they call hateful fall asleep, she thought. But it never did. Her whole being was Anishinaabe. She was Illusion. She was Mirage. Ombanitemagad. Or what they called her now—Indian. As in, *Do not speak Indian,* when she had been speaking her own language. It was hard to divide off parts of herself and let them go. At night, she flew up through the ceiling and soared as she had been taught. She stored pieces of her being in the tops of the trees. She'd retrieve them later, when the bells stopped. But the bells would never stop. There were so many bells. Her head ached, at first, because of the bells. My thoughts are all tangled up, she said out loud to herself, Inbiimiskwendam. However, there was very little time to consider what was happening.

The other children smelled like old people, but she got used to it. Soon she did too. Her wool dress and corset pinched, and the woolen underwear itched like mad. Her feet were shot through with pain, and stank from sweating in hard leather. Her hands chapped. She was always cold, but she was already used to that. The food was usually salt pork and cabbage, which cooked foul and turned the dormitory rank with farts, as did the milk they were forced to drink. But no matter how raw, or rotten, or strange, she must eat, so she got used to it. It was hard to understand the teachers or say what she needed in their language, but she learned. The crying up and down the rows of beds at night kept her awake, but soon she cried and farted herself to sleep with everyone else.

She missed her mother, even though Mink had sold her. She missed Wolfred, the only person left for her. She kept his finely written letters. When she was weak or tired, she read them over. That he called her Flower made her uneasy. Girls were not named for flowers, as flowers died so quickly. Girls were named for death-less things—forms of light, forms of clouds, shapes of stars, that which appears and disappears like an island on the horizon. Sometimes the school seemed like a dream that could not be true, and she fell asleep hoping to wake in another world.

She never got used to the bells, but she got used to other children coming and going. They died of measles, scarlet fever, flu, diphtheria, tuberculosis, and other diseases that did not have a name. But she was already accustomed to everybody around her dying. Once, she got a fever and thought that she would also die. But in the night her pale-blue spirit came, sat on the bed, spoke to her kindly, placed her soul back into her body, and told her that she would live.

Nobody got drunk. Nobody slashed her mother's face and nose, ruining her. Nobody took a knife and stabbed an uncle who held your foot and died as the blood gushed from his mouth. Another good thing she thought of while the other children wept was that the journey to the school had been arduous and far. Much too far for a head to roll.

⸸

WOLFRED TOLD the story of Mackinnon's sudden illness and how he and the girl had plunged into the wilderness seeking help, which was dispatched. The Indians had already found Mackinnon scattered outside the trading post, and they reported that in his fever he'd sought cold snow, died there, and been torn apart by dogs. His head? Wolfred wanted to ask, but fear stopped his tongue. Wolfred was authorized to take up Mackinnon's position, and so he left the settlement and traveled north. He left Mackinnon's gold watch, wedding ring, and money in their hiding place. He did well at the post, though the heart of the trade had moved on. Sometimes at night perhaps he heard Mackinnon's hoarse breath. Sometimes he whiffed the rank odor that used to swell from Mackinnon's feet when he removed his boots. Wolfred kept beautifully detailed books of transactions. Often, he wrote to the girl in Michigan, *My Flower, Chère LaRose.* He was influenced by French and Metis descendants of the voyageurs he came to know. They tried to persuade him to forget her. He did not, at any rate, take a wife. Although he helped himself liberally to women's charms, there was no forgetting her.

He kept writing letters so that she would remember her promise. He wrote of their experiences, for as they had traveled he had marveled at her skills and authority. Wolfred spent longer periods of time living with, hunting with, speaking with, and sharing ceremonies with her people. They gave him medicine to get rid of Mackinnon, which seemed to work. He stopped hearing the breath rasp at night, stopped smelling the feet. He was turning into an Indian while she was turning into a white woman. But how could he know.

THE DAY did come, the death day. One year had passed already. Landreaux and Emmaline had no idea how the Ravich family would spend that day. LaRose was with the Iron family, as Peter had planned. They did what they could the night before, gathering the children for a pipe ceremony in the living room, and everyone talked. They passed the sacred pipe, one to another. The children turned the pipe to each direction when it came to them. They were careful. They knew to handle the pipe. Hollis said that because LaRose went over to the Raviches he saved them. Willard said he missed LaRose. Josette said both things her brothers said were true, and that she was glad he'd brought Maggie closer. Snow said LaRose had saved both families. He was a little healer. Emmaline could not speak. Landreaux said nothing, but a demonic sadness in him grew and grew.

On the very day of it, Landreaux found that he could not get out of bed. All strength and will had left his body. A black weight of sleep pressed down. The boys came to the door of their parents' little bedroom right off the kitchen. Dad, they said. Dad?

He heard their feet shuffle at the foot of the bed. Then the girls came in. They touched his hair, his hands. He kept his eyes shut. When they left, tears leaked down the lines along his mouth, down his neck, and pooled along his collarbone. The heat of his body dried them. He was unusually hot, he found. To his joy, he had a fever. He was really ill. After the older children left on the school bus, Emmaline sat beside him.

She thought of lying down beside him, but something had gone out of her. She searched her heart, and found only weary calculation of the difficulties that his misery would make for her that day.

I have to go to work, she said. LaRose is here. Can you take him to school in an hour?

Yeah, the aspirin will kick in, said Landreaux. I'll be okay.

Emmaline sat with him, stroked the hair back from his forehead. LaRose was eating oatmeal with raisins, leaving the raisins for last.

You're sure you can do it?

I'm sure. I'll just stay quiet here half an hour. Then I'll get up.

He heard her tell LaRose good-bye, heard the door shut, the motor growling as she left the house.

INFINITE RIDE

The buck knew, Landreaux thought. Of course it knew. Last year it knew. Landreaux had been watching, with his gun sometimes and sometimes not. Many times he had found that the buck was also watching him. He

234 · LOUISE ERDRICH

would stop, feeling its gaze on the back of his head, and turn to see it motionless, its eyes deep and liquid. If he had listened, or understood, or cared to know what he understood, he would never have hunted that buck. Never. He would have known the animal was trying to tell him something of the gravest importance. The deer was no ordinary creature, but a bridge to another world. A place where Landreaux would never stop seeing his friend's son in the leaves, never stop strange thoughts from visiting at the most inopportune moments.

How to explain that shot? He'd wish himself out of existence to take it or not take it over again. But the harder, the best, the only thing to do was to stay alive. Stay with the consequences, with his family. Take on the shame although its rank weight smothered him.

Sometimes he was afraid he'd crack and say suddenly that he'd been drinking that day, even though that was wrong. It was maybe worse. He'd not been thinking. He hadn't waited, or maybe he'd been waiting so long for the buck that the actual moment seemed an afterthought. But it was a moment of stupidity, really, wasn't it? Still, to Landreaux his crucial lack of attention at that moment was as bad as being drunk. Not a soul understood it was as bad, except Dusty. He knew, of course, or his spirit knew. He had told Landreaux in a dream.

Afterward, Zack Peace had given Landreaux that Breathalyzer test. He'd done it, routinely, after Landreaux had been taken in. Zack had glanced at the readout, then turned and looked steadily at Landreaux. People always suspected those who worked with terminal patients of taking their drugs. But he had been clean for weeks. Clean. He'd sworn off that anodyne. The number was normal, but there was something about Landreaux, his reactions, alternating between raving fits and calm, his burp of laughter, once. Maybe high? But there was no sign of substance on him. And anyway, Zack knew that in the aftermath of an event like this, nothing seemed normal. Everyone was whacked-out on horror and adrenaline. He had looked up to Landreaux from childhood and he was Emmaline's favorite cousin. Zack included the negative test in his report, which would help exonerate Landreaux. Yet, he was troubled. They hadn't spoken of it since. They hadn't spoken at all.

Today, on this day, Landreaux had to tell someone the truth. His head was ringing. He was sick of hiding it. In the past year he'd realized that there wasn't a right person. There were, of course, two people who were safe to tell, who could share the weight. Yet he did not want to lose Father Travis's respect. He didn't want to see Emmaline's face after he released those words.

So that left nobody. Zack, who knew, wouldn't speak to him. He had to tell, and that is when LaRose came into the room.

Daddy. LaRose sat down on the bed. Get up!

I'm sick today.

LaRose felt Landreaux's forehead, just like a grown-up, and made his father smile.

Little doctor, do I have a fever?

You need a sweat lodge, said LaRose, because he wanted to make all of the preparations.

Okay, said Landreaux, let's do it. We'll have a sweat lodge, just us two. You can skip a day of kindergarten, I guess, for a sweat lodge. Yeah?

Sure I can.

But first I gotta tell you something.

LaRose waited.

This is a secret, a big secret. We have to swear it is our secret, okay?

LaRose grew very serious. They shook hands four times.

Okay, I'm trusting you.

LaRose opened his eyes wide at his father and did not blink.

I wasn't, ah, right in my head the day I killed Dusty. I didn't mean to, but I don't know, maybe my aim was off. The point is, I was clumsy that day.

LaRose frowned and his father's heart stabbed.

Did you see Dusty there? LaRose asked. Did you see the dog?

What dog? said Landreaux.

Dusty fell from a tree branch, said LaRose. I saw the place. One night in my dream I saw the whole thing. Dusty followed the dog into the woods. The dog saw you. Ask the dog.

Landreaux's brain began to hurt.

You always had a good aim before. My other Dad said so.

Peter.

Yeah. He said you would have hit the buck.

That's true, said Landreaux. The buck is still there. I've seen it roaming in the woods.

Dusty told me you shot him on accident, said LaRose.

Landreaux opened his arms to his son, and LaRose crept close to lie against his chest. They breathed together. LaRose loosened, took a big sigh, fell asleep, but Landreaux stayed awake, staring at the ceiling. The sky fell, as it did each moment. Shame covered him. He saw that he was supposed to share LaRose all along because the boy was too good for a no-good like him. LaRose, again. LaRose had saved him before. On the day the bus left for boarding school, he had been only a few years older than his son was now. It seemed impossible that his parents had let him go. They didn't tell him, but they were on their way to live, and die, in Minneapolis.

Landreaux's parents had left him at the bus with his things and driven away in his grandfather's car. He was nine years old. The school people took his sack of clothes and belongings as he got on and that was the last he saw of it. He was going to a school run by the Bureau of Indian Affairs of the U.S. government, said his parents. They'd both been to mission schools and didn't like them. They thought the government school would be much better. Plus they could visit him. They could take a different kind of bus if they moved to Minneapolis.

The seats of Landreaux's bus were green and tough, hot because it was still August and the bus had been sitting in the parking lot. Halfway to the school there was supposed to be a lunch, and it was true. They got off at a park. The older kids ran around laughing. Waxed-paper parcels were handed out. The sandwich was soft white bread. There was butter and the cheese was orange. There was an apple. His stomach glowed. He asked for and got another sandwich, the same. He ate it all, drank iron-tasting water from a pump.

After he climbed back on the bus and was counted, he sank onto the floor. He crawled under the seat. The bus rumbled back onto the highway and Landreaux made himself comfortable there beneath the seat. He could make out a name emphatically formed many times on the metal inside of the bus there.

LaRose. LaRose. LaRose.

Girls behind him murmured, happy. Other children started crying, soft, in low hiccups. A four-year-old softly vomited. Some were staring out the window, mesmerized. Some kids laughed and chatted, expectant. Other children were going numb. Curled underneath the bus seat, Landreaux stared at that name. The letters were drawn in heavy pencil, traced over and over. LaRose. He dozed off and soon he was sleeping heavily on a full stomach. He did not wake when the bus stopped, when all of them got off. He did not wake when they shaved his head for lice and left him in the shower while they found him new clothes without bugs. Not even in bed that night, the next morning either, did he wake. He never woke up. He was still sleeping on that bus.

Take It All
1967–1970

Romeo & Landreaux

The dormitory building was made of tightly mortised red bricks. It was a simple boxy building, the main entrance opening in the center. When Landreaux pushed the dull steel of the main doors, the inside pressure changed and a hoarse vibration of sound escaped. A low sigh, the ghost of Milbert Good Road. The floors were pale linoleum tiles polished to a gloss. In late afternoon, the heatless sun blazed down the central corridor. Little boys were on one side, big boys on the other. There were large divided barrackslike sleeping quarters to either side of the hallway. There were two bunk beds to a room, four boys. The bathrooms and showers were halfway down the hall and the matrons' glass-fronted offices were set watchfully at either end.

Down in the basement there was a laundry room with banks of washers and dryers chugging day and night.

One of the matrons in the little boys' wing, plump and freckled with blazing thick white hair in a short bowl cut, explained to Landreaux the system of demerits. His name was added to a chart in a bound book, at her office desk. If he didn't wash or if he wet the bed, if he overslept, if he was noisy after lights-out or backtalked or went out of school boundaries, or most especially, if he ever ran away, demerits would be marked by his name. Mrs. Vrilchyk explained that if he had too many demerits he could lose recess, trips to town. If he ran away it would be much worse, she said. He might not get his privileges back. Landreaux had heard they made boys wear long green shame dresses, shaved their heads, made them scrub the sidewalks. But no, another boy had told him on the bus, they had done this in a different school and now they'd stopped. Mrs. Vrilchyk was still talking. Running away was dangerous. A girl had died two years ago. Mrs. Vrilchyk, whom everyone called Bowl Head, said that the girl was tossed in a ditch. There are bad people out there. So don't run away, she said. Her voice wasn't mean, or kind, just neutral. She patted his shoulder and said that she could tell he was a good boy. He wouldn't run away.

Every time she said the words *run away*, Landreaux had a feeling about the word: *runaway*. The word bounced him up inside.

He took the bundle of clothes and bedding. A man matron stood in the bedroom and showed the boys how they were supposed to make their beds. He was an Indian, like an uncle, but with little eyes and a hard, pocked face. The matron stripped the bed he had made and told all of the boys to make their beds that way. He was called from the room. The boys who were to share the room started pawing the sheets and blankets into shape.

Except a pale, hunched boy. He sat on the edge of his bed and said, in a low voice, *Go to hell, Pits.* He kicked the bedclothes on the floor and stamped his foot on them. So this was Romeo. At four or five years of age he had been found wandering beside the road on the same reservation where Landreaux grew up. Nobody knew exactly who his parents were, but he was clearly an Indian. He was burned, bruised, starved, thought mentally deficient. But once he was sent to boarding school, it turned out he was one of the smartest boys. He snarled to show he was tough, but he was not. He was in love with Mrs. Peace and was working in her class to make her notice him, take him home with her.

Adopt him. That was his aim, maybe high but not impossible? After all, he had graduated from the pee boys.

Romeo had stopped pissing in his sleep because he'd stopped drinking water. Just a cup in the morning and a cup at noon. Was he thirsty? Hell, yes. But within a month of enduring this great thirst he was no longer a pee boy and it was worth it. Not a drop passed his lips after noon feed, even if he got too dizzy to run around, even if his mouth turned dry and tasted of rotting mouse. It was very worth it not to piss the bed.

He heard them talking in the other bunks.

Can't have a top bunk, Romeo. Might drip.

But Landreaux looked at Romeo, gave an open, friendly smile, and said, Nah he looks steady. I'll sleep under.

Landreaux put his bedding in the bunk below.

Romeo was flooded with a piercing sensation that started as surprise, became pleasure, and then, if he'd known what to call it, joy. No boy had ever stood up for him. No boy had ever grinned at Romeo like he might buddy up with him. He had no brothers, no cousins at school, no connections at home except a dubious foster aunt. This moment with Landreaux was so powerful that its impact lasted days. And it got better. Landreaux never wavered. Because Landreaux called him steady, Romeo became steady. Landreaux was instantly cool with his careless slouch and rangy confidence, and he acted, simply, as though Romeo had always been cool right along with him. Because of Landreaux, Romeo stood straighter, got stronger, ate more, even grew. He began drinking water later in the afternoon. Stayed dry. Landreaux was ace at archery, hit bull's-eye every time. Romeo could do math in his head. They became known. Other boys admired them. Many times that year, Mrs. Peace took them home with her. She was the mother of a little girl named Emmaline, who seemed to adore them equally. Landreaux ignored Emmaline, but Romeo adored her back. He sat on the floor with her, played blocks, dolls, animals, and read her favorite picture book whenever she pushed it into his hands. Mrs. Peace laughed and thanked him, because, she said, the book was repetitive. Romeo didn't care. The little girl hung on his every word. As they grew, his love grew also, but she forgot about him.

Mrs. Peace's home had a yard with a knotted rope dangling from a tall tree. The boys took turns clinging to the ball of rags at the end of the rope. They twisted each other up tight and then swung out, untwisting in great loops, until they got sick. After their stomachs settled, they ate meat soup and frybread, corn on the cob. Mrs. Peace made them read *The Hardy Boys*, which she'd taken from the library just for them, sometimes out loud. Romeo was a better reader than Landreaux, but he hid that. He listened to Landreaux strain along, his whole body tilting as if each sentence was an uphill walk. The friends were contented all fall, all winter, all spring. They stayed two summers, and were best friends. Around year three, however, Landreaux began to talk about his mother and father. They had never visited. He talked about them in fall, then winter. In spring he began to talk about going to find them.

That's running away, said Romeo.

I know it, said Landreaux.

This one girl? She run away by crawling under the school bus, hanging on somewhere under there. She sneaked out when it got to the reservation. She run back home. Her mom and dad kept her because of how she taken the chance. They were afraid of what she might do next if they sent her back.

The boys were talking back and forth in their bunk beds, hissing and whispering after lights-out.

I dunno, said Landreaux. You could fall out. Get dragged.

Flattened like Wile E. Coyote.

Ain't worth it, said Sharlo St. Claire.

You're too big anyway. Gotta be small.

I could do it, said Landreaux. This was before he started eating and got his growth.

I could do it too, said Romeo.

Couldn't.

Could.

We should do it quick then. School bus going back in a week. Nobody else gonna take us, said Landreaux.

Isn't so bad here in summer, said Romeo. His heart hammered. What if he got "home" and there was nobody for him? Yet there would be no Landreaux, here, if Landreaux left. That was unthinkable. Romeo knew how his life was saved and knew the scars along the insides of his arms represented something unspeakable that he could not remember. He didn't want to leave the school and didn't want to hang beneath the bus.

Look, Landreaux. In summer, we go to the lake and swim and stuff? Right? That's fun.

They watch you alla time.

Yeah, said Romeo.

Well, said Landreaux. I am sick of their eyes on me.

Even Romeo knew that Pits was after Landreaux, cuffed him around, so it was more than the seeing eyes.

Next day on the playground, Romeo looked at Landreaux.

Whatcha think?

Landreaux nodded.

Romeo saw the dullness behind his eyes. This opacity of spirit—well, Romeo would never have called it that, but many years later Father Travis was to call it exactly that as he considered the man hanging his head before him. Romeo knew only that when Landreaux shut that spark off behind his eyes, it meant he was asleep and would do anything no matter how dangerous. It made Landreaux look extremely cool, and Romeo felt sick.

During the weekend, they got in good with Bowl Head, who let them deliver a broken step stool to the woodworking shop. The buses were parked just beyond. After they dropped the stool off, they sneaked behind the corner of the building and then crept to a school bus, rolled beneath. They could see immediately where you might hang on.

Maybe, said Landreaux, if you were shit-ass crazy. Maybe a few minutes. Not for hours and hours.

Though you might hol' on longer if you knew falling off would kill you.

Don' look like much fun, said Romeo.

Don' you believe 'bout that girl? said Landreaux.

But there was something irresistible in Landreaux's intense planning. He could not stop thinking, talking, how they might strap themselves on with belts or ropes. How it might get hot or might get cold. Need a jacket either way.

⋆

THE DAY came. Romeo and Landreaux ambled into the go-home line and lingered at the very end. Bowl Head stood by the open bus door, scanning her checklist. Each student in the line held a sack of clothing. Romeo and Landreaux had sacks too. At the last moment, they ditched, sneaked around the tail end of the bus, rolled into shadow, then wormed into the guts of the machine. There was a flat foot-wide bar they could hang on that ran down the center, and beside it two catch pans that could help them balance. They put their bags in the pans and fixed themselves in place on their stomachs, feet up, ankles curled around the bar, face-to-face.

A thousand years passed before the bus roared violently to life. It bumbled along through the town streets. The boys could feel the gears locking together, changing shape, transferring power. As they pulled onto the highway the bus lurched, then socked smoothly into high gear.

They lifted their heads, dazzled, in the vast rumble of the engine. Their ears hurt. Occasionally bits of stone or gravel kicked up and stung like buckshot. Seams in the asphalt jarred their bones. Their bodies were pumped on adrenaline and a dreamlike terror also gripped them. On their stomachs, feet up, ankles curled around the bar, face-to-face, they clung fear-locked to their perch.

The pain burrowed into Romeo's eardrums, but he knew if he lifted his hands to his ears he'd die falling off. The pain got worse and worse, then something exploded softly in his head and the noise diminished. The boys tried very hard not to look down at the highway. But it was all around them in a smooth fierce blur and the only other place to look was at each other.

Landreaux shut his eyes. The dark seized and dizzied him. He had to focus on Romeo, who didn't like to be looked at and did not ever meet another person's eyes, unless a teacher held his head and forced him. It wasn't done in Landreaux's family. It wasn't done among their friends. It drove white teachers crazy. In those days, Indians rarely looked people in the eye. Even now, it's an uneasy thing, not honest but invasive. Under the bus, there was no other place for the two boys to look but into each other's eyes. Even when the two got old and remembered the whole experience, this forced gaze was perhaps the worst of it.

Romeo's rat-colored buzz cut flattened and his pupils smoked with fear. Landreaux's handsome mug was squashed flat by wind and his lush hair was flung straight back. His eyes were pressed into long cat-like slits, but he could see—oh, yes he could see—the lighter brown splotches in Romeo's pinwheel irises, mile after mile. And he began to think, as minutes passed, endless minutes mounting past an hour, a timeless hour, that Romeo's eyes were the last sight he would see on earth because their bodies were losing the tension they needed to grip the bar. Arms, shoulders, stomach, thighs, calves—all locked but incrementally loosening as though the noise itself were prying them away from their perch. If they hadn't both been strong, light, hard-muscled boys who could shimmy up flag-poles, vault fences, catch a branch with one arm, and swing themselves into a tree, over a fence, they would have died. If the bus hadn't slowed exactly when it did and pulled into a rest stop, they would also have died.

They were speechless with pain. Landreaux gagged a few words out, but they found they could hear nothing. They watched each other's mouths open and shut.

They cried sliding off the bar as blood surged back into muscle. From beneath the bus, they saw Bowl Head's thick, creamy legs, and the driver's gray slacks. Then the other kids' boney ankles and shuffling feet.

They waited on the tarred parking lot ground until everyone had gone to the bathrooms and was back inside. The doors closed, the driver started the bus idling, and that's when they rolled out from underneath. They dove behind a trash barrel. Once the bus was gone, they staggered off into a scrim of thick blue spruce trees on the perimeter. For half an hour, they writhed beneath the branches and bit on sticks. When the pain subsided just enough for them to breathe, they were very thirsty, hungry too, and remembered they'd left their sacks stuck beneath the bus. They sharply recalled the bread they'd squirreled away with their clothes.

The rest stop was empty, so they left the bushes and went in. They drank water from the taps, pissed, wondered if they could hole up inside for the night. But there was nowhere in the bathroom, really, to hide. Digging through the trash, Romeo found a bit of candy bar. The chocolate just got their juices flowing. Walking out the door, they noticed a car turning off the highway. They sneaked around back and flung themselves beneath the trees. A family of four white people got out of the car with two brown paper bags. The children put the paper bags on the picnic table, and then the family went into the restrooms.

The instant they vanished, Landreaux sprinted for the bags. Romeo ran to the car to look for other food, and saw that the keys were still in the ignition. He signaled to Landreaux, who walked over with an easy step, slid behind the wheel, turned the key, and pulled out as if he'd done it all his life.

Romeo and Landreaux turned off the highway onto a county road. It quickly turned to gravel. Landreaux kept on going. They ate the sandwiches, deviled eggs, everything except the two apples, and kept the lemonade bottle, the hats and jackets. They left the car parked down a side road in some bushes, and doubled back to a set of train tracks they'd crossed. They started walking west on the cross ties. When it got dark, they found a shelterbelt, put on the extra jackets, and used the caps for pillows. They ate the apples and drank a third of the lemonade. Three trains passed in the night, much too fast to hop. In the morning they kept walking.

One thing I wonder, said Romeo, and hope I never know.

Whuh, said Landreaux.

How Bowl Head really cuts her hair. With a bowl the exact same size of her head or what?

That hair went brown to white in one day, said Landreaux.

The thick brilliance of her hair was truly remarkable.

Romeo did not believe it happened in one day, but he asked how.

What I heard was she went back of the dining hall and saw Milbert Good Road the way he looked after he had drowned on that school trip. He asked why she never runned for him when she saw him go under. The water wasn't more than up to her stomach. People said she was parasite.

Paralyzed, murmured Romeo.

She yelled for Mr. Jalynski an he jumped in. Ermine jumped in, waded in, all the kids good at swimming went in, all the other grown-ups. They never found him til later. They said it was a water moccasin.

Romeo said nothing, but sometimes he wondered about Landreaux. Some kids had heard a teacher from Louisiana mention the deadliness of a water moccasin. Some kid made up that it was a moccasin made of water that slipped around your foot and pulled you under. Romeo knew it was a snake and Milbert had drowned because he couldn't swim. Landreaux was cool, but, parasite? Water moccasin? These lapses made Romeo uneasy. Not only that, they just hurt his brain.

This train couldn't just run on forever, with no reason, Romeo complained. Must be a grain elevator someplace.

They could see a farm many miles away. A square hedge of green on the horizon, blank flat earth all around. The sun was low and they had drunk all of the lemonade, jealously watching each other. But Landreaux gave Romeo the last swallow, saying, Kill it, reluctantly, looking away. They'd had nothing to eat for hours but the juicy ends of tall grass along the tracks.

Maybe we could get there by dark, said Romeo.

Pretty sure there's a dog, said Landreaux.

But they went.

From a handsome shelterbelt of evergreens and old lilac, they watched the house—two story, painted white, a trim of scalloped wood all around the first story and four plain columns holding up a meager, dignified front porch. A light went on in back. The screen door creaked open and flapped shut. An old white-muzzled black dog tottered stiffly into the yard, followed by a tall old woman. She wore a whitish dress, saggy gray man's sweater, and sheepskin slippers. The boys noticed the slippers because she walked by them on the edge of the mowed grass. The dog dropped behind and stopped before them, nose working, eyes cataracted and opaque.

Pepperboy, get over here, said the woman.

The dog stood before them a moment longer. Seeming to find them harmless, he took painful mechanical steps toward his master. The two continued around the yard. They made ten rounds, moving more slowly each time, so that the woman and her dog seemed to the dizzied Landreaux to be capturing the last of the light slanting out of the trees, taking it with them while breasting continuous waves of darkness. At last the night became absolute and the woman and dog were nearly invisible. Each time they passed, the dog stopped to measure the boys, and then caught up with the woman again. On the last round, the boys heard them shuffle near. This time when the dog stopped, the woman's black silhouette loomed.

You hungry? she asked. I made some dinner.

They didn't dare answer.

She walked away. After a few moments, the boys rustled out of the grass and followed her to the door. They stood outside as she went through.

Might as well come in, she called, her voice different, unsure, as if she thought perhaps she hadn't really seen them.

The boys stepped into the kitchen, and stumbled back at the sight of the old woman in the light. She was striking—lanky and overly tall, deeply sun-beaten, her face a folded fan of vertical lines. A thick shock of white hair tipped like a crest over her forehead. The sides of her hair were neatly pinned back and her ears stuck out, drooping pancake ears burnt crisp over a lifetime. She was more than old, she was powerfully old. The milky blue of her eyes faded spookily into the whites, giving her the authority of one risen from the grave. Not only did the woman look so strange, but there was a phone in the kitchen. How long before she called the sheriff? The boys were jittery enough to bolt.

Why, you're wearing new clothes! the woman suddenly said, and smiled toothily, gently, as if she knew them.

The boys looked down at their dirty old clothes.

She turned away to the open refrigerator, and began removing foil-covered pans and dishes. She handed them back to the boys, who stepped forward.

Stick 'em in the oven, she said.

Landreaux opened the oven of a clean porcelain stove and the boys placed dish after dish inside. The oven was cold. Romeo examined the dials and turned it on. The numbers went up to 500. He chose 425.

There, said the woman, rubbing her hands. Now what else?

She opened a cupboard, took out a box of saltine crackers and a tin of sardines. She put them on the table. There was already a sweating icy pitcher of cold tea.

Get some glasses.

She waved her hand at the dish drainer and sat down. The dog rose from a woven rug in the corner and came to lie at her feet. While the boys gulped the tea, she unstuck the key from the sardine can, shakily inserted it into the slot, and rolled back the top halfway.

Forks? She jerked her head toward the drawers left of the sink. Landreaux brought the forks. Romeo guessed the right cupboard and brought to the table three large yellow plates with full-skirted ladies and top-hatted gentlemen dancing around the edges. The woman forked a piece of sardine from the can, mashed it onto her cracker. She nodded at the boys to do the same. The food stuck in their craws at first, then their hands seemed to grab unwilled, loading cracker after cracker. They stuffed all the sardines down but the last, which they left for the old woman. She had been watching them, smiling, her teeth dim and broken.

Go ahead, I got enough, she said. The boys split the last bit.

Mister's dead, she told them. It was the heart. Mine is going strong but I don't care if it does quit. How's your mom and dad? she asked Landreaux. They dig their cellar?

Landreaux looked at Romeo, raised his eyebrows.

They dug it? said Romeo.

The woman nodded.

Good, that's how you keep your food for winter. We told 'em. That cold was hard on the Indians. Mister said, they're dying off. One goes every day. So I'm glad to see you boys, glad you made it over here. Your family is the good kind of Indian. Mister always said when they're good they're the best friend you ever had. A bad one will steal you bare and they're wicked when they're drunk. You boys have always been good. Good boys.

The phone rang, jolting them all. The woman licked her lips and stood to answer it, a black wall phone, numbers worn on the dial. She held the receiver grimly to her big ear.

Just fine, she said. She was glaring at the box of the phone as if whoever had called was inside of it.

Haven't eaten it yet, she said, her face uncertain as though it was a trick question. Yes, the stove's off, she said meekly. I'll go take it out. Yes, yes. I'm hungry.

A crafty look came over her face and she turned to wink at the boys. Hungrier than I ever been!

Okay, night.

She hung up the phone and said hmmph. The warming smells of all the different foods had filled the kitchen, but she didn't notice. She sat down at the table again, frowned into space.

Should we take out the food? asked Romeo.

The woman's mouth worked silently, then she startled.

Take them dishes out, will you, boys? Let's eat!

Mashed potatoes, gravy, creamed corn, creamed spinach, chicken potpie with peas and carrots, corn relish mistakenly baked to a pretty good taste. A thick pork chop, which the boys divided, corn bread, soft buttered carrots, macaroni with cheese, macaroni with meat, macaroni with tuna. A thick piece of steak meat with mushrooms. More gravy. It all went down. Some of it tasted questionable, but hot and good at the same time. And on the counter underneath a dish towel was an apple pie, plump and oozing thick sweet juice, uncut.

The old woman relaxed, leaning back to marvel as she watched them eat and eat and eat.

You boys always could eat, always could, she murmured.

When they were done, sitting back, stupefied, she said, We don't have much to warsh except our plates and forks. Ceel says to leave them soak. Says he'll have to do them over anyways. Then I suppose you boys have to be getting back to your people. You could take summa this along, what's left. Your brothers and sisters might go for it. I don't need it. Can't stop cooking for a crew of people. So, you pushing off?

We . . . we can't go home, said Romeo. Could we stay here? With you?

The woman looked from one boy to the other.

You never done that before, she said.

It's kinda dark, Landreaux ventured.

The old woman laughed. Your dad says Indians can see in the dark, but maybe you ain't learned yet. Sure. Do me a favor. Go sleep in that big room upstairs with the green bedcover. Mess it up good and don't make it in the morning. I like having my radio music at night, down here. I like listening on the couch until I nod off. It's a good couch, but Ceel always checks if I slept there. On account of my back. Like hell. Go on! Go on! She shooed them upstairs, laughing.

That'll fix Ceel's leg, she said, turning the dial on the radio until she found some slow waltzlike music. She turned off the light and settled back in the pillows.

The boys, exhausted and well fed, slept long into the morning and woke to voices downstairs. The young man's was loud, petulant, and he wore clomping shoes. They could hear footsteps rattling around, the young man's voice fading but always audible. The woman's voice was small and placating, like she'd been on the phone. They couldn't tell what she was saying.

They heard him in and out of the kitchen, saying the same thing over and over. You couldnta eaten that much! And I came over here to clean your fridge out and you couldnta eaten that much!

The young man must have rummaged in the garbage.

You didn't toss that food. Unless maybe you threw it in the woods.

The old woman said something.

Okay, okay! You wouldn't do that. Did you sleep down here on the couch again, Mommy? Well, did you? Did you? I told you not to, didn't I? You want throw your back out, make me haul you to the chiropractor when I got so much to do? Huh? Don't pretend you can't hear me. Don't turn your head away that way.

She must have admitted she'd slept on the couch, because the young man, her son, scolded her harder. The boys were stunned, listening. Though they'd heard grown-ups fighting, this way the son sarcastically talked down to his mother disturbed the very order of love.

Okay then, the son said meanly, okay thank you for being honest with me. Okay then I don't need to go and straighten upstairs.

By which they knew the old woman had remembered they were there.

She spoke some more, and must have finally convinced her son.

Maybe I did think there was a whole lot more food than there was. Huh. Well, I'll just leave this sack off for you. Don't cook it all at once, huh? You eat on this for a week. There's still what you got left in the freezer. But hey, this pie. Mommy, now don't lie to me! Never, ever lie to me. You make these whole damn pies but you never eat that much pie.

They heard her when she loudly said, I picked those apples off my tree! Stewed 'em, froze 'em. I can make a pie, can't I?

And the son's suspicious questions. There's only two pieces left! What's going on? You have a visitor?

The old woman must have made some story up about the dog because the son next said, He throw up? Was it in the house?

Ceel stomped around some more, looking for the puke, but apparently the dog was too old to climb stairs because Ceel didn't come upstairs to look. He left quickly. Roared off in a big shiny white pickup. The boys peeked over a window ledge and watched the son drive a whole section of land before he was only a puff of dust.

They came downstairs. The woman was standing by the window watching the place her son had disappeared. She turned around, her face alight with emotions the boys exactly knew: the fury and shame of kowtowing to a righteous person who controlled your destiny. Threw their goodness in your face. It wasn't something they would ever name, but it would matter for all the rest of their days. The boys knew the old woman the way she seemed to think she knew them. They stood looking back and forth at one another in the living room. At last the woman seemed to collapse a bit. She passed her hand tremblingly across her chest.

I'm glad to see you boys, she said, sudden tears in her eyes. She laughed, relieved, and they saw how afraid she was that her son would realize how deeply lost she was in this world.

You hungry again? Her skeletal grin.

Later on, that morning, she spoke.

Oh, it was good land up there. We started in Devil's Lake. A sweet lay of land. Sloping pasture, flat acres. You just had to turn the sod. Water only fifteen feet down. We had a dug well. Pure. Mister bought the land straight off your mom and dad in '12 when their taxes come due. All the farmers were buying up Indian land cheap that year. You all moved to your grandpa's but got a poor farm there. You might remember your mom was pretty then, Indian braids, how she come for a bit of food just like you boys and I always had something for her. Old coats, dresses, blankets, worn-out stuff for quilts. Even gave her the needle and threads. I loved your folks. Anything they hunted down, they'd bring some over, too. They died so quick. Just faded out. One thing, another. They all got sick.

And you boys, where did you go? She sat up straight and peered at them with frail intensity. Where did you go?

The boys paused, drew breath. She was staring at them, anxious.

We went to boarding school, they said.

Oh yes, she said. Of course you did. Fort Totten. Did they feed you enough?

Fort Totten had closed years ago.

Though they could always eat more, there had been food enough at their school. One of the reasons Romeo had loved it there. No, food wasn't why Landreaux had run away. It was more to do with living smothered by alien rules, and with his grandparents who had loved him but maybe no longer existed, and with that thing he had seen in the old woman's face—fighting to keep herself. Landreaux was reminded of Bowl Head's know-better smile when he did something Indian. And

Landreaux felt the other part of it powerfully, too, the way the woman's son treated her, her desperation over which reality to choose.

You fed us good, said Landreaux.

The woman looked at them with her hard, folded face and her eyes from the spirit world.

You want something? Take it. She gestured all around. Take anything, before he takes it. He wants to sell it, the acreage, the house. What we lived for. And you were always such good boys. Quiet boys. Ducked your heads away. Like that, like you're doing now, she said to Romeo, to Landreaux. Take it. Take it all.

JARS OF water, money, bags of food. Romeo and Landreaux walked back to the railroad tracks and continued west. In forty years the tracks would carry mile-long black steel sausage cars full of fracked oil—the trains wouldn't stop until they blew up or reached a port. But when the boys ran away there were only occasional freight trains loading grain cars at town elevators. It only occurred to them once they walked the tracks and passed hundreds of acres of sprouting wheat and corn that there was no reason for a train to load up at a grain elevator early in the summer.

They stopped at a friendly cottonwood tree, sat and stuffed themselves with boiled eggs, sandwiches, cheese, pickles. The old farm lady had given them money from a secret sock stuffed with rolled bills. She had also tried to give them her husband's watch, a ring with white stones, a bracelet made of yellow stones, and a clock that she said was antique. Landreaux would have taken these things but Romeo politely refused.

Man, were you nuts back there? Romeo said to Landreaux as they ate. If the cops ever caught us with that farmer lady's stuff they would lock us in prison.

Landreaux shrugged. We should count the money.

The top bills on the rolls were tens and the inside bills were twenties and a couple of hundred-dollar bills, at which they marveled.

Oh no, no, no, said Romeo. I bet that Ceel knows about this. He will sic the cops.

Landreaux was dazzled. He kept counting. Over a thousand dollars.

The boys carefully divided the money. They pried up the insoles of their shoes and put the hundred-dollar bills and the twenties there. They each kept seventy dollars out, in their pockets, and walked on and on, treading down the cushiony money in their shoes, until they came to a town. It was a fairly large town and had a Ben Franklin dime store. They went in. The store lady followed them around; they were used to that. It didn't faze Landreaux, but Romeo insolently waved a ten-dollar bill at her. Landreaux bought black licorice pipes. Romeo bought red wheels. They paid and went down the sidewalk to the edge of town and back, Landreaux pretending to smoke. At the eastern end they passed a small café with a sign, BUS. Landreaux was afraid to buy a ticket. Plus they argued about where to go. Home? Not home.

We should go to Minneapolis and get a job, Landreaux said, because he'd heard people say this.

Romeo stared at Landreaux.

Nobody's going to hire us, he said. We're supposed to be in school. If they see us, the police might even arrest us.

How did Landreaux get this far, he wondered, without understanding how things work? But Landreaux kept talking about Minneapolis and jobs until he gave in and they bought the tickets, which were so expensive that Romeo knew for sure this was all stupid. When they boarded the bus, he said, What are we doing? We risked our life not to get on a bus.

But the bus rumbled off and they were trapped on it. At least the seats were cushy and could recline back. Their stomachs were full. They drowsed, then fell into a dead sleep. They woke for the lunch break, bought soup, and gulped it down fast. Watching Romeo suck his soup down, Landreaux thought, as he had many times, how much Romeo looked like a weasel with his wedge-shaped face, close-set eyes, and avid jaws.

There was flat North Dakota and then rolling Minnesota farms. They fell silent, mesmerized by the pretty land, the neat little towns of brick and stone. Then, down an empty highway, Landreaux saw her. He grabbed Romeo and pulled him over to the bus window. A woman walked along the breakdown lane, toward them. Landreaux had seen her as just a pinpoint far away, but there was something familiar. When she was close enough he realized it was Bowl Head. Her hair was white, short, and stuck out exactly the same. They ducked as the bus whizzed past her. Landreaux scrambled to the back of the bus to see if she had recognized them. He bumped two grown-ups necking underneath a blanket on the flat backseat. Bowl Head was in the distance but she was running, he thought, definitely running after them. He knew that she was a slow runner. He had seen her chase a boy named Artan. Although Bowl Head was slow, she was steady; she never stopped. Artan ran circles around her, but she still caught him because she outlasted him, never quit, never faltered in her pursuit.

He was shaking when he sat back down with Romeo. When Landreaux told him what he'd seen, Romeo put his hand on Landreaux's arm and said it wasn't Bowl Head.

Lots of white ladies look like her, don't you notice?

Landreaux calmed down, but he couldn't stop thinking the strange thought that Bowl Head was a spirit, a force, an element set loose by the boarding school to pursue them to the end of time.

The bus brought them to the city.

When they had boarded, the driver had asked who was meeting them in Minneapolis. They were struck silent. Mom and Dad? Relatives? He'd asked. They nodded in relief. They were about to step past the driver now, but he held them back.

Wait here. I'll escort you to your parents, he said. Okay, boys?

Again they nodded. When the driver went down the steps to open the luggage compartment they slipped off the bus and entered the station. They mingled with a group of people scanning the little crowd held to one side of the walkway by a rope. The boys ducked under the rope, darted through the glass doors, and then they were out in the street.

Noise pressed down from every side, pushing them along. Romeo tried to watch the metal signs and stay on First Avenue. They had seen stoplights only a few times in their lives. Now stoplights everywhere. They copied what other people did, drank at a public drinking fountain, looked in windows or at framed menus outside of restaurants. Walked as if they knew where they were going. At a tiny corner store they bought bottles of pop and boxes of buttered popcorn. All of a sudden they came to the end of their downtown city street. There was a building made of rose-red bricks and a sign, BERMAN BUCKSKIN. A gravel parking lot, chain link, scarred walls. Beyond that a tangle of weeds, scrub, spindly trees.

They went into the weeds. A path sloped down to a broad river. They made their way down the bank to the concrete abutment that anchored the bridge. There in the brush, they saw evidence of a camp—some driftwood logs placed around the smear of a dead fire, blackened rocks, blankets stuffed underneath some boards, two large sagging cardboard boxes and bags containing empty cans and bottles. Stained pieces of carpeting were laid out where the ground was level. They drank their orange sodas and ate the popcorn. They added the bottles to the others, tore the boxes into tiny bits and threw them in the river. They watched the curls of paper float east. It was getting dark.

Let's go up there, said Landreaux.

They tilted their heads back and looked into the iron trusses. Rusted ends of rebar in the eroded concrete pilings stuck out enough for hand- and footholds. Landreaux pulled a raggy blanket from the boards, draped it around his neck, and climbed. The blanket reeked of rot and urine. Romeo shook out a blanket, but the stench nearly choked him and he left it. The top of the concrete piling was big enough for the two of them, but dropped straight down to the river on one side. There was four feet of space between their heads and the iron girders that held the wooden trestle and rails. The train would pass over to one side of them. It would be loud, but then they'd already been inside the workings of a school bus.

They woke and squirmed together when the train passed over. After that, they couldn't get back to sleep right away and lay awake, listening. Everything died down—the traffic, the throb and bleat of the city. It was so quiet they could hear the river muscling its way past to a rushing place, a dam or waterfall. They slept hard again. Sometime close to dawn, the light just lifting, Romeo heard people talking below. He prodded at Landreaux carefully, as Landreaux was liable to thrash around when coming to. They craned over the edge of their nest and tried to hear what the people below were saying.

Slam, said a man.

Fuckin A.

Eight dollars, man. Nine dollars.

Good looks, good looks.

Well, it wasn't your breath, said a woman.

It's that Red Lake whammy.

Chippewa skunk oil, said the woman.

And you love it.

I don't love it, but I might roll around in it.

Oooo, down girl.

The voices started laughing and laughing, whooping until they gasped. Something the woman must have done. Over the course of the next week, they learned that this special predawn hour was the only time they could hear the voices of the people in the camp. The city was still sleeping, the air hollow. The water gave off a fog that carried sound up to their ears. At all other times the voices could be heard only as a rising and falling mutter punctuated by blunt pops of laughter and, once, a flurry of screaming and shouting, a fight that seemed to have come to nothing as the members of the camp, always five and sometimes six, ate or slept on their carpet beds or in boxes, hidden in the weeds. Most of the people were Indians.

Romeo and Landreaux developed habits opposite those of the scraggly people in the camp. An hour or so after full daylight, when the bums were unconscious, the boys climbed down. They skirted the fire circle and the sleepers. Sometimes they swiped a bit of food, plundered a bread bag; once they took an open can of baked beans. They stepped onto a thin path that led along the river until it neared another camp, maybe a rival camp, maybe the source of the fight. The boys veered up the bank before they got too close. Once up on the street they crossed the river along a low parapet on an old bridge that was ready to be torn down. On the other side of the bridge there was a neighborhood where milk was delivered. Every so often they could lift a bottle. When the stores opened, they bought bread and a pound of baloney. In a park, an alley, or on the sunny steps of a decrepit church, they divided up the loaf and the baloney, ate it all. They never tired of this breakfast.

There were three separate movie theaters to walk to. Every afternoon they saw a matinee, gathered all the half-eaten boxes of popcorn afterward, and stowed them by their seats to eat during the next show. Sometimes if the movie was extremely good they hid behind the exit curtains until the evening shows came on. They saw: *Bigfoot, The Aristocats, Beneath the Planet of the Apes, Airport, House of Dark Shadows, Hercules in New York, Rio Lobo, A Man Called Horse* (six times; it affected them deeply), *Little Big Man* (eight times; it affected them deeply), and *Soldier Blue.* (It affected them deeply but they were asked to leave. It was not for children because it featured a woman crying over an Indian's severed arm. They became obsessed by this unspeakable scene.)

Because they had to see this movie again, they sneaked into *Soldier Blue.* While they were watching for the arm, a woman entered late and sat down a few rows in front of them. Her pale hair puffed out around her head. They slumped down in their chairs, peeked between the backrests in the row ahead. Suddenly she swiveled around. Her teeth lighted up in the dark. Her Bowl Head hair glowed and rose, detached from her body. Her hand went up. They thought she was going to crawl over the seats toward them. But another person came to sit beside her and she turned back to the screen. She hadn't seen the boys. They crept out. Romeo's pants were slightly peed in, but Landreaux was much worse and thought he might puke.

See, said Landreaux.

I know, said Romeo. But get hold of yourself. It looked like Bowl Head but it couldn't have been her, man. Couldn't have!

Still, they were disoriented and wandered sickly back to the river. They blundered into the camp, into the middle of the regulars they had been hiding from and stealing from for nearly two weeks.

A man put Landreaux into a headlock, but he smelled so bad that Landreaux puked for real and was let go.

A woman with long wild hair tackled Romeo around the ankles and pulled him down.

A man in sunglasses spoke.

Sit, he said.

He struck the ground with a long white stick propped on his shoulder. He gestured at the stomped grass around the dead fire.

Someone kicked Landreaux and he collapsed.

Romeo shrugged the woman off and sat too.

Mystery solved, said the sunglasses. He laughed. Don't you little pricks know you can't steal from stealers? We're stealers and such. We steal people blind, get it? Blind!

The others laughed like people who had heard that joke before. The boys had never seen a blind person's white stick, so they didn't get the joke.

Now speak, the sunglasses ordered. Speak your business here.

We're visiting our relatives, said Romeo.

This struck the stinky man as extremely funny. When he laughed, the boys could see he had two sets of teeth in his mouth, one behind the other. His mouth was so full of teeth that it seemed hard to open. He closed it carefully. In spite of nervous fear, Landreaux kept his eye on this man's mouth, hoping he would open it again.

You're runaways, said the sunglasses man.

Yes, said Landreaux.

You been here a while. We noticed stuff missing. But we thought it was the white bums at the other camp. Run from boarding school?

Yeah.

Sunglasses nodded. Then took off his glasses, rubbed his morning-glory blue eyes and put them back on. The rest of him looked Indian, so his eyes were startling. Very beautiful and startling. He was a lean, ropey, blue-eyed Indian with a kung fu mustache.

Okay, cool, he said.

You can stay, said the stenchy toothbound man who'd grabbed Landreaux. He built a fire with grasses, then twigs, then little branches. Immediately his fire spurted flames and made a comforting crackle. He pushed a circle of rocks just so, and added chunks of wood, tending fussily to their position while the shaggy woman painstakingly opened a #10 can of Dinty Moore beef stew with a short screwdriver. She stabbed the screwdriver viciously into the top of the can, over and over, trying to connect the holes so she could pry up the lid. The fire had blazed down to coals by the time she got it partway open, and the boys had told their story to the sunglasses. Another woman wandered quietly into the camp, two bags in her arms. She was tiny and birdlike, pitiful, with a face full of boils. There was also a silent Indian powerful in grease-slicked cowboy clothes. He sat apart watching the others with tiny, searching red eyes. He had a stomped-on-looking face.

This man spoke suddenly in a rasp-file croak and took out a long gleaming bowie knife.

You little fuckers steal my blanket?

Romeo and Landreaux surprised themselves by crumpling onto the ground. They slumped like puppets. Landreaux sobbed in sucking breaths and Romeo made tiny helpless irritating noises.

Oh shit, the man said, cleaning his nails with the knife, I killed 'em.

The others laughed, but not in a mean way.

Shut up, you, said the shaggy woman. They're just kids. They sleep up there. She pointed up at the railroad bridge with her lips. It's not even safe, she grouched. They should have somebody looking out for them.

The stomped-on-looking powerful Indian put away his knife. Sorry I scared you little fuckers, he said. Tomorrow I'll get youse a nice box. You can sleep down here.

The shaggy woman threw the stick she'd been stirring the can of stew with into the weeds and took some small utensils from within her shirt. She dipped stew into old pie tins still crusted with piecrust and gave them to the boys.

You give me back my spoons once you finish, hear?

The boys nodded and ate, tears dripping into the stew.

They climbed up onto the piling that night and slept. Maybe the stew, the blue eyes, or the arm caused Landreaux to thrash and howl so hard he woke Romeo in the middle of the night. Landreaux was still asleep when he started rolling off the top of the piling. Romeo grabbed his arms and Landreaux suddenly woke up. There was a moon out, and they stared into each other's eyes the way they had beneath the bus.

I got you, said Romeo.

Landreaux made a desperate noise.

Never fear, said Romeo as he skidded toward the edge.

He felt calm, loving, and powerful. That moment would endure in his memory. It was the last time in his life that he did a heroic thing. Romeo tried to stab his feet into the concrete and willed his arms to stop quivering. But Landreaux was heavier than Romeo. Every time Landreaux swung his leg to find a desperate foothold, Romeo was drawn closer to the edge. At last, with a wild jerk, Landreaux gained his balance. In doing so, he flipped Romeo over his head into space. Landreaux tried to cling but fell backward. They could have hit the water and waded to shore, or maybe drowned, or hit the base of the piling and died, but instead they hit the weedy earth. Romeo broke Landreaux's fall, and Romeo started screaming. Landreaux went instantly to sleep. When he came to in the morning, with a headache, Landreaux crawled out of a piece of canvas to look for his friend. Romeo was wrapped in a bag by the cold fire and he looked dead. The shaggy woman came out of the grass and poured some whiskey into Romeo, plus she crushed up a pill and mashed it into a bit of stew. Stuffed it clumsily down his throat. Romeo fell quiet and looked dead again.

What's wrong with him? asked Landreaux, touching the trussed bag gently.

We foun him like this.

The woman was extremely drunk. She tried to pat Romeo's hair but kept missing his head.

We didn't know what to do so we tied im in the bag. He says his arm and leg. Landreaux pulled the bag cautiously down Romeo's leg. There was no blood, but the leg looked sickeningly wrong, even in his pants. And his arm was also crooked. His shoes were gone.

Let's bring him to the doctor, said Landreaux, unnerved.

But Romeo's head lurched up and he shrieked. No, no, no, no! Landreaux crab-scrabbled backward.

You were right. She's here!

Romeo ground his teeth, eyes mystically flashing.

She come after us. Now I seen her.

Who?

Bowl Head, man, hissed Romeo.

See? The shaggy woman had also stepped back, impressed. What ya gonna do? She joggled the whiskey bottle.

Sonny knows where to get some more. We jus keep him here, loaded for the pain, eh? Until he's better. We don want cops poke aroun here.

Landreaux crawled close to Romeo, touched his gray face. Romeo's skin was cold, wet, and hard as rock. Landreaux waited, watched until he took a breath, then another. Landreaux's eyes burned—he knew very well that Romeo had tried to save him. The sudden shame of having caused his friend's injuries was unbearable.

I'm gonna find a way to haul you to the hospital. Wait here, he said, and ran off, his friend's pain swelling his heart.

Landreaux bolted up the embankment. He stopped where they had fallen, and snatched Romeo's shoes from weeds. Then he sprinted across the bridge in a panic. He slowed down, took the money from the inner soles of Romeo's shoes, put the bills in his own shoes. He began to wander the neighborhoods they knew. He walked for hours, searching for a cop. He became so weary that he didn't see the police car pull ahead of his path, or the officer who emerged, until he was close enough to be grabbed by a man who knew how to grab. Landreaux could feel that. It was reassuring that he could not get away, and Landreaux relaxed. He began to talk. He told the officer all about Romeo and the bums' camp and how he needed help, how his friend looked dead.

The policeman put Landreaux carefully into the backseat of the car, which was hard plastic with a heavy mesh barrier. Someday there would be Plexiglas and Landreaux would know that too. There was a radio with a handheld microphone. The police used it, asked questions, relayed the information. Then they drove back across the river. An ambulance pulled up, and then another police car. Landreaux sat in the squad car while the others beat their way down the embankment. After some time passed the police came back.

They bugged out, said one officer.

Landreaux scrambled out of the car and sprinted into the brush, wormed through the loose links of a fence, dodged down an alley, across a street, and was caught trying to cross a parking lot. The officer tried to calm him.

You got to find him!

Landreaux yelled, blubbered, moaned, and finally fell silent. They drove him to the precinct headquarters and stuck him in a chair with a glass of water and a sandwich. He sat there for a day, then another half day. But even though he was tired of waiting, he scrambled up when the original Bowl Head walked into the station. His hair prickled up the back of his neck and his stomach tried to puke up the sandwich. He knew he had been right. Bowl Head was more than she appeared to be, even supernatural.

Much later on, when Landreaux first got high behind the water tower, he saw again that he was right, that she was the spirit of the boarding schools. She meant well and her intentions were to help him be a good boy, but a white boy.

When Landreaux begged the police for pity, she said that all the runaways acted like this. She signed some papers. A policeman walked him to the car, and he saw that Pits was riding in the passenger's seat. The policeman put Landreaux in the backseat of the car and told him that he'd be all right now. Landreaux sat petrified, couldn't even eat the lunch that Bowl Head bought him at a restaurant, though she urged him to and said he looked thin.

When they were almost halfway home, Pits said something and Bowl Head pulled the car over. Pits opened the back door and yanked Landreaux out, shoved him down the ditch and up the other side to a riffle of trees.

Go, he said.

Landreaux did not dare move. He heard Pits pull down his zipper. A moment later hot piss spattered the back of Landreaux's pants.

That's for losing Romeo; he was a good kid, said Pits.

Landreaux bolted away, down the ditch, back to the car. After they'd been driving for a while, Pits said something in a low voice to Bowl Head. She shook her springy white hair no, that he should not say what he said anyway.

Pew! Landreaux's a pee boy now!

The emergency-room doctor at Hennepin County Medical Center thought that Romeo's arm could be pinned together, but the leg had to come off. He stabilized Romeo and sent him to surgery. The surgeon there, Dr. Meyer Buell, had studied infectious diseases and was more conservative when it came to legs. He found out that Romeo was an American Indian. He knew that Romeo was descended of the one Indian in ten who had preternatural immunities, self-healing abilities, and had survived a thousand plagues.

I believe in this boy, he declared. Even though he is the scrawniest, stinkingest, maybe the ugliest kid I've ever seen, and in the worst shape, he is from a long line of survivors. He has the soul of a rat.

This was not an insult. Meyer knew rats, medical and feral. As a boy, he had been shipped from Poland to relatives here, right after the war. He respected rats. He admired their cunning will.

This will be a long operation, he said to his nurses as they helped him prepare. I will save this sad leg.

Every other morning for two months, Romeo waited for the all-seeing, stirringly kind brown eyes of Dr. Buell. He would enter the room, pause, and say with a slight accent, How goes the sad leg today? With his immaculate hands, his knowing hands, Dr. Buell un-bandaged and peered at, even smelled the parts of Ro-meo's arm and leg he could examine outside the cast.

One side of you will be weak as a baby when the cast comes off.

Everything hurts, it hurts so bad, said Romeo. Where are my shoes?

Don't worry about your shoes, said Dr. Buell, for the hundredth time, in the kindest way possible.

He did not give Romeo pills anywhere near as pow-erful as he had known. It would be years before Romeo again tasted of the substances fed to him by the shaggy woman, but when he did, he felt reunited with the only mercy in this world.

Wolfred & LaRose

The Old One

I t was ancient and had risen from the boiling earth.
It had slept, falling dormant in the dust, rising in
mist. Tuberculosis had flown in a dizzy rush to unite
with warm life. It was in each new world, and every
old world. First it loved animals, then it loved people
too. Sometimes it landed in a jailhouse of human tissue,
walled off from the nourishing fronds of the body.
Sometimes it bolted, ran free, tunneled through bones,
or elaborated lungs into fancy lace. Sometimes it could
go anywhere. Sometimes it came to nothing. Sometimes
it made a home in a family, or commenced its restless
touring in a school where children slept side by side.

One night after prayer at the mission school, where
the first LaRose, the Flower, slept with other girls in
rows, in a room coldly bitter except for their plumes

of breath, tuberculosis flew suddenly from between a thin girl's parted lips. In the icy wind that creaked through a bent window sash it drifted over Alice Anakwad. Hovered over her sister Mary. It dipped and spun toward the sloping bump of LaRose under a woolen blanket, but the current of air dropped it suddenly. The old being perished on the iron railing of her bed. Then a sister being tumbled explosively forward in a droplet of Alice's cough, vaulted over the railing of LaRose's bed, swooned downward in the intake of her breath.

†

WOLFRED WAS waiting to greet her when she stepped off the wagon that brought her down to St. Anthony. She had left the missionary house for the mission school six years ago, wearing a shift and blanket.

Now behold!

A tight brown woolen traveling jacket, kid leather gloves, a swishing skirt, and underneath it stockings, pantaloons trimmed in lace she herself had knitted, bone corset, vest. She had been paid for years of hard labor with old clothes. She wore a shaped felt hat, also brown, decorated with a lilac bow and the iridescent wing of an indigo bunting. Her shoes had a fashionable curve to the heel that had nearly lamed the mistress of the house.

Exactly as she hoped, Wolfred did not recognize her. He gave her an appreciative glance, then looked down, disappointed. His gaze gradually returned to her. After a while, his look cleared to a stunned question and he stepped forward.

It is I, she said.

They smiled at each other, unnerved. His face reflected her glory with a satisfying humility. She stripped off a glove and extended her hand; he held it like a live bird. He hoisted her trunk on his shoulder. They walked the dusty margin of the road. Wolfred showed her the cart, his Red River cart, two-wheeled and hitched to a mottled ox. The cart was made entirely of wood, ingeniously pegged together. Wolfred put her trunk in back and helped her up onto the plank seat beside him. He snapped his whip over the bullock's right ear and the beast drew the cart onto the road, which became a rutted trail. The wheels screeched like hell's millions.

The trail led back to the trading center of the Great Plains, Pembina, then farther, out to where Wolfred had decided to try his hand at farming. As she rode in the disorienting noise, which made speaking useless, a melting pleasure stole up in her. First she unpinned her hat, puffed out the lilac bow and balanced it carefully upon her thighs. Her skin had yellowed from lack of sunshine. Now light struck her shoulders and burned along her throat. She closed her eyes. Behind her lids a blood-warmth beat, a shadowy red gold. She balanced herself with a hand on Wolfred's arm. The mission teachers believed that educating women in the art of strictly keeping house and disciplining children was essential to eliminating savagery. A wedge should be placed between an Indian mother and daughter. New ways would eliminate all primitive teaching. But they hadn't understood the power of sunlight on a woman's throat.

The warmth revived in LaRose the golden time before her mother was destroyed. She looked critically at Wolfred. He seemed to have become an Indian, true. The teachers would have cut his hair off and relieved him of all he wore—a shirt of flowered red calico, fringed buckskin pants, a broad-brimmed hat, moccasins beaded with flowers and finished off with colored threads. Wolfred's skin was tanned to a deep nutshell color and he'd lighted a pipe. The smoke was fragrant, the tobacco mixed with sage and red willow bark. He winked when he felt her sidelong gaze. She tried to laugh but her stays were too tight. Why not laugh? She reached beneath her shirtwaist and loosened her corset, right there. She kicked her shoes off, plucked the pins from her hair. The corset and shoes had been the worst—never to take a deep breath, and each step a stabbing pain. Who was looking? Who to care now if she wore moccasins, burned her corset, gambled with the fifty buttons that closed the back of her dress? She would eat fresh meat and no more turnips. Wolfred's teeth flashed. How long he'd waited— in a manner of speaking. Anyway, he hadn't married any of those women. Was he now too rough for her? Excited, he wondered. He slowed the ox. He stopped the cart. The wind boomed yet there was silence on the earth.

Wolfred turned to her, held her face gently.

Giimiikawaadiz, he said.

Suddenly, clearly, she saw them naked on a river rock in sunshine, eating berries until the juice stained their tongues, their lips, until it ran down her chin and pooled along her collarbone. She saw their life. She saw it happen. She yanked Wolfred close. He carried her through tall grass and they lay down where it hid their nakedness. They rolled in berries, smashing them like blood, like childbirth. Everything would happen to them. They'd be one. They'd be everyone.

I want a wedding dress like this, she said to Wolfred, and showed him a picture that was used to raise money for the school. Her friend was in it. All the clothes were borrowed, but her hair was real. LaRose had combed her friend's hair out and arranged it to cascade down her shoulders. Later, she had pulled it up into a bridal knot.

I think she died of tuberculosis, she said. Like everybody else I knew. I never heard from her after she went back home.

A cough boiled up in her own chest, but she breathed calmly and tapped her sternum until the tightness released. She was getting well. She could feel her strength casting the weakness out.

Wolfred built the cabin that would eventually be boarded into the center of the house containing the lives of his descendants. The cabin was made of hewn oak, mudded between with tan clay. There was a woodstove, a cast-iron skillet, oiled paper windows, and a good plank floor. Wolfred made a rope bed and LaRose stuffed a mattress with oak leaves and pillows with cattail down. The stove in winter glowed red-hot. They made love beneath a buffalo robe.

After, LaRose washed in icy water by the light of the moon. She stretched out her arms in the silver light. Her body was ready to absorb wanton, ripe, ever avid life. She crept back into bed. As she drowsed in the pleasant heat of Wolfred's body, she felt herself lifting away. When she opened her eyes to look down, she'd already drifted up through the roof. She fanned herself through the air, checking the area all around their little cabin for spirit lights. Far away, the stars hissed. One dropped a speck of fire. It wavered, wobbled, then shot straight into LaRose. She bobbed back down and lay next to Wolfred.

And so they brought a being into the world.

She cut up her fancy clothes for baby quilts. She took apart her corset and examined the strange, flexible bones. Wolfred fashioned them into head guards for the cradleboard. The shoes were bartered to a settler's wife for seed. The stockings and hat were given to a medicine man who dreamed the child a name.

The next three children arrived during thunderstorms. LaRose howled when the thunder cracked. Energy boiled up in her and the births were easier. Each child was born strong and exceptionally well-formed. They were named Patrice, Cuthbert, Cleophile, and

LaRose. It was clear they would all possess the energy and sleek purpose of their mother, the steady capability and curiosity of their father, variations of the two combined.

She scoured the floorboards of her house, sewed muslin curtains. Her children learned how to read and write in English and spoke English and Ojibwe. She corrected their grammar in both languages. In English there was a word for every object. In Ojibwe there was a word for every action. English had more shades of personal emotion, but Ojibwe had more shades of family relationships. She made a map of the world on a whitewashed board, from memory. Everybody factored, copying their father's numbers. They all sewed and beaded, especially once the snow came down and isolated them. The children chopped wood and kept the stove stoked. Wolfred taught them the mystery of dough making, the wonder of capturing invisible wild yeasts to raise the bread, the pleasant joy of baking loaves in wood ash and over fire. The oiled paper windows were replaced by glass. The land would become reservation land, but Wolfred had homesteaded it and the agents and priest left them alone.

When her youngest child was a year old, LaRose's urgent cough exploded past her strength and pain shot through her bones. Wolfred made her drink the butter off the top of the milk. He made her rest. He wrapped her up carefully and set hot stones in the bed. She improved and grew strong. She was herself for years. Then one spring day she collapsed again, spilling a bucket of cold water, and lay wet in the cold grass, wracked, furious, foaming bright arterial blood. Yet again, though, she recovered, grew strong. She fooled the ancient being and wrested from it ten more years.

Finally, in its ecstasy to live, the being seized her. It sank hot iron knives into her bones. Snipped her lungs into paper valentines. Wolfred spooned into her mouth the warmed fat of any game he brought down. He still made her rest, wrapped her carefully every night, and set hot lake rocks around her feet. Every night she said good-bye, tried to die before morning, was disappointed to awaken. He arranged a plaster of boiled mashed nettles between strips of canvas, and lowered it onto her chest. She improved, gained strength, but was herself for only a month. On a cool late summer day with insects loud in the hay field, tangled song in the birch trees, she folded herself again into the grass. Staring up into a swirl of brilliant sky, she saw an ominous bird. Wolfred wrapped LaRose in quilts and laid her on a bed of cut reeds in the wagon bed. The children had piled the bed thick and high. They had covered the boards with two heavy horse blankets, then with their quilts. LaRose saw this bed they had made for her and stroked their faces.

Take back your blankets, she said, in a horror that she would spread what ate her.

Air them out, she cried. Air out the house. For a time, sleep in the barn.

They touched her, tried to calm her.

I am warm, she smiled, though she wasn't.

Wolfred heard there was a doctor in newly built St. Paul who had a treatment for the disease. He took LaRose overland in the wagon. There, after a two-week journey that nearly killed her, she met Dr. Haniford Ames.

In an immaculate examining room, the mild, pale doctor took her pulse with calm fingers, listened to her breathe, and explained what he'd learned from a southerner, Dr. John Croghan. In a great cavern in Kentucky, he had originated cave therapy for consumption, or phthisis. The purity and mineral health of the air in caves was curative. Dr. Haniford Ames had hollowed out and built four stone huts in the Wabasha caves of St. Paul, and there he kept his patients, feeding them well and making certain that their surroundings were clean and beneficial. When he met LaRose, the doctor was at first opposed to bringing her into the treatment regimen. Because she was an Indian, he was certain she could not be cured, but Wolfred was adamant. They waited eight days. A patient died and Wolfred handed over all the money they possessed. She was admitted. Her whitewashed stone room was tiny, with space just for a pallet and washstand. The front opened onto an expansive rock ledge where she would lie all day watching the untamed, torrential Mississippi River. LaRose smiled when Wolfred set her on the soft, fresh mattress. From the bed she could see across the river to the horizon, to the east, where bold pink clouds urgently massed.

Her brain seethed with fever; she was excited, alert. She asked for paper, quills, and ink. For two nights Wolfred slept at the foot of her bed, rolled in a blanket. All patients slept on this long stone outcrop of a porch because Ames believed that night air, also, strengthened the lungs. LaRose wrote and wrote. When he went home, Wolfred took the papers, which were stories, admonitions, letters to her children.

They had messages from her whenever there was a post rider. She was eating. She was resting. Dr. Haniford Ames was using the latest science to govern her treatment. He was judicious with the laudanum, was considering surgery. The doctor had lost a sister and a brother to the white plague. Though he'd been ill right along with them, he was now recovered. If he could have dissected himself to find out what had caused him to live, he would have. When he found the eastern doctors too conservative in their thinking, he packed his entire laboratory and headed west. There, he would have the freedom to pursue a cure. He would find out what had saved him while his loved ones wrackingly died. As far as he could tell, there was nothing unusual about him. He was not robust. His only exercise was walking, in all weathers, to set his thoughts at peace. His diet was slothful—he ate whatever he could, gorged on sweets. He even smoked. No, there was nothing outwardly special. Everything about him was uncolorful, unprepossessing. There must be something inside of himself that he could not quantify. His brother had been a mountain climber, ropey and long limbed. His sister had been a great beauty, who swam in the Atlantic waters off Cape Cod and rode intractable horses. She had had a mystical belief in herself and it had surprised her very much to die. It had surprised Haniford as well, and because of it he had been resigned to his own death. To be alive still startled him.

When he met LaRose, he met another conundrum that would shape his life. Disease was rampant among her people, and nearly every disease was lethal. He believed in science, not this idea of manifest destiny, which kept appearing in the newspapers. He was upset when pious land-grabbers declared that the Will of God was somehow involved in so effectively destroying Indians who squatted in the path of progress.

Funny how often the Will of God puts a dollar in a pocket, said Dr. Ames.

Some found him offensive. He did not care. He had ability, he had life, he would put both to use.

Because no Indians were ever cured of the disease, he doubted that LaRose would survive. Because as he came to know her, LaRose reminded him of his sister, he decided that he would cure her anyway, and threw himself into her case.

From her bed on the stone promontory, LaRose watched the weather change. Dr. Ames had eaten fish in cream sauce when he was ill. LaRose ate fish in cream sauce. He had walked, so she walked, though up and down the cave's short stone corridor was all she could manage. When Wolfred left, she was already improved. Dr. Ames wrote to say that she was responding well to the experimental collapse of one lung—he had some hope. Her letters told Wolfred that she was stronger, that she was allowed to walk twice a day now, that she was still eating fish in cream sauce. Then a letter arrived in which she told Wolfred she had seen Mackinnon.

Wolfred fixed food for the children in a manic rush and saddled his horse.

Mackinnon's head appeared at dawn, across the great river, a speck, tumping gently in place all day, preparing. Every sunrise, day after day, she woke to see that the head was waiting, greedy, steam boiling around it in a cloud. One afternoon, the head lurched into the water. Sometimes it disappeared for days. But always, it surfaced again. The tattered ears, like oars, pulled Mackinnon laboriously against treacherous currents that surged in eddies and rapids. When the river upended or sucked the head down a pool, she took heart. But it always spun back. Her eyes sharpened and she saw clearly over the distances. The head bobbed in circles, the nose snuffling and twitching until it stopped, sensing her. If she fell asleep, the head moved closer. So she tried to stay awake. Inevitably, sleep took her. Every time she woke, the head was closer still. Soon she could see that over the years it had deteriorated; one eye was white and blinded, fire had scarred and puckered the skin, blacked the pocked nose. Hair bristled in the paddle ears and vacuum nostrils. As night came on the hairs burned like straw. Gentian light flashed in the waves. She caught its scent—not of decay but strong brine. Mackinnon had pickled his head long ago in salts and alcohol, and could not be killed.

The nurse came and bound LaRose in sheets, covered her with heavy blankets warmed with bricks, strapped her safely in to sleep. Weak as water, strong as dirt. It was taking so long to die that she had become strengthened by the effort. She was ready. The head climbed, grunting its way up the rock cliff. She couldn't flee the bed, but she used her mother's teaching. She thrashed out of her body, unsticking her spirit. Mackinnon's head worried at the stones with its teeth, lashing back and forth. Gurgling with eagerness, it gnashed itself over the brim of the ledge, and was upon her. Too late. She broke out of her body and spun up through the rushing air, just as Mackinnon sank his pig tusks into her heart.

Wolfred arrived later that day. All the way there, he had felt her arms, and the weight of her behind him in the saddle. He had talked to her, told her to stay in her body. But the scent of bergamot and her warm breath between his shoulders persisted—these things made him despair. There was a tiny waiting room. He was brought there to learn the news, which was told to him by a plump, florid nurse. Indeed, his wife was sadly departed. The nurse did not have time for details. She patted his hand, and left him to bear the news in private.

Wolfred had prepared his mind for this by picturing the actions he would take. He would wrap her body tightly, carry her to his big horse. He would ride home with the reins in one hand, her on the saddle before him. Her head would rest on his chest and her hair would absorb the tears that melted down his throat. He couldn't get Mackinnon's head out of his thoughts. But she would at last be safe now, beyond reach. Her children would never have to endure what she had suffered. He would care for them with his life. In his thoughts, he told this to her, his words warm in the air, searching out her spirit.

He saw himself turning down the road home. He would slow to a hopeless walk. He dreaded telling their children, although they might know for she would have visited them, he thought, in their dreams. He would dismount, he decided, turn his wife across the saddle, lay her to rest upon the earth.

Then he would bring the children to address her. When he'd left, it had rained the night before and the ground was still wet in places. He closed his eyes, saw himself mixing a little mud up with his fingers. He would touch her face, smear the mud across her cheeks, down her nose, across her forehead, the blunt tip of her chin. If he'd owned a bronze shield, he'd have thrust that into the earth at the head of her grave. After she was buried, he would wander the woods, drinking from the hives of wild bees the bitter honey that had driven Xenophon's soldiers insane.

LaRose, he said out loud in the stuffy waiting room.

Where was that nurse?

He didn't want his beloved to be hurt in the next life, by men, the way she had been in this life. Later, he would burn all her things to send them with her.

Walk to the edge and wait for me, he said into the air. Wear your hat with the feather.

Where was that nurse?

Wolfred came clomping down the road, numb. His children ran to him. They had been keeping watch. Seeing their ever rational father disoriented confused them. They immediately became needy, loud, insistent. Wolfred rolled off the horse and put his hand across his face. They did not ask if their mother lived, they asked where she was. It took until he was inside the cabin, seated in a chair by the stove, until the fire was built up, the horse brushed down. It took a long time for him to say any word. His silence fueled their anxiety to such a pitch that they went still. Into that stillness, at last, his words struck.

Your mother has died. She is buried. Buried far away.

He held them, petted them, allowed them to weep against his vest, his arms, until they were exhausted and crept in misery into their bed. Only the youngest, LaRose, her mother's namesake, stayed curled near him. At one point, staring into the coals, her father shook himself. LaRose heard his whisper-rasp.

Stolen. Your mother was stolen.

⁂

UNTIL THE second LaRose was grown, she sometimes imagined that her mother, although stolen, perhaps by God, might actually be living somewhere. She knew it wasn't true, of course, but the thought nagged at her. When at last she questioned her father about it, he became upset and got the whiskey bottle down off the top shelf. Wolfred only drank a spot from time to time. He never became a drunk, so his drinking of the whiskey only meant he was preparing to speak of something difficult.

You're the only one who ever asked, he said.

You told me she was stolen, said LaRose.

Did I?

Wolfred had never remarried, though women threw themselves his way. For many years, he had talked of their mother incessantly, which had kept her alive to the children. He hadn't spoken of her now for perhaps a year. This daughter, this LaRose, had been recruited by a man named Richard H. Pratt, who had passed through the Mandan Hidatsa Arikara reservation and traveled through North Dakota as well as through South Dakota. He'd started a boarding school in Carlisle, Pennsylvania. She wanted to go because she knew that her mother had gone to a boarding school. It was a way of being like her mother, who had vividly and with desperate insistence taught her daughter everything she knew.

WHAT SHE LEARNED

Before the first LaRose died, she had taught her daughter how to find guardian spirits in each place they walked, how to heal people with songs, with plants,

what lichens to eat in an extremity of hunger, how to
set snares, jig fish, tie nets, net fish, create fire out of
sticks and curls of birchbark. How to sew, how to boil
food with hot stones, how to weave reed mats and make
birchbark pots. She taught her how to poison fish with
plants, how to make arrows, a bow, shoot a rifle, how
to use the wind when hunting, make a digging stick,
dig certain roots, carve a flute, play it, bead a bandolier
bag. She taught her how to tell from the calls of birds
what animal had entered the woods, how to tell from the
calls of birds which direction and what type of weather
was approaching, how to tell from the calls of birds if
you were going to die or if an enemy was on your trail.
She learned how to keep a newborn from crying, how
to amuse an older child, what to feed a child of each
age, how to catch an eagle to take a feather, knock a
partridge from a tree. How to carve a pipe bowl, burn
the center of a sumac branch for the stem, how to make
tobacco, make pemmican, how to harvest wild rice,
dance, winnow, parch, and store it, and make tobacco
for your pipe. How to carve tree taps, tap maples, collect sap, how to make syrup, sugar, how to soak a hide,
scrape down a hide, how to grease it and cure it with
the animal's brains, how to make it soft and silky, how
to smoke it, what to use it for. She taught her to make
mittens, leggings, makazinan, a dress, a drum, a coat,

a carry sack from the stomach of an elk, a caribou, a woods buffalo. She taught her how to leave behind her body when half awake or in sleep and fly around to investigate what was happening on the earth. She taught her how to dream, how to return from a dream, change the dream, or stay in the dream in order to save her life.

❧

CARLISLE INDIAN Industrial School in Carlisle, Pennsylvania, was overseen by a tall hatchet-beaked former captain of the Tenth Cavalry. Having succeeded in educating prisoners at Marion, Illinois, and having worked with young Sioux men and women at Hampton Institute, having in effect foiled those whose ideas were identical to Frank Baum's, Richard Pratt promoted his students to sympathetic reformers, writing that the hope and salvation of the race was *immersing the Indians in our civilization and when we get them under, holding them there until they are thoroughly soaked.*

The second LaRose was saturated. She was smart. After the agony of getting used to her corsets she pulled them tight and wore gloves—because her mother had on special occasions worn gloves. She learned to clean white people's houses during Carlisle's outing program, gouging congealed dust from corners with a knife. Polishing the gray veins of marble floors. She made the woodwork glow. Sparkled up the copper boilers. Also, she wrote in lovely script and factored into the thousands. She knew the rivers of the world and the wars the Greeks fought, the Romans fought, the Americans fought, beating the British and then the savages. A list of races she had to memorize placed white the highest, then yellow, black, and finally savage. According to the curriculum, her people were on the bottom.

So what. She wore hats and buttoned up her shoes. She knew the Declaration of Independence by heart and Captain Pratt himself had spoken to her of the Civil War and why it was fought. She gave recitations including a poem about the angel in the kitchen. She learned mathematics and memorized the shape of the countries on the globe. She learned American history and the levels of civilization ancient to modern, which culminated in men like Captain Richard Pratt. She learned how to survive on bread and water, then coffee, gravy, and bread. Mostly she learned how to do menial labor—how to use a mangle, starch, an iron. She worked ten-hour days in 120 degree heat. She learned how to sew with a machine. How to imagine her own mouth sewed shut. For speaking Anishinaabe. She learned how to endure being beaten with a board. How to eat with a fork, a spoon, how to lard bread correctly with a knife, how to grow vegetables, how to steal them, how to make soap, scrub floors, scrub walls, scrub pots, scrub the body, scrub the head, scrape a floor clean, a commode, a pantry shelf by shelf, what rats were and how to kill them, how to supplement her diet by stealing from the surrounding farms or gathering nuts and acorns, hiding them in her bosom. During those early years, Carlisle sold its farm produce and fed the students oatmeal, oatmeal, oatmeal.

She learned how to stand correctly, shake hands firmly, pull on gloves and take them off finger by finger. How to walk like a white woman on hard shoes. How to use and wash out stinking menstrual rags when Ojibwe women never stunk of old blood as they used and discarded moss and cattail down, bathed twice a day. She learned to stink, learned to itch, learned to boil her underwear for lice and wash only once a week, once every two weeks, three. She learned to sleep on cold floors, endure the smell of white people, and set a proper table. She learned how to watch her friends die quickly from measles or chokingly from pneumonia or shrieking from the agony of encephalitic meningitis. She learned how to sing funeral hymns, and she sang them for a Sioux boy named Amos LaFromboise, for

a Cheyenne boy named Abe Lincoln, for Herbert Lit-
tlehawk, Ernest White Thunder, Kate Smiley, and for
a suicide whose name she carefully brushed from her
mind. She learned how to go hungry and how to stay
full even if she had to eat bark—the innermost layers
of birch. She learned, like her mother, how to hide that
she had tuberculosis.

Pratt also said: *A great general has said that the only
good Indian is a dead one, and that high sanction of
his destruction has been an enormous factor in pro-
moting Indian massacres. In a sense, I agree with this
sentiment, but only in this: that all the Indian there is
in the race should be dead. Kill the Indian in him, and
save the man.*

They hadn't started the killing early enough with this
LaRose, though. She knew "The Battle Hymn of the
Republic," and yet her mother had taught her how to
use fierce and subtle Ojibwe poisons. She knew how
to catch and skin any animal she saw. Her mother
had snared the head of a demon white man and burnt
its eyes out. Her mother had called for her mother's
drum and cured a man who wandered in black vertigo. Her mother had made a new drum for her
daughter. Nobody took it because she left it with her

father. Now this LaRose had seen the ocean. Now her work out east was done. Her mother had taught her to put her spirit away for safekeeping when that was necessary. Out of the treetops, she brought back and absorbed her many selves. She was complete. She could go. Beneath the bobbing plume on the cast-off hat she was given for a month's wages cleaning pots, she moved demurely along the railway platform, in her purse a ticket home.

She wanted to change everything about everything when she got home. She was able to amend a few things in small ways. She lived with her father, Wolfred. She married a cousin. She was a teacher and the mother of a teacher. Her namesake daughter became the mother of Mrs. Peace. All of them learned two languages, four levels of math, the uses of plants, and to fly above the earth.

* * *

HER FATHER sipped his whiskey. He still hadn't spoken, but now a pile of papers rested under the hand that didn't hold the whiskey cup.

Will you tell me, at least, where she is buried? asked LaRose.

I can't tell you that, said Wolfred.

Why? She came close, touched his shoulder.

Because I don't know.

In spite of her conflicting thoughts, LaRose had always tried to be realistic, to imagine a grave, a stone with her mother's name on it, a place she could eventually go to visit. What her father said made no sense.

That can't be, she said.

It is true, he said. Then he repeated the words she had forgotten and remembered many times since she was young.

She was stolen.

He patted the pile of papers, looked straight at her.

Daughter, it is all right here.

1,000 Kills
2002–2003

The Letters

Mrs. Peace at her sparkle-chrome kitchen table. The lacquered surface covered with beading trays, cigar boxes of beads, stacked papers. Snow and Josette carefully slipped very old letters into page protectors. Most of the paper that Wolfred Roberts had written on through the 1860s, then 1870s, was still thick and supple. Some was more brittle, lined, torn from ledgers.

That old-time paper was made so well, said Mrs. Peace. Stuff nowadays crumbles in a few years.

It's the acid, said Snow. There's acid in most paper now.

Wolfred Roberts had written fair copies of the letters he had sent in order to recover his stolen wife, fiercely building an archive in his quest. The dates were on the letters, and there was a record of the dates they were mailed, and dates upon which he received replies, if there were replies.

The original backup plan, said Josette.

He used his training as a fur trade clerk, said Mrs. Peace. Keeping track of every transaction. My aunt told me that he kept these letters in a metal box, locked. She was young when he died, but she remembered that little key. It was kept in an old sugar jar, the handles broken off. He worried that kids would mess around with these papers. This here was all he had of her, proof he looked for her.

Mrs. Peace locked the plastic pages into a ring binder. The first letters were addressed to Dr. Haniford Ames. Each of the letters from Wolfred, later from a lawyer also, requested the remains of LaRose Roberts. Her chipped incisor, fractured and knit skull, injuries from the vicious kick of a dissolute fur trader, as well as her tubercular bones, would make her distinctive. His letters searched after her, then the letters went on. Wolfred's daughter, the second LaRose, kept them going. There were also letters from her time in Carlisle. And then the letter writing passed on to her daughter and then to Mrs. Peace. For well over a century these letters had searched after the bones of Mirage, the Flower, LaRose.

LaRose had some use, first of all, in Dr. Haniford Ames's research. Letters from Dr. Ames politely refusing Wolfred's requests attested to the value of her body in the name of science. Her bones demonstrated the unique susceptibility of Indians to this disease, and also how long she'd fought it. Over and over, her body had walled off and contained the disease. She had been, said the doctor, a remarkable specimen of humanity. For a time, also, LaRose had become an ambassador to the curious. Ames, according to the lawyer, had no right to take LaRose on the road as an illustration for his scientific lectures on the progress of tuberculosis. Ames had willed all of the human remains in his possession to the Ames County Historical Society in Maryland, where he spent his old age. The bones went on display.

After the letters from Wolfred, the bones were kept in a drawer next to the bones of other Indians—some taken from burial scaffolds, some dug out of burial mounds, some turned up when fields were plowed, highways constructed, the foundations of houses or banks or hospitals or hotels and swimming pools dug and built. For many years the historical society refused to return the bones because, wrote the president, the bones of Wolfred's wife were an important part of the history of Ames County.

LaRose's bones went on display once again and were abruptly removed after an unsolved break-in. Later still, the human remains of the first LaRose, who had known the secrets of plants, who could find food in any place, who had battled a rolling head and memorized Bible verses, that LaRose who had been marked out for her intelligence and decorated with ribbons every year, and marked out also as incorrigible by two of her teachers at the mission, that LaRose who had flung off her corsets and laughed when she walked again in moccasins, not heeled shoes, that LaRose attended to by pale-blue spirits and thunder beings during the births of her children, the LaRose who loved the thin scar next to Wolfred's smile, that LaRose, what remained of her on earth, was, to the president of the historical society's great regret, somehow lost.

AUGUST LIGHT poured long through the trees. The ticks were dead. The grasses flowed in the ditches and LaRose could not stop his thoughts. He was compelled to sleep on the spot of ground where the boy he replaced had died. This inner directive was so strong that LaRose lied for the first time in his life in order to accomplish it. He told Emmaline that he was supposed to go to Peter and Nola's over the weekend. He invented a friend from school because they didn't know kids from Pluto, he talked about a birthday party, and he made it sound plausible. He felt a flicker of wonder that his lie was so easily delivered and so instantly believed. Peter would pick him up while she was at work, he said. Emmaline was disappointed. She often brought LaRose to work with her on weekends and he helped in her office, in the classrooms. At noon they went to Whitey's and bought mozzarella sticks or a petrified-tasting fish sandwich from Josette.

No, said Emmaline at first. No, you can't go.

LaRose looked into her eyes and said, Please? That look got him things. He was learning to use it. Maggie had taught him.

Emmaline took a deep breath, let it out. She frowned but gave in. LaRose hugged his mother good-bye and kissed her cheek. How long would that last, Emmaline thought, pushing back the flop of hair he now affected. The dark wing hung to his eye.

See you next week, Mom. He gave her an extra hug, extra-sweet. There was something in that hug that made her step back. Holding him by his shoulders at arm's length, she scanned him.

You okay?

He nodded. Already caught.

I just feel kinda bad but kinda good, he said. Which meant nothing but was also true, so he could say it with conviction. She was still uncertain, but she was also late for the usual emergency meeting. After his mother left, LaRose went back into the bedroom, took a blanket from the storage closet. He rolled the blanket up and tucked it beneath his arm. He unzipped his backpack full of action figures, added a spray bottle of mosquito repellent. In the kitchen, he turned on the tap and filled a canning jar with water.

In all of these things, LaRose was precise and deliberate. He was becoming an effective human being. He had learned from his birth family how to snare rabbits, make stew, paint fingernails, glue wallpaper, conduct ceremonies, start outside fires in a driving rain, sew with a sewing machine, cut quilt squares, play Halo, gather, dry, and boil various medicine teas. He had learned from the old people how to move between worlds seen and unseen. Peter taught him how to use an ax, a chain saw, safely handle a .22, drive a riding lawn mower, drive a tractor, even a car. Nola taught him how to paint walls, keep animals, how to plant and grow things, how to fry meat, how to bake. Maggie taught him how to hide fear, fake pain, how to punch with a knuckle jutting. How to go for the eyes. How to hook your fingers in a person's nose from behind and threaten to *rip the nose off your face.* He hadn't done these things yet, and neither had Maggie, but she was always looking for a chance.

When he reached the place, he spread out his blanket beside the tobacco ties, cedar, disintegrating objects, leaves, and sticks. It was a hot, still day, the only breeze high in the branches. The mosquitoes weren't the rabid cloud of the first hot summer hatch, and once he sprayed himself they whined around him but didn't land. At first, they were the only sound. The stillness, the too-quiet, made him uneasy. But then the birds started up again, accepting him into their territory, and he sat down on his blanket. He realized he had forgotten to bring any kind of offering—you were supposed to do that. For sure you were supposed to do that if you went into the woods. You had to offer something to the spirits. He had himself, the pack of action figures, the mosquito spray, his blanket, one song, and the jar of water. The song was the four-direction song he'd learned from his father. He held the jar of water up the way he'd seen his mother do this, offering the jar to each direction. He sang his song as he poured the water out on the ground. He carefully capped the empty jar. Then he lay back and looked into the waving treetops and bits of sky. The trees covered almost all the sky but what he could see was blue, hot blue, though down here the air was warm but not blistering. If not for the mosquitoes that got in an ear or went up his nose and occasionally bit through the repellent, he would have been comfortable.

The chatter of birds, the light hum of insects. He lay there listening to his stomach complain, waiting for something to happen. Toward late afternoon his stomach gave up and the wind came sweeping along the ground. It was harder for the bugs to light on him. He fell asleep. When he woke it was extremely dark. He was thirsty, wished he'd brought a flashlight or some matches. But his parents might have seen a light, he told himself. He'd done the right thing. He was uneasy, thought of going back. But they would find he'd lied and never trust him again. He'd never get this chance. So he lay in his blanket listening to the leaves rustled by small animals, his heart plunging in his ears. Late summer crickets sawed. A few frogs sang out. There were owls. His parents talked about the manidoog, the spirits that lived in everything, especially the woods.

It is only me. He whispered to the noises and their nature changed. They became a whispery chorus, willing to accept him. He fell asleep, at last. He slept so fervently that he couldn't remember dreaming when the loud birds woke him in the morning. Now he was thirstier, and hungry, but also deliciously weak. He didn't want to move at all. His body needed food; it was stretching out. Everybody said he was getting his growth. It would be so easy to show up early at Nola's and say that he'd been dropped off. He'd done what he needed to do—that one night. But he decided to stay because he was strangely comfortable. His throat was so dry and scratchy that it hurt to swallow, but he didn't care. The heat of the day clenched down, pressed through him.

After a while LaRose heard, or felt, someone approach, but he was held too fast in the hot lethargy to move. He did not feel afraid. Most likely, it was his father. Landreaux liked to range around the woods too. But it wasn't—in fact it wasn't one person at all. It was a group of people. Half were Indians and half were maybe Indians, some so pale he could see light shining through them. They came and made themselves comfortable, sitting around him—people of all ages. At least twenty of them. None of them acknowledged or even looked at him, and when they started speaking he knew that they were unaware of him. He knew because they talked about him the way parents do when they don't know you can hear. He knew right off it was him they were talking of because someone said, *The one they took for Dusty*, and another asked, *Is he still playing with Seker and the other Actions?*, which of course he was, but which he tried to hide. All of a sudden one pointed.

He's right there!

They glanced at him and acted like relatives who suddenly notice you.

Oh my, he's big now.

The woman who said this was wearing a tight brown jacket, a billowy skirt, and a hat cocked to one side decorated with the wing of a bird. There was another woman with her, holding her hand, who looked very much like her. She pointed out LaRose and they spoke together. The older woman spoke Ojibwe. There was approval in her voice, but something about her was also quick, formidable, and wild. She bent close, looked at him very keenly, examined him up and down.

You'll fly like me, she said.

There were a few Indians who looked like from history, wearing the old kind of simple clothing. They spoke Ojibwe, which LaRose recognized but could not understand very well. They seemed to be discussing something about him because they nodded their heads at or glanced at him in speaking. They agreed on something and the woman who knew English spoke to him. She spoke kindly, and her eyes rested on him in a loving way. As he looked into her fine, bold features, he recognized his mother. Intense comfort poured into LaRose.

We'll teach you when the time comes, she said.

In one of the presences he could see traces of the four-year-old picture he had seen sometimes in Nola's hand. It was Dusty, his age now.

Are you okay? LaRose asked the boy.

Dusty shrugged. *Nah,* he said. *Not really.*

Can you come back? Remember we used to play?

Dusty nodded.

I brought some heroes and stuff.

Yeah?

LaRose opened his pack. He took out the action figures and Dusty examined them. They began to play, quietly because adults were right there.

If you come back, you can be Seker.

Dusty's face brightened and he ducked his head.

A short time later, everybody got up and left. Just walked off in all directions, murmuring, laughing. LaRose sat up and looked after the woman in the hat. He folded his blanket in half, then rolled it up again. He swung the backpack on, put the roll under his arm, and began walking. He felt fine. He took the trail to Maggie's house and got in through the back door before Nola even knew he was home. Went into the bathroom and put his mouth under the tap. Just let the astounding water pour in.

LaRose?

I came in through the back, he called down.

I didn't hear anybody drive up.

They dropped me off at the road.

He lay down in bed. The sudden comfort made him pass immediately into a hard, dreamless sleep.

AFTER HIS favorite childhood teacher and the other ladies had committed sabotage, Romeo could never again get wasted with the same conviction. Their betrayal skewed him. The fluid arrangements he had made all of his life, the scams and petty thefts, did not come naturally. To make things worse, or better, he was not sure, he got the job he'd applied for. The real, true job. He was chosen for this job over others. At first, surprise made him industrious. Then he got interested in the stories that took place all around him. He worked extra hours because it was like existing in a living TV drama. To get into the different wards, and find new information, he did more than lean on his push broom. He emptied trash incessantly, especially during staff meetings. He polished floors with a big electric floor polisher because people liked the floor polished. They trusted him more after he polished. He swept, wiped, cleaned up puke and blood with proper protocol. He began to like following rules! He loved wearing rubber gloves! People began to think he had sobered up, and he let them think that. He went more regularly to the AA meeting on the hill, with Father Travis. Everybody was a washout there. Now he was one of the success stories.

Then one day somebody said there would be drug testing at work. Even for sanitation engineers. Someday, not now. But it was coming. Romeo snarled, threw down his broom, and walked all the way into town. The job was also bearable because he was fortified. And yet, it had been a long time since his old injuries had been officially treated. Maybe he could work the system and get newer, stronger, legit prescriptions. His mood improved. His steps directed him to the Dead Custer, though even with his job he didn't like to spend his money on bar drinks. Maybe there would be somebody he knew there, with cash, maybe on a bender and anxious for a drinking buddy.

Once his eyes adjusted to the dim interior, Romeo scoped quickly for the priest. He wanted to talk to

Father Travis, not about the drug testing, but about the latest news. But the priest wasn't there. He was amazed to see his son at one end of the bar.

He sat down next to Hollis.

What's this? he asked.

It's my birthday, said Hollis. I was born in August, remember?

Of course, of course, cried Romeo in surprise.

Hollis had entered school late because, when he was little, they were always on some mission involving lots of car backseat beds, party houses, Happy Meals. Romeo had forgotten to send him to school, but only for the first couple of years. Hollis was now turning eighteen before his senior year. He slid his driver's license from his wallet to show the bartender, Puffy.

I am ordering my first beer!

Stand me too, my son.

Why don't you buy me one for a change, said Hollis. Being it's my birthday.

I would love to honor you but I am busted to bits. Romeo slumped.

Hollis ordered two beers.

What're sons for? Hollis wearily said. But don't try scamming on me, Dad.

No, no, I never would.

Right.

Except I got this arm here. Romeo winced, rolled his shoulder.

Your arm and leg. Hollis looked down at the leg. The last time he'd seen his father, that leg had been encased in black fake leather vinyl. Now it wore the sturdy brown cotton/poly of an honorable job.

You know how I got this? How it was Landreaux?

Yeah. You told me lots of times.

Since that day, always been a sad ol' leg. Romeo laughed, he couldn't help it. He was moved by the prospect of drinking a beer with his son. His son had not walked out the door. Romeo ducked his head, bobbed it up and down, smiling at the beer.

It is good to sit with you, my son.

I graduate this year, you know.

Wowzer, said Romeo.

I'm joining the National Guard. Got an appointment.

Speechless, Romeo gestured at Puffy to bring the beers, quick.

Ever since they hit the Towers, said Hollis, I've been thinking. My country has been good to me.

What? Romeo was scandalized. You're an Indian!

I know, sure, they wiped us out almost. But still, the freedoms, right? And we got schools and hospitals and the casino. When we fuck up now, we mostly fuck up on our own.

Are you crazy! That's called intergenerational trauma, my boy. It isn't our fault they keep us down; they savaged our culture, family structure, and most of all we need our *land* back.

Hollis took his first legal drink of beer.

Oh yeah, true. But I keep thinking how I could save people in a flood. Motor them out on a pontoon, their little children in life jackets. Their dogs jumping in the boat last moment. I keep seeing that. I mean, National Guard. I probably won't leave the state.

Hope not, said Romeo, weakly. This acceptance thing was part of being a father, he guessed, and it was more difficult than he'd imagined. He had a jealous thought.

What about Landreaux? He tell you to join up? Because of Desert Storm and all?

Not really, said Hollis. He was on the supply side of it. Medical. Never went out on the Road of Death, just got things ready for the guys, serviced lifesaving equipment and such. But there's more, anyway, to this decision I'm making. I'll learn welding, bridge construction, maybe truck driving. Heavy equipment. I want to get some money together, and those benefits. Go to UND later on. Maybe travel to the Grand Canyon or Florida, even. Out of state, anyway.

Romeo nodded and sweat.

I've not been the greatest, he mumbled. Who am I to say?

It's okay, Dad. I know you went to boarding school. People say that fucked you up so . . .

Romeo reared his head back.

Say? People say? They don't know. Leaving boarding school was the thing that fucked me. I loved my teachers and they all said I was college material.

Right, thought Hollis. He didn't hate his father—he knew some worse fathers. Mostly he grew exasperated and just had to get away from Romeo. He had no quarrel with his mother, either, only wanted to know who and where she might be. He fit in with the Irons, maybe too well, because he found himself thinking constantly of how great it would be if Josette liked him and maybe someday married him.

You got a sweetheart?

Romeo asked this in a shy doggy voice, afraid that his son would say something sarcastic. When Hollis didn't answer, he thought he'd offended him.

I know I ain' been a great dad to you, Romeo went on, but you can count on me now.

Hollis looked at his dad, so scrawny, so anxious to be loved, and dropped his gaze, embarrassed.

You can count on me too, Dad, he said.

Romeo frowned into the dregs of his beer and blinked back tears.

That's one for the books, he said. He put his hand out for the soul shake and Hollis could break his grip only by ordering them both another beer. Hollis asked Puffy to change the channel on the TV over the bar to CNN, because he knew his dad liked it. Someone complained about the news channel, but Puffy hushed him. Sure enough, Romeo sat up and peered intently at the screen.

After a few minutes he slumped back and leaned confidentially toward Hollis.

So that hijacker Atta was maybe meeting some Iraqi in Prague, maybe? A year ago April.

What's that about? Hollis asked without interest.

It seems to me like Rummy's scattering crumbs, said Romeo. Rummy's hoping reporters peck the crumbs up. But come on, Czech intelligence?

Romeo pressed his kung fu 'stache down his chin like a sage pondering.

Hollis shrugged.

They wanna clobber Saddam, said Romeo. Saddam's a greedy crazy dude, but not like Doe Eyes. That's definitive!

Doe Eyes was Romeo's nickname for Bin Laden.

Hollis let his mind drift while his father enlarged his speculations on the motives of this or that public figure or politician. He didn't hear the nervous fear for himself in his father's voice. Hollis drank his beer sip by sip, not wanting to leave because once he got home, he'd have to find the summer-read book, *Brave New World*. Couldn't even remember if he had a copy. Josette and Snow had stacks of paperbacks, probably including that one. He'd get the book off their shelf. He'd speed-read. Maybe Josette would help him write his paper. Hollis saw himself staring at the PC screen, Josette leaning over his shoulder. A critical frown. Her breath in his ear. Happy birthday. That sweet voice she used with LaRose.

Shut up, brain! Hollis tugged his own hair to jolt himself back. Here he was with his actual father, on his own actual birthday. It occurred to Hollis he might ask about his mother, again, although it was always the same—a song of memory lapse, a dance of drunken veils. These days he asked the question mostly to hear his father's inventive swoops and swerves.

Hey, it's my eighteenth birthday. So, Dad. My mother. What was she like? What was her name?

Her name? Mrs. Santa Claus Lady. She brought you, right? Seriously, my son, I don't remember. Those were insane times, my boy. But seriously, once again, she was holy shit beautiful. She would walk into an establishment. The heads would swivel off their necks.

The eyes would beg like a pack of starving mutts. The shit-ass fuckhounds. I was shocked when she allowed herself to be approached. By me.

Romeo shook his head, wagged his finger in the air. Ah, but you see . . . it was the drugs. Clouded her judgment. I hope she is alive today, my son, but the evidence of her addictions casts doubt on that. Don't do drugs or nothing because . . .

Wait, Dad. Hollis ordered again, then another beer for his father. Wait, but according to what you're telling me I would not exist if my mother's judgment had not been clouded by drugs.

Ergo, laughed Romeo; his clattery heheheh went on until he wagged his finger again. Ergo sum.

That's what for what?

Therefore I exist.

She took drugs, therefore I exist.

Ain't life odd? But still, please refrain from getting mixed up with substances.

Okay, Dad, said Hollis, not even sarcastic. So you're not going to tell me her name even on my birthday?

Hollis felt the cheer leak away and decided to sacrifice his beer, slide out the door before he got mad. Not getting mad was a life policy with Hollis.

He paid Puffy, pushed his beer over to Romeo.

Live it up.

Hollis walked out the door and Romeo watched him go, wounded. Here he was, a loving father in the reject chair again. The beer was nice, anyway, a consolation, and free. But as the door closed, Romeo suddenly pictured his blood-kin son making his way over to the Irons'. And giving Landreaux his filial loyalty. Landreaux, who was responsible for his whack arm and his leg that ached and sometimes trembled. To consider this caused Romeo to gulp down both beers. A mini-relapse! He could tell about it at the next meeting. He abandoned the barstool, tried to keep his balance, and set out for home in the throes of a mellow buzz. By the time he reached his room and removed a low-level painkiller from his stash, he was almost weeping with the contradictory joy of having celebrated his son's eighteenth birthday and the knowledge that Hollis preferred Landreaux's family and house to his own dad's apartment. With a year-round Christmas tree.

So much betrayal. So many lies. Although Romeo could not remember if he'd actually asked Hollis to live with him.

Resentment is suicide! This group slogan often helped interrupt a chain of tigerish thoughts.

Romeo rocked back in his minivan captain's chair, appreciating what he'd wrought. There it was, a glittering sight. The year-round fake tree cheered a father's lonesome heart. Still, he could not get positive. Snap out of it! Romeo glared at the walls hung with special things on nails. Such attractive sacred yarn and chicken-fluff dream catchers! He spoke to the faltering TV picture where old Mailbox Head was trying to jolly an interviewer. Such finesse! And the arrogant aplomb.

No one to trifle with, Slot Mouth. Nor am I. Nor am I, ol' buddy ol' pal Landreaux Iron. According to my exceedingly detailed memories of our so-called runaway escape, said Romeo to a sky blue dream catcher with iridescent threads, the reason which I am rubbing Icy Hot into my sad ol' leg, you Landreaux Iron have much to answer for, things you never have addressed!

The good stuff penetrated and his leg felt immediately warm. Pain melted away into the luxury seat. Yet things did not feel very good at all when Landreaux's avoidance of their mutual past was considered.

You ol' war bitch, cried Romeo, happily, waking later to Rummy's interview, sound off, the glow of his mango-scented sparkle tree. Having drifted off, he was now comfortable with the resentment he'd stifled before. Landreaux maybe should have not acted high and mighty to the point of stealing my son Hollis's affections. Leading my son to join the military, even! Landreaux was the one who dragged me into his plan, and he should have not pretended all his life that he didn't remember. Landreaux should have shared and shared alike the stuff that he could acquire. Landreaux should not have imagined people had short memories, or would forget. Because people had long memories and never stopped talking around this place. Romeo had heard them and Romeo knew. Landreaux should have not imagined it was over and done with—because a man had ears, tough little pinned-back ears that pricked up when people whispered. A man had a brain that decoded guarded talk between professionals. A man's heart, shriveled raisin, prune of loneliness, burnt clam, understood what it was to lose out on love. And lose to a lying liar. Romeo bet his livid black heart could burst Landreaux's baggy heart sack. If he could just get something solid on Landreaux to bring him down.

The Green Chair

The boredom of late summer covered Maggie like an itchy swoon. Thirteen, but living in her girl body. No breasts. No period. Too old to act like a child, too underformed to feel like a teenager, she wandered. She packed herself a sandwich, a can of pop, and took off. There were old paths through the woods, made long ago when people still walked places, visited one another, or hiked to town, church, school. There were new paths made by kids with trail bikes and ATVs. If there was no path, Maggie crept in and out of tangled bush, slipping into places of peace or unrest. When she went off the paths, anything could happen but nothing bad ever did. Nobody noticed. LaRose was sometimes with his other family, and Peter was at work.

When had her mother stopped looking after her? Stopped checking? Stopped spying?

Maggie sat in a tree and watched what she decided was a drug house, black muscular dogs chained to the porch. She watched for a week to see if any drug freaks went in or out. Finally a car drove up. A woman she recognized got out. It was her kindergarten teacher, the only teacher she'd loved. Kindergarten was the one year she had been good in school. The muscular dogs tossed themselves over on their backs for Mrs. Sweit to scratch their bellies. When she went inside, the dogs followed her like children. Maggie keenly wished she could tag along with them, but she had to turn away knowing that inside the house Mrs. Sweit was feeding the dogs milk and cookies. She was reading them stories. She and the dogs were cutting lanterns from construction paper. Maggie went home.

The next day she saw a bear digging up some kind of roots beside a slough. Another time a fox arched-leaped high in the grass, trotted off with a mouse. Deer stepped along with their senses bared, stopping to twitch ears and nose-feel scents, before moving from cover. She watched the dirt fly behind a badger digging a den. White-footed mice with adorable eyes, blue swallows slicing air, hawks in a mystical hang-glide, crows tumbling on currents of air strong as invisible balance beams. She began to feel more at home outside than inside.

One day she was sitting high in a tree, pulling apart a wood tick. Something large flowed at her, ghost-silent. She flattened against the bark. Hung on. She felt fingers rake her hair lightly and the thing rushed up, soundlessly sucked into the leaves. She didn't scare easy, but her breath squeezed off. She scrambled halfway down and huddled against the trunk. It was coming at her again, she could feel it. An owl with great golden eyes lighted on the branch before her, clacked its beak, fixed her with supernatural hunger. She looked straight back. At that moment her heart flung wide and she allowed the owl into her body. Then it sprang. She threw her arms up and it left razor cuts on the backs of her wrists. Her screams impressed it, though. It kept a distance while she climbed the rest of the way down. It swooped her once again, raising the hair on her scalp as she barged through the scrub.

She slowed to a walk as she neared the house. When she came out of the woods, she saw that her mother's car was in the driveway. She went through the house, but there was nobody home. Outside, in the backyard, she saw the dog sitting alertly outside the barn, staring at the door. The dog felt her gaze and turned. It ran to her, whined, then ran back to stare anxiously at the door again.

Maggie didn't call her mother's name or make noise—the owl inside her now. On a pathless path leading to a place of peace or unrest, Maggie went to the barn. Her soundlessness probably saved things. Sensing with bared senses, she pulled open the small side door and stepped inside. There was her mother in a shaft of light. Nola stood on the old green chair with a nylon rope around her neck.

Nola was wearing her purple knit dress with silver clasp belt, maroon pumps, subtly patterned stockings. Nola's breast was looped with necklaces, her fingers deep in rings, wrists in bracelets. She had worn all of her jewelry so that nobody would ever wear it again. Perhaps Nola had done this periodically for weeks or years. Maybe this time she had stood there all morning, collecting the sickly courage to kick away the chair.

She could still do it. Maggie would not have the strength to hoist her or the quickness to cut the rope. Nola still might do it right in front of her. There would be no point in running forward. Maggie didn't move, but fury choked her breath.

God, Mom. Her voice came out squeaky, which made her even madder. Are you really gonna use that cheap rope? I mean, that's the rope we tied around the Christmas tree.

Nola kicked her foot back and the chair joggled.

Stop!

Nola stared down at her daughter from the other side of things.

In Maggie's eyes, her mother saw the owl's authority. In Nola's eyes, her daughter saw the authority of the self and the self alone.

The foot lifted again. Beside Maggie, the dog quivered, at attention.

Okay, said Maggie. Please stop.

Nola hesitated.

I won't tell, said Maggie.

Nola's hesitation became a pause.

Mommy. Maggie's eyes blurred. The word, her voice, shamed her.

If you come down, I'll never tell.

Nola's foot came back down and stayed motionless. The air was radiant, hot, stifling like the secret between them. Complicity made Nola remove the rope, step down. Claustrophobia made Maggie throw up.

She puked for two days, sick every time she saw her mother and entered again the tight metal box of their secret. Nola held the glass bowl, wiped her daughter's face with a damp white dish towel. Tears overflowed her mother's eyes as she put the towel and bowl away. Mother, daughter. They fell into each other's arms like terrified creatures. They clung together like children in the panic cellar.

※

THE NATIONAL GUARD ARMORY was old and friendly, but they were building a new facility out of town. The equipment was used and even somewhat shabby, but they were soon to receive a shipment of the latest armaments, high-tech ordnance. The office space was cluttered and the files were bulging, but soon there would be new file cabinets, computers, desks, and copying equipment. Hollis sat at a scratched desk across from Mike, who was treating him like a long lost brother. Mike was square-headed, solid, with sparkly little blue eyes and thin pink lips. His blond hair was short, but not Marine high and tight. Hollis had resigned himself to losing his lanky rebel hair, and going straight to basic training, but Mike told him that there were plenty of options. He laid them out. The National Guard wanted Hollis to secure his education and would work with him at every stage. It felt so adult, so take-charge, to examine these shapes for his future, make decisions, lay out a plan, sign papers, and finally shake hands.

After signing, shaking, and introductions to others in the armory, Hollis was invited to the afternoon's youth symposium. Mike made him an honorary uncle for his three-year-old son and introduced Jacey, his wife, who looked uncannily like her husband. Everyone split up into their family groups and each group attempted to build a tower out of marshmallows and uncooked spaghetti noodles. It turned out that Hollis was very good at this. He planned an elaborate base using the noodles and marshmallows like fragile Tinkertoys. While their toddler ate Cheerios and hollered for marshmallows, Mike and Jacey carefully broke the spaghetti into the lengths that Hollis required. He laid five brittle rods together so they could reinforce one another, like a pasta beam. He'd worked at Wink's Construction that summer tying rebar. Their tower was the tallest of all and it did not even wobble. Sergeant Verge Anderson chose their marshmallow tower as most worthy, and showed it to the other family groups at the end. He pointed out the double construction, the reinforcement, the alignment, the precision. Mike introduced Hollis, gave him the credit, and everyone applauded. Sergeant Anderson said that Hollis had the right stuff to become a combat engineer, if he so chose, or go on to have any sort of career he wanted, and that his country needed him and his presence honored the North Dakota National Guard family—people working together to ensure the safety of their fellow Americans.

Hollis drove back home with a schedule for drills, a schedule for his payments, a schedule for acquiring his uniform and materials for study, a schedule for each step in becoming a member of the National Guard. As he drove, he thought of Landreaux, who had told him that the army was easy to get used to, seemed natural after boarding school. He thought of the times he'd hunted with Landreaux, before the accident, how careful Landreaux had been in teaching him. Landreaux had told him that in basic training his instructor had ordered the western boys to step out, the rural boys from Wyoming, Montana, the Dakotas. He'd set them aside to work with one-on-one, because they'd always be his best shots. Landreaux's grandfather had taught him to hunt so early in life that it all came back, he said. Landreaux hadn't shot anyone in Desert Storm— he had worked way back in the support sector, filled out their medical forms and done routine health checks, taken care of superficial wounds, and promoted overall general health. Hollis was pretty sure he'd never have to shoot anyone either. He'd do the opposite. He'd save people. In a crisis Hollis would know what to do and be the one to depend on. In a vague way, he understood that saving people could be just as dangerous if they ever got into a real situation.

When he stepped into the house he smelled fried rabbit with onions and bacon. He smelled burning sage and saw that Snow and Josette were smudging themselves, for some special mysterious reason. Emmaline put her thin arms around him. Coochy punched him, punched him harder when he didn't respond. Hollis felt his heart swelling with love so he put a fake choke hold on Coochy. LaRose yelled.

Take it outside! I'm making a hogan.

He was gluing pieces of construction paper into a frame shoe box. He was making a diorama of Native American dwellings for Emmaline's office.

Josette quit fanning smoke on herself, looked over his shoulder, tipped her head back and forth.

Make sure you put a cactus in there.

No, said Snow. A sheep. And a FEMA trailer.

Plus a volleyball, Josette said. Those Navajo girls are killer.

Dine girls, said Snow. I think they live in super nice new suburb houses, actually. Put in a cul-de-sac and sprinkler system.

Sprinkler system?

Josette looked disturbed.

Nah, you're right. They wouldn't waste their water.

Damn straight! Phoenix is stealing their water! I read about it! Put in big pipes sucking away Dine water! LaRose, you can use drinking straws!

LaRose looked up at Hollis and said, Brother, will you get them out of here?

LAROSE WAS at his Ravich family, in the lilac bush cave. Maggie squeezed into their green shadowed hideout and sat with him. They'd lined the space with dried grass, like a nest.

I have to tell you something, Maggie said.

LaRose had brought a frozen twin pops out to eat, the kind you could break into two Popsicles. He gave her one half, though she didn't like banana flavor.

How come these are the ones always left?

Because you don't like them.

Yeah, they're gross, said Maggie.

She licked the bogus flavoring and watched LaRose. His eyelashes were so long and full they cast shadows on his cheeks. But he wasn't a cute boy. He was soft and beaky.

I'd kill to have your eyelashes.

Josette and Snow already said they'd kill for my eyelashes too. Why don't you pull them out and paste them on your eyes? I don't care.

Yeah, okay, said Maggie. But see, Mom tried to kill herself.

LaRose bit straight into the banana ice and cold pain shot up between his eyes. Maggie put her hand on his shoe and spoke into his face.

Mom was standing on a chair in the barn; she had a rope around her neck. She was going to hang herself to death.

LaRose frowned at his running shoes. He took a smaller bite, then ate the rest, closing his eyes when the ache bloomed inside his forehead again. He put the stick in the neat pile he was saving to build a fort for his action figures. Maggie put her stick in his pile.

Can you help me? Tears shot into Maggie's eyes but she blinked them out. She drew her legs up and hugged her kneecaps. Her head flopped down and her hair snarled over her face.

I know what to do, he said, though he didn't know.

Maggie rested her hand on the ground, splayed toward his. After a while LaRose reached into his pocket and took out a smooth little gray rock. He put the rock on her palm.

What's that?

Just a little rock.

You're always picking up rocks. Like, what can this rock do? She threw it down.

We gotta watch her. We gotta stop her!

I know, said LaRose. He opened her hand and put the rock back. It's a watching rock. You give me the rock if I should watch her. I give you the rock if you should watch her.

She opened her hand. Now the stone was cool and took half the weight off her. Maggie was so tired of sobbing herself sick, and gorping until she could only puke yellow. It was the only way to keep her mother focused on her. Now LaRose seemed very sure. He seemed to know what to do.

But you're just a kid, said Maggie. How can I trust you?

I'm not just any kid, LaRose said. He waited, thinking, then he trusted Maggie and whispered in her ear.

I got some spirit helpers.

Yeah, right. He made her laugh until she hiccuped. She put her head up and shook her hair out of her face. She was so pretty, with her neat little features, her teeth lined up straight.

You promise you can help?

It's going to be okay, said LaRose. I know what to do.

He said this firmly, although he still didn't know exactly what to do besides watch Nola. Sam Eagleboy had told him to sit still and open his mind if he had a problem. LaRose would come back to the grass nest that evening, after Maggie was gone. He would concentrate on the problem. Even if he couldn't see them, he would ask those people he met in the woods. He would find out what the situation called for.

Two nights later, LaRose startled awake. He sneaked into the bathroom and switched on the light. He flushed the toilet. While the water was running, he eased open the medicine cabinet. There were all kinds of pills in there. Pills in amber plastic bottles. LaRose didn't know which ones she might use, but tomorrow he'd write them down and get Maggie to find out which ones were poison. Peter usually shaved with his electric shaver, but for special occasions he had a double-edge safety razor. Two packets of Shark double-edge blades were stacked behind an underarm deodorant. LaRose took the razors. He brought them back to his room and hid them underneath his comics. The next day LaRose put the packets of razors in his pocket and went outside. He found an old coffee can and went out to the woods to bury the razors inside of it.

While Nola was outside, he went into the kitchen and removed the chef's knife. The next night he went downstairs and cleaned out Peter's tackle box, removing those skinny-bladed supersharp filet knives.

Where's my chef's knife? asked Nola the next day.

Nobody knew. But LaRose knew. He was allowing Nola only dull paring knives. He dug a hole with Nola's small gardening spade and buried the knives, wrapped in a piece of canvas, alongside the coffee can. There was a list growing in his head.

When everyone was gone, LaRose carried an aluminum step-ladder into the house and opened it beside the gun case. He climbed the ladder, groped around the top of the case, found by touch where Peter had secured the key. He untaped the key from behind a decorative piece of molding, then climbed down, and opened the gun case doors. All the guns that Peter kept carefully loaded were fixed in notched stalls.

LaRose did exactly as Peter had taught him. He lifted out the .22 and held the barrel in his left hand, the stock in his right. He pulled the bolt back and down, curved his right hand to catch each bullet as it rolled out. There were three cartridges inside. Always three, Peter's rule. If you can't kill it with three bullets, you shouldn't be shooting a gun. LaRose put each cartridge softly on a pillow. He worked the bolt back and forth a few times, peered into the chamber to make sure it was empty, then put the Remington back exactly as it had been before. LaRose repeated this action with each of the other guns—working most carefully with the one Peter favored. LaRose locked the case, climbed up the ladder to retape the key. He put the ammunition in a glass canning jar, watertight in case he ever had to dig shot, slugs, and bullets up for use. He checked to make sure he'd replaced the guns in exactly the same order, and that he'd left no fingerprints on the glass. He went out to bury the jar in one of his many digging places. He was satisfied.

He threw away pesticides, rat poison, replaced the pills that Maggie said Nola could overdose on with look-alike vitamins. He removed all rope. There was so much rope around—here and there, in Peter's end-of-the-world stash. LaRose Hefty-bagged and dropped it into the back of the pickup when he knew Peter was getting ready to go to the dump. While he was at it, he tossed in a couple pairs of the sturdy bought-ahead shoes that Maggie hated.

A week after, he woke again thinking of the oven. Was it gas or electric? And how exactly did it work that putting your head inside could kill you? The danger there was maybe low, but then, bleach! Poison, right? Why hadn't he thought of it?

LaRose crept out of bed and sneaked into the laundry room. He poured the skull-and-crossbones bottle down the utility sink drain and put the empty jug out in the garage. He crept back into bed and slept hard.

Maggie was the one who had trouble sleeping. In vast schools of infinite classrooms, on ever branching roads, towns that stretched across worlds, she tried to find her mother. She would startle awake knowing that her mother was trapped behind a padlocked door, lost on a lost road, wandering in a lightless city. One night Maggie spent hours biting and scratching off her nail polish. Next morning her face was covered with light green flecks. When she came down for breakfast, her mother touched a flake of green off her face and looked at it.

What's this?

Instead of walking away without answering, enfuried that her mother had dared to touch her face and ask a question, Maggie just said, Nail polish.

The normal, nonsarcastic answer fell sweetly on Nola. She loved Maggie with all of the ripped-up pieces of her heart now. Nola turned to the cutting board and started sawing away at potatoes with a steak knife. Things were disappearing. She was losing things right and left, running out of things, failing to buy things, forgetting. But these matters were not as important as other people seemed to think. They were not crucial. In fact, they didn't matter at all.

❧

EVERY DAY after the gray dawn or the blue dawn, Hollis stomped sleepily out to the dusty mold-green Mazda with its sagging fender, mashed door. He'd bought this car for six hundred dollars. This car would carry Hollis, Snow, Josette, and Coochy to school in a week. On weekends it carried him off to his first National Guard drills. He and Mike had decided on a delayed-entry program—combat training delayed. School. Drills one weekend a month throughout the year. After graduation, basic combat and advanced individual training. Then he'd get going on his Guard job—maybe combat engineer. He still wasn't positive. And get the money together for a move, he supposed, although he didn't still want to. He was happy on the blow-up mattress. Even though his ass touched floor halfway through the night, he loved his sleeping corner. He wanted to keep living with the Irons after he graduated, maybe forever. Besides everything else, Hollis was forever hungry. Emmaline and the girls cooked big, tasty meat-rich stews, thick corn and potato soup, bannocks. Also, that long ago spark of holiday interest in Josette had caught. She had, for real, helped him with his summer read and even written most of his paper. He was the one who had leaned over her shoulder peering at her confident typing. Now a steady glow was his. More than a glow, really. Sometimes, flames.

First day of school. Hollis dressed and schlumped out to the kitchen, where he thought today, maybe, was the day. Maybe he would reveal his mad hopeless love for the mad hopeless glory of Josette.

Always, as soon as he came in the room, she began pouring cereal.

Hey.

Hey.

She was strong, had a wicked jumping overhand volleyball serve, her curves were powerful. She could put a thousand voice-layers into that one morning greeting and so could Hollis. The shadow in her Hey said, *I'm into you!* They rarely said more than Hey and Hey. But the way it was said would stay with each of them as the day wore on. Their Heys were a pilot light that could possibly flare up if Josette ever took her eyes off the cornflakes falling into her bowl.

If that occurred, Hollis imagined a stare-down in which the animal tension became unbearable. But maybe it wasn't supposed to happen that he was taken in by good people and he then poached the daughter of the house. Who was younger. So he took his bowl of cornflakes back to the boys' room, and waited for the girls to call when they were ready for school.

That same morning, Emmaline woke with a clenched heart and could hardly breathe. When? She asked the star quilt hanging on the wall, and then answered herself. Now. LaRose was supposed to go back to the Ravich house, but when Emmaline touched his heavy brown hair she knew for sure. There had to be an end and this was it. From behind the closed door of her bedroom, she called the Ravich number. Peter answered.

I can't stand it anymore, she said.

Peter felt the heavy sadiron of his heart lurch. He waited but it was stuck on the wrong side of his chest.

Ah, god, please, Emmaline.

I just can't do it anymore. It was never supposed to go on forever, was it? Her voice began to shudder. She gathered herself, stood straight, tucked her hair behind her ears.

Listen, said Peter, stepping aside to look out the window. School is starting. It will get better.

I'm enrolling him here. With other Indians.

Nola was already up. She was outside fixing up the old chicken coop, painting it. Her thin arm swept back and forth.

Please let's just keep going for a little while longer. Peter stopped. He was about to beg her for LaRose. That would make him angry. He would become hateful were he driven to that.

Nola's so much better, he said. She's finally getting over Dusty. She's, ah, integrating. Right now she's painting the chicken coop.

This detail pricked at Emmaline. Painting a chicken coop? Why was that some kind of leap?

Almost three years, she hasn't talked to me, said Emmaline. We're sisters. She acts like half sisters aren't real sisters. She's my sister and she won't talk to me. But that's not even it, not really. I'm enrolling him here, in the reservation school, where his family goes to school. LaRose is with us now.

Oh, Emmaline, said Peter, in an unguarded way that brought Emmaline back because she liked Peter fine; he was solid, and had never hurt anyone. She trusted Peter's goodness and was sure that in past times he'd kept the lid on Landreaux by just taking his own slow way and leading his friend along the innocent dirt road of a Peter kind of life.

I understand, said Peter, careful. He had to stay in control. He knew enough not to escalate this, not to become emotional. Why don't you keep him with you a few more days? I'll explain to Nola.

She won't understand, said Emmaline.

No.

Still. I am taking him back, said Emmaline. It's time.

She came out of the bedroom and spoke to the others, who were nearly ready: she told them that she was going to take LaRose to their school.

You're going to school with your sisters, she said brightly to LaRose. Surprise.

He looked from Snow to Josette, who widened their eyes in a silent message, *Mom says.* He went back to the boys' room to get dressed. They were talking out there in the kitchen now. Things were always like this. Although LaRose was used to going where he was supposed to go, and doing what he was supposed to do, sometimes they just threw these big surprises at him.

Coulda told me. Like more than a minute ago, he whispered.

He put on fresh jeans, a clean T-shirt. He smelled his yesterday's socks, threw them down, and took a pair of Coochy's from the sock pile.

Peter stood frozen, the phone droning in his hands, gaze fixed on the cipher of a woman out there painting a chicken coop with old white leftover gummy paint. Even though she wouldn't talk to Emmaline, his wife was better, he thought. Maybe. Maybe men just think women are better if they have sex with us, but even so. A few nights ago she put her hands on him, stroked him without saying one strange word. And they had loved in utter peace. He came back into his body. He could not inhabit himself without her. He had that roughed-up Slav shell and inside a milky tender heart. He had guarded it carefully before Nola. There was nobody else for him but this one woman—he might hate her sometimes, but he would go to hell for her and save her cakes.

Two days later, he tried to have the conversation.

I just don't like her, Peter, I don't, because she is a self-righteous bitch.

Why do you say that?

Peter had read magazine articles that advised questions when you wanted to divert a way of thinking in another person. Or you wanted to stall.

Why? he asked again, then ventured. She's your sister. You could try.

Okay, I'll tell you why I can't *try*. She's got that program director's attitude for one thing. Like, here's Emmaline. Posing at her desk. Wehwehweh. I can listen. Listen with my hands folded and my head cocked. You know? Emmaline puts on her listening mask and behind that mask she's judging you.

They were outside, at the edge of the yard. Nola ripped up a stalk of grass and put the end in her mouth. She narrowed her eyes and stared out over the horizon, that line at the end of the cornfields, between the sweeping coves of trees.

For emphasis she dipped her head to each side. Right. And left. Judging me.

She tossed the stalk of grass away.

Oh, I guess I could. Talk to her. If she would give back LaRose.

Peter glanced at the ground, disguising his hope.

It's been four days. I get it, said Nola. I really do.

I never said.

But I get it.

Peter nodded, encouraged.

I mean, it's wrong, but I get it. She's holding him hostage because she wants my attention. She wants me to be like, Oh, Emmaline, how are you, how is your project, your big deal, your this, your that, your girls that Maggie likes so much? How generous you are, Emmaline, what a big-time traditional person to give your son away to a white man and almost white sister who is just so pitiful, so stark raving. So like her mother that Marn who had the snakes. People never forget around here. And they will never forget this either. It will be Emmaline Iron the good strong whaddyacallit, Ogema-ikwe. The woman who forever stuck by that big load Landreaux and even straightened him out so he could, so he could . . . I'm just saying I would kill him for you. I see your face when you're chopping wood. I'd kill him for you if it wasn't for LaRose. So their damn unbelievable plan worked its wonder because now I'm better.

Peter questioned that now, but said nothing.

And nobody's going to kill the big freak. He's too fucking tall.

He's only six three, murmured Peter. I'm six two.

I hope our son doesn't get that tall. I hope LaRose doesn't turn into a killer hulk.

It's been a while now, said Peter.

Yeah, the years have gone by, haven't they, Nola said. Her top lip lifted in the mad little sneer that sometimes jolted a shiver of lust in Peter.

C'mere, he said.

Why? She ripped another piece of grass out and stuck it between her lips. Maggie was over at the Irons' house, as usual. They were alone.

Peter took the stick of grass from her mouth and lightly struck her cheek with it. She was still. He searched into her face. Kissed her until she kissed him back. She nodded at the house. He picked her up and carried her to the barn.

Not there, she said.

He carried her in anyway. They passed the old halters on hooks, the junked refrigerator, the green chair, the empty stalls. He threw bales down in the last one, a canvas tarp over the bales. There was that good smell of an old barn where animals had eaten, shat, breathed, an old clean barn full of hay and sun. He untied and removed her paint-streaked worn-out running shoes, peeled down her tight jeans, slipped each foot from the creased-up ankles. He knelt before the bale, lay her back, crooked her legs.

She looked over his shoulder. The crossbeam black oak. The rope gone. Gone. Nola flung her arms straight over her head. Her breasts tipped up.

He placed her feet on each side of his chest, placed his hands under her hips, pulled her onto him, rocked into her. And then they both went back and farther back, to the beginning, where there was nothing else, no bad things happened, where there was no child to grieve, no loss, no danger, where a few wasps hovered over but did not land on Peter's ass, and the sun shafts lighted up with falling ever falling dust.

And why couldn't she just see the peace and glory in it anyway? Why did she have to think of all the dead and one fine day herself among them, sifting through bright air? She wouldn't do it. The rope was gone! How? Don't ask. No, no, of course. Not now. LaRose told her how much he needed her. Maggie watched over her. She could feel it. She had a new life. Still, she had to think about it sometimes, a little, it wasn't wrong, was it? Just to fall endlessly and rise forever on soft currents of warm air stirred by bodies of the living. There was nothing wrong with giving over to the melty swoon of it, the null. There was nothing wrong with having more in common with the dust than with her husband, with Peter, was there?

I thought I'd call, said Nola on the phone. Just because it's a rainy day. Just wondering how LaRose is . . .

Then she heard LaRose laughing in the background. One of the girls had maybe answered. It wasn't Emmaline. Nola's voice wouldn't come out of her throat. She set the phone down and passed her hand over her eyes.

Are you okay?

Maggie came into the kitchen. Mom, you are staring at the phone. Was there a phone call?

Maggie still had the stone LaRose had pressed into her hand when he left. It was on her bedside table. She didn't want it there, or anywhere. She had total responsibility for Nola, and she was weary.

No call.

Nola hugged Maggie. She was hugging her too hard and she knew it.

Honey, she said, LaRose is being kept against his will.

Maggie just hugged her mother harder. *I mean, what to say?*

Akk, said Nola. You're getting strong.

Maggie laughed engagingly. Well, you too. You were squeezing me!

They won't let him come back to me. He's my only son. Am I too crazy, Maggie? Is there something wrong with me? Is that why? I love him so much. There's nothing else in my life.

Nothing else. Well. Maggie turned herself off. She spoke in a cool, careful voice.

Dad loves you. I love you. Mom. You have us.

Nola squinted and peered forward as if Maggie were standing at the end of a long tunnel. Maybe at the end there was LaRose or someone else, because for a moment she did not recognize her daughter. She put her hand on Maggie's face in a gentle way that creeped Maggie out, but Maggie did not move. She stayed in control.

You know what you need? Maggie kept her voice low and normal. It's kinda cool and rainy. You need some hot chocolate.

I need to speak to Emmaline.

First the hot chocolate, with whipped cream.

Nola nodded thoughtfully. We don't have cream.

Well then, marshmallows.

LaRose likes marshmallows, said Nola.

So do I, said Maggie.

Okay, said Nola.

Pouring the heated cocoa milk over the marshmallows, Maggie heard her mother press the buttons on the telephone, then hang up again. Nola came into the kitchen and sat down with Maggie.

It's really hot, don't . . .

But Nola had already gulped. Her eyes widened as the scalding cocoa passed across the roof of her mouth and continued down, a blistering streak. Maggie jumped up, poured cold milk in a glass. Nola took a drink of cold and sighed. Then she closed her eyes and put her hand over her mouth.

Maggie's teeth clenched her words back. She didn't say that she was sorry, but she was sorry. She was sorry that she couldn't do the right thing. Sorry that she couldn't do what her mother needed done. Sorry she couldn't fix her. Sorry, sometimes, that she had come across her mother in the barn. Sorry she had saved her. Sorry sorry sorry that she thought that. Sorry she was bad. Sorry she wasn't grateful every moment for her mother's life. Sorry that LaRose was her mother's favorite, although he was Maggie's too. Sorry for thinking how sorry she was and for wasting her time with all this feeling sorry. Before what happened with her mother, Maggie had never been sorry. How she wished she could be that way again.

Maggie went to find Snow and Josette. It was after school for them. Hers would start Monday. She, at least, could go back and forth and see them and see LaRose. The girls were outside. LaRose had gone to town with Emmaline, they said. She should help them with this thing they were doing. The grass, or weed base of the yard, was torn and gouged. It was hard and trampled. The girls had set up a ragged old volleyball net. Maggie helped them spray-paint orange boundaries on the dirt and mashed weeds. The court was done. While they talked, they bumped the ball back and forth. Maggie had only played in gym. Josette taught her how to bump, showed her how to set. Snow spiked. They practiced serves.

Don't even bother with an underhand, Josette said. Watch.

Josette set her pointy left foot forward, drew her right elbow back, like she was going to shoot an arrow. She smacked the taut, filthy, velvety ball around in her hand four times, then tossed the ball high overhead. As it fell, she skipped up and slammed it with the heel of her hand. It curved low and fast over the net, bounced down where you wouldn't expect it.

Ace!

That's her trademark, said Snow.

I wanna learn it.

Holy Jeez, said Josette, after Maggie tried to serve.

Maggie missed six times and when she connected the ball just dropped down feebly, didn't even reach the net.

You gotta do push-ups if you want any power.

Drop down, gimme ten, yelled Snow.

Maggie did four.

This girl needs building up, said Snow.

Yeah, you need some upper body. Josette felt Maggie's arm critically.

Coochy came outside.

Having your girl time? He mocked them, stepping back in a graceless pretend serve. When he turned to walk away, Snow served a killer to the back of his head.

It must have hurt but he just kept walking. He was bulking up his neck to play football.

Two points, said Snow.

Josette popped the ball up on her toe and tucked it beneath her arm.

Beaning Coochy is two points, she said to Maggie. Just hitting him is one.

I wanna bean, said Maggie. Show me that serve again.

At home, Maggie checked in on her mother's nap, waited at the bedroom door's crack until she saw slight movement. Then she went out to the garage. The big door was open, the air blowing around some papers on the floor. Her father had the hood of the pickup propped up. He was changing the oil and air filters, draining out the sludgy residue.

Hey, said Maggie. Can I change schools?

No, said her father. But grown-ups always said no before they asked why.

Why? he asked. Because of LaRose?

I have to go to the same school as my brother, right? Also, other reasons. Kids at my school hate me.

That's ridiculous, said Peter, though he knew it wasn't.

There's this girl Braelyn one year older, and her brother in LaRose's old class, and his brother Jason, who's older. That whole family hates me, plus their friends.

You never said anything before.

Maggie shrugged. I can handle it, that's why. But I'd rather change schools.

So you want to go to reservation high school? He laughed. Even tougher there.

Dad, they have more afterschool programs now. Pluto's a dead town. Our state's so cheap. You know they'll probably consolidate and we'll be on the bus an hour more.

What she said was probably true, but Peter didn't like to think that way, except he did think that way.

Reservation's getting federal plus casino money.

Peter wiped his hands on an old red rag and closed the hood. He looked down at Maggie, a whippet, finely muscled, her intense stare.

Where'd you hear that?

I heard it from you, Dad.

Did I say our state was cheap? I wouldn't say that. Plus, their casino's in debt.

You said the farmers around this part of the state don't have any money. You said there's more money on the reservation these days. You said . . .

Okay. That really isn't true. I was, you know honey, I was frustrated.

Grown-ups always say that when they lose their temper.

Now you're the expert on grown-ups.

Maggie knew it was time to shift strategy.

I can go there because of Mom. Descendancy status and everything. And, see, I wanna go to high school with Josette and Snow. Be on their team.

But you hate sports.

Not anymore. I like volleyball.

That's not a sport, really.

Sometimes grown-ups didn't get it. They remembered volleyball as a laid-back backyard barbecue pastime, or a gym requirement. They had no idea how fierce and cool the sport had become, how girls had taken it over. Maggie decided to change up on her dad again.

I can't see Emmaline really keeping LaRose all the time.

Really?

If he goes to their school that's a difference. A compromise. And if that's the deal, I shouldn't be left out. I should be going there. He should have all his family in one school.

There are tough kids at that school. Drinking. Drugs?

Drugs are everyplace. Plus, remember? I'm an outcast. I'm severely hated.

Now Peter laughed. Maggie couldn't even pretend to pity herself. There wasn't a whine in her. He was proud of her and she knew it.

Awww, Dad, come on. Snow and Josette have traditional values and all that. They're A students. They'll have my back. Plus their big brother Hollis. And there's Coochy, I mean Willard. We should all be together, Dad. It would really help LaRose.

Peter kept wiping his hands. The cracks in his palm and the wrinkles in his knuckles absorbed the oil so his hands looked like ancient etchings of hands. His tired blue eyes rested sweetly on Maggie. He knew his daughter. He remembered the years of teacher conferences. The teachers were wrong. She was not disturbed. High-spirited. That was it. She was too high-spirited for their dull expectations of girls. So. Could things get any worse? Maybe she was right. Keeping LaRose was some kind of last-ditch test for Emmaline. Maybe allowing the kids from both families to go to one school would help Emmaline come out of it. Things would balance. Whatever happened, Snow and Josette had become like sisters to Maggie. They were half cousins. Cousins and sisters. It struck him that this was the first time since Dusty that Maggie had really wanted something, asked him to help her. So he said yes. And yes, he'd try with Nola.

OLD RUMMY. He's giving out hints again. See?

Father Travis watched the gray-skinned gray block of talking head. They were sitting out a morning of weird September heat at the Dead Custer.

It's not supposed to be this hot, Romeo complained.

It is what it is, said Puffy.

Romeo hissed in exasperation. Everyone was saying *It is what it is* as though this was a wise saying. They would say it with a simple hand lift. To get off the hook, they would say it. They would say it when too lazy to finish a job. Or often when watching the news.

And it ain't what it ain't, said Romeo.

Father Travis didn't register this comment. He just sweated, stoic, with a jar of Puffy's special iced tea. Last night he'd entered the whirling energy, the black aperture, silence. Before the screams, he was suddenly with Emmaline, naked, their bodies moving and planing, slick with sweat. Father Travis rolled the cold jar across his forehead.

Romeo squinted at the TV, nodding.

There's that clue. Chemical weapons. They showed some diagrams. Fuzzy gray recon pictures shot off a satellite.

They're pulling together a case, he muttered.

Father Travis cocked his head and looked sideways at the shapes pictured on the screen. On 9/11 he had watched the Towers dissolve and thought, *They've learned.* After that, over and over, he'd sifted down in his dreams with the others, his body flayed by the acceleration of the building's mass. He watched the news, flipping channels. It was like the barracks bombing never happened. Nobody made the connection. What was the connection? It hurt to think. He felt himself disintegrating. One night that September, he had gone off the wagon. He drank the bottle of single malt scotch an old friend from the Marines had sent to him. He'd stayed in bed the next morning—sick for the first time in his history as a priest. It had felt like the thing to do.

Hey Father, said Romeo. Can I ask you something?

No.

How come you quit trying to convert me?

This was an opening for Father Travis to say something mildly insulting that they would pretend was a joke but know was true.

I didn't want to have to baptize you, said Father Travis.

How come?

I'd have to sponsor you. Promise to stand between you and the devil. But there is no space, nowhere to stand.

Haha! Romeo preened in delight. No place to stand! Between me and the devil!

This remark would make the rounds, Father Travis knew. Romeo would repeat it to everyone he saw in the hospital corridors. Knowing that, Father Travis usually gave more thought to what he said to Romeo. But right now he was having trouble. He couldn't sit still, anywhere. He had to get out of the Dead Custer. He had to get out of every place. He had to get out of his skin.

I have to go.

Was it something I said? Romeo was joking. It was always something that he said. He caught the priest's arm. Wait. What would you say to a kid joining the National Guards?

Which kid? Father Travis managed to sit down.

My kid, Hollis, the one Landreaux and Emmaline have, you know.

I'd say he'll learn a useful set of skills, get out of Dodge for a while . . .

. . . what do you mean, out of Dodge?

He'll go to Camp Grafton, or Bismarck, Jamestown training sites, depending on what he wants to do.

Not like a war then?

Father Travis was surprised. His attention sharpened.

I don't think the Guard has ever been called up for a war. Although LBJ was within a heartbeat of doing it for Vietnam, right? But he instituted a draft. Tested the will of the people.

Who said fuck you.

Yes, and I'm sure the Pentagon learned from that, said Father Travis, thoughtful.

If Bush threw the Guards in . . . . Father Travis paused. He'd voted for this president because his father had been a decent and a prudent president. Bush Sr. had understood that getting out of a war was, like marriage, far more difficult than getting in.

Romeo gulped down his healthful iced tea and Father Travis clapped him on the shoulder as he got up to leave.

❧

SMALL TOWNS and reservations nearly always had a tae kwon do school, even if no Korean was ever there or even passed through. Great Grandmaster Moo Yong Yun of Fargo had planted the discipline throughout the tristate area. Father Travis had studied in Texas with Grandmaster Kyn Boong Yim. He'd earned his third degree black belt before seminary. A few years after settling into his job, with his teachers' permission, he opened a dojo in the mission school gym. He had learned that he couldn't stay sharp himself unless he taught. He had arrangements with several affluent schools that shipped outgrown uniforms and donated color belts. His classes took the place of the usual Saturday catechism classes. Now he just gave handouts on church doctrine. It was much more satisfying to teach combinations and run through drills, to yell numbers in Korean while fiercely punching air.

During classes, Emmaline waited for LaRose in an orange chair with an hourglass coffee stain. She always brought work—kept a laptop open or worked through a stack of papers. Sometimes she put everything down, stared at the class, driftingly smiled, and then caught herself. After the class, Father Travis always found a few words to say about LaRose. He's making progress, for instance.

Emmaline tipped her head to the side, raised her eyebrow.

He's getting strong, said Father Travis.

He's okay, isn't he?

You did well.

LaRose took her hand. Emmaline's eyes were fixed on Father Travis.

I kept him this time.

Father Travis nodded and tried not to think of Nola just yet.

Emmaline asked, unexpectedly, How are you?

Priests don't get that question, or not in the way she asked it. He raised his eyebrows. He laughed, weirdly bubbly, maybe in a frightening way.

Don't ask, he said, abrupt.

Why not?

Because.

His heart jolted to life, ridiculously banging against his ribs. He put his hand on his chest to calm it down.

Something's bothering you, said Emmaline.

No, I'm fine.

Really? Because you look disturbed, said Emmaline. Excuse me.

No, really. Sorry. I am fine.

His ploy was feeble. He regretted it.

Emmaline turned away. She and LaRose walked off holding hands. Her thoughts slowed. Why had she asked that question? Why had she turned away when he deflected it and gave a bullshit answer? It was exactly what priests were supposed to do. Keep their personalities subservient to their service. Endure whatever God gave them to endure without complaint. Was a priest ever not fine? Who could tell?

Father Travis watched them go. He had studied his feelings regarding Emmaline. This wasn't about his vows. It was about her family, her and Landreaux, the fact that he had counseled them, married them, baptized their children. They trusted him to be all things except, actually, human. *Be all to all in order to save all.*

Thanks, St. Paul. Better to marry than to burn, and this burns. But she's the only one I'd ever want and she's already married. So take the heat! Just live with it, he told himself, you fool.

She had asked him how he was, said that he looked disturbed. How pathetic that such an ordinary question and simple observation should make his heart skitter.

Father Travis shut down the gym lights. It was his shift for the Adoration of the Holy Sacrament. He padlocked the door and walked over to the church, entering the side basement. He walked through the lightless dining hall toward the faint glow in the stairwell. Popeye Banks was nodding off in the pew, and startled when Father Travis jostled his shoulder. He stumbled out, yawning, put his hat on at the door, and called good-bye. Father Travis sat down on one of the comfortable memory-foam pillows he'd bought for the people who kept the Adoration going 24/7. Then the dim hush, the arched vault, the flickering bank of candles, and his thoughts. But first his hands, shaky. His chest was stopped up. His breath weak. He put his hand to his chest and closed his eyes.

Open, he said.

He always had trouble opening his heart. Tonight it was stuck again. It was a wooden chest secured by locked iron bands. An army duffel, rusted zipper. Kitchen cupboards glued shut. Tabernacle. Desk. Closet. He had to wedge apart doors, lift covers. He was always disappointed to find a drab or menacing interior. To make a welcoming place of his heart was mentally slippery work. Sometimes cleaning was involved, rearrangements. He had to dust. He had to throw out old junk to make room. It was all so tedious, but he worked at the project until he had the whole damned lot of Emmaline's family in there and could slam it shut, exhausted, with Emmaline in the center and safe from him.

Emmaline and LaRose got in the car and pulled out onto the road home. Kids always say what's on their minds while you are driving.

How come you changed my school?

Do you like Mrs. Shell?

Yeah, course, but how come I'm still with you?

You mean not going back to Peter?

And Nola, and Maggie. How come?

Because. Emmaline said it carefully. Because I want to keep you with your family, with us now. I miss you too much. She glanced over quickly at LaRose.

Your dad, your brothers and sister, they miss you too. They know I'm keeping you.

He was staring out the windshield, his mouth slightly open, transfixed.

Is that okay with you, my boy?

He took a moment. He was thinking how to put this.

You just pass me around, he said. I'm okay with it, but it gets old. Problem is, Nola, she's gonna be too sad. It might be death if she gets too sad, Maggie told me. Plus Maggie and me, we're like this. He put two fingers together, the way Josette did. We keep her mom going when she can't get out of bed and stuff.

Everything that LaRose said shocked Emmaline. He's a little man, she thought. He's grown up.

So I gotta go back there, Mom. I like Mrs. Shell. She's not picky. But I need to go back to Dusty's family.

You remember him, Dusty?

He's still my friend, Mom. I got his family on my hands, too. So can I go back?

Really, my boy?

She thought she'd better stop the car and throw up. Plus her head hurt suddenly because her boy remembered Dusty, spoke of him with such immediacy, felt this level of responsibility. It was too much to put on him, but there it was.

Yeah, Mom, it's too late to go back on your promise.

She did pull over, but just put her face in her hands and was too overwhelmed to cry. Anyway, she never cried. That was Landreaux's job. He cried for both of them. Emmaline tried to cry, tried to well up just to get some relief. But she was Emmaline.

LaRose patted her arm, her neck.

It's okay, you're gonna make it, he said. If you just get going you'll feel better. One step after another. One day at a time.

LaRose was used to mothers' despair and these were the words that Peter used with Nola.

⚓

LANDREAUX DROVE his son to the Ravich house. He could see that the change in routine had made LaRose anxious, and restoring the old order was the right thing. Still, Landreaux had trouble letting LaRose go. He hugged his son just before LaRose swung out of the car with his pack on his shoulder.

It's all good, Landreaux muttered.

He was not all good, would never be; yet there were slender threads of okay.

Landreaux watched LaRose run up the steps. Maggie was at the door jumping up and down. LaRose bounced straight in. Neither Maggie nor Nola had ever waved at or acknowledged Landreaux. It was necessary to be invisible to them, but not to his son. At the last moment LaRose stuck his head out the door and waved good-bye.

The little things that get you. Choked-up smile from Landreaux.

He will be okay, he muttered, pulling out and driving away. This was a phrase he repeated like a mantra when things were not okay. After a while it made him feel better and after a time it worked.

⁂

MAGGIE HELD the stack of new school notebooks in her lap. She was in the passenger's seat. LaRose was in the backseat. Nola was driving them to school because they weren't on the bus route. Last year they could have walked over to the Irons' house, just over the reservation boundary, and taken the bus with them. But the bus no longer stopped there because Hollis drove. Maggie hoped that Hollis would get a bigger car so she and LaRose could ride along. She was tense. Sitting beside her mother going sixty-five miles per hour, she tried not to hyperventilate. Maggie held her breath every time a car swished by in the other lane. Let it out when the danger was over. She had developed propulsive convictions since finding her mother in the barn—like if she held her breath when cars came, her mother would not swerve and kill them all. Or if Maggie held her breath even longer, Nola might swerve but she and LaRose would miraculously survive the crash. Right now, with all the school supplies in the car, and her mother so pleased about having bought new fine-point markers, packages of notebook paper, labels, even a magnetic mirror for the inside of her locker door, Maggie felt the danger of a murder-suicide was pretty low, still she held her breath.

Maggie was dizzy by the time they stopped at the school entry. The doors swished open, the kids were talking. LaRose went one way, she went another. Josette and Snow had flipped a coin to see who got to be her First Day Mentor. Only kids with a top average could get that honor. You got an automatic late pass to your own classes, because you showed the new student around, went to each class to make sure they found the room.

Snow had won. She was standing tall and serene in the entry, wearing a hot-pink tank top layered over a slinky purple T-shirt, waiting with a class schedule and a lock for Maggie's locker.

Don't sweat it, she said. Maggie thought she might look nervous, so she tossed her head and grinned.

Hey, Cheeks, said Snow to a stagey-looking boy with earrings and tattoos, meet my little sis.

Hey, Sean, said Snow to a boy with floppy pants, sagging jacket, and wildly inappropriate Hooters T-shirt, meet my sis. Sean, you're gonna get kicked out for that T-shirt.

I know, said Sean.

Hey, Waylon, said Snow to a scary massive dude with heavy eyebrows, plush lips, football linebacker vibe, meet my little sis. You guys are in the same class.

He put out his hand to shake, formal.

Ever so pleased, he said.

A girl behind him laughed. Get away from her, Waylon! She was tall like Snow, her eyelids hot blue, hair to her waist, balloony blouse, tight jeans.

This is Diamond. The three girls walked to Maggie's first class. It was Physical Science taught by Mr. Hossel, a painfully thin young man with scarred red hands.

We think maybe he blew himself up, whispered Diamond, in a chemistry accident. Nobody knows.

He's enigmatic, said Snow.

They left Maggie alone; she went in and sat down. Eyes rested on Maggie, she could feel them, and it felt wonderful. Nobody knew her. Nobody hated her yet. Light, she felt light. Shed of an insufferable responsibility. Nola off her hands for the whole day. Nothing she could do. No way to stop her mother. No way to know. And LaRose safe also in his own classroom so he wouldn't find Nola dead and be scarred for life. Maggie smiled when she told her name to the class and smiled when they muttered. It wasn't a mean mutter, just an information-exchange mutter. She smiled when the teacher introduced himself to her and smiled when the class shifted their feet. She smiled down at her new notebook as he went over the day's assignment and reminded them that his rules included no makeup application during class. Two girls lowered their mascara wands. Maggie dreamily smiled at Mr. Hossel as he told her what she needed to bring to class. Startled, he caught her smile, and thought she might be a little odd, or high. But the class began to murmur, so he went on trying to interest them in the laws of motion.

THE POWERS

Tryouts for the team were that Saturday.

C'mon, Josette yelled from the pickup. Snow was driving. Maggie got into the jump seat just behind. They drove to the school and parked by the gym entrance. The gym was huge and there were three courts with nets rolled up in the steel rafters so that there could be several different games played at the same time.

The eighteen girls trying out for the team wore ponytails centered high on the back of their heads, and wide stretchy headbands of every color. Some looked Indian, some looked maybe Indian, some looked white. Diamond grinned at Maggie. Six feet tall and in full makeup, she danced around, excited, snapping gum. Another girl's ponytail, even tightened up high, hung nearly to her waist. She was powwow royalty. Regina Sailor was her name. Snow was five ten and her ponytail was also long—halfway down her back. Maggie decided to grow her hair out. Diamond was powerfully muscled and the powwow princess had extremely springy crow-hop legs. Maggie decided to work out more. The coach was small, round, smiley, maybe a white Indian. He wore a bead choker. His thin hair was scraped into a grizzled ponytail. He was Mr. Duke.

Coach Duke started the girls off with warm-up exercises. Josette paired off with Maggie and Snow paired with Diamond. The powwow princess, very striking with winsome cheekbones and a complex double French braid, looked at Maggie with cool scorn and said, Who's that.

She's my sister, Josette said. She's a digger, too. You watch.

The coach made them number off twos and ones, for a scrimmage. Josette and Snow were twos. Maggie tried to stand in a spot where she would be a two, but she got stuck as a one. She was on the same team as Diamond and the princess. They seemed to know where they played best and took their positions. Diamond passed Maggie the ball and said, Serve!

Maggie's throat went dry. She slammed the ball on the floor—it didn't bounce crooked like in the yard. The ball came right back to her hand as if it liked her. She tossed the ball high.

Wait.

Coach hadn't blown his whistle.

Okay. He tweeted.

Maggie tossed the ball up again, knocked it into the net. But the others just clapped and got down to business. Her face was hot, but it seemed nobody cared.

There went the next serve. The princess returned it. Josette set the ball and Snow launched, legs gangling, spiked the ball left of Maggie just the way she did in practice. There wasn't time to slide under it so Maggie dove fist out, konged it up high, and rolled. Diamond messaged that one deep but Josette was there with a bouncy blonde, who again fed the ball to Snow, who again whacked it straight at Maggie.

Ravich! she screamed.

Maggie dug it out again with a kamikaze dive.

Holeee, screamed the powwow princess. Another girl set and the princess slammed a pit ball past Snow's lifted arms right into the sweet spot of gym floor nobody could reach.

Kill!

Maggie couldn't serve or jump. She couldn't hit for squat. She wasn't graceful, but she got to where the ball was, wherever it went, and popped it up. Sometimes she pounced, sometimes she frogged, sometimes she stag-leaped to cork it overhead, backward, if a teammate smacked it out of bounds. And her placement was good. Her craziest save was playable. She gave everything—every fret, every gut clench, every fear—freed herself for a couple of hours, made the coach laugh, and picked up the team with her slapstick retrievals.

Okay, you might be on the bench a lot at first. Don't worry, said Josette, when they found out she'd made the varsity team. You mighta got more play JV. But we need you.

You're suicidal out there!

Snow laughed. They were driving back. Neither of them saw Maggie's face freeze at the word, saw her eyes lose focus. She was suddenly in the barn—her mom standing high in the slant of light. Zip. She ricocheted back into the car. She was afraid that she felt too good, too happy, and that would make her mom feel the opposite. She watched the road, anxious as the sisters gabbled. Snow was driving fast enough, but still, she needed to get home.

RANDALL HAD a friend who had inherited a permit to cut pipestone at the quarry in South Dakota where the pipestone lived. This friend gave pipestone freely to Randall, who gave it to Landreaux, who made pipes for him. But this was a pipe for Landreaux's own family. They all took the pipes into the lodge whenever they went. They treated the boys' pipes like people. All the children were given these pipes early on, but didn't smoke them until they were grown. LaRose was the last child without a pipe, so Landreaux was making one. He used an electric saw, then a hasp file on the red stone to rough it out. Later, a rasp, finer files, and a rattail file for the curve in the bowl. He would use graduated grades of sandpaper. At last he would use fabrics, then polish the bowl with his palms and fingers for a few weeks. The oil from his own hands would deepen the color. It was a simple pipe. Landreaux didn't believe that pipes should be made in eagle head, otter, bear, eagle claw, mountain goat, turtle, snail, or horse shapes, as he'd seen. They were supposed to be humble objects to pray with humbly.

Landreaux felt that working on a pipe was a form of prayer, but prayer where you could multitask. He often brought a pipe bowl to work on when he sat with his clients as they went through procedures, waited for tests, watched TV in hospital lounges or at home.

Today, he brought the pipe to work on when he went to Ottie and Bap's. He got Ottie's hygiene taken care of first. He showered Ottie and carefully protected the still healing fistula that would help access large veins in his chest. Landreaux also bathed Bap's dog just because she'd be pleased. Bap was visiting their daughter in Fargo. Ottie rolled up to the television, pointed the weak-batteried remote, and flipped erratically through the channels while Landreaux made them sandwiches, nothing juicy. Sometimes Ottie said he longed for an orange so bad he wanted to cry. He was on a low-fluid diet. Ottie found the cooking show he liked, and they ate while watching the flashing knives, close-up batter whipping, sizzling, critical tasting. But Ottie was still washed out from dialysis the day before, couldn't finish his sandwich, and soon even the show couldn't hold his interest. He wanted to talk, though. He switched off the tube and asked how things were going for Landreaux. His voice was thready and soft.

Guess I have to say the whole situation's stable now, but goddamn, said Landreaux to Ottie, who smiled at him with dim eyes. Landreaux had the pipe bowl in his hands, but he couldn't get calm.

I shouldn't swear while I'm working on this pipe, he said. Randall says it might get offended. The pipe's supposed to be treated like a grandma or a grandpa.

You're too reverential, all that. Grandpa Pipe won't get pissed off, said Ottie. Grandpas take pity. Plus this isn't really a sacred object yet. Has to be blessed.

True, said Landreaux.

Swear away, said Ottie.

Sorry, said Landreaux to Ottie. Sometimes it gets to me all over again.

Ottie knew that Landreaux could get on a jag.

Hey, I wonder.

Ottie groped to change the subject.

When did you and Emmaline first meet?

He surprised himself. Maybe it was an unusual thing for one guy to ask another. They had him all plumbed up like a toilet. Dying so slowly was boring.

So?

At a funeral, said Landreaux. It was Eddieboy's funeral, her uncle. During the wake, while Eddieboy lay there looking his best, Emmaline got up and spoke for him. The things she remembered: like this raccoon he tamed that sat on his head like a hat. The way he let kids be his workout weights, lifting them up and down on his arms. The green plastic shoes. These things brought him alive, you know?

I remember Eddieboy.

People were smiling and nodding at Emmaline's memories like you're smiling and nodding, said Landreaux. Eddieboy's morning Schlitz—and he never drank at any other time. Those Hawaiian shirts. How he used to go *yabadabadoo* at the end of jokes. I watched Emmaline and thought that someone who could raise those mental pictures at a sad time and make people smile was a good person. Plus, a looker.

For sure, said Ottie. I bet the feast was good for Ed-dieboy.

Potato salad, macaroni shells. Ambrosia. Of course we ate together, then I left. I was working in Grand Forks as a night clerk. I'd got her address and I wrote her every night on Motel 6 letterhead paper. She kept all my letters.

I wrote Bap too! What'd you say in your letters?

Landreaux was smiling now.

I would die for her, eat dust, walk the burning desert, that kind of thing. Maybe I said I would drink her bath-tub water. I hope not.

Ottie still looked expectant, so Landreaux went on.

Oh well, you know. We tried each other out, I guess. No, it was more like we disappeared into each other for a while. Vanished out of the ordinary world. To be honest, for a while we drank hard, drugged some. Then got sober. We wanted a baby, then Snow was born tiny and we had to lean on each other to make sure our baby lived. Emmaline was in school. We made it through that. Earlier in this time we got Hollis. Along came Jo-sette. Eight pounds! We came back here and got into the traditions, to stay sober at first, then to bless our family. We went deeper into it, got married traditional before the kids, got married by Father Travis way after.

Coochy came along, then LaRose. One thing had led to another in a good way until . . .

Don't skip ahead, said Ottie. You lucked out with Emmaline, but maybe it wasn't just luck. You're a good man, too.

Ottie had perked up during Landreaux's story, but now a powerful wave of fatigue hit him. Abruptly, he fell asleep; the air whistled between his lips. Landreaux fixed a travel pillow around Ottie's neck so that he could sleep comfortably in his chair. The past was stirred up in Landreaux. It had been a long time since he'd thought of the way he and Emmaline were in the beginning. Even to remember, now, both hurt and pleasured his mind.

Up until Emmaline, he had been living in his sleep. Dozing on his feet yet doing a thousand things. And then she had roughly shaken him and when he dared look into her eyes he saw: together they were awake. She began to inhabit him. He felt too much. Had strange thoughts. If she left him, he would go blind. Deaf. Forget how to talk and breathe. When they argued, he turned to air. His atoms, molecules, whatever he was made of, started drifting apart. He could feel himself losing solidity. How had she done this? Sometimes at night, when she left the bed and he was anchored in half-consciousness, he couldn't move. Terror built in him, a panicky, anxious, stifling misery that abated only when he felt her stirring about beside him again. If Emmaline had not loved him steadily in return he would have died of the experience of falling in love. It was like he had been born in a cave, raised as a wolf child or a monkey with a bottle strapped on a wire for a mother. To feel was nearly too much to bear.

Landreaux thought about the Fentanyl patches kept in the back of the bathroom drawer. They were for Ottie's unhealable stumps.

Sit tight, said Landreaux to himself.

He gripped the pipe bowl and watched his knuckles whiten until the need, the need, the need passed down a level, which was the dangerous moment when he would think he had conquered the need but that sly part of him could bypass the conviction. The desire, the shame, the fear that stopped his breath was settling. He had been infected with feelings and his body held them like a live virus. But he could turn them off, go to sleep again, find safety in a self-compelled oblivion. He put the stone to his forehead until he felt safe. He took a deep breath. That erratic thing in him had settled down. He talked it down some more.

Now, you stay there. Leave me alone, he told it.

Landreaux handled the pipestone lovingly. It was the blood of the ancestors through which Emmaline and his children existed in this precarious world.

❧

MAGGIE WALKED LaRose back to his brothers and sisters on an October weekend. The radiant leaves had blown off quickly the night before, and stuck to the bottoms of their shoes. Maggie stayed on at the Iron house to do homework with the girls, and because she was invited to their beauty spa. Josette and Snow were going to turn their kitchen into a relaxing world of skin and hair regimens.

The treatments could be assembled out of the pantry and refrigerator. Sugar facial. Salt exfoliation for the feet. Cinnamon and honey lip exfoliation. Egg-white facial that would tighten your skin. Cucumber eye mask. Frozen tea bag eye mask. Lemon hair rinse. Mayonnaise hair moisturizing treatment. They decided that they were going to do that one first.

Snow set a jar of mayo on the table along with a roll of plastic wrap. She poured a quarter cup of oil into a bowl. Maggie sat down in a kitchen chair, a towel over her shoulders, and Snow massaged mayonnaise and canola oil into the crown of Maggie's head, then down each strand of hair. Maggie wanted to laugh. The smell was annoying but Snow's massage felt so good that she fizzed up inside. She closed her eyes and sealed her lips. It would be weird to laugh. Snow wound the plastic wrap around and around Maggie's head. She tucked the ends tight, then wrapped a towel tightly over the plastic into a turban.

Now you can go sit in Dad's recliner and Josette will do the frozen tea bag treatment on your eyes, and the salt exfoliation on your feet. After that, Josette's going to do the mayo treatment on my hair, then we all do the egg-white face mask.

I want one too, said Emmaline when she saw the girls painting the egg whites onto their faces, and onto LaRose. They lay on the couch, or on towels on the floor. They listened to the radio while waiting for the egg white to dry. As it dried, it started pulling on their skin.

Can you feel it?

I can, said Maggie, her eyes shut beneath the melting Lipton tea bags.

Kinda hurts, said Josette after a moment.

That's because it's stimulating your collagen.

Emmaline sat up. Can I take it off now?

Maggie took the tea bags off her eyes. Mine's dry.

Ow! Don't smile, said Josette. But she laughed. The dried egg white on Snow's face had cracked in a web of tiny lines.

Get it off!

They washed off the egg white and admired the smoothness of one another's skin. They unwound the turbans, washed their hair, and couldn't get the mayonnaise out. Maggie looked into the mirror and saw that the tea had left raccoon marks around her eyes. Within the stains, her eyes gleamed as if with fever. She looked mysteriously ill. She examined the porcelain finish on her cheeks.

Wow, said Emmaline. My face is all dried out. It feels like my skin is going to fall off.

Me too, said LaRose.

She stared into the mirror and started rubbing Oil of Olay onto her forehead.

Now the manicures!

Josette brought out a tray of nail enamels.

I'm leaving for town to get Coochy. Do your homework, said Emmaline to the girls. And this egg-white mask? I think it aged me ten years. Her skin was still tight and strange.

I'm going with you, said LaRose.

You're from the olden days, said Josette suddenly, bending over to hug LaRose. You got an old spirit.

Just that egg white, said LaRose.

Know what he said? You guys, know what he said? He said what we used for TV in the olden time was stories.

Come on, said Emmaline.

No, really, he said that!

I mean come on—let's go.

Maggie and Snow jumped in the car and got a ride into town. They wanted to buy cinnamon for the lip treatment, and they had to get more shampoo.

We smell like freakin' sandwiches, said Snow.

Whose idea was this, the mayo?

Mine.

Really?

Actually, Josette's, but she's sensitive, you know?

Maggie hadn't thought of Josette as the sensitive one.

My mom's sensitive, said Maggie, and wished she hadn't. Anyway, they were both sitting in the backseat of the car, where Emmaline couldn't hear. Snow was silent, but Maggie could tell she was thinking of what to say. After a while, Snow spoke.

Your mom, she's okay. I mean, she's done pretty well, don't you think, considering?

Mom's hard to deal with, said Maggie. She stopped herself from chipping at her new nail color. Pale sky blue.

Snow didn't tell her how she and Josette had re-coiled from that witchy vibe Nola had given off those first years. She said that Josette liked how Nola planted flowers.

She's into that, said Maggie.

Snow's approval of something that her mother did had a strange effect on Maggie. Her stomach seemed to float inside her body. Yet there was a jealous itch in her brain. She looked at Snow, at the elegant way she held her mayonnaise-smelling head, the slim flex of her shoulders, the perfectly layered T-shirts. She needed Snow to understand.

My mother actually doesn't like me, you know, said Maggie. She loves LaRose.

Snow's eyebrows drew together, her lips parted; she stared into Maggie's face. Just when Maggie was about to shoot her mouth off, say something tough, swear to stop what she saw in Snow's eyes might turn to pity, Snow reached an arm around Maggie's shoulders and said, Oh shit, baby-girl, we gotta stick together. Look.

Nicking her head toward the front seat, she shaped her face to indicate LaRose and Emmaline.

He doesn't even have to call shotgun anymore, said Snow. Guess who's always stuck in the backseat when-ever Mom's got time with LaRose?

Maggie stuttered; it was like an unexpected present thrust into her hands.

I never knew.

It's a fact of life, said Snow. We call her out on it all the time. She doesn't get it. Hollis and Coochy, they're tight. And we got each other, me, Josette. And, hey.

She rocked Maggie toward her comically.

We got you covered too.

After they left, Josette started prying up the packed powdery dirt beside the front steps of their house. The rest of the yard was damp, but this part stayed dry because of the overhang of the roof. Maybe it wasn't the best place to plant because of that, but her vision demanded fulfillment. Her parents had no feel for gardening, for home beautification. They were focused on the human side of things—medical, social, humanitarian, and all that. But over the past year, whenever she had picked up LaRose, Josette had seen how Nola got some new flower to bloom every week or so. They weren't just ordinary flowers, and Josette didn't know their names. Somehow they bloomed one right after the other, all summer and even into fall. Between these unusual plants were the constant marigolds and petunias, which she did know. Nola was growing vegetables out back of her house, too, climbing vines that twined up chicken wire. Rows of plants were set off by straw paths where the chickens pecked. It all looked to Josette like a magazine house. Of course, Nola had a part-time job only. Anyway not like her mother. Emmaline's job was endless. Josette would take charge.

Yesterday, she had brought home seeds and some tiny, droopy marigolds from the grocery store. They were in a bin marked free. This was her vision. There would be colorful bursts of flowers beside the door to their house instead of a junked bicycle and rusted scooter that could not be used by a kid on a gravel road. Those things, she had hauled back into the woods.

The dirt, though, was not like the dirt at Maggie's house. It was filled with tiny rocks and the color was gray. The water just turned it to soup.

Dirt's dirt, right?

Josette sat back on her heels.

She put the seeds in, gingerly pulled the marigolds from their sectioned plastic pot. She set each one gently into a hole and sifted the gray dust from beneath the eaves over the roots. She watered everything, nearly washing the plants away until she learned to trickle the water from the bucket. She leaned back on her heels again.

Grow, little flowers, grow.

She loved the scent of them, pungent and warm.
She heard Hollis's car from a long way off, struggling
toward the house. The engine was plaintive, but patient
with the slight hill. Soon he pulled up in the driveway,
got out.

Hey, he said.

Hey, she said back.

What's that?

Oh, just making a garden, said Josette. Thought I'd
brighten things up.

He admired it from every angle. He praised the
marigolds. He didn't tell her that the first frost would
kill them off and they wouldn't come back the second
year. Or that planting seeds was useless in the fall. But
he wondered how it was she didn't know that. Why
hadn't she picked up on these pieces of knowledge in
her life? The air was warming, but the spindly plants
with their leaves yellowing already were doomed.

So, he said when she brushed herself off and stood
and looked at him.

So what's there to eat?

Is there any soup left?

They walked inside and rifled through the refrigerator, lifted the tops off stove pots, found the hidden
cookies, leftover bannock. Josette smelled intensely of

something that made Hollis hungry. He tried to make a sandwich, but there wasn't any mayonnaise. Josette toasted some bannock in the iron skillet. They sat down to eat.

Hollis sprinkled a spoon of sugar on his bannock. Josette tried to chat.

This old sugar bowl, you know? It belonged to this house from way back. My great-great-et-cetera-grandpa from olden times used to keep a key in it.

Although Hollis already knew about the no-handle sugar bowl, he said nothing. Josette kept talking.

It was something from the first LaRose. She lived here when it was still a cabin-shack. All we have of hers is this little sugar bowl, I guess, except some letters and records. Grandma's got those.

Your family goes way back, huh.

Josette looked at Hollis and because of the way he said this, in a softened voice, staring at her with a peculiar serious regard, she remembered what Snow had said about Hollis liking her. Which was disturbing. A stormy sense of this moment's weird potential gripped her and she screeched, making him jump.

Everybody's family goes way back! Fuckin A. Back to the future, man.

She began to laugh with what she thought of as a dangerous sexy growl, and he looked at her in wonder.

OLD STORY 1

The old people were parked around the room in folding chairs and wheelchairs. LaRose's namesake grandmother, the fourth LaRose, was frying frybread. She lifted each golden pillow of dough from fat and set it in a nest of paper towels. Emmaline put the squares on plates and handed them to each elder. The boy LaRose brought around the butter, the chokecherry jelly. He set out the coffee mugs: the Tribal College mug, the Up Shit Creek Without a Paddle mug, the scratched casino mug, and the brand-new casino mug with the slot-machine fruits. The coffee-machine coffee was still dripping into the glass pot. LaRose watched it. He was pudging out a little before he shot up another inch. Malvern Sangrait squinted at him and nodded each time he did something.

Oh that boy, oh that boy, she whispered. He's made of good ingredients. Maybe, after all, your Emmaline stepped out on Landreaux.

Shut up, bad lady, said Mrs. Peace.

The last few pleasant years with Sam Eagleboy had taken none of the meanness out of Malvern. She watched Mrs. Peace tong the frybread out and tried not to say anything about her technique. Still, other words popped from her mouth.

Is that your jelly or your daughter's jelly?

We put it up together, said Emmaline.

How come you ain't living with your mother? Is it he, Landreaux, against it? How come your mother ain't living in her own house?

You asked me that a hundred times, said Mrs. Peace, and I told you I like my habits. Like living here, alone except for you and your mean mouth.

Ignatia wheeled in with her tank of oxygen.

God save the queen, said Malvern.

Naanan, said Ignatia, holding up her tiny claw hand for LaRose to pretend to slap.

Ignatia's face glowed like a young person's when she decided to smile.

I got a good story for you, she said to LaRose. In the middle of the night I remembered all the pieces. This story came off my own grandmother, too, maybe when I was your age. That long ago. I forgot all about this story until the other night.

Let's hear you say it then, said Malvern, pouting, jealous.

I can't, said Ignatia with a proud little wag of her hand.

Why not? Malvern leaned close, eyed her narrowly.

Ignatia drew herself up, tucked her chin to deliver the teaching.

There is no snow on the earth. The legless beings do not yet sleep.

Ooooo, you sound like an old-time Indian, you, said Malvern. Her eyes lighted with malice. Nothing was worse than being called out on sacred tradition by another elder.

You know we *do* wait until snow's deep on the ground, said Mrs. Webid.

I *do* know that, said Malvern, enraged now. It was me who originally remembered that rule and Ignatia who tried to break that rule. The beings who might bring our stories to the lowest levels of the earth, to the underwater lions and the giant snakes and other evil beings, they have to be froze in the ground, sleeping.

There's one more piece of frybread left, said Emmaline.

Let her have it, the one who tells the stories out of season, said Ignatia, pursing her angry lips at Malvern.

Gawiin memwech, said Malvern. Let's give it to the one who tried to steal my husbands, all six of them, one right after the other one. She tried to snatch away the fathers of my children by jiggling her stuffs at them! For shame!

They never saw nothing they didn't want to see. Ignatia gave a choking snarl. You were so mean you scared them limp. They couldn't take it. They swarmed after me.

Giiwanimo!

Don't you call me liar. Your pants are smoking!

Emmaline cut the piece of frybread in half and slathered it with butter and jelly. She put a piece in each woman's hand. The antagonists gnawed off bits, glowering and guttering, and for a moment it looked like they might soften. Then Malvern blurted.

Giiwanimo! Giin! Your *underpants* are burning! Hot pussy, you, at this age. For shame!

Ignatia threw her buttered bread at Malvern and it stuck to her breast, right at about her nipple. She looked down and snorted.

Here, let me help you, my darling, said Sam Eagleboy. He lifted the bit of bread off, then spit on his handkerchief and scrubbed slavishly at her bosom. Malvern pretended to bat his hands away.

Sam automatically popped the frybread in his mouth.

Sam ate the whiteman's food! Mrs. Webid leaned excitedly toward Malvern. He must love you pretty bad, eh?

A man who will do that will do anything, said Ignatia. I should know. Her face screwed into a wink.

✦

NIGHT SHIFT? Yes, I believe . . . I am certain. I will be. Quite happy with those hours, said Romeo, nearly dumbstruck with excitement.

Sterling Chance had a round, worn, dignified face. His hands were calm between the stacks of papers on his desk.

You are working out real good here, Romeo. Don't always get to see that. We don't just clean and repair stuff, you know, we are kind of the guiding force around here. If we don't do our job, nobody can do a damn thing to fix people, right?

So far, Romeo had tinkered with and revved up an emergency generator. He had hot-wired the ambulance. He had gently broken into file cabinets and even an office when nurses had forgotten their keys. He had squeezed a breathing pump for a kid with asthma during a blackout. He had figured out stuck windows, coaxed fluorescence out of touchy bulbs, unclogged toilets, and dehairballed showers. All without uttering one single swear word that could be heard outside the sanctum of his head.

You're polite, said Sterling Chance, with gravity. That also counts.

As Romeo walked out of the maintenance office, his prospects expanded.

Not only would he not be alone, at home, at night, which had gotten tedious, but certainly there would be only sleepy supervision at the hospital. Certainly the rules would relax. During the first week of work, he found that he was right. All around Romeo, over the upside-down hours, there was talk. Gossip ruled the night shift. Not mean gossip, like at the Elders Lodge, just valuable updates. You had to talk to stay awake. And you had to move around to stay awake, too, so Romeo might as well do some work. He continued to normalize servile behavior in order to get close to many conversations—any of them might be useful. He let himself be seen polishing the floor on his hands and knees.

You know, we've got a floor-polishing machine, someone said to him.

Thank you, but I have my standards, he replied.

The emergency team had a little picnic table set up outside their garage door. Of course, they had life-and-death matters on their minds, but really, what careless people! Romeo had to pick up the bits of paper they crumpled, the cigarette butts of course, the candy and sandwich wrappers that blew down off their lunch. He did this even after the sun went down, as they sat beneath the floodlights. Then he had to slowly, slowly, dispose of these items. He had to smooth out and stack each piece of trash before he lowered it reverently into the bin. Romeo placed himself near the emergency team, around the emergency room, anywhere he could get near the EMT on duty or the nurses who might have a bit of information to spare, or the doctors. He blended into the hospital furniture with his mineral-colored outfits. He wore a tan turtleneck to hide the blue-black skulls around his throat. His gray stretchy jeans were the color of dirty mop water. Probably, they were women's jeans. He didn't care. He didn't tell his own stories, he just encouraged others. He didn't make himself obvious in any way. He wore black rubber sneakers he'd found abandoned on the highway. Mornings, on the way home, head brimming, he entered his disability sanctum and emptied his pockets of papers—jottings on Post-it notes, papers drawn from the trash, even copies of a few files left out overnight. He kept his notes in piles. Pocketed another box of colored thumbtacks. Kept on tacking the pertinent scribblings up on the softened drywall of his rotting walls.

From these scraps of conversation Romeo learned: There was a kind of disease where you acted drunk, but it was just your own body making alcohol. Eating food off the edge of a sharp knife had resulted in an ambulance call for Puffy Shields. A baby was born with hair all over its body. Another baby was born holding a penny that the mother had swallowed. Old Man Payoose had a son on methamphetamine. That son had stolen the old man's money and while that boy was high had shoved a carrot up his own ass, which was what brought him to the ER. A lady whose name he tried to catch used small round lake stones to exercise her vagina. A tribal member, a roofer, had breathed several nails into his lungs and wouldn't let the doctors take them out. There was too much salt in everything, including the air. A little girl froze to death because she couldn't get back into the house where her mother was passed out. Although she was pronounced dead at the scene, a doctor CPR'd and warmed her blood and brought her back from the spirit world. Now the girl knew things, like that other kid, LaRose. A teenager froze to death sleeping under the porch of his father's house. They tried, in hope, but couldn't get that boy back. An old woman got lost taking out the garbage but she didn't quite freeze because she buried herself underneath the snow.

But wait. Romeo mopped his way up to the door of the dispatcher's office, where the ambulance crew sometimes did paperwork or just talked. He heard

Landreaux's name. He strained, leaned closer, held his breath and tried to make out the words.

Not the femoral, said someone.

For sure?

Not that one either.

What day was it?

A Wednesday? A Tuesday?

You coulda fooled me.

Then they started talking about the carrot again.

Romeo strained his work-weakened mind. Tried to memorize. When he had to move on, he swiftly wrote down what he'd heard on pages torn from a waiting-room magazine. Into a file folder rescued from the trash, he slipped all that he found. Possibilities. Creative possibilities. He took pride in how he organized his own reality.

⚓

MAGGIE SNEAKS into LaRose's room and curls up at the end of his bed.

I think it's going good. I think she's happier, says Maggie.

Me too. She's not making the cakes.

And she might take a job with Dad at Cenex. I heard them.

You gotta stay nice to her.

Are you saying . . . Maggie's voice is low . . . are you saying she wanted to hang herself because of how mean I was?

Course not. But you were.

I was a bitch. I am a bitch. That's what they call girls like me. Not so far, I mean, at this school. There's bitchier bitches here. But it will happen.

LaRose sits up. No, you're just tough. You gotta be.

Lemme show you tough!

She jumps up, bounces the bed, and smacks him with his pillow. He lunges for her and they wrestle off the bed, onto the floor. They stop laughing when their bodies thump down hard. Nola calls out. Maggie is out the door into her own room quick as a shadow.

The parents' door creaks. Nola's voice floats from down the hall.

Some books fell, says LaRose from his bed. It's all right, Mom. You can sleep now. I'll be quiet.

Maggie?

Whaaaa? Mom? She answers from her own room, pretending she's groggy and crabby. All is quiet. Falling asleep, Maggie thinks about LaRose. She thinks about him every night. He calms her down. He is her special, her treasure, she doesn't really know what he is—hers to love.

Suddenly he is there, at her bedside, finger at her lips. He's never done this before.

She turns toward him.

I wanna ask you something, he says.

Okay.

Who were those boys, you know, in the other school. Whenever. Those ones who held you down. Who did that stuff?

She looks over at LaRose's skinny boy arms and hair so thick it won't stay down. His question makes her sick. She thought she was over it, but turns out she's been holding a pool of slime in her body. Now it seeps from her pores, a light film. Are there tears? She wipes her face. Damn. It still gets to her. And they remember, those guys. Last year Buggy said to her, fake innocent, *Hey, Ravich, you still want it? You still want it like you did before?* Another time, coming down the hall toward her, Buggy had grabbed his crotch. At least he flinched when she went in for the kick.

She tells: Tyler Veddar, Curtains Peace, Brad Morrissey, Jason "Buggy" Wildstrand.

I think I've seen those guys, says LaRose.

Plus there is this Wildstrand sister, Braelyn, just a year above me. She's mean, pretends she's hot, wears a ton of makeup. Plucks her eyebrows into half hoops. I hate her. I'm so glad we changed schools. She used to give me the stink eye. The finger. For nothing! I know Buggy said something to her, told Braelyn it was my fault.

I never forgot what you said that night, says LaRose.

You didn't? The oozy snot dries off her. Their prying fucky fingers fly off her skin. You remember? What'd I say?

Can a saint kill?

A saint?

You meant me. Even though I'm not a saint.

LaRose, oh shit. I didn't mean you should kill them.

Don't worry. I'm not gonna kill them exactly, but yeah, now I'm stronger.

No, you're not, she says. Please!

Tyler is now a high school wrestler. Curtains is ungainly and slow but a hulk. Brad Morrissey plays football. Buggy is nerveless, cruel, and very smart.

It's over. Over! It does not affect me. Besides, they're kind of brutal. They're mean assholes. Promise you're going to leave them alone.

Don't worry. LaRose holds his voice down, modest. You know I work out with Father Travis. I have my green belt now.

Oh my god, don't you try anything!

Ssshhhhhh.

He disappears.

MATERIAL OF TIME

Peter brought Nola to his Cenex job and she began to work beside him a few days a week. She ran the registers, stocked the shelves and refrigerator cases, kept the bathrooms fiercely spotless. Not an item was out of place, all labels visible. The coffee station glowed like an altar. As she worked, Nola's daily ration of sorrow dissipated into thousands of small items—the creamer cups, wrapped straws, adjustable candy hooks, the slushie machine and donut display case. Sometimes she stared long at the hot dog broiler turning endlessly until gold beads of sweating fat glistened on the skins of the lethal wieners. Sometimes she read and pondered the ingredients on the flimsy snack packages. When she counted the ice scrapers or replaced a shoplifted tire pressure gauge or studied the placement of magazines, it seemed that in righting the tiny things of life she was gaining control of herself, perhaps at a molecular level, for she was made up of all this junk, wasn't she? The beef sticks, which she chewed in the car ride home, the fluffy chemical cups of French vanilla latte from the automatic dispenser. She drew an extra-large cup for herself every morning and sipped all day—the taste growing harsher, the dry acid eating at her.

Then Peter started drinking gas station lattes too. They laughed together at their latte addiction. The laugh flew out of Nola's throat, harsh and rusty. It dissolved when it hit Peter's chest. Nola saw it. That night, she rested her head there and closed her eyes.

A COLD rain was blowing, not sleet yet, or snow. Fat drops smacked Nola's face as she came back to the house one afternoon. LaRose was upstairs, the door to his room halfway shut. Walking by the door Nola heard him talking, or rather, having a conversation. He often spoke while he was playing in his action world. He used Legos, blocks, magnets, an old erector set, Tinkertoys, cast-off bolts and odd bits of metal, even butter tubs and cracker boxes, to create a complex citadel. This magic edifice was attacked and defended by members of alliances that shifted and formed in his hands when he played with the many plastic creatures he had found in Dusty's toy bucket or been given. Tetrahellemon, Vontro, Green Menace, Lightning, Mudder, Seker, Maxmillions, Warthog, Simitron, Xor, Tor, Hiki, and the Master.

He was shy about his games. He never played around people, usually closed the door entirely, sometimes spoke in whispers. But today LaRose was so absorbed in the invented drama before him that he didn't hear Nola approach, or sense her listening.

Let's connect our fists and rocket over the dinosaurs.

You can't push me!

I repeat.

The plasma boat got our back. We're safe.

Get Xor out! Quick! He's getting weak!

Triceratops forced him in his jaws!

Good one, Hiki. The Master likes.

Don't use that one, Dusty.

He lost his powers yesterday. He's recuperating in the chamber.

Green Menace will stop the infest!

The cycle has begun and we must complete the universe.

Maxmillions. Take Maxmillions.

Yeah, you're Seker. Hold the exam button down.

Then mouth explosions. Bchchchchch! Pfwoooozhzhz! And the quiet clashing of molded plastic.

Nola sank silently down against the wall beside the open door. Her face was peaceful, her eyes downcast; her lips moved slightly as if she was repeating a name or prayer.

She heard everything. An epic battle between light and darkness. Forms passing through the material of time. Character subverting space. The gathering and regathering. Shapes of beings unknown merging deeply with the known. Worlds fusing. Dimensions collapsing. Two boys playing.

The next day, Nola splashed gasoline on the rotted lumber and ten-year-old tax records and bank statements she had gathered in the burn pit. It was a sparkling, mild, windless day. She threw in a burning twist of paper. There was a dull whump. When the fire was burning hot, she pushed in the green chair.

That's all over, she said out loud.

Whenever she was alone, tears had filled her eyes. No drug had helped, and even LaRose had not helped at first. But after listening to him play with Dusty yesterday, she woke this morning and got out of bed before she knew she'd done it. There had not been that agonized mudlike hold the bed usually had on her. Then later this morning her old self stirred. Something unknown, internal, righted itself. She felt unalone. Like the inner and the outer worlds were aligned, as with the actions of the action figures. Because the fabric between realities, living and dead, was porous not only to herself. This pass-between existed. LaRose went there too. She was not crazy after all. Just maybe more aware, like LaRose was, like everybody said he was. Special.

Something good he was doing for her by playing with her son from the other kingdom.

Plans sprang up. She would get fancier chickens, not just her old reliables. She would get barred rocks, wyandottes, Orpingtons, some of those wild-looking featherhead Polish chickens. She would make the garden bigger, better. They already had that ugly dog who wouldn't leave her alone. So an old sweet horse. Flowers, shrubs, bats now that bats are good, bees now that bees are good. Bird feeders. Trap the feral cats, but then what to do with them. No. Let them hunt rats, keep the barn safe. A cow, two maybe, for milk only. She hated sheep. No sheep, no goats. Rabbits, though, in a stack of rabbit hutches and from time to time she supposed Peter would remove one and kill it for supper. She'd make him skin it, too, cut it up in pieces. She would fry it, sure, but wait, their eyes! Big soft eyes! Too much. Too much, too soon. If you could eat a rabbit, you could eat a cat. If you could eat a cat, you could eat a dog. So it went, on up. No, she'd just have chickens, she thought, staring into the flames. That was all the death she would be able to bear. Slow down, she counseled herself. You have time to live now. She looked around, behind her, toward the woods.

See? She whispered. I burned the chair.

WISHING WELL

Wishingwellwishing wellwishing wellwehyahheywhen-yahhey. Ojibwes have a song for everything. This was Romeo's lock-picking song. He sang beneath his breath as he unlocked a hospital file cabinet with an unbent paper clip.

It is truly wonderful, he thinks, that such precious information is considered secure when protected by a lock so jiggly, and cheap-john enough to break. Or merely find a key to this generic lock if he so wishes. Or saw it off. But he has the time and inclination to pick this lock, which will make his entry invisible.

For ten quiet minutes Romeo toys with the innards of the lock, humming and whispering his lock-picking song until the tumblers line up and the mechanism yields.

Within the cabinet his secretarial finger-flipping produces the copy of a file it would be hard to obtain otherwise, the original probably residing in tribal police headquarters. From which zone he is barred except as an arrestee. Funny the trust that resides in him as a recovering alcoholic. Everybody loves that recovery shit, he thinks, as he slides out the paper he needs and replaces the file just in case anybody thinks to look for it although nobody ever will, as this was considered an open-and-shut sort of thing, a tragic accident.

He puts the document into a flimsy black cloth bag, another freebie he's cleaned up from the tribal security conference, where he witnessed tribal police officers using their Homeland Security grants to practice double-cuffing each other on the floor. The pack also holds ten sealed squares of expired noodles, the kind with pungent little foil skibs of flavoring. He's also scored three blueberry yogurts from the staff fridge at the hospital. Romeo heads up to the Catholic day school to see about lunch leftovers—he has been lucky there. If he could find some protein source to complement the noodles, and perhaps a wilted carrot or two, he'd have a hearty soup. An onion would be a plus!

Romeo scores a flabby cucumber and some chicken cooked so dry it almost flakes, but the soup will soften it. And there is nothing wrong with boiled cucumber. Back home, he switches on his television and the hot plate. Feeling domestic, he rinses out his enameled tin saucepan in the bathroom sink. He opens three packets of noodles, douses them with water and flavoring, pares the cucumber into bits, cutting against his thumb. Behind him, CNN seems stuck on yellowcake.

Yellowcake, he sings.

Weyoheyoh weyoheyhoh

Yellowcake

Yellowcake

Make my sweet tooth ache.

Then, remembering all of the yellow cakes he's devoured at funeral dinners and always with that chocolate frosting in tiny elevated swirls, he becomes nostalgic. Settling in before the television he meanders back to the times he went to visit Mrs. Peace so long ago and accepted squares of cake from the hands of little Emmaline. If he had ever declared his love to her once they were grown, would it have mattered? Would she have gone out with him, not Landreaux? Every year she moved farther above him, ever more out of his league. Not that he cared to be in any league, anymore, where women were concerned. My junk is monk, he thought. LOL. He'd learned LOL at work. In the olden days, there had been a chance. When he was considered smart. When there was cake passed on a little flowered plate from her hands to his hands. He can taste it, the melting scoop of vanilla soaking into the sweet loam of the slice. Like her dearness soaking into his porous heart. He's not high, just living with that memory.

Not just to bring down Landreaux, he suddenly thinks, staring at his detective wall. But more. Maybe something true. I am not just a scabbed-over pariah. People should know.

The ramen hisses up, boiling over. Romeo busies himself rescuing his dinner. He gets his spoon ready, an old heavy metal cooking spoon from the government school. With a rag for a pot holder, he brings the pot of soup over and sets it upon a folded towel on the floor next to his chair. Waiting for his soup to cool, Romeo fixes his attention on the news. More yellowcake uranium powders. Italian what? Military Intelligence. What? Apparently Saddam has purchased Niger uranium powders, yellowcake uranium powders, which look like what they sound like, yellowcakey powders used for nuclear weapons. Then McCain comes on and Romeo puts the spoon back. McCain says that Saddam is a clear and present danger and that his pursuit to acquire weapons of mass destruction leads McCain to have very little doubt that Saddam would use them.

Romeo nods and vacuums in the noodles, along with these words. McCain has suffered and survived. McCain knows whereof he speaks. Romeo loves to say that name, so cowboy. McCain would never put the young people of American reasonlessly in harm's way. Romeo upends the cooled pot, drinking the soup dregs.

The file he took such pains to steal remains in his tribal security conference bag. Just before settling into a concocted dream state, Romeo remembers. He pulls the bag over to his mattress and switches on the cock-eyed lamp. He pulls out the paper and glances over the coroner's report on the accident that occurred just about three years ago, on the reservation side of the boundary line only by a few dozen yards. His eyes cross. He's barely following the letters. He knows anyway what's in it, knows from the conversations he has pieced together on his bulletin board, knows just what happened, can see what happened, if he wants to, in his mind. But he doesn't want to. Who could. He shoves away the document, the black bag, the responsibility that he has assumed. He shoves away the fact that his country sounds like war. Then suddenly, halfway into a dream, he gets it.

There is more than they dare say. More the carotid than the femoral, more than these tubes and cakes. Condoleezza, her eyes glitter when she says the word *cavort* as in *cavort with terrorists*. The image of Saddam cavorting when the Holy Towers were destroyed. They know something they won't tell the public. Don't want panic. McCain knows what it is. McCain must think the Towers were only the beginning. Behind all the flimsy bits of pretend truth there must be a real truth so terrible it would cause a stock market crash. But what if that truth is some kind of bubble truth? What if behind the truth, there is nothing but a heap of pride or money or just stuff?

Romeo has seen the havoc that occurs when commodities of all sorts are going bad and people need to use them fast—in cafeteria the strange amount of celery, the overflow of tapioca, in clinic the medications, so useful but of fragile potency past a certain month. What if.

What if there is a use-by date on a heap of war stuff?

THE BREAKS

In his single bed with his head resting on one hard polyester-fill pillow, Father Travis tries to sleep. Under a woolen Pendleton, a flashy turquoise Chief Joseph blanket he was given by the Iron family when he blessed the vows of Landreaux and Emmaline, he gives up. He opens his eyes and stares into a soft-sifting darkness that seems to rise and fall in the room.

No trappings of authority, no special hotline to God, he tries to pray. He has been through so many definitions of his God now that he has to scroll around to find one to address. First there was fervent protector of his childhood, the God of kindliness. Then there was a blank space where he did not think of God and trained his body to act in the service of his country.

God resumed as the unknowable exacting force that allowed a bomb to take his friends' lives but gave a thin boy the power to rescue Travis. Afterward, there was the God who spoke one night about fractured mercy, waters of being, incline of radiance. He was invited to a conference attended by immortals, who spoke to him and dressed his arms with colored ribbons. Scarlet and blue whizzed and yellows ruptured, spilling brilliance through the room. That was pain in West Germany. But he was somewhere else, from time to time, watching the familiar body on the white sheets. *Oh, you should have been a priest.* He was sure he'd heard those words from the mouth of God, in the hospital, but later he realized that his mother might have said this as she prayed beside him before he came back alive, before he entered a drabber, more monotonous daily agony.

Was there a Polish God? The God of sausage and pierogi. A mystical, shrewd, earth-dwelling God who always took things hard. His parents' God, the one they'd left him with not long after he was ordained. Having seen him back into his life, they'd felt that it was all right to leave, he'd guessed, because bam bam, a stroke, a fatal disease, and they were out of existence.

You should stop making Gods up, imagining them as a human would imagine a God, he says to himself, again. Address your prayers to the nothingness, the nonfigurative, abstract, indifferent power, the ever-so-useful higher power. Talk to the unknowable. The ineffable author of all forms. Father Travis finally dozes thinking of all the trees, all the birds, all the mountains, all the rivers, all the seas, the love, all the goodness, all the apple blossoms falling on the wind, then the dust of the world swirling up and falling, the stillness on the waters before it all began.

Father Travis bolts up, slumps over, head in hands.

It is over, he thinks.

In the morning, there will be a call from the Most Reverend Florian Soreno, His Excellency, Bishop Soreno, who will tell Father Travis what he already knows.

THE FEARSOME Four still meet, only now they really are fearsome. They get together in Tyler's garage. They have another electric guitar to compete with the old one. Their noise is louder and they smoke weed, drink beer, share cigarettes, talk. They have girlfriends, but only Buggy's lets him do everything he wants. He tells them all about it, and the other boys save his stories in their heads. They have not forgotten Maggie, but it's different with her. She beat on them!

Back then, they respected her. Now when they think about it, they'd like to kind of dominate her. Show her. They got big and she stayed spindly. The way it goes. But then, she's unpredictable and quick. Her nut kicks now living on in legend. Buggy had to get some outpatient surgery. His parents considered sending the doctor bills to Peter and Nola Ravich. But Buggy didn't want everyone to know. Also, Maggie's family is now associated with those Irons from the reservation. Maggie's got her danger girl Indian sisters, Josette and Snow. The Fearsome Four are much aware. Yes, those girls go to another school but they could come right over with a posse, ambush their asses, no problem and there's those older brothers, Coochy and the one who worked in construction, Hollis—ripped dudes. Bummer though it is, Maggie is off-limits unless one of them gets ridiculously high. They hardly even talk about her, except for sometimes, in low voices, wondering if she ever told anyone about what they did.

It didn't go too far, anyway.

Nothin' nothin' really. We never crossed, you know, a line there.

For sure. No line was crossed. Was it?

Dude, we hardly touched her. She just got mad for no real fucken reason!

Will you guys get off it? That was so long ago. Nobody remembers. Nobody cares.

Anyway, says Buggy, she wanted it and she still wants it.

The other boys are silent, taking in this line of reasoning. They all nod, except Brad, who stares off into the air like he hasn't heard them. Though he has for sure heard what they said, he is Christian, and that doesn't sound right at all.

Block. Punch. Side kick. Knife-hand. Block. Punch-Punch. Snap kick. Block. Block. Poor kid, thinks Emmaline, LaRose's got Landreaux's exact nose, okay on an adult but too big for a boy's face. Yet he is a handsome kid. And those eyelashes. Landreaux's, again wasted. Expressive brows. His sisters shouldn't put makeup on him, but they do. A year's growth and he won't let them. Maybe Emmaline should stop them now.

Father Travis stands beside her. She rises from her chair.

He wasn't going to speak of it. He was going to make a simple announcement. Next Sunday Mass. Or the Sunday after. But—

I'm being transferred.

Leaving.

Yes.

Her gaze is fully fixed on him.

When?

I'll help the next priest for a few months. After that,
I go.

Where?

I don't exactly know yet.

He laughs uncomfortably. Mutters something about
a new line of work.

Emmaline turns away, and when she turns back,
Father Travis is unnerved to see that she might be
crying. It is hard to tell, because she's talking at the
same time as tears well up and disappear without spilling. Father Travis knows that Emmaline rarely weeps.
When she cried on that terrible day in his office, it was
a rent soul leaking quietly, eclipsed by Landreaux's
tearing sobs. She tries to speak but she is incoher-
ent, which undoes him. Even when emotional she has
always made sense before. Emmaline shakes her hair
across her face, creases her brows, bites her lips, tries
to hold back words, then blurts out nonsense. Father
Travis listens hard, trying to understand, but he is
rocked by her emotion. She stops.

I'm blubbering! I'm having trouble absorbing this.
You've always been here and you've done so much.

Priests blow through here, but you've stayed. People love you . . .

She looks down at the balled-up tissues in her hand, not knowing how the clump got from her purse to her hand, stunned that this wave of language poured out of her and what did she say?

What did I say?

I don't know, but I've fallen in love with you, says Father Travis.

She sits down hard in the plastic chair.

Behind them, LaRose is still practicing his forms. Punching air with increasing ferocity, so he doesn't hear. Everyone else is gone, so nobody sees the priest kneeling before her, offering the large white handkerchief he keeps on his person for out-of-office emergencies. Emmaline puts the square of white cloth on her face, holds it to her temples, and cries beneath it. There is no question now. She is really crying beneath the handkerchief. Father Travis waits for a sign. This is what he began doing when he was a soldier. This is what he has been doing ever since he became a priest. Kneeling, waiting for a sign, comes so naturally to him now that he hardly notices. He focuses on not taking back or apologizing for what he just said. He leaves it all with Emmaline.

That's not fair, says Emmaline from beneath the cloth.

LaRose is still fighting invisible foes. Kicking the practice dummy so hard it tips and rolls. This one's for Tyler, then Curtains Peace, another donkey kick for Brad. LaRose whirls to punch Buggy. They blast backward from the force of his attack. They land stunned, writhing on the mats, try to bumble away. One sneaks up from behind. LaRose can see behind his back! Wham. Cronk. Lights out.

❧

HOW DOES an eight-year-old boy find out where high school boys hang out? White ones? In an off-reservation town? There is a long highway between them, and a lack of access deep as a ravine. He asks Coochy, but his brother doesn't know who they are at all. He asks Josette, but she doesn't care to answer. Or, is there some reason she raises her eyebrows? As does Snow. They keep their eyebrows up together, staring at him in a creepy way like they are frozen, until he backs out of the room.

He asks Hollis.

Those assholes? Why?

LaRose doesn't have an answer.

Did one of those guys do something to you?

No.

Sounds like maybe something happened.

No.

Come on. You can tell me.

Nothing happened.

So why're you asking?

I just wondered.

Okay, so nothing happened. Then there's nothing you need to know about those guys except avoid their asses.

Sure.

I mean it. Hollis watches LaRose closely as he walks out of their bedroom. It's weird that a little boy would ask about those guys—about Curtains, that freakin' jerk who tried to hit on Snow by asking if she wanted to go for a drive in his rusted-out conversion van. Or Buggy, that Indian-hating blackout who walked by Waylon after they trashed the Pluto team in football and called Waylon blackout and Waylon laughed and put the hammer on Buggy and Buggy yelped to his friends, He's scalpin' me! Blanket Ass is scalpin' me! And, because he might have killed Buggy and gone to jail, Waylon slung him away and got into his car.

And so on. Tyler, or was it Buggy, one of those guys once called Josette a squaw, so Josette is already intent

on killing him, or them, any one of them, but Hollis
wants to get there first.

GETTING A block or spiking from anywhere was all
about jumping, crucial if you were not tall.

That's what Coach Duke told Maggie.

Out in the barn, Peter marked a stall post with chalk.
In the beginning, the height she could jump, reaching up with her arms, took her only a couple of inches
above an imaginary net. But every week, she gained a
tiny fraction. Coach Duke noticed.

Hey, Ravich, come over here, he said after practice.
You've put a few inches on your jump. Are you practicing?

She told him about her chalked post. He gave her
jumping exercises.

He showed her squats, ankle bounces, step-ups, and
his favorite, the four-star-box drill. Coach Duke's heart
beat to inspire. It tuned him up when kids worked at
getting better. That Maggie had set herself these personal goals, improving her jump to make up for height,
got Coach Duke so happy that he called her parents
that same night.

Peter answered, and when the coach said who he was Peter's stomach clutched, sure that Maggie was getting kicked off the team. But no, this was a good call. The first good call about Maggie that her parents had ever received.

Every night after school, now, she got a pass from setting the table. Peter and LaRose set the table as long as Maggie went out to the barn to do her exercises and jumps. The dog sat in the doorway concentrating on her pogo leaps. At first it was hard to jump for five minutes. Then hard to jump for ten. Then fifteen, twenty. Dark came early. She turned on the barn light and massaged her legs. It got cold. She wore a parka and sweatpants to keep her legs warm, so they wouldn't seize with cramps. Her muscles became hard springs. She practiced serves—running, leaping, at the height of her leap punching the ball just so, at the dog, who politely stepped aside and never got beaned.

Once, as she vaulted toward the dog, she thought that if she'd had a knife sharp enough, and with the height she could now achieve, she could have jumped up and cut the rope. *Her mother falls, gagging. Maggie kicks her in despair.* Maggie saw it all happen. Then she heard her mother call.

Turn out the barn light. Come in. Come in now, Maggie. It's dinnertime. Your food is getting cold.

OLD STORY 2

Mewinzha, mewinzha, said Ignatia, right after the first soft snow securely blanketed off the living from the dead. Long time ago. This was before the beginning of time. In those days everything could talk and people had powers. At that time, there was a man living in the woods with his wife and his two little boys. They lived good on what they had; they were doing okay. But then the man noticed, when he was getting ready to go out and hunt, his wife was putting on her whitest skin dress, her quill and bone earrings, all her beautiful things. The first time he thought that she was preparing herself for him, but when he returned with meat on his toboggan, he saw that she was wearing her old clothes again. He was jealous. The next time he prepared to go hunting, she put on her finery the same way. But he doubled back. He hid himself, and when she left their boys behind and went out into the woods, in her fancy clothing, he followed her secretly.

This man's wife goes up to a tree. He watches her. She strikes the tree three times. Out of the tree comes a snake. A big one. Yes, a big snake. The wife and the snake begin to love each other up then. The man sees his woman and the snake together and oh my, she loves that snake better than she ever loved her husband.

Don't talk bad!

Oh, shut up, Malvern.

The two women frowned at each other, and at last Malvern nicked her head at LaRose, made some motions with her lips that Ignatia interpreted.

See here, LaRose, the snake and woman they want to hold hands but the snake don't have any hands. They want to kiss but the snake don't have any lips. They just have to twine around together.

Ignatia moved her arms around to show LaRose how this could happen.

What kind of story is this? asks LaRose

A sacred one, Ignatia says.

Ohhhh-kayyyyy . . . LaRose has learned the okay of a skeptical eight-year-old from wise-ass sitcom eight-year-old boys.

I know this story, said Malvern. It is a frightful story. Not a good story to tell a young boy.

Maybe, said Ignatia. But it is a story of existence. This boy can know it; he is brave enough.

She went on telling the story.

The man was very jealous of the snake. So the next day he went hunting, and when he came back he said to his wife that he had killed a bear. He told her to go and fetch the meat. When she was gone, he put on a skirt and went to the serpent tree. He struck the tree three times, and the serpent appeared. Then he stuck his spear through the serpent, killing it dead. He brought the snake back to his lodge, cut that snake into pieces, and made that snake into snake soup.

Snake soup?

Yes, my boy.

They ate snake soup in the olden times?

The old women frowned at each other.

Ignatia said that in the olden times the kids had no TVs. They just shut up and listened to stories and didn't interrupt.

Malvern said that his question was good and she would answer it.

They ate the snake soup just this one time, she said.

Okay, said LaRose. I mean, I had to ask. It's unusual.

So moving on with the story, said Ignatia. When the woman finally returned, she said that there was no dead bear in the place he'd told her to go. There was no meat. She had searched, but found nothing. Her husband told her not to worry because he'd made soup.

Wait, said LaRose. Made soup out of the snake she . . .

Loved, yes, said Ignatia.

That's like . . .

Point of the story, said Malvern.

Did she eat it? LaRose stared at them, pained.

Ignatia nodded.

Oh, said LaRose. This just gets worse.

IT'S NOT much of a life, said Ottie in the car. But it's something.

This dialysis makes people crazy, Landreaux said, but you're holding up good.

I'da checked out if it wasn't for Bap.

She loves you.

People who were chronically ill either dulled out and watched TV or cut to the chase in surprising ways, Landreaux found. The dulled-out ones were easier. But Ottie had been asking these questions and was so pleasant and forgiving that it was, almost, possible to tell the truth.

We're in love. The good stuff lasted, said Landreaux. For me.

I get it, said Ottie.

I'm like you, Ottie. Probably check out if not for her. That don't go both ways. He laughed, but it was a heart-worn laugh.

Emmaline would not check out if he did; she would survive for the kids. For herself. Also, the good stuff was in question. Emmaline had put a wall up, Landreaux thought. He even pictured it—brick but at least there were gaps, maybe windows. Sometimes she reached both hands through, unclenched, and Landreaux hurriedly clasped her from the lonely side. He understood the wall as blame for what happened. He did not understand when she said he was asleep. His eyes were open. He was driving. He was pulling up in Ottie's driveway.

Landreaux got Ottie into the house and settled by the window, where Bap had put a bird feeder. Landreaux went out and refilled the empty feeder. He could hear winter in the sharper scolding of the chickadees. After he got into the car, he thought of the two oxycodones in his pocket. He'd skimmed them off one of the new prescriptions he'd filled for Ottie. Only two. He'd throw them out. But he didn't. He drove home. Was this a night he had to drive anybody anyplace? No. He plucked out the one pill. Swallowed. Only one, hardly anything. This would barely mellow him, still.

You resist and resist and resist and wear yourself down. For all these years he had been substance free, but lately, well, this summer, the deterioration of his clients and the helplessness of waiting for Emmaline's touch further diminished him. That was an excuse. He should be stronger. He'd made the Stations of the Cross last spring and wondered why Christ's torture was called his passion. Jesus suffered drug free. He'd seen Emmaline go through drugless childbirth. She wanted drugs but only got lucky with Josette. Twice the trusted, competent anesthetist was not on duty at the IHS hospital. She didn't want a bad spinal, an everlasting epidural or headache. Without one, the pain took up everything, she said. When she went to visit friends in the maternity ward, the smell of the place made her blood pressure shoot up, her hands shake. Light-headed, she had to sit. Some physical memory. But all worth it, she said, as women always did.

Maybe Jesus thought so too, Landreaux thought as he walked toward the house. Or maybe he looked at all the sorry-ass fuckups he saved, like Landreaux, who couldn't stand the pain, and said, Why?

Landreaux resolved to flush the other pill down the toilet. He heard shouts. When he walked in the door, Snow and Josette were slapping open-handed, blocking each other. At least they weren't punching or pulling each other's hair. He kicked his boots off and stepped between them.

He grabbed each girl by one wrist but they reached around him with their flapping hands. Finally they quit, sullenly ripped their arms free, and agreed to talk from opposite corners of the room. Josette stuck her lower lip out, slumped, arms crossed. Her foot jiggled. Snow sat knock-kneed looking at her orange-glow fingernails.

What's the deal? said Landreaux.

Snow says I like Hollis.

Well he likes you, said Snow.

So?

He's my brother. It's gross.

Josette drew her arm back and made a fist. There was a face drawn on her fist. Lips where her thumb met her crooked forefinger. A nose and eyes, too. Snow lifted her arm and made a fist. A face was also on her fist. She kept her teeth clenched and barely moved her lips.

You have no DNA in common. You grew up together and he still likes you—bedhead, bad breath, gray old underwear in the laundry—it's a miracle.

I have never let my underwear be seen, said Josette, with considerable dignity. And it is not gray.

Stop, begged Landreaux. His head was softly ringing.

Josette collected herself.

I suppose we can talk about this like mature adults? she said.

There's only one in the room, said Landreaux.

In the first place, said Josette, I know Hollis has a crush on me. That's immaterial.

I'm gonna go nuts, said Landreaux.

Because I don't have a crush on him, Josette said. Who knows, I might be a lesbian.

Like you'd even know, said Snow.

Landreaux's heart muttered. Lesbian?

You guys don't KNOW me, said Josette.

Okay, said Snow. Nobody KNOWS you. You're SO mysterious.

You know me, said Josette to her balled-up hand. I can tell you everything!

I love you for yourself, said her smeared fist.

Get outta here, said Landreaux. You're making me loco. I want to make myself some coffee and read my paper.

Like you always do! Josette and Snow, a team again, jumped up and rushed him. You're so predictable. Why can't you bust loose? Drink tea? Read a comic! C'mon, Daddy, be creative!

They knew they could make him laugh, and when he did they attacked him, jumping on him, pretending to fling him on the floor. He fake fell, cowered in a dramatic I-give-up, hands in the air.

Mercy! He begs for mercy! Show him no mercy, growled Snow and began to fake punch him so he fake reeled back, holding his stomach, laughing until the girls left him on the floor.

Okay, Daddy, try to pull yourself together. Go do your wander. Or here's a newspaper full of want ads. Or boring news. Just don't TELL us about every boring thing that happens in the tristate area. We'll go make you that weak coffee you like to guzzle. We're gonna cook, too. We got some meatball meat. Noodles. Mushroom soup. You'll flip.

Landreaux sat back in his chair. His back ached from lifting Ottie, rolling, bathing, seating Ottie. Then it didn't ache. The pain left. His heart rate slowed. He didn't mind anything now. This was the first time in a long time he'd goofed off, let the girls wrestle him down. He felt lighter, almost happy, and he didn't need the other pill, but after Snow brought him a cup of coffee, he felt his fingers tease it from his pocket. Then it slipped from his fingers, onto the floor. Some better person tried to crush it with his heel. But the heel was in a sock and the pill was coated with a hard-ening agent, which resisted until Landreaux walked over to the entry, got his boot, and hammered the thing to powder. Even then, on the vinyl tiling, there was a perfect little patch of whiteness, which, if he went down in a yoga crouch, nose to the floor, he could inhale. But how would that look to his girls, ass in the air? He sat down again and swirled his foot around on the powder until it was absorbed into the floor so that the desperate man would have to put his nose to the ball of the foot of the sock and sniff the powder out with mighty whiffs and he was safe, yes safe, because Landreaux had taken this process down too far a level even for himself.

ONE DAY LaRose closed in. He had written down the last names of the Fearsomes and narrowed down their probable locations from a telephone book. He lied again, got a ride from Peter, who dropped him off in Pluto to visit a friend whom LaRose ditched after an hour. The town was small, some blocks now bull-dozed clear of houses that had collapsed. Empty. It wasn't hard to find the various houses after all, but he was looking for the one with the garage that Maggie had once described. When he saw the Veddars' garage, and looked in the window, he knew that was the place. He walked in the side door. Nobody was there, so he decided to wait. He fell asleep on the broken couch. When he opened his eyes, it was Tyler shaking him.

LaRose lets his punch fly—he's been dreaming of it.

Ow! Tyler steps back, puzzled, rubbing his jaw. Why'd you do that?

LaRose leaps up on the couch. They are all there! He channels Maggie's claw hand moves, hears Father Travis's shout in class: Loud kiap! Loud kiap. To strike fear into the enemy.

LaRose gives his choking war cry. Kiap! Then another, more confident. Ready stance! Heart rammed in his throat, pulses thudding.

Why'd you do that? Tyler turns to the others. He socked me!

For Maggie!

Buggy has snapped a beer open. Maggie! Hatred warps his face. He's the meanest. Brad Morrissey is the biggest, but he isn't mean at all anymore, except in football. He has certain codes of honor now, because of Jesus and football. He only kills people in football. And Curtains is just confused.

What's your name, little kid?

LaRose launches himself onto Curtains's back, climbs his shirt, tries a choke hold.

Get him off me!

Accidentally, but on purpose, Buggy slaps LaRose so hard that he flies off Curtains and lands on his back. When LaRose hits the floor with a violent smack, he bounces out of his body. His lungs squeeze shut. He is hovering above, looking down at himself in wonder.

Brad is bending over LaRose, concerned. Why'd you do that, Buggy? He's, like, not breathing.

LaRose hovers, watching to see if he'll take a breath. Freedom, buoyancy, repose. Oh yes, and take that breath before Brad gives him mouth-to-mouth. As soon as he fills his lungs, LaRose is sucked back into his body with a gentle thhhhpppp. He lies still until he's sure he's intact. He stands up, dusts off his pants, picks up his backpack, and leaves. He means to walk home, but Brad Morrissey insists on giving him a ride. They say not one word until the Ravich driveway.

The way you defended your sister was awesome, says Brad.

LaRose turns and knife-hands Brad on the nose, drawing blood. Then he gets out of the car.

You should go out for football someday, calls Brad as he pulls out, mopping at his face. LaRose walks into the house, up the stairs to his room. He needs to be alone. Something has happened.

✦

THERE ARE five LaRoses. First the LaRose who poisoned Mackinnon, went to mission school, married Wolfred, taught her children the shape of the world, and traveled that world as a set of stolen bones. Second, her daughter LaRose, who went to Carlisle. This LaRose got tuberculosis like her own mother, and like the first LaRose fought it off again and again. Lived long enough to become the mother of the third LaRose, who went to Fort Totten and bore the fourth LaRose, who eventually became the mother of Emmaline, the teacher of Romeo and Landreaux. The fourth LaRose also became the grandmother of the last LaRose, who was given to the Ravich family by his parents in exchange for a son accidentally killed.

In all of these LaRoses there was a tendency to fly above the earth. They could fly for hours when the right songs were drummed and sung to support them. Those songs are now waiting in the leaves, half lost, but the drumming of the water drum will never be lost. This ability to fly went back to the first LaRose, whose mother taught her to do it when her name was still Mirage, and who had learned this from her father, a jiisikid conjurer, who'd flung his spirit all the way around the world in 1798 and come back to tell his astonished drummers that it was no use, white people covered the earth like lice.

OLD STORY 3

What tastes so good? This was the man's wife asking.

The blood of your husband, the snake. I have made him into broth, said the husband.

The woman was furious and ran to the tree where her snake lived. She knocked three times, but it did not emerge and she knew it was killed. While she was gone, her husband plunged the two little boys into the ground, for safety.

That doesn't sound very safe, said LaRose.

This time Ignatia didn't answer, just kept on with the story.

When the woman ran back, her husband cut off her head. Then he rose into the air to flee away into the sky.

How could he do that? asked LaRose.

In those olden old days, said Ignatia, remember, before this earth existed, those people had all kinds of power. They could talk to anything and it would answer.

I mean how could he cut off her head, said LaRose.

But Ignatia had resolved to ignore all questions.

After a while, said Ignatia, the woman's head opened its eyes.

Scary, said LaRose, with respect.

The head asked the dish where her children were. She asked all of the belongings in the lodge, but they would not tell. At last a stone did tell her that her husband had sunk the children into the earth, and that now they were fleeing underground. The stone said that he had given them four things—power to make a river, fire, a mountain, a forest of thorns.

So the head began to follow those children. It cried out, *My children, wait for me! You are making me cry by leaving me!*

Ignatia's voice was wicked and wheedling. LaRose looked aghast but leaned closer.

Really scary, he said. Keep going.

The little boy was riding on his big brother's back, and he kept telling his little brother that the head was not really their mother. Yes it is! Yes it is! said the little brother.

My children, my dear children, do not leave me behind, called the head. *I beg you!*

The little brother wanted to go back to the mother, but the older brother took a piece of punk wood and threw it behind him, calling out, Let there be fire!

Far and wide, a fire blazed. But the head kept rolling through fire and began to catch up with them.

The boy threw down a thorn. At once a forest of thorns sprang up, and this time the rolling head was really blocked. But the head called to the brother of the snake, the Great Serpent, and that serpent bit through those thorn trees and made a passage. So it managed to catch up with him.

The brother threw down a stone and up sprang a vast mountain. Yet that rolling head got a beaver with iron teeth to chew down that mountain, and it kept on pursuing the children.

The brothers were very tired by now and threw down a skin of water to make a river. By mistake it landed not behind them, but in front of them. Now they were trapped.

LaRose nodded, caught in the story.

But the Great Serpent took pity on them and let them onto his back. They went across the river. When the rolling head reached the river, it begged to be carried across. The Great Serpent allowed the head to roll onto its back, but halfway across the serpent dumped it off.

Sturgeon will be your name, said the Great Serpent. The head became the first sturgeon.

What is a sturgeon? asked LaRose.

It's an ugly kind of fish, said Ignatia. Those fish were the buffalo of our people once. They still have them up in the big northern lakes and the rivers.

Okay, said LaRose. So that's the end?

No. Those two boys wandered around and by accident, the younger boy was left behind. He was all alone.

Now I must turn into a wolf, said the little boy.

That's interesting, said LaRose. Just to become a wolf.

When his older brother found him, then the two walked together. This older brother became a being who could do many things—some places he is known as Wishketchahk, some as Nanabozho, and he has other names. He was kind of foolish, but also very wise, and his little brother the wolf was always by his side. He made the first people, Anishinaabeg, the first humans.

Huh, said LaRose. So what's the moral of this story?

Moral? Our stories don't have those!

Ignatia puffed her cheeks in annoyance.

They call this an origin story, said Malvern, also annoyed, but precise.

Like, ah, like Genesis, said Ignatia. But there's lots more that happens, including a little muskrat who makes the earth.

And our Nanabozho, he's like their Jesus, said Malvern.

Kind of like Jesus, said Ignatia. But always farting.

So the rolling head's like his mom, Mary? And this whole story is like the first story in the Bible?

You could say that.

So our Mary is a rolling head.

A *vicious* rolling head, said Ignatia.

We are so cool, said LaRose. Still, getting chased like that. Maybe caught. Maybe slammed on the ground. Getting your wind knocked out.

It is *about* getting chased, said Ignatia, with a long suck on her oxygen. We are chased into this life. The Catholics think we are chased by devils, original sin. We are chased by things done to us in this life.

That's called trauma, said Malvern.

Thank *you*, said Ignatia. We are chased by what we do to others and then in turn what they do to us. We're always looking behind us, or worried about what comes next. We only have this teeny moment. Oops, it's gone!

What's gone?

Now. Oops, gone again.

Ignatia and Marvern laughed until Ignatia gasped for breath. Oops! Oops! Slippery!

What's gone?

Now.

Oops, laughed LaRose, slipped past!

And then, just like that, Ignatia died. She gave them a glowing look and her feet kicked straight out. Her head fell back. Her jaw relaxed. Malvern leaned over and with her nurse's paw pressed the pulse on Ignatia's neck. Malvern looked aside, frowning, waiting, and at last took her hand from Ignatia's throat, pushed Ignatia's jaw back up, and pulled down her eyelids. She then cradled Ignatia's hand.

Take her other hand, said Malvern. She's starting out on her journey now. Remember everything I say, LaRose. This will be your job sometime.

Malvern talked to Ignatia, telling her the directions, how to take the first steps, how to look to the west, where to find the road, and not to bother taking anyone along. She said that everybody, even herself, Malvern, who had never told her, loved Ignatia very much. They held Ignatia's hands for a long time, quietly, until the hands were no longer warm. Still, LaRose felt her presence in the room.

She'll be around here for a while more, said Malvern. I'm going to get her friends so they can say good-bye too. You go on home now.

LaRose placed Ignatia's hand upon the armrest of her chair. He put on his coat, walked out the door, down the hall. He went through the airlock doors, then out the double front doors, into the navy-blue frost-haloed air. He was supposed to meet his mother at the school, so he walked along the gravel road and crossed the uncertain pavement, the buckled curb. The cold flowed around him and down the neck of his jacket. His ears stung, but he didn't put his hood up. He moved his fingers, shoved in his pockets. There were so many sensations in his body that he couldn't feel them all at once, and each, as soon as he felt it, slipped away into the past.

THE PICTURE diagram on Romeo's wall was slowly taking shape, with bits of information plucked forward or pushed back. Romeo's television had lost sound, but no matter. He only watched the mouths move and read the closed captions. It was better because otherwise their voices, the emphasis they put on certain words, could distort his thinking. He still liked the word *yellowcake*, and the unknowable place it was from. Niger! But already they were past that. As bright October shifted to the leafless icy dark of November, there was scarier talk of weapons of mass destruction.

Oh please! Everybody in North Dakota lived next door to a weapon of mass destruction. Right down the road, a Minuteman missile stored in its underground silo was marked only by a square of gravel and a chain-link fence above. You passed, wondering who was down there, deep and solitary, insane of course, staring at a screen the way Romeo was staring now, at the mouth of Condoleezza Rice and knowing, as nobody else but Romeo knew, that this was a hungry woman who strictly controlled her appetites. This was a woman so much more intelligent than any of the men around her that she played them with her concert hands like chopsticks on her piano. Even Bulgebrow Cheney with his frighteningly bad teeth—and he must have millions so why could he not get new teeth—even Cheney was her mental slave. Didn't know it, but he was. Her eyes glittered. Her mouth a deep blood red. She had no feelings for any man. She ate them. Talked of rods. Smoking guns.

Romeo adored her.

Of them all, she was the smartest and most presidential. Could they see it?

From his pockets, he emptied the night's take onto a cafeteria tray. He went through it meticulously now, pushed aside tiny blue pills, fat white pills, round green pills, oval pink pills. He was quite sure that another clue was hidden in the story he'd heard just that evening about the way a person bled to death from only surface wounds. That fit into the findings somehow. A tack. A placement. A string that would attach the phrase and the possible meaning. He'd cross-medicate, then medicate. It was beautiful, like an art project, this thing he was doing.

MAGGIE BADGERED her mother into teaching her how to drive to school. Nola instantly got used to it. Every morning, after her father left, Maggie went out and started the Jeep. Nola put a long puffy coat on over her robe, thrust her sleepy bare feet into Peter's felt-lined Sorels. With a thermos go-cup of coffee in hand, she settled comfortably into the passenger's seat. LaRose took the backseat. On the half-hour drive, it was Nola's job to make encouraging noises and dial through the radio channels, finding the Hallelujah stations. Rush rants. Perky pop and stolid farm reports. It woke Nola up, freed her from the sticky webs of benzodiazepines. The radio and its familiar chaos flipped a pleasure switch in Maggie's brain. Because she had her mother belted in safe beside her and LaRose safe in back, because she was in charge, she was light with relief. She hummed and tapped her fingers on the wheel. Through snow, through black ice, slippery cold rain, Maggie was a fully confident and careful driver.

When she got to the school drop-off, her mother kissed her dreamily, then walked around to slip behind the wheel and drive home. Maggie let her go. She let LaRose go. She walked down the high school hallway, flipped her hair, and now said hi to many girls. She called home sometimes, from the school office, just to hear her mother's voice. On one hand, Maggie was now a stable, caring, overprotective daughter—adjusting slowly to the fear smother of her mother's fragility. On the other, she was still a piece of work.

A disciplined piece of work.

She was cute in an early-supermodel-Cheryl-Tiegs way except her hair was dark, her eyes either gold or black, and except that sometimes there was hot contempt in her skewed gaze. She made it her business to study boys. How their heads, hearts, and bodies worked. She didn't want one, but she could see herself controlling one. Maybe each of the so-called Fearsome Four, hunt them down, skewer their hearts. Have them for lunch although she was trying to be a vegetarian—because good for the skin. She was strict with herself.

Somehow, hulky Waylon got past all that. He stood by her locker and watched her exchange a set of books—morning books for afternoon books.

So are you okay here? Anybody bothering you?

She found it surprising that he would ask her this question, and weirder than that, she answered yes. Though nobody had bothered her at all.

Waylon's interestingly lush features focused. He had an Elvis-y face, which Maggie knew only because Snow actually liked that old music. He was thick and broad, with soft skin over cruel football muscle. His hands were innocent, expressive, almost teacherly. His summer football practice crew cut was growing out into a thick fuzzy allover cap of furlike hair. He was taller than Josette but not quite as tall as Snow. Maggie stared at his hair intently, then decided that she liked his hair, a lot.

Waylon's look had turned somber.

Who? he said at last.

What?

Who bothered you?

It wasn't kids here, said Maggie. It was kids at my old school.

He nodded gravely, without speaking. He let his face talk, lowering his brows to let her know he was waiting for more. Maggie liked that, too.

There's some guys, call themselves the Fearsome Four?

Waylon's jaw slid sideways and his teeth came out sharply, gripping his bottom lip. He leaned his head to the side and squinted his sleepy eyes.

Ohhh yeahhh, he drawled. I know those guys.

Those guys bothered me real bad, said Maggie with a comfortable, bright smile. Especially Buggy. Wanna walk me to class?

Waylon swayed slightly as he walked, as if his heavy body needed to be set upright after every step. With Maggie beside him, so tensely pretty and purposeful, people looking at them, shy pleasure made him blush.

Whenever Nola and Peter had gone to teacher conferences at Maggie's school in Pluto, it was the same: careless homework, trouble in the classroom, mouthing off, probably she wrote the c-word in a bathroom stall. However, test scores always perfect. That meant she was smart enough to change her behavior, if she wanted to. Clearly it was all on purpose, said her teachers. Peter had always left Maggie's classroom gasping for control. Nola was silent, clutching his arm, her lips moving. They would walk unsteadily down the hall. After LaRose started school in Pluto, however, LaRose's teachers had consistently erased Maggie's distressing reviews.

Ah, LaRose! Maybe not an A student, but a worker, quiet, and so kind. Respectful, easygoing, pleasant, a little shy. Those eyelashes! What a sweet boy. Dreamy sometimes. And accomplished! He could draw anything he wanted. Sang, off-key but with expression. A talent show favorite with Johnny Cash tunes, the boy in black. Just a love, the teachers gushed, he makes it all worthwhile. They knew the teachers meant worthwhile dealing with Maggie, how the struggle for her soul was worth the effort once they got to LaRose.

Maybe things would be different now that Maggie was in ninth grade. Now that she had more freedom. Now that her whole other family—Hollis, Snow, Josette, Willard, and LaRose—was in her new school also.

Peter and Nola each ate a tasteless cookie from the plates set out in the hallway. They sipped scorched coffee waiting for the first teacher to finish with the parents before them. At last they entered the classroom.

If she's trying to find her footing here by kicking in doors, that's not an appropriate choice, said Germaine Miller, English teacher.

I am trying my hardest not to fail her, because I can tell she's bright, said Social Studies.

If only she would do her homework! Cal Dorfman shook his head over math scores.

Nola explained that Maggie did math homework every night. Peter said he'd even tried to check it but she was so independent now. The three looked from one to another in distress. The teacher sighed and said that Maggie probably didn't turn her homework in because she lacked organizational skills. From now on he would stop the class every day until she coughed up a homework paper. So it went.

Except for Physical Science. Mr. Hossel gave a pallid smile when they introduced themselves. But Mr. Hossel was already talking about what a hardworking daughter they had and how they must be extremely proud of her deductive skills, her logical mind, her disciplined approach to handing in homework and how well she worked on group projects. She seemed fascinated by the laws of motion, for instance, and she was excellent at calculating speed.

Nola gaped, Peter flushed. Mr. Hossel grew more animated.

She is *super* eloquent describing the electromagnetic spectrum, he cried.

We are Maggie Ravich's parents, they reminded Mr. Hossel.

The science teacher scratched his hands, poked at his glasses, and went on.

I wish more students were like Maggie in terms of class participation. What impresses me is that she's fearless. Shrugs off mistakes. That's unusual in a young person—they are terrified of being laughed at— you know this age! But Maggie will play with an idea. Throw something out to spark discussion. At what exact moment does inertia become momentum? *Can we measure that moment?* It goes to the heart of everything, said Mr. Hossel with a pensive sniff.

Again he repeated those golden words: You must be very proud of your daughter.

Then he showed them her A.

Peter and Nola beamed out of Mr. Hossel's classroom. They crossed the parking lot holding hands, brought together by the contradictions.

Finally, a teacher who *gets* her, Peter said.

He really was . . .

Nola faltered.

He really *was* talking about Maggie, wasn't he?

Maybe at school, she only shows her real self to him, Peter answered. She trusts Hossel the way she trusts us.

I see all of those things in her, the bravery, you know? The discipline. This teacher has just opened some door for her. I don't understand, honey, but with this experience the sky's the limit! She always had it in her, didn't she. Always had it.

We weren't wrong.

Nola clutched his hand tighter. They got into the car and drove home, silent, Nola gripping Peter's knee.

As they pulled into the driveway, Maggie opened the door, waving with a happy smile. Usually, her cheerful greeting after teacher conferences was an attempt to mitigate the misery she knew she had inflicted on her father. Up until this year, she hadn't cared if she pained Nola. But now she did care. She wanted to avoid bringing down her mother's mood. She didn't want to trigger a relapse. While they were gone, she'd made oxtail and vegetable soup, plus the little frybreads Josette had showed her how to make. Maggie loved, or at least pretended to love, making soup and frybread. LaRose charmingly stole pieces as they cooled, tossing the oily, hot bits of fried dough hand to hand. Maggie chased him around the kitchen island. Nola laughed at this, giddy. Peter should have been giddy too, but something about the scene was disturbing. It was as though the two were putting on a show for Nola, giving her a warm glimpse of normal brother-sister hijinks. They glanced at their mother, from time to time, anxious to make sure she was pleased.

That weekend, in celebration of Maggie's Physical Science A, Nola wanted to bake a cake with her daughter's name on it. Maggie told her that eating cake gave her diarrhea.

But you love cakes, said Nola.

Mom, I wanted to make you happy. But no cakes.

Maggie had read about obsessive-compulsive behavior in a library magazine and had resolved to keep her mother from embarking on addictive binges—plus she did hate cake because of all the cake making after Dusty was killed, and after LaRose appeared. Cakes brought bad feelings, especially cakes bearing names. She didn't want cakes in the house.

Let's watch a vintage movie, like an eighties movie, and eat popcorn?

Because of the sale bin at Cenex, they had several unwatched VHS movies. Soothing ones from the older days, like *Ferris Bueller's Day Off*, *Sixteen Candles*, *The Breakfast Club*. Maggie talked to Nola about how she still related to these movies as a teenager although they were of this unthinkable time and place where cell phones were only in cars and big as shoe boxes. Yes, they talked. Or rather, a version of Maggie talked as though she were Molly Ringwald finally coming to terms with life's complexities. And Nola talked to her like a parent slow on the draw but ultimately loving. Peter came home and witnessed them slouched in pillows, one of them out fast asleep and the other smiling thinly into the air.

He sat next to Nola, the smiling one, and quietly asked.

What is going on?

What do you mean?

She just kept smiling, didn't look at him. Spooky.

What are you watching?

Peter gestured at the movie on the screen.

Nola opened her mouth and shook her head, entranced at some dialogue between two teenagers. She leaned her head on his shoulder and Maggie stirred in the pillows pushed up against her mother so the three were now connected, sitting there like normal people.

Maybe this is it, thought Peter. I feel weird because it's all so normal. I'm the odd man out, the only one who cannot understand that we are now going to be all right.

What were you saying? asked Nola once the moment of on-screen drama had passed.

Nothing, said Peter. It's just me.

THE WARS

The Pluto boys were already the Planets, so the Pluto girls were the Lady Planets. Their colors were purple and white. Their mascot was a round planet with legs, arms, a perky face. The reservation team was the Warriors, but the girls weren't the Lady Warriors, they were just the Warriors, also. Their colors were blue and gold. They didn't want to have themselves as a mascot, so they had an old-time shield with two eagle feathers. This was printed on their uniform. The volleyball shirts were close-fitting nylon, long-sleeved so that hitting balls on their forearms wouldn't leave them bruised, though they were often bruised anyway. They wore tight shorts and knee pads. Coach Duke made them wear headbands and ponytails because no matter how disciplined they were, girls still got distracted and touched their hair. The girls had come to idolize Coach Duke and his mingy ponytail. The Warriors had won every game of the season except their first game with the Pluto Planets. The nights turned colder, colder, and suddenly they were 8–1, with a grudge. Tonight they were playing the Pluto team again and ready to win.

I don't like that they call scores kills, said Nola. Nothing should die.

Peter took her hand.

Nothing dies, said Peter. It's just a word.

They were crushed into the stands, parent knees in their backs, parent backs against their knees. Nola had packed a small padded cooler with sandwiches. An ice pack slipped into the side kept the sodas stuffed around it cold. She'd even bought green grapes, so expensive this time of year. Peter helped her take her coat off, or lower it anyway. There was no place to put it so she wrapped the puffy sleeves around her waist. The gym was stuffy and there was only one stand, so the parents of the opposing teams had to sit together. They tried to group themselves according to the team they'd come to support, but inadvertently mixed.

The teams warmed up, doing stretches first, then a pepper drill—pass, set, spike, pass, set, spike. Next each player jumped and spiked the ball off the coach's toss. At last, both teams got court time to practice serves. The Warriors' strategy was to look weak to the Pluto team. They would even pretend to argue.

Ravich, hissed Josette. *You awake?*

Invisible wink. Elaborate pout by Maggie. Lots of ball smacking. No smiles at each other. Then the girls lined up.

She's so small, Nola whispered, always struck by the contrast between Maggie and her teammates.

And the Planets are . . . but Peter caught himself.

He was going to say massive or planetary. They were big, solid, formidable girls. Maggie had told them to watch for Braelyn.

I see her, said Nola loudly. The harsh eyeliner!

Peter put his arm around her and spoke, low, in her ear. Remember? The other parents? He hadn't seen Braelyn's parents for a while, but was pretty sure they were behind them.

Oh! Nola pulled an imaginary zipper across her lips.

Landreaux and Emmaline came in, found a place to sit, wedged in with a group of Warrior parents. The Warriors saluted first the parents, then their coach, then passed the opposing team fake-touching hands through the net and saying good luck to every Planet. Good luck, good luck, good luck, you wanted it, said Braelyn to Maggie with a smile pasted on her face. She passed swiftly, looking straight ahead.

Did you hear it?

Snow had been directly behind Maggie.

Hear what?

You wanted it, thought Maggie. Buggy had told his sister. Shake it off. Maggie had a little thing she did, a shimmy to get rid of a bad feeling or a failed hit. It was an almost invisible instantaneous all-over shake. Josette knew about it, though. The team made a circle, put their arms around one another. Coach Duke stood holding his clipboard in one hand. His other hand sliced the air with each deliberate sentence. He told them volleyball was just a game except for right now when it was more than a game. He reminded them about relaxed intensity. Focus. Bold acts. Knowing when to take their time setting up a spike. He told them to stay loose, keep focus. They were a family, sisters, warriors who would beat this team, restoring honor. Stop everything except being right here, right now, he said. And use your voice. Call the ball. Slap hands on the floor and stay positive.

Diamond was team captain. She looked at each one of them in turn. They silently rose and each put three fingers in the air. Everyone thought they were pointing to the Holy Trinity, but it was their special move, a W for Warriors. Then they roared Warriors, Warriors, Warriors, jumped high, smacked hands.

Josette was first up to serve. She loved the moment when the team slung off its false girly vagueness and became a machine.

Rock that serve, baby! Emmaline's voice was then consumed by the other parent voices.

Josette flew up and bashed it. But one of the brutal redheaded Planet twins, Gwenna, caught it on one forearm. A mishit, but a setter managed to play it and

Braelyn boomed it down the seam. Snow nonchalantly lobbed it, Diamond set with a precise fingertip pass to Regina, and that was that. Regina could drop the ball on a dime. An actual dime. For fun they had set up shots for her, twenty dimes on the floor. She kept every one she hit, and made two dollars.

A medium blonde named Crystal, pretty, twisted to return Josette's next serve and shanked. So it went. Josette got six serves in before the Planets called time-out.

They'll blast back now, said Coach Duke. Maggie, you're our secret weapon right now. They haven't tested you. So be ready. Josette, they will try to get your next serve if it kills them, so give 'em heck. Regina, if you get a chance . . .

Don't say it, Coach.

Take a dump, said Diamond.

Let's call it a surprise left-hand attack, okay? And everyone, remember, an assist is as good as a kill.

Maggie didn't think so. After each game she totaled her kills on a piece of paper taped to her bedroom wall. The scorekeepers added them up too, and if a girl reached 1,000 she got a foot-high golden trophy. Maggie wanted one. Newspaper headline: Girl of 1,000 Kills. She had developed her jump to ballerina height and perfected a sliding tip. The merest tap, never push, a deflection of trajectory that sometimes happened so quickly that it was uncanny. She could score without remembering how the ball came at her. Sometimes she'd even feel its shadow and think the shadow off her hand onto the floor of the opposing court. When she was rotated into the hitter's position up front, the other team always wanted to show the tiny girl what. With her slippery, eccentric, high-leap blocks and tips, Maggie got to show them what.

Josette's serving surf was upset by the interruption, as the Planets' coach intended, and Maggie felt the energy on the court shift. The Warriors crouched, pep-talking one another, passing around *Call it call it call it* so they'd remember to use their voices. Braelyn was at serve. Square-shouldered, chubby-jawed, goth-eyed, she didn't look at Maggie or seem to aim at her, but Maggie was ready anyway. Braelyn got an ace off her. The ball had hesitated, Maggie could swear, and changed direction. She flushed. But once she knew Braelyn's trick she could handle it. She watched the ball come off the heel of Braelyn's hand this time and saw where it would break. Maggie was there, but the ball wasn't. That was two points. Back-to-back aces. The Planet parents were shouting. Her parents were tense and silent. Maggie shimmied all over and stepped back into the game.

She kept her eyes on the serve and pried a weak rescue off the floor, something Josette, on her knees, could put into play for Diamond. But the Planets returned the shot and there began a long, bitter, hard-fought, manic volley with miracle saves and unlikely hits tamed into dinky wattle-rolling blurps off the top of the net that drove the parents nuts. They leaped up gasping, yelling, but it was friendly pandemonium. By the time Regina finally won a joust with Crystal, everyone was in a good mood. Except Crystal, who hissed at Regina, a startling freckled cat. Regina turned away and said, *Freaky.* The players bounced into formation and although the Warriors continued their five- or six-point lead they fought hard for it. Luck was with them in close calls, causing a few Planet parents to grumble. The Warriors took the first two games. Then the Planets bore down, the luck went their way. So did the next two games. The tiebreaker fifth game was now on.

Most volleyball games were competitive but affable, everyone straining toward good sportsmanship. Coach Duke had even sent home a code of conduct that the player and her parents had to sign. But during the fourth game there had been hard hits, harder looks, a few jeering yells, smug high fives on points. By the fifth game, an ugly electricity had infected the gym.

Nola knew which parent was for which team. There was no placatory murmur, *Nice hit,* when the opposing team scored a point, no friendly banter. Nola had yelled hard but held back her glee, as the coach's flyer counseled, when the other team faulted. She had tried not to contest line hits. Tried not to call *out* when she thought she knew better than the player where the ball would strike. She had tried, as Coach begged, not to dishonor the game of volleyball.

Nola surreptitiously ate a grape. It was disappointing, with a tough tasteless skin, a watery chemical pulp. She tried another. Maggie didn't always serve, but the coach did not remove her from the lineup. There she was, up. The Warriors had lost the first two points. This serve had to stop the Planets' momentum. The pressure! Why Maggie? Peter shouted encouragement, but Nola was silent. She stared hard at her daughter, trying to pass luck into her daughter by force of love.

Maggie served into the net. Desolate, her mother threw her hands into her lap like empty gloves.

The Planet parents with the knobby knees in the Raviches' backs, the Wildstrands, cackled in pleasure. Peter caught Nola as she turned, put his arm around her.

Don't go there, honey, he said into her hair.

The Warriors were relaxed and intent on the next serve. Coach had directed them to breathe from the gut, focus, and high-five every play even if it ended in a lost point. His philosophy was based on developing what he called *team mind meld*, where each player visualized exactly where her teammates were on the floor and where each player had the power of the whole team inside of her. But Nola only saw that Maggie was now stuck. Right in the line of fire. A sob of anxiety caught in Nola's chest. But a buttery warmth now spread across Maggie's shoulders.

Maggie looked so small and vulnerable, with her sylph frame and spindle legs. She could have been standing on the court alone. She crouched, arms out. Crystal served straight to her and Maggie set for Regina's surprise left dump. Point. Next serve, from Snow, the other redhead burned the ball down Maggie's left but Maggie flipped underneath and socked it high. Josette assisted Diamond, who landed a swift spike. Another point. Another. Tie. Braelyn stepped up and flared her vixen fury eyes. Maggie's stomach boiled. Braelyn slammed the ball twice on the floor, impassive and stony mad. With a flick of power she sent Maggie her booby-trap special. It was supposed to break just over Maggie's head and land behind her, but Maggie knew Braelyn's arm now and with a surge of exuberance lifted off her feet. She swerve-spiked the ball into the donut. Kill.

Nola had been standing the whole time. A parent nudged Peter and he tried to pull her down.

Kill! She screamed into a spot of silence. Kill! Kill! Kill!

Maggie heard it and the butter swirled down around her heart. Peter tightened his arm around Nola's shoulder, whispered in her ear, but she was someplace else. And this, oddly, filled him with relief. Because this was not fake or unreal, there was no hidden meaning. This was the Nola he knew, not the supersmiley one. This was the family dynamic, not the manufactured happy family with no aggravation, no anger, no loud voices, no pain allowed, where he felt alone.

He was for sure not alone now because Nola was going batshit.

Sit the goddamn hell down! It was the woman behind her.

Nola heard that command with a grape in her cheek. She turned, opened her mouth to give a dignified piece of her mind, and out it flew, exactly like a glob of green snot-spit, landing on the mother's broad pink nose. A shocked pause. The father lifted himself, a squarish, bearlike man with sloping shoulders, a walrus mustache, a trucker hat that said *Dakota Sand and Gravel*. He put his arms out to shove Nola down, but having perfected her move on Father Travis she leaned forward and popped her breast into his grip. Trucker Hat yelped.

Get your paws off me, shrieked Nola.

Peter saw only the hands. Mrs. Trucker Hat was still wiping grape off her face when Peter let his fist fly. It felt so good to let the rage out, then instant remorse as Trucker Hat bent over, face in hands. Nola, however, went numb with pleasure. The game was stopped and thin, apprehensive Mr. Hossel was forced to extract the four parents from the stands. Nola dreamily slid out, clinging tight to Peter's arm. Both failed to see that their daughter had blazed a beanball straight at Braelyn as the whistle sounded to stop play. Distracted, Braelyn let down her guard and sustained a facial. Now her nose was bleeding all over the floor.

The referee held up a yellow card and out went Maggie to the boos of Planet moms and dads. The Planets, hearts blistering, played with vengeant energy but lost control, faulted, missed easy returns, tried for nasty cut shots without the setup, and lost by eight points. The Warriors high-fived it and made a subdued exit. It didn't feel exactly good, like a win; it felt like something bigger and darker had just played out.

They didn't know the half of it, thought Maggie, still quiet with joy at the sight of Braelyn's blood on the floor.

When Peter and Nola were escorted out, Landreaux and Emmaline followed. Braelyn's bearlike father with the sore nose, and his wife, who was stocky and had a sensible Prince Valiant haircut, walked over to their pickup. There was no one in the lot to make sure the parents didn't start another brawl, but the fight was out of the Wildstrands. And Maggie's parents were embarrassed to be escorted out by Maggie's science teacher. Mr. Hossel turned his soul-wounded gaze upon them, gestured apologetically with his scraped hands, and turned away. Nola was hyperventilating.

What if he takes back her A because of us?

We can bring Maggie back, said Emmaline to Peter, if you want to bring Nola home.

No, no, leave me alone, Nola gasped out. But Emmaline didn't step away or change expression. Although her teeth were chattering, Nola wouldn't get in the car. Mist had frozen in the air. Sparkling auras hung from each halogen light, cloaking the cars, frosted windshields, and gleaming asphalt with the peace of another world.

Emmaline nodded at the idling pickup. Braelyn's parents! Mrs. isn't even supposed to go to games. Last year she got suspended.

Before Nola could move, Emmaline put her arms around her and then released her so suddenly that the hug was over before Nola could even react.

We should stay here until the girls get to both cars, said Peter.

It wasn't Maggie's fault, said Landreaux. The ref blew the whistle while her hand was in the air.

The four of them stamped and beat their hands together against the cold.

Come on, said Peter, we'll watch for Maggie from inside the car. He coaxed Nola to him, cajoled her along.

Nola gave Emmaline a long look as she turned away. It was something, the way Emmaline had hugged her. It hadn't felt bad or good. She didn't know how it had felt. Maybe normal was the way it felt.

Snow and Josette walked Maggie out the gym door. Braelyn passed but they stink-eyed her and she strode to her parents' pickup.

How come she's got it out for you?

She's from my old school. I gave her brother Buggy the ball kick.

How come? asked Josette.

Maggie looked down at her feet and hunched her shoulders.

Oh, said Josette.

Guess they're still mad, said Maggie.

No shit. She was gunning for you, said Snow.

They watched the pickup, with Braelyn in it, roar from the parking lot.

Oh my god! Holeee!

Diamond caught up with them.

You know your dad punched out Braelyn's dad? Your mom spit on her mom?

You got a badass family, Diamond said.

Maggie jumped into her car's backseat.

Mom? Dad?

Maggie?

Nice game, said Peter.

***

FATHER TRAVIS turned Emmaline's words over.

Unfair. Not playing by the rules. Was that what she'd said when he'd talked to her after the tae kwon do class? He kept imagining that she'd replied with the same words as his, and stayed . . . But Emmaline had shoved his handkerchief back and left with LaRose. Her face, remarkably, had been neither red nor swollen, betraying no emotion, no sign that she had spoken wildly. Nor had she answered his declaration.

What did I do? Why did I say that I am in love with her?

Every time Father Travis asked himself this question shortly after their meeting, he was still too exhilarated to answer it. But as week after week passed and she didn't show up at class, sent one of the older sisters or brothers with LaRose, he began to regret his words. He began to wonder if he'd even said them, or if she'd understood, or perhaps was crying for some other reason.

One night when Snow walked into the class with LaRose, Father Travis stepped down too hard. His foot pressed into the floor as if a support beneath the wood had given. His knee buckled. He went down in surprise, but righted himself and taught the class with complete concentration. That was what he liked about tae kwon do in the first place—there was no room for any thought but what came next.

After everyone had clapped for one another and he'd dismissed the class, LaRose approached him. He liked the boy, his fearless and confiding way, and his hard work. Though he had no talent, LaRose plonked his way through the forms and eventually memorized the drills. His kicks and punches rarely possessed conviction; they were just motions he made in the air.

LaRose stood before his teacher, at attention.

Sir.

Yes?

I had a fight, and I lost.

I'm not teaching you to fight, you know that. I'm teaching you to defend yourself.

Well, sir, I was doing that.

So someone was hurting someone weaker, and you tried to defend that person getting hurt?

Someone did something to someone else, so I went there to fight the bad guys.

This bad thing someone did? Was it right then?

No. A few years back, I guess.

That's not defending, then. That's revenge.

That's what revenge looks like, she said that.

Who?

LaRose didn't answer.

Okay. I can guess.

These guys did bad things to her. I went to their garage. I punched one guy, but then another guy knocked me down and almost stopped my breath.

Father Travis walked LaRose to a corner of the gym, where they sat down together on a pile of floor mats.

How old were these guys?

LaRose said they were in high school now, and that Brad, oops, one of the guys, had driven him home afterward and told him that he should go out for football.

Brad, huh? Morrissey. I know those guys. So you went to beat them up. This is just what I tell your class never to do. You've broken the discipline. I should take your belt.

LaRose hung his head. His shaggy hair flopped forward.

They hurt her very much, LaRose whispered.

Father Travis took a deep breath and held it until he could control his voice.

You told the truth, so you earned back your belt, he said, and now you must tell me everything.

I don't know exactly, said LaRose, except she took so many showers, after, to get clean. They made her feel like a broken animal.

Father Travis tried to keep his hands from tightening by putting two fingers to one temple and closing his eyes. The infection of fury rose in him.

Father Travis?

I'll have a word with them, said Father Travis, opening his eyes. A word or two. Not a fight, you understand?

Waylon, Hollis, and Coochy decided to drive over to Hoopdance for a hamburger at the truck stop. In case they saw Buggy or any of his friends, they brought tube socks and rocks. The rocks were in the glove compartment and the tube socks stuffed in the cup holder. If things got bad, they'd put the rocks in the socks and come out swinging. But in the truck stop most booths were filled with elderly farm people talking loudly, sinking their upper plates carefully into the day's special. The boys ignored the steam table and the tiny salad bar. They sat in a back booth. They had helped Bap and Ottie clean out their garage, and they had money in their pockets. Halfway through their hamburgers, Buggy entered, alone. He didn't notice them. He paced around a bit, finally sat down at the counter, then jumped up again right after he'd ordered. The boys stuffed down the rest of their food, signaled to the waitress, put money on the table, and got out the door. Buggy was talking to the short-order cook. They sat in Hollis's car waiting for him to come out.

After a few minutes, Father Travis pulled up next to them in the white church van. He saw them as he got out, said hello, and walked into the truck stop. They saw him sit down next to Buggy on a counter stool. When Buggy jumped up to leave, Father Travis put a friendly hand on his skinny shoulder and Buggy sat down hard.

The boys saw this clearly.

What's he doing?

Maybe Buggy got a vocation.

They watched the two at the counter, Buggy talking and gesturing but hunching forward until his face was practically in his hash browns. Every so often, Buggy swiveled around, darting glances to every side as if somebody might be listening in, though most people in the booths were nearly deaf, tuning their hearing aids up or down, filling themselves with weak coffee. Finally, Father Travis handed some bills to the cashier and they walked out of the truck stop together. Buggy fidgeted, standing next to Father Travis, until Curtains drove up. When Buggy got into that car, Hollis started the engine. He was pulling out when Father Travis stepped over, stood right in their way, and put his hand on the dented hood. Hollis killed the engine. Father Travis came around the driver's side and Hollis rolled down the window. Stepping back, Father Travis motioned for them to get out of the car. They did, and stood awkwardly, not wanting to meet his eyes.

I understand, Father Travis finally said. But don't do it.

They shot looks at one another.

Buggy's beyond intimidation. He's breaking down, but still dangerous, so don't go near him. His parents kicked him out. He did something to his sister. He's just got the one friend left. I think you should let things play out. If you go after him, you could end up with assault charges, and that would stay on your record. Hurt you when you apply for college.

Waylon hadn't seriously considered going to college, and it warmed him that the priest thought he might.

Once Father Travis had driven off, the boys got into Hollis's car, talked for a while, and then drove out to look for Buggy Wildstrand, but he had disappeared.

Two weeks later, on a warm day, Coochy heard where Buggy was hanging out and they drove over there. The place was down a long unpaved tractor road and became no more than a mud rut as they crossed a slough. Past that, trees closed in and Hollis said, Isn't this the place where that kindergarten teacher lives? Mrs. Sweit?

She had, notoriously in the area, fled town that past year.

Waylon and Coochy didn't answer because they saw the house. It gaped open. The windows that weren't broken were lined with stained blankets. Three crumpled black garbage bags lay in the thawed rocky muck and snowed-on shit of the yard. As the boys walked carefully forward they smelled and then saw that the bags were the sunken carcasses of dogs stretched out at the ends of chains.

This is bad. Let's not go in, said Hollis.

Coochy and Waylon were already on the porch. Hollis stepped up behind them. Sharp chemicals and deadness hung in the air. They pulled their T-shirts up over their noses, stood in the entry.

The place was spectacularly trashed. Kitchen cupboards were torn apart. Every surface was piled with plastic jugs, snarled tubing, or melted plastic. Petrified gunk hung down from the ceiling and was flung up against flares of charred Sheetrock. The cold floor was heaped with clothes soldered together with food, mined with broken dishes, crushed cans, shattered bottles. They stepped carefully through bagged and unbagged garbage, pizza boxes, ancient pizza like slabs of reptile skin, gluey pop, gnawed bones, and human shit. Against the opposite wall of what might have been the living room there was no motion, but a sensation of something alive came over Hollis and his neck prickled. Waylon tore a blanket off the nearest window. They saw two people, one snared in garbage, asleep maybe. The other staggered upright. It gathered energy and they could see it used to be Buggy.

His eyes flickered like neon in his yellow skull; his mouth was a black hole. His hands clutched and unclutched. One hand dug at his scabby and bleeding arm.

You came here to kill me, said Buggy.

No, said Hollis.

We're gonna leave now, said Waylon.

Coochy stepped back.

Buggy lunged, silently flailing and striking as he bore Coochy down. Waylon tried to pull Buggy off and Buggy reared up, head-butted Waylon, and then slugged Hollis so venomously that he dropped, gasping in the slippery filth. Buggy kicked and hammered them with such dazzling intensity that they barely made it out of the house and to the car. It was all done in hideous silence. Hollis gunned the car in reverse; Buggy flew after them with giant leaping strides. He threw himself onto the hood of the car and mashed his face on the windshield, pop-eyed, tongue swirling on the glass. Hollis had to wrench forward, hit the brakes, and jerk backward to fling Buggy off. Hitting the ground at an odd angle slowed him. But as they drove off Coochy looked back and saw Buggy crouching, as if to spring after them along the ground on all fours like a movie demon.

They drove for about a mile and then Hollis said that Buggy was supposed to graduate as class valedictorian.

Maybe, said Waylon, he will come in second now.

Salutatorian, said Coochy.

Hollis flipped on his windshield wipers to try to clear the glass of Buggy's spit. But his car was out of wiper fluid and the spit smeared in a streak.

Just like a bug, said Waylon. But nobody laughed.

⚜

IN MARCH there was the war. Father Travis started to watch the shock and awe, then switched it off. He was trembling inside, couldn't think. He turned out the lights, knelt beside his bed, and bowed his head onto his folded fists. He tried to pray but his body was enthralled by a sticky, hot, beetling-red rage. The air in the room went thick and whirled with freakish energy. He jumped out of bed, put on his running clothes, and dashed down to a field near the school and hospital where he could run in circles all night if he wanted. It wasn't a large field and he'd made only a few circuits when he registered the light in Emmaline's office.

He told himself he would not, but he found himself going there. He told himself he'd just make sure she wasn't there, or if she was, that she was safe. He told himself that if she was there, if he glimpsed her, he would immediately leave. But when she came to the door of the empty building, he did not leave. When he stepped in, he knew that she had been expecting him ever since they'd last spoken. Everyone else was home right now watching the war, so he and Emmaline were alone.

She walked straight back to her office and he followed. Once inside, she didn't close the door. The light was harsh. She sat down at her desk and gestured at the other chair.

They didn't say anything for nearly five minutes, nor did they look at each other. He listened to her breathe and she listened to him breathe. He shifted slightly, leaned forward. A small, strained gasp escaped her, almost inaudible.

✦

THE RECEPTION on Romeo's TV was so lousy that he was sure Condoleezza had not been consulted on the presentation of the war. There were some green glows. A filthy sky. Wolf Blitzer repeating the words *intense bombardment* and a list of the three thousand types of precisely precise precision weapons guided only to the hardened bunkers of the enemy who ran around waving white sheets in disarray. Complete disarray was happening except for maybe on that hill. They kept talking about the hill where Iraqi intelligence was gathered and how they'd shaved that hill down by a couple of feet. Shaved it? Using missiles, artillery, hit after hit, then what was left? They used napalm to finish off everything alive or that might ever live there. Then the ground troops and the light show. Yet the reassuring news that no homes were being damaged, no collaterals damaged, no buildings even, only ruined tanks and other weaponry to be found. The fast-breaking-news ticker tape along the bottom said that people were getting beaten away from U.S. embassies all around the world. How useless, thought Romeo. You cannot stop a warlike people from doing what they like to do. Besides, frugality. Those giant flares were probably due to expire next week.

Romeo looked around himself, at his life, at his dinner. He was eating leftover pizza heisted from the hospital fridge. The pepperoni had dried to rigid disks. The cheese was tough. It wasn't bad, but Romeo wished for digestion's sake he had procured a vegetable. He had paychecks deposited in his bank account now, but he didn't like to go to stores. He didn't like to feel the payment for things coming from himself. What was he saving for?

The same footage, over and over. Why hoard his money? The world could be ending either there, or here.

Why save?

He really didn't know. The amount of money just kept growing. Perhaps one day Hollis would look at the bank account that shared his name and say something.

Maybe he'd think that Romeo wasn't such a shithead father after all.

That's what, said Romeo to CNN, that's who I am saving for. That's why I am eating this petrified cheese and this tagboard pizza. That's why I have no sound on my TV.

The war was on at the Iron house. Josette screamed, *Fuckers fuckshit fuckers it's about the fucking oil!* Hollis was out with friends and came back late. Maybe a little drunk. At the Ravich house only Peter watched. He said that LaRose shouldn't watch, so Nola went upstairs with him. Maggie was not interested. The dog laid his head on Peter's leg and closed his eyes under Peter's hand, mesmerized as the voices droned in self-important excitement.

Suddenly, shoved aside, the dog circled and plopped down with a disoriented groan. Peter paged through the slim directory, dialed.

The man he had punched at Maggie's volleyball game, Braelyn and Buggy's father, answered.

Wildstrand here, said the voice.

Hi, said Peter. This is Peter Ravich. Sorry I punched you. Hope your daughter's okay too.

Peter put the phone down.

Why'd I do that?

He asked the dog. The dog's brown-black eyes shone with rich appreciation. After a few moments, the phone rang. Peter picked it up.

Wildstrand here. I never meant to touch your wife. I know it.

Wildstrand hung up this time. Peter let the dog out and in, shut things down on the first floor, checked the doors.

He called up the stairs. There was no answer.

Dusty's gone, he said.

He bent over and the dog leaned into his arms.

Peter walked up the stairs and found them, each in bed, faces visible in the crack of light from the hallway. LaRose a shadowy lump in the bottom bunk, face buried in the pillow. Maggie with puddles of jeans and underwear on the floor, books splayed, papers, notebooks. Yet on her dresser the bottles of nail polish in strict rainbow array. He stepped into his and Nola's bedroom. Soap and stale sleep. Nola on her back like a stone queen on a coffin. She didn't stir as he eased into the bed and settled himself with stealthy care. By morning gravity and his greater weight would roll her down to him, and he would wake with her sleeping in his arms.

✧

EMMALINE PACKED for a conference in Grand Forks. She took nothing more than the usual overnight things—a change of clothes, her makeup case, shoes to walk in if she shopped at Columbia Mall. On the drive there, she could have played the tapes that were in the car—but each album or mix reminded her of other times. She played nothing, and didn't give herself a problem to think through, either, as she often did on these drives. She just steered herself along. The wind out of the northwest was dry and bitter. Off the dunelike billows along the ditches, snow blew and sifted across the road. Emmaline only glanced from time to time at the continually vanishing tails of snow. A driver could be hypnotized by their loveliness.

When she reached Grand Forks, she drove straight to the University of North Dakota. She gave her presentation, talked to several colleagues. Soon she excused herself to check into her hotel. She'd taken a room in a generic place across the river where no one from the conference was likely to stay. She gave her information, signed the check-in slip, and went up to her room. She took off her jacket, shoes, and stockings. Then she lay down on the bed. Quickly, she got up.

But she was weary and eventually she pulled back the covers and lay down again, still dressed. She curled up on her side and dozed until the phone rang. Her hand hovered until the third ring, but she picked it up and gave him the room number.

She let him in and he closed the door carefully. They stood before each other. He was dressed of course like a normal person. They didn't speak. After a while she reached out and tugged the arm of his jacket. He took it off. She touched his shirt. He took that off too. Scars webbed his chest and thickened where they disappeared. She waited and he touched her blouse. She undid the little white shell buttons. He pushed the material off her shoulders. She shrugged and it fell. Once that happened, everything was easy and they slipped together like the snow along the way, endlessly rushing across the pitch-black surface of the road.

⚓

CHEAP FAMILY photographs were advertised that spring—Saturday morning in the Alco parking lot. Maggie insisted. Peter said it was hokey. They had plenty of photographs. Shelves of framed photographs.

But none are by a trained photographer, said Maggie.

Peter pointed to the lines of school photographs.

All of us, Dad, in one photograph. It will make Mom happy.

She's okay, isn't she?

Oh come on, Dad!

Peter hesitated. They hadn't taken a family photograph since Dusty. Also, he didn't know if this would be a secret photograph, to keep hidden from Landreaux and Emmaline. Because LaRose would be in the photograph, it would be a symbolic thing. Peter had worked to keep things like this low-key—neither family claiming LaRose overmuch. He was even more careful since Emmaline had temporarily reclaimed LaRose. He said no. But Maggie stared at him in her spooky, smiley, perfect-daughter kind of way.

Will a family photograph make you happy? Peter asked Nola as she entered the room.

We should do it! Maggie threw her arms out to spark her mother. Nola sparked.

Yes! I'd just love a family photograph.

I need a beer, thought Peter.

Lately, Maggie had given him several characters to play: Bumbling Dad, even though he was the handiest man he knew. Wet Blanket Dad, even though he just liked to check in on reality once in a while. Careless Dad Who Lost Things, even though he was beginning to understand that somebody else had long been losing stuff. Maybe he really was Emotionally Lost Dad because he understood that Maggie was taking care of Nola all of the time, in ways he could not define. He couldn't tell, couldn't remember what she'd been like before, anyway. So maybe he was Absentminded Dad. And Spaced-Out Dad because he liked to avoid these questions. He was Best Boy Buddy Dad, although LaRose was clearly the character mainly playing Nola's son. She doted on him. Her eyes followed the fork he ate with. His back when he left the room.

In the case of this picture, however, to make everybody happy, all he had to do was wear his best shirt and smile.

Or maybe a suit, said Maggie. Do you have a suit? We are all dressing up, Dad. You need a suit. You need a tie.

Peter found his wedding suit and tie.

Nola came out in a purple dress with a silver buckle at the waist. Maggie lowered her head and stared at her mother. Charged ions moved. Nola turned around and went back into their bedroom. What just happened? Peter wondered. He would never see that plum-colored dress again. Nola was now wearing a tan suit, white shirt, black heels. She looked like a flight attendant or a presidential candidate.

You get my vote, he said.

Mom, that outfit begs for those twinkly green earrings, said Maggie. And a scarf! Nola returned to the bedroom.

LaRose did not have a suit, but he did have a dress shirt. Maggie slicked his hair back with water. Nola said he looked like the exceptional boy he was. Everybody beamed. Maggie had on a matching sweater and shell, hot pink, and a short, sassy, eggshell-colored faux leather skirt. She was wearing a white headband and white plastic go-go style but nineties boots that had belonged to her mother. Peter found it disorienting when Maggie wore clothes that he remembered Nola wearing during college, in those years when he took keen notice of her clothing and her in it.

I'm a lucky man, he said, looking them all over and meaning that sincerely.

Nola and Maggie gazed at him indulgently. In their script they often didn't understand what he was saying but rolled their eyes away from him with the gentle exasperation of two mothers.

With just the right amount of oxy, Romeo looked at things as a movie drama where revenge was justice, saw himself outside of himself, even heard the music, furtive or swelling. And see? Peter was all dressed up in heroic clothing to act his part in a heroic portrait, thought Romeo. But a startling message approached.

Romeo made his way toward Peter Ravich, whom he'd spotted in the Alco parking lot. To keep walking, he had to keep arguing with Landreaux in his head. Still, still! Landreaux had never talked to Romeo about the old times, and was too high and mighty to give Romeo a sign he even cared one shit about the sacrifice that Romeo made, trying to save Landreaux, even to this day. Plus he was stealing Hollis and Emmaline and all that Romeo should have. Getting away with stealing these because they all believed in a false Landreaux, a saved and sober Landreaux, a Landreaux who could do the worst thing possible and still be loved. That Landreaux must fall.

I tried to warn him, tried and tried again.

Now Romeo stood before Peter Ravich.

Can I talk to you?

Peter vaguely remembers Romeo, but doesn't know from where. Romeo himself does not recall that he once approached Peter while the man was pumping gas into his vehicle, and scammed him as he frowned at the whirring readout of numbers. He told Peter that he had lost his wallet and needed ten dollars' worth of gas to bring his grandmother to the hospital. Peter had unfolded his lean wallet and given him five. Now, stooping and shadowy, Romeo cuts Peter away from his family.

This is private, he says.

Romeo's skinny tail of hair is neatly braided, by himself, braided wet from a shower obtained by stealth from the casino campgrounds. He has broken into his supply of swag and wears a T-shirt stiff with new-ness, featuring a huge plastic press-on eagle, comrade to an Indian-headbanded turtle, both bursting fiercely through a dream catcher. A red bandanna is tied crisp around his throat, the indigo skulls peeping discreetly over the folded cloth. Romeo has clipped sharp the drooping wisps of his wisdom 'stache. His jeans are slung low, barely on his hips. He speaks calmly, though clearing his throat every other word.

Apologies, he says, this will only take a minute.

I'm supposed to be over there, says Peter.

I'm a friend of Landreaux's.

Oh?

Well, not a friend, as you will see, but a former friend before I found out what Landreaux was up to.

Romeo pauses; he is proud of that *as you will see*, which Mrs. Peace once called foreshadowing. He makes a pious sorry-face, like he's sad to give the news of Landreaux's hidden character to one who believes in him.

In fact, feeling inspired, Romeo uses that line.

I know you believe in him.

I . . . yeah, sure . . . what's going on? Peter glances at his family and smiles uncertainly, waves at their impatient faces.

You see, I am a hospital worker, says Romeo in a formal way. For that reason, I accidentally hear how things really go down from time to time in real life.

Peter feels the pull of where this is going and tries to extricate. But Romeo is an assured narrator and already has him with the suckage of story. Romeo puts his hand to his heart.

I apologize if this causes you to revisit trauma, says Romeo, but you weren't told the truth. And I just feel— me being me—that you, as a parent, deserve the truth.

Now everything is very slow or even paralyzed, like time has quit its business and there is only Romeo, and only Peter, and dread like a gong in Peter's head.

So that day three years ago, says Romeo.

Cut the shit.

Peter's shoulders hunch and square, his chest expands, his neck swells, his heavy hands itch to grab that red bandanna and twist to choke the words off. This guy is slime. This guy is doing violence here. At the same time, this is something Peter can't help coming to know. It will be there whether he hears it now or walks away. It will exist behind the sorry-to-tell-you mini-frown with the smugness boiling up behind Romeo's unctuous manner.

It's not shit, says Romeo, calm. He expected this resistance from Peter, so he goes in more slowly. Poor Landreaux. Romeo sighs. Sometimes he tries to self-medicate, you know? Looks like he tried to that day. I heard the guys who were on the ambulance crew that day. I obtained access to the coroner's report.

Coroner?

Yes, nobody told you? Nobody gave you that report? You were perhaps unaware?

Peter's legs go weak. No. Maybe it was filed away or burned. It had not occurred to him. The unthinkable had been, at least, straightforward. Peter had seen the tree where it happened. It had all made unbearable sense. He hadn't wanted to know any details. He'd had his hands full, back then, with Nola spinning off in space and Maggie clutching him like she was drowning. Then fighting him off. Then clutching him. There was no sense in looking at the paperwork of death. It would not have brought his son back. Reports were the cold logistics of death and he'd been dealing with the hot truth of grief.

So, no.

I do have it here, said Romeo in a hushed voice, then repeating the TV phrase. I was able to obtain the file. I can tell you what it says, basically. Romeo's voice is dry and competent. He marvels at how intelligent he makes himself sound—his brain though wormholed is a smart brain, after all.

It says that Landreaux's shot missed Dusty's head, heart, lungs, liver, aortic artery, femoral artery, and stomach. It says that Dusty was not killed by the shot but by the tearing shrapnel of the branch he was sitting on. Shallow wounds, sir. He bled to death while Landreaux was restraining your wife in the house. It doesn't say this in the report, but the guys speculate Landreaux's judgment—tragically!—impaired. If Landreaux had not run or panicked, but stopped to treat the boy's bleeding, which as a personal care assistant he certainly knew how to do, he would probably have saved Dusty's life.

And . . . here Romeo embroiders for further effect . . . and, if your wife had been allowed to run back there, even she might have saved the boy.

Peter feels the paper in his hands. He opens the thing, filled out in squirrelly handwriting. His brain will not read the phrases in sequence, though the words Romeo just used pop out here and there. The paper falls. Romeo picks it up and tries gingerly to press it back into Peter's hand, but there is no response, so he steps back. Peter's arm is long and now is the time Romeo might get slugged.

As Peter stares through Romeo his face goes fragile. Peter's skin crinkles and lines form, flushed brown as old parchment, and he is suddenly very, very old. Romeo takes another step back from this amazing special effect. Then Peter's daughter calls.

Daddy! It's our turn.

Peter closes his mouth. His eyes focus. He walks past Romeo and goes to stand before the photographer.

At the end of his driveway, Peter. Motionless, balanced, hands dangling at his sides. He does not wave at or even see the few cars that pass, the ones that are not Landreaux. Behind him, the pickup, his hunting rifle in the gun rack across the back window. He's wearing blue jeans, a shirt, his old red and black checked jacket. Head buzzing. Hollow roar of blood in his ears. Had he remembered to relock the gun case? He'd grabbed the gun so quickly. Yes he had, yes. He asks himself this question every three minutes. Part of him already knew what Romeo would say and had been waiting for this. It didn't feel like news. It felt like corroboration.

Every noise is magnified. The dog shuffling in the un-
dergrowth. He watches the birch and popple trees. The
leaves shiver with light. He cannot remember his son's
voice. He cannot call a happy image to his mind that is
not a photograph. But he can see his son in the leaves,
and where before Dusty was at peace, gone instantly in
one shock, now his eyes are open, he is calling. He is
afraid. Peter bangs the side of his head, trying for another image. The good times. Not a photograph. The
real times. Why had he not memorized the moments?

This moment, anyway, he has stone cold.

He lifts his arm, waves Landreaux down. Does not
move. It is apparent to Landreaux that Peter has something to say so he pulls over and gets out, worried.

What is it?

Peter turns, opens the passenger-side door of the
pickup.

Get in, he says.

Landreaux does.

Peter slides into the driver's side, starts the vehicle,
pulls out.

Where are we going?

Hunting.

It isn't hunting season, says Landreaux.

Yes it is, says Peter.

On their way to federal land, Peter tells Landreaux all that Romeo told him in the Alco parking lot. Landreaux does not argue with the narrative because in the sudden crush of images, he doesn't know, can't remember. Was he high that day? No. He doesn't think so. No. He knows he wasn't. No. But does that even matter? He is guilty whichever way. He took the shot. And if he could have saved the boy . . . Landreaux puts his splayed fingers on his face, as if to push pieces of himself back together. They drive in silence. Peter's skin is gray as rock. But his hands are loose and warm on the steering wheel. Forty minutes pass in seconds.

The pickup lurches down an old logging road and comes out on a ridge, an opening in dense second-growth woods. Together, many years ago, they had hunted in this place. There was an old clear-cut full of browse, and one time Landreaux had perched in a tree stand on the southern end, waiting, as Peter beat down toward him from the north. They had taken a fine buck.

Now they get out of the truck and Peter reaches back in for the rifle.

I'll find that stand down there, says Peter, gesturing toward the southern limit. He nods to the north, calmly meeting Landreaux's eyes. You walk down from that hill toward me. I'll be waiting.

Landreaux turns toward the hill. A giddy ease steals into him. That all of this will soon be over. Peter is a good shot. It will be like vanishing. No more hiding his miserable truth. No struggle with the substance or not the substance. No waiting for Emmaline to love him again. Although the kids . . . set them free? He doesn't think he can exist, anyway, seeing forever what he now sees and knows about that day. His thoughts loop. Yes. Peter's got sights on his rifle. Landreaux won't even hear the shot. To die will be nothing. It seems like a favor, almost. Landreaux takes his time. He sleepwalks peacefully up the hill. When he gets halfway up, he tells himself to turn and walk down. It is here that he has some trouble.

The unwelcome desire to live nearly thwarts Landreaux as he gazes down into the woods where Peter is waiting. He sees the birch, the crisp film of new green. The trees quiver with light. His grandfather had tapped birch trees in spring, and they drank the cold sap, which tasted of life. The bark, the inner layer; he had eaten it when he was hungry and his parents were out drinking. Close by, he sees that dark stands of bur oak could hide him. Peter's shot would never penetrate that wood. The frogs start singing again down that hill—telling him to run. But he does not run. Blood drains from his heart. His arms and legs go transparent. He glances down to see if he is shot yet. He is both keenly downcast and relieved to see there is no blood. Thoughts tell Landreaux he can still get away. He is out of range. He can run. Why, then, does he drop his head forward and walk back down the hill?

He is stubborn, and he is angry, and he will not give Peter the satisfaction. With a composure that surprises him, Landreaux orders his shaking legs to move, and they do move. As long as he points his head down the hill, it turns out that the rest of him will follow. He keeps his eyes on the ground. Shy trillium and garlic mustard, swamp tea, snowberry, wintergreen, wild strawberries. Landreaux stoops, picks a few of the berries, puts them in his mouth. The taste is so intense that he nearly drops, right there, to crawl into the downed trees, rough brush. But he doesn't. Step after step. Fear fizzes in his blood. He mutters, Kill me, you fuck, kill me now—trying to keep the anger. He tries a death song like old people talk about, but his throat shuts. Kill me, you fuck, kill me now, take the shot, take the shot, take it now. But one step follows another. Sometimes he stumbles, but he picks himself up and keeps going.

WHEN ROMEO leaves the Alco parking lot, he wanders, now empty of purpose. All of his being was concentrated on this one attainment.

It is finished, he says.

He has triggered events over which he now has no control.

My work here is done.

Who to visit, what to do? Nothing appeals. And now that the adrenaline is spent, this is a low day, all energy in the air sucked away in spite of sunshine. Romeo should sleep before his shift. He only got a couple hours last night. But he can resort to several chemical enhancements to keep moving. He doesn't feel like sleeping right now. These are hours of destiny. If he could only talk to another person! But as usual, nobody wants a visit from Romeo. His treasured captain's chair sits empty in his gracious home—he could go there. He could arrange the window blankets, put the light on, read the tribal news or some of the literature he's picked from the hospital trash. People toss perfectly good books away. In theory. When he opens them they're always crap.

Where to? Where to, my man?

The AA meeting beckons. Destination? Romeo recalls that the group was maundering on about the step

516 · LOUISE ERDRICH

that includes a searching and fearless moral inventory. Romeo's favorite. He loves to listen to his compatriots' new inventory items every week. Romeo's avid listening skills sustain the group narrative. His later comments provoke humor and tears. The staginess of the meetings suits him and always improves his mood. So off he goes. Catches a ride up the hill, slouches around the side of the church, down the steps, along the corridor and into a homey room with mildewed carpet. Chairs in a circle, waiting. Nobody here yet. Romeo sits down and realizes that he may not have the means to get himself into the right mood to withstand assaults of fellowship. He has some means, which he exits into the bathroom to safely take advantage of, and feels himself fortified when he returns.

Still, nobody. And a dry Mr. Coffee.

The sun leaks in and there is the smell of funeral power-cooking down the hall. Good eats later. The hard chair becomes more comfortable as the chemical fortification builds. Plus, there is gloating to accomplish. The attainment of his ends is now Romeo's to nibble on. Thinking back, he calls up each word, each exchange, each emotion loosed in the Alco parking lot. These moments are his forever, his to taste singly. He lingers over the initial confusion, the dawning dread, the vertigo, the resolution, which will mean a big fat comeuppance at last for Landreaux. Maybe death, even, fast or slow, though unlikely. And would he want that for real? He had set things in motion. That's all.

My work here is done.

I like that, says Romeo out loud.

He leans back with his head resting lightly in crooked arms, legs outstretched, the sad one shorter and now quiet. This is the pose of satisfaction Father Travis comes upon as he enters the meeting, and sits across from Romeo, who slumbers in that unlikely position. Eventually, the priest calls his name and wakes him up. The meeting was supposed to start ten minutes ago.

Guess it's just us two, says Father Travis.

Hardly worth it.

Romeo is disappointed—there will be no entertainment.

On the contrary, says Father Travis. A chance for special attention to your growth in the program, Romeo.

I am supposed to be somewhere, says Romeo.

You're supposed to be right here, says Father Travis.

They pass the page-protected ritual greetings and organizational prompts back and forth. They read the steps aloud. Father Travis says, You're up.

I'm up?

You're the speaker of the day.

I got nothing.

Sure you do.

Romeo wants to say the fuck with that, but his mouth surprises him by uttering other words.

Okay. I'll start.

His mouth, his tongue, his voice box, seem to be working separately at first. His Adam's apple shivers, the skulls vibrate, his voice quakes. What's going on? It is as if a different Romeo is speaking, an interior Romeo. This unknown alternate Romeo has staged a coup. This Romeo Two has infiltrated his communication infrastructure. Are the drugs betraying him? What did he take again? What shape of pill? Romeo thinks it was a big white oval but there also were some smaller yellow articles. Perhaps crisscrossing side effects. Romeo is startled to silence even as Romeo Two becomes voluble, moved to unload certain acts undertaken for certain reasons. Romeo Two's mouth claptraps, his voice shifts gear, high and higher, until Romeo One understands in despair that Romeo Two has frog-leaped all the way to that holy step somewhere beyond three, maybe four, five, where you tell God and another human the exact nature of your wrongs. Talk about combined side effects. Where among the vertigo, gastric pain, incontinence, shortness of breath, and possible kidney failure was telling the truth? Meanwhile, Father Travis, another human, and God's representative on earth, is caught up in the fever of Romeo's surprise recital:

I wasn't always this scumbag a person, Father Travis. Once, I was somebody. Once, I was considered the most intelligent kid in my class. I was the treasured confidant of Landreaux Iron himself when Landreaux was a cool guy. This was before his sad-sack days. It was when he was new at boarding school. Landreaux at the time had a kinda rock-star quality, always leaning on a board. Then Landreaux tempted me to run away. A fiasco that would change my life. That would . . .

Tears, not the eye-welling teasers he used to gather the information-spilling sympathy of others, but choking, wretched, wracking. His voice scratches out. Ruin my life! Romeo tries to take control of Romeo Two, but it's too late to stop. They merge. He keeps talking.

In our mutual adventure, Landreaux fell upon me from a height and broke my leg and arm—you know the story. Everybody knows the story. Landreaux's fate is to cause death and destruction to those around him, while he always slips free into the sunset. Or to Emmaline. I mean, there we were at school. This was after we had run away. We were caught, we had surrendered. I had come back from the hospital with my whole side wrecked, arm in an itching, stinking, long-term cast, leg pinned together inside, and afflicted with the nervous damages I bear to this day. First thing, I see Landreaux.

My man! I call out to him. My man!

He looks right through me. Maybe he feels bad for what he did. But not sorry! He looks right through me.

Father Travis, that right there is why I fell from grace. Not because of my crinkled armbone or my sad ol' leg, not because I lost brain cells in the fall, not because I am at heart a raging addict who'd do anything to feed his want, though that's true also. But, Father Travis. That's not why.

You ever heard of omphalosite? You know what that is? It's a kinda parasitic twin. It has no heart. Depends on the twin's heart for circulation. Just lives off the twin and usually dwindles away before anybody even knows it exists. That's how it was with me—like Landreaux was the beating heart and I the fainter twin and when he didn't know me anymore my circulation stopped. I became a dead person, Father Travis. I was dead inside after that first year when Landreaux suddenly did not know who I was, suddenly would not answer to my call, suddenly outcast me when I needed him the worst. I needed him to come to my aid and stop a nickname from sticking on me. It took all my doing to slide out from under or slap down those nicknames. I battered Crip to the earth and went after Stooper. Sank my fangs

into Wing and I defined myself. I stayed Romeo. I did
it, but it cost me, and now here behold: I am who I am.
Not a good person, not a bad person.

Father Travis listens, impassive, his eyes cast down.

Well, maybe, says Romeo. Could be I am a bad
person. Unforgiving all these days and years. But when
I see Landreaux living large with the girl who marked
me out, who might have loved me at one time the way
I love her, then I am deader than I was dead before. I
become the gray worm. Just a digestion tube, really.

So Romeo loves Emmaline too, thinks Father Travis,
and the sudden fact that he and his friend the weasel
are afflicted and exalted by the same emotion makes
him raise his head and settle his eyes on Romeo. That
little gesture of attention causes in Romeo a deeper un-
flooding.

Truth he doesn't even know is true tumbles out.

I put the mark on Landreaux just now, Father Travis.

What do you mean?

Romeo loses track. What does he mean? Put the
mark. He stammers, under the influence of truth-tell
side effects, to piece together what he has with utter
certainty divulged to Peter Ravich. He spoke with such
confidence. His delivery had been dignified, fluid, im-
pressive. Oh yes. Now he remembers. Romeo puts on
his honest face.

So you know that Landreaux Iron had relapsed that day. Yes! Romeo raises his hand, testifying. We know he's struggled, and he's fought, and I more than anyone understand that. Acknowledge it, Father Travis. I more than anyone dislike bearing unpleasant news. But, yes, it takes a strength of character. Even if Landreaux had that strength, which I know he does, Father Travis, because I know Landreaux well, even so there are times. This was one of the times. His shot blasted a tree branch, splintered it, and the boy was struck as with shrapnel. But shallow wounds, many of them, here, here, here, etc. Not one of these wounds hit a major vein or artery. The cause of death, exsanguination. However, had Landreaux not fled the scene he might have stopped that bleeding. Had he not overpowered the boy's mother, she might have reached her son in time to stop the bleeding. This boy might be alive. I made copies of the coroner's report, which bears this out. It is signed by Mighty Georgie herself, yes, Georgie Mighty, unavailable right now, most sadly, or she herself could bear this out as it was also corroborated by the state coroner, who happened to be in the area and was called in on this case, so yes. Most sadly . . . .

Romeo drifts a bit, then rouses himself, riffles in his pocket, draws out the report.

Father Travis puts his hand out, takes the paper. He reads the paper. He holds it long enough to read it several times over. At last he lifts his eyes to meet Romeo's dozing-off eyes.

It doesn't say that.

Romeo blinks.

It doesn't say that.

Romeo sits up in his chair, mouth clamped.

I put it all together! Romeo speaks firmly. Father Travis!

It doesn't say that, Romeo. The words you used are written here, but they don't add up to your story. It just doesn't say that.

Please don't take this away from me. This is my only thing!

He peers stubbornly at Father Travis.

You are mistaken! Romeo slaps his knees. Mistaken!

Romeo rounds up all of the scattered bits of who he is, or was, and flings them on the table.

Father Travis, he says with authority, I gathered every word from trusted sources. I assembled the whole report from pieces of information relayed to me by people who were on the ground that day. That terrible day. Even if the report doesn't say exactly what I said, there is corroboration. It's not like I wanted to find these things out.

These things aren't things. Father Travis gestures at the paper. They're not here.

These words, these connections, these facts. They fell into place. Little by little. They added up! Into an inevitable story. I made diagrams. I procured a box of tacks. Tacks were in my wall. Still there. I drew lines between words and then elided . . . do you know that word? The meaning of that word?

Yes.

Don't you love that word? I fit these connections to other connections until a huger connection emerged.

What are you talking about? *Elide* doesn't mean that. It means erase.

Or slur together!

Yes, like when you're drunk, slurring, erasing part of your word.

Well, says Romeo, maybe. Erased the meanings between the salient points. Could have.

And then what?

And then, and then, well. Peter Ravich was there in the Alco parking lot, okay?

Romeo searches his hands, polishes his wrist, and tells Father Travis every detail of what he'd told Peter Ravich. He is still talking when Father Travis gets up. Romeo keeps talking after Father Travis walks through the door. Keeps on talking to the empty coffeepot and waiting chairs, to the walls, to the sun shafts through basement window, to the food smells, to the hands, the knees, the air. Keeps on talking because once he finishes he does not know what will happen next, what awaits him anywhere in his own life, and because he cannot leave with these embarrassing sheets of snot and tears still running down off his face. He stands to follow Father Travis, still talking. Climbs upstairs and through the center aisle of the church, still talking, too stunned at himself to genuflect. Steps out the front door of the church.

From there, he can see down the hill into the marrow of the reservation town. High and mentally blasted as he is, he sees into each heart. Pain is dotted all around, glowing from the deep chest wells of his people. To the west the hearts of the dead still pulse, burning soft and green in their caskets. They stream out pale light from the earth. And to the south there are the buffalo that the tribe has bought for tourism purposes. A darkly gathered congregation. Their hearts also on fire with the dreadful message of their extinction. Their ghostly gathering now. Like us, a symbol of resistance, thinks Romeo. Like us, now rambling around in a little pen of hay getting fat. Like us, their hearts visible as lamps in the dust. To the east, also, the holy dawn of all the earth, every morning of every day, the promise and the weariness. He is so tired, Romeo. Because of course Peter will kill Landreaux. He saw this, has always known it. He doesn't want to look north because he realizes he's thought in the counterclockwise fashion that belongs only to the spirit world, where, it appears to him now, he belongs. His place of rest.

So thoroughly relieved and convinced is Romeo in that instant, and so fully does it seize him, the idea of his death, that he casts himself violently headlong down the twenty cement church steps, to the very base.

FATHER TRAVIS drove the parish outing van along the BIA road across to County 27 and pulled into the Ravich driveway. Landreaux's Corolla was parked to one side of the drive, and Peter's pickup was gone. Nola came out the front door and stood on the fussy little stone pathway to the drive, hands on her hips, full makeup, brightly frosted hair, immaculate pale outfit. She held his gaze pleasantly. As if she'd never seen him before.

Hello? Can I help you?

Is Peter home?

No.

I need to speak to him right away.

Nola gave him a suspicious flounce, and called Maggie. She came out, also smartly dressed.

What's wrong?

Maggie could tell immediately that everything was not all right. Not all right again. And she had tried so hard with the family photograph! But clearly, something had happened with her dad. He'd acted weird the whole way back. And now the old Vin Diesel priest.

Can you tell me where your dad went?

I'll look around, she said to Father Travis. Just wait.

Maggie walked through the house with her radar on. Her mother kept everything so exactly in its exact place that Maggie could always feel, before she even saw, what was different about a room.

Maggie came back outside.

He took his best deer rifle.

Thank you, said Father Travis.

✝

WAYLON DROVE up just after Father Travis left, and Maggie turned off her radar, right there in the driveway, where he met her. She had asked him over to help her work in the cornfield. Peter had plowed last year's stubble into the field, but there were already weeds up in the rows. She went inside, and changed into work clothes, put on SP 30 and came out. Together, they walked to the field. It was warm. They each had a hoe they'd keep sharp using the files stuck in the back pockets of their jeans. Maggie's were short cutoffs. She was a faster or more indifferent weed killer, so she got ahead of Waylon right away. He left a few pickers in the black dirt and stumbled after her. Maggie's white shirt was tied off at her belly. Her foal's legs shot down into thick socks, heavy tie boots. A battered straw cowboy hat shaded her face. Her lips were moving to some song in her head. Both of them had heavy brown cotton gloves in their back pockets but they swung their hoes bare-handed. The scent of dry crushed plants, torn dirt, piercing and pure, followed them over the earth. Waylon was proud of his shoes—Jordans—which he shouldn't have been wearing in the field. His dad had bought them and didn't have the money. He'd had to sign something to get them—but he wanted people to know that Waylon's family could afford them. Fine dirt was sifting into the shoes and his sweating feet turned the dust to paste. He kept on swinging the hoe, slicing off pickers, shuffling along behind Maggie in his pasty shoes. One moment he was thinking about washing the shoes out later with a hose, or maybe a wet cloth, and if he would ruin them. The next moment everything changed.

Maggie's white shirt is slung off. She is chopping weeds in just her bra—sky-colored cups holding two small creamy scoops. She is pale all over because of the sunblock slathering that went on before an incident of possible sun exposure. Her skin is marless. Not a freckle, a fleck of mole, or even a blemish. Only the blue dot on her shoulder. Which Waylon sees when she turns away. That dot. He knows what it is. She told him. And his heart is pierced as with the needle-sharp pencil. He puts his hand to his chest, takes his hand off, even looks at his fingers, but there's no blood. Just her, obliviously swaying with her hoe, occasionally leaning forward to viciously whack a deep-rooted thistle.

The sunblock hasn't kept her back from glowing a supple golden. Her spine sweatily glistens down into the tiny cutoffs. Her legs are milky white and deerlike. There is dirt up the insides of her calves, thighs, adhering to her sweat like shadow.

Waylon sits down between the rows, on sunny dirt. A small black jumping spider lands on his knee. Stares at him with fierce, pent sorrow. Then pops away. Waylon doesn't move. He rubs his head as if to rearrange his thoughts.

Maggie moves down the row.

Get up, lazy-ass, she says. Don't make me do this whole field by myself.

Waylon leaves the hoe on the ground, gets up, and stands before her. She squints up at him, smiling her bad-luck good-luck smile. Right then they are the only people in the universe, yet Waylon is too shy to say out loud what he leans over to whisper against her neck.

Maggie could wind herself through the bush, no matter how snakey and dense, but Waylon was like a big calf and stumbled after her, hair flopping, eyes wide, lips pink and lustrous, skin darkly glowing with sweat until at last she pushed her hand on his chest to make him stop.

Okay, this is the place, she said. My place.

It was an old oak so huge that it had choked out all other brush but the long pale grass they lay on underneath.

Do you love me? asked Waylon.

No, said Maggie.

You're lying, huh. You love me.

I said no. Maggie laughed.

He put his hand around her face and adored her chin. She was thinking about her volleyball kill score—

she had got up to 200 last season. It would take at least another couple years to hit 1,000.

Okay then?

All right then, said Maggie. Let's try it. I mean, if it hurts too much you have to quit.

She leaned toward him and he tried not to grapple with her, not treat her like he couldn't wait, not lunge or buck, tried to be all manly and collected, but it was all too unbelievable. She was just so small but just so quick. She got on top of him and moved aside her panties, unzipped him and got him out and started to try.

Put it in, she said.

They couldn't get it in. She got off, lay down, opened her legs. He got on top and tried that way. It worked better, but she screamed.

Get it out!

He moved backward.

Okay, she panted. Try again.

Waylon sweat and worried, trying to slow down but stay hard all at once. Then it was suddenly better and she relaxed under him and said it was okay and she could handle it.

So move, she said.

His uncles had teased him, *Hold back, you got to hold back.* They had eased their arms in slow cranks like pulling a boat back to an idle. So he tried to hold back, yet to keep moving. This was only the third time for him, and he had promised himself he would hold back by counting, thinking of numbers, as he was bad at math.

That's good, said Maggie.

He thought of the wrong number and lunged too hard. She cried out, dug her nails into the small of his back, so deep he could feel the blood. He stopped. His eyelids drooped, but he wasn't at all mean, he was just trying to hold it.

Okay, said Maggie. Now go.

He moved and moved in a trance of happiness. She moved with him underneath that tree and suddenly she lifted out of the pain. She was right at home with herself. She was Maggie. The owl had entered her body and she was staring out of its golden eyes.

FATHER TRAVIS forced himself to back the van from the Ravich driveway without laying rubber, to shift calmly from reverse into drive. Then he gunned it to Landreaux's house, jumped out, and knocked on the door. Emmaline appeared, shadowed by the screen. He tried not to rest in the cool shade of her gaze, her presence behind the mesh door. She said come in. He stepped inside. She stood too close to him. No, it was a normal distance. Any distance was too close.

What's happening? Is everyone okay?

Father Travis could not think of how to put words to the buzzing in his head.

They're okay, except I need to find Landreaux. He . . . Romeo . . . he had this idea or notion he's been putting together that Landreaux was, well, he was high when he killed . . .

No, said Emmaline, standing taller. He was not. Romeo makes things up.

She stood taller, stepped back from him. She made more distance between them. He wanted to cross that, step toward her, but wrenched back to stay focused on Landreaux. Emmaline read him. She folded her arms and drew into herself. Wisps of her being had dispersed and she gathered them abruptly in. In that moment she went back to existing as one with the father of her children. She was expressionless, waiting.

Romeo makes things up, she said again.

I know, said Father Travis. But he sounds convincing. He told Peter.

Emmaline's arms dropped away, to her sides.

Where are they?

I need to know where they'd go if they went out hunting.

Her eyes went a pale green and she knew what was happening.

Federal land, west.

Emmaline told him how to get there but she didn't ask to come along. She just stood there holding herself together.

☙

LANDREAUX APPEARS first to Peter's naked eye as movement, a faraway shift of greeny blur as he parts leaves. Then he gets Landreaux in his gun sights and watches. Peter's hands are cool and steady because they belong to the other man, the one who pictured doing this and did not, the man who split Landreaux's skull a thousand times chopping wood. The other man who dreamed what Peter is doing now.

Landreaux is still far away, stepping carefully along. He stops from time to time and pulls aside a branch, giving Peter a clear shot. When he sees that Landreaux isn't going to obstruct him, Peter feels the reason they were friends. He sees Landreaux's lips move and is glad that Landreaux is praying. The way it has to end feels right. An agreement signed by both parties. Witnessed by two sons. He lets Landreaux come close enough for him to take the infallible shot. Closer and closer yet.

There it is. Peter squeezes the trigger gently with his heart exploding. Nothing. He knows his rifle's loaded because he always keeps it loaded. He never did unload it and nobody knows where he hides the key—so he puts the crosshairs on Landreaux's third eye. Shoots. Nothing. Peter wills himself to pull the trigger again. But now his hand won't do it. Won't do it. Landreaux's face fills the sights.

Peter lowers the rifle but holds it close to him. He watches Landreaux still stepping wearily toward his death. From a human distance, now, Peter sees LaRose in Landreaux's solid, hip-slung walk. Funny, he never noticed. Then he sees more. Sees all he has kept himself from seeing. Sees the sickness rising out of things. The phosphorus of grief consuming those he loves. A flow of pictures touches swiftly, lightly, through his thinking—all lost things; then all the actual lost things: the aspirin, the knives, the rope, all deadly in Nola's hands. And the bullets deadly in his own hands.

LaRose.

The picture of those small capable boy hands now fills Peter. Those hands curving to accept the bullets. Loading and unloading his gun. And the ropes, the poisons. Those hands taking them from their places and getting rid of them. The missing rat poison, strychnine, the missing bleach. LaRose saving him now, saving both his fathers.

Well, Landreaux. Peter turns from the murderer. Landreaux doesn't need any help to die. Let him hoof out his dread alone. Let him walk. Peter will be the only one who knows he pulled the trigger. The knowledge engulfs him. There is a slough glittering in the new air. Peter walks to the edge, runs, hops, and tosses the rifle like a spear toward the sun-sequined water.

As it crashes in, he feels one moment of lightness. He lifts his arms. He holds his arms up waiting for the energy of absolution. Nothing comes. Nothing falls from the warm, sunny, ordinary sky except the same knowledge. He pulled the trigger. Nothing happened. He killed Landreaux. Nothing happened.

FAR OFF, down the broad county gravel road, Father Travis spots a small figure moving along the ditch. When he recognizes Landreaux, he feels the cold tension leave his arms. Weakness, so foreign he doesn't know what he is feeling, washes down his body, from his heart, draining his nerves. He pulls over and switches off the engine. His heart is still vibrating, his nerves on alert. Whatever happened, Landreaux is right there in front of him.

A dissonance in his thinking surfaces.

Along with his relief, there is a bizarre disappointment related to the fleeting thoughts that passed through his mind, rejected, but popping up again. Basically, what if. What if Landreaux was just gone. What if, well, it meant he was dead. Okay. What if Landreaux was dead. Forget what would happen to everybody else.

What if Landreaux was dead and Emmaline needed me now.

What if there was no Landreaux, just Emmaline, what if.

All along the road these thoughts had come and gone, but Father Travis had not reacted to them. It was seeing Landreaux, kicking along the road, shambling toward him, that made the thoughts real.

Not that he'd asked for the thoughts. Sure, he'd rejected and rejected, but the thoughts had come into his mind again and again. He clenched his hands on the steering wheel and lowered his head, shut his eyes. Everything was all right because Landreaux was alive, but he'd had those thoughts.

Who are you?

Father Travis addressed himself in a small voice, in a whispery voice. He looked up. Landreaux still walking toward him. Larger. Larger.

I could still run him over, said Father Travis to the windshield.

After a hopeless moment, watching the big man trudge toward him, Father Travis felt the wildness burst from a space below his heart. The sound came out weird. Like a jackal. Something in a zoo. He didn't recognize this sound he was making until it looped into a kind of laughter.

I could hit the gas!

He was still laughing when Landreaux got to him. When Landreaux opened the passenger door. Father Travis took a look at Landreaux's big ol' sad-sack face, exactly the face Romeo had described, and gave a sobbing guffaw. Slammed his hand on the steering wheel. Laughed and laughed.

Landreaux shut the door and kept walking.

He made it home around dark with questions still rattling in his head. Did Peter really try to kill me? Or was he just putting fear into me? Father Travis? Was it all a joke and what was true? Josette had put a wobbly tin fence up along the side of the house, and he caught his foot. Nearly fell up the steps. So maybe Emmaline, sitting at the kitchen table, thought for a moment he was drunk, but when he walked in she knew he was just clumsy.

Whatever the answers to the heavy questions were, he was weightless now. He'd got lighter and lighter all the way home until suddenly, at the doorway, he'd lifted off the ground, kicking off his shoes at the door. He went straight to her, bent over and put his arms around his wife sitting in the chair. She put her hand up and held his arm. The kitchen light was harsh. She closed her eyes and leaned back. He pushed his chin lightly along the crown of her head.

You smell like outside, she said.

She kept her hand on his arm, frail gesture. Hardly the way a woman treats her husband when she's become aware that it might be her cousin Zack who comes to the door. Hardly. Something, though. The hand on his arm hardly represented what had been their passionate marriage, their once-upon-a-reservation storybook time. She just held his arm. He leaned over her, his elbows on the back of the chair. Leaning wasn't much, when compared to how they used to push a chair under the doorknob in a cheap motel where the lock was broken. They used to think they were something special. Lucky. They used to say they were sure nobody else had ever been this happy, ever been this much in

540 · LOUISE ERDRICH

love. They used to say, We will get old together. Will
you still love me when I'm shriveled up? I will love
you even better. You'll be sweeter. Like a raisin. Or a
prune. We'll be eating prunes together. That's the way
they used to talk. But now they were tasting the goddamn green plums, weren't they. Bitter. What about
me? Will you love me? I don't know, it depends on
where you shrivel up. That's the way they used to talk.

Landreaux straightened up and got two glasses of
water. He sat down in another chair. Emmaline felt a
surge of fear that suddenly contained what might be,
could be, identified as possibility. She took a drink of
water and closed her eyes. She saw a slough thick with
reeds, muck bottom, tangled, both deep and shallow.
She saw the ducks batter their way across and up. She
saw herself, Landreaux beside her. She saw them both
wade in together.

WHEN FATHER Travis returned to the church
grounds, having spoken to Peter Ravich, having made
Peter read the coroner's report, the new priest was
there. He was wearing an elaborate medieval priest
outfit with chain for a belt and shoes that looked
like carpet slippers. He was from a newly formed

order. He was young, with a creamy complexion, apple-blossom cheeks, bright cornflower eyes, and corn-silk hair cropped to the skull. His voice was startling, high-pitched, but commanding of attention all the same.

I suppose you're Father Travis, said the new priest. A frowning flush mottled his cheeks.

I suppose I am, said Father Travis.

I am Father Dick Bohner.

Oh no, thought Father Travis.

I am your replacement, said Father Bohner.

You should go by Richard here, said Father Travis.

Dick is my name, said the new priest fiercely.

Of course it is, said Father Travis.

Things will be changing around here, said Father Bohner, flushing still more violently. Saturday mass should have started ten minutes ago.

You're late then, said Father Travis.

Father Travis walked away to pack his suitcases. He had come with two hard-sided Samsonite cases. Somehow, in the packing, he found that he had downsized. He had only enough to fill one suitcase. His cash, what there was of it, was in a bag behind a loose ceiling tile. He called Randall Lafournais, who drove down to Fargo every week, and arranged a ride with him. Father Travis decided to get off in one of the train stop towns, buy a ticket on the Empire Builder to Fargo, Minneapolis, Chicago, and then continue on east by train and south by bus to Jacksonville, North Carolina, and Camp Lejeune. He would walk down the boulevard among the memorial trees. He would visit the broken wall and touch the names engraved there.

As he was folding clothes, he realized that after all he had very little money. The phone rang. He let it ring and then pounced suddenly, brimming over, laughing:

Shit-broke soldier of God here! What can I do for you?

The person on the other end of the line was an Indian who laughed with him and hung up.

You love a woman you can never have, he thought, dropping the phone. Suck it up and deal. But his blood expanded and his heart seemed ready to explode. He sat on the bed, put his head in his hands. He thought again about the money. After a while he got up, stood heavily over his last few belongings laid out on the bed. He picked up the slippery blouse he'd asked Emmaline to give him, put it to his face, then added it to the suitcase. He snapped the suitcase shut. It was a heavy, dull red thing.

The Gathering

You Go

Josette and Snow wanted to give Hollis a big three-cake graduation party. For that, they decided that they needed a yard and a flower garden. Josette's English teacher said that she could have the classroom geraniums. Carmine geraniums. Today, Josette transplanted the classroom flowers and scattered the seeds of the marigolds, which Hollis had plucked last fall and saved for her. She also threw grass seed onto the pounded-dirt volleyball court. Snow had bought a hose for the outdoor spigot and she tried to water, but the seeds just swirled around in clumps.

I think you have to open up the dirt, said Coochy, looking at the whole thing critically.

We're hunter-gatherers by nature, said Josette. Farming's not our tradition.

Wrong, said Snow. Historically, we grew potatoes, beans, pumpkins. We had our own seeds and stuff. Invented corn.

We called it maize, said Josette, significantly. She paused. So we lost our traditions, then.

Just our family did, said Coochy. Lots of Indians have gardens. Grandma even had a garden. It was over there.

A verdant patch of weeds blew in the wind. Maybe there were flowers, but the girls didn't know what leaves to look for. They eyed the bare dirt mournfully.

Maybe we can bring out rugs.

No, said Josette. I want a lawn. God damn it. I'm going over and talk to Maggie. Her mom's got lawn magic. The least we could get is a lawn, right?

Dad and Mom know how to make a lawn, said Coochy.

They don't have time. Or the inclination, said Josette, a little pompously. She was always like that with Coochy, showing off her words, her understanding. He was her little brother, so she went on lecturing him.

It just isn't a priority for them. However, if we're giving an out-and-out celebratory barbecue for Hollis, we can't be mingling on a bare dirt volleyball court.

I getcha, said Coochy, watching her stride off on her strong, short legs.

Good-bye, Professor Headupyourass, he called.

Josette went the long way, the mile down the high-way, and turned down the Raviches' drive. The dog barked three times, then recognized Josette, and came to meet her, head down, butt wagging. Maggie was there with LaRose. They were out on the grass, crouching over with tools. When they saw Josette, they threw down the tools. LaRose ran to her.

Hey, said Josette.

She had never really visited, just picked up LaRose.

Come on, said Maggie, trying to cram down a smile. Let's go inside, get ice cream.

Actually, I wanted to ask your mom how to make a lawn.

They're gone to town. C'mon, we're hungry.

Josette followed them into the house. She'd never been past the front door. She looked all around, at the tan carpet, tan couch, at the brown and golden throw pillows, plumped and lined up.

This is where LaRose lives his other life, she thought.

There were old, polished, antiquey things. Heavy milk white pitchers. Carved wooden clocks and picture frames. In one of the pictures, LaRose and Maggie sat in front of Peter and Nola. They were dressed up and smiling—not stiffly but naturally, as though they had always been together. Josette passed her hand over a shining end table. Every piece of furniture was bare on top, or maybe had one decorative item on its surface. A glass horse. A series of dull green ceramic boxes, various sizes. The bookshelf had a few books arranged by what, color? All were stacked and aligned with exacting precision. The dining room table was bare. Not even a doily. The kitchen counters didn't have random bottles of medicine or bread bags or tools spread across them. Everything was contained in cabinets. Maggie opened a cabinet door, to get cones. Josette saw clear storage jars containing various shapes of pasta. At first the house was like a movie set. An ad in a magazine. Then it began to weigh on her. Maggie took a box of ice cream out of the freezer drawer of the refrigerator. Josette peered over her shoulder and saw that freezer bags of vegetables were stacked and labeled. Maggie made cones of blackberry swirl ice cream, gave one to LaRose. She refolded the tabs on the box, replaced it. Then she rinsed the scoop and put it into the dishwasher. Josette was holding two ice cream cones, standing in the kitchen, when she began feeling weird.

Can we go back outside?

They went out the sliding glass back door, sat on deck chairs. Down on the grass Josette saw a pile of wilting dandelions, and that the tools had forked metal ends.

What were you doing?

We have to get a hundred dandelions every day, said LaRose.

Not every day, said Maggie.

Seems like it, said LaRose.

How many do you have? Josette felt slow-witted. The concept threw her.

Oh, we have seventy-eight already, said Maggie.

Then what do you guys do?

She shrugged. I dunno. Throw 'em in the big weed pile behind the barn. Then more grow on the lawn. Some people poison them but Mom lets the chickens out here. Can we come over to you guys' house?

I like this flavor, said Josette. Won't your folks be mad?

I can leave them a note, said Maggie.

Well, I still need to know how to make a lawn, said Josette. How do I make a lawn?

I don't know, said Maggie. The lawn was always here.

Don't make one, said LaRose. I'm not forking dandelions at two places.

Want to help us make a party? Graduation party for Hollis? I was thinking barbecue. That's what the lawn is for.

Wish I could roll up this one, said Maggie. It never gets used.

Wish we could borrow it, said Josette.

She licked into the sugar cone, then ate the cone down to a tiny nib. The lawn was thick, green, soft-looking, like a blanket. Josette saw herself rolling it up piece by piece. She would carry the lawn over, light and airy, on her shoulder. She would spread it out behind the Iron house, take down the volleyball net, for a while at least. People would walk barefoot on the soft grass. There would be . . . oh, paper lanterns. All colors—coral, yellow, sky blue. Tiny lights inside of them.

You should wait for your parents, she said to Maggie. Come over later. Thanks for the cone. I've got to go.

Maggie didn't like it, but after Josette left she went to the yard with LaRose and stabbed the dandelions.

Why do people hate dandelions so much?

You always ask that, said Maggie.

You never have a good answer.

It's because I honestly do not know, said Maggie.

Dandelions are cheerful, and they try so hard.

I know, said Maggie, sitting back on her heels.

Let's go on strike.

Strike? You mean quit.

Yeah.

Maggie took her dandelion fork and his dandelion fork. She hefted them and threw them in the woods.

I think that's a good idea, she said, dusting off her hands. Let's go on strike!

Let's stop being grown-ups, said LaRose.

Josette walked back along the highway, her mind blurring out the image of the carpety Ravich grass. There was plenty of grass beside her, in the ditches, the new grass growing out of the dead grass. She thought of her house, where she could put something down and pick it up later, where Mom always bugged everybody to straighten up but still the shelves held a spill of books and papers, an eagle fan on a rectangle of red cloth, abalone shells, sage, tobacco ties, red willow baskets, framed pictures, a bird's nest, cedar, Disney figurines. Maybe it was too much. She walked down into the ditch, and then up to her scruffy gray house. She stopped. Surveyed her valiant little flowers. The classroom-toughened geraniums hadn't died yet. There were white violets dug from the woods, Johnny-jump-ups from her grandmother's flower box, some budding purple onion-smelling plant, chives. And the yard, oh well. Some weeds were growing in. She'd keep watering it. In the shed there was an old push mower. A gas-powered weed whacker. Dandelions were everywhere, and they were green, very green, and she'd let them grow until they touched leaves and grew together. She'd mow them too. Mow everything, she nodded, looking around the place and smiling. There would be splashes of color around the front door. It was the cake people came for, anyway, and she had that solidly covered. She and Snow were buying the cakes with their own money. One would be chocolate with white icing that said *Happy Gradua-tion*, with a frosting diploma that said *Hollis*. The next would be yellow cake with chocolate icing that said the same. The third would say *You Go!* and the frosting would be desert camouflage.

Dessert camouflage, said Josette when they ordered the cakes. Get it?

Groan, said Snow.

Their mom was going to a meat locker in Hoopdance where she could get the right cuts for slow-cooker bar-becue. Landreaux was sent around to borrow cookers from Ottie and Bap and random relatives. The frybread was coming from Grandma Peace. They would make the coleslaw, the potato salad, and Hollis said he'd get the ice and two big coolers. He'd get the sodas.

Don't tell Dad, said Josette. And get some diet ones.

Hollis was in on the planning now. He'd found out about the party just the week before. One of his friends at school had told him he was coming.

To what?

To your party.

What party?

Oops. Shit. Was it a surprise, man?

I don't know.

Along came Snow.

We were going to tell you!

Or maybe surprise you!

Josette said, We couldn't decide. We kept arguing about what to do.

God, said Snow. I'm so glad you know.

We were sure Coochy would let on.

No, Hollis had said, dazzled. I didn't know. A party.

Now he was in on the rest of the planning.

Should I, said Hollis. Can I . . .

What?

Invite my dad.

Oh my god, of course, said Snow.

He's already on the list, said Josette. We dropped off an invitation.

You guys made invitations?

Don't choke up, Hollis.

For a moment, Josette was her real self. Smart-alecky. Then she remembered that she might be in love with Hollis. Her voice went softer, studiously casual.

Yeah, we ran them off on Mom's school printer. They're just, you know, basic.

No, they're not, said Snow. She made them really elegant. She put all different fonts of lettering and RSVP and all of that.

Can I have one?

Sure, said Josette. You can check it out. I think I got everything right.

That's not it, said Hollis. I want one so I can frame it. I'm going put it up on my wall. Wherever I have a wall, where I end up next.

He trailed off.

Oh, just stay, said Snow.

Josette looked into his thin face, tried to say *yeah* in a casual way, but her voice scratched out in her throat and she turned the sound into a cough. Why did this happen to her, always? This leaping joy? Then this sudden clutch? She tried to laugh it off but her laugh snagged in her nose, became an ugly snorting hack like a crabby old man's. Could it get worse? Snow was looking at her with a *get it together* expression. Hollis was embarrassed for her, staring at the side of the yard. She took a deep breath. Dignity. Dignity please.

Sorry about that. Allergies. Of course you should stay.

Then she looked straight at Hollis again and all her heart came into her face. If he had not been so polite, trying to make like he didn't notice her honk. If he had just turned back in time to see the look on her face. He would have known. He would have known in all certainty. Her love was pouring straight out of her eyes. But he was still staring at the yard when her expression froze, then neutralized. He was thinking, *Maybe I can grow some grass there, in those bare spots. Maybe she would like that.*

⚜

JOSETTE WANTED to make a medallion using tiny, faceted beads, but so far she had only managed to bead a circle about the size of a dime. Snow was working on a pair of moccasins, and on a quilt, which she helped her grandmother sew in strips every so often just to see the quick progress of a thing. They had a soft cutting board, a razor-sharp cutting wheel, and a big plastic fabric guide. Making long strips of cloth with one razor swipe was satisfying. Mrs. Peace was sorting, as she did endlessly, through her tins of letters and papers. She was surprised to have received an extremely cordial answer from the historical society, which had changed names and venues through the years. The president had promised to look into the matter of the first LaRose.

Because of that law, said Snow. Museums have to give us back our sacred stuff, right? And our bodies. Native Graves and Repatriation. I did a report.

So macabre, said Josette, chasing the tiny beads around a jar cap with her needle. Snow didn't even mark out the word as on the latest vocabulary quiz, because they always used interesting words now. They were known for it.

I want her back, murmured their grandmother. She can rest down the hill with her family. We'll get LaRose her own lantern.

Oh no, I have to rip this out again.

Josette slumped over and rested her head on the table, beside the cigar box of beads.

How come I suck at this? What kind of Indian am I?

She sat up, threw down the circle of plastic and Pellon with the tiny circle of unevenly stitched beads.

Don't do that, Snow said, retrieving it. You'll lose the needle. Grandma will sit on it. Snow took her sister's beadwork, plucked up beads with the end of the needle, and began quickly connecting them, adding circular rows of copper, gold, and green. Relieved, Josette watched the circle enlarge.

You're so good at beading, she said comfortably. I like to watch you.

You picked hard beads to use, said Snow. Cutglass 13s.

Josette touched her sister's added circles.

So perfect. Makes me sick.

Snow wagged the circle toward her, and Josette flinched away.

Keep going! Please!

Snow took back the medallion, the size of a quarter now.

After she'd beaded a few more rows on, she glanced at Josette and asked who the medallion was for. Josette didn't answer. The sewing machine whined as Mrs. Peace put her slippered foot to the pedal.

Dad? Coochy? LaRose?

Thanks so much, said Josette to her sister, holding out her hand. I'll take it back now.

Oh, sweet! It must be a surprise for me. Snow held the medallion out of Josette's reach. You're such a good sister! Making me a present! Awww, ever cute. I don't deserve this!

For sure you don't, shouted Josette. Give it back!

Is it for Hollis?

Josette snatched the circle and pricked her finger. She began to bead again, then dropped the medallion and put her finger in her mouth.

See now? You made me bleed on it.

Ooooo. Old-time love medicine.

Bad medicine!

Mrs. Peace lifted her foot from the sewing pedal. She snapped her thread against the cutter.

You don't drop woman's blood on a man's belonging, she said.

Mmmm. Snow wagged her eyebrows at Josette. Miigwech for sharing that wisdom, Nokomis.

So Grandma, said Josette, poking her needle laboriously in and out. I thought only moon blood could hurt a man's things. But it's all of the blood inside our womanly bodies?

Oh, what do I know. Mrs. Peace shrugged. I was a teacher in the whiteman schools. New tradition rules come up all the time. You'll laugh. Sam says to Malvern that she should wear a skirt to ceremonies so the spirits know she is a woman. Okay, says Malvern, soon as you wear a diaper thing, a breechcloth, or keep your pecker out so that the spirits know you are a man. And while you're at it, you men should go back to using bows and arrows and walk everywhere you go. These traditions? You'd have to ask Ignatia-iban, but she's off in the spirit world.

Mrs. Peace said this with energy, and waved her arm at the window as though Ignatia were off on a vacation enjoying herself.

So, a medallion for Hollis, said Snow. Does that mean . . .

We ever talked that way? No. But maybe I want to do something special for him. You got a problem with that?

Course not, said Snow. Here, let me help get that next color on.

Again, Josette surrendered her work and watched her older sister straighten out the beads and add more.

Can we put a movie on, Grandma?

You got one of those mechanical people movies?

We're so psyched, said Snow. We found *Terminator* in the sale bin.

Mrs. Peace crowed. Make my day!

That's Clint Eastwood, said Snow. He plays real guys. And he's ancient.

Not to me. He's just a pup.

You like Arnold, too.

Arnold's in it? I'll be back.

Yes!

They recited the lines and didn't have to look up to watch it, although at key sections they glanced at the screen and meditatively drew their threads across the scored and crosshatched block of beeswax. The wax strengthened the thread.

Don't forget to make a mistake, said Snow to Josette, you know, to let the spirit out.

Only the Creator is perfect, said Josette dutifully. You think bleeding on my beadwork is a mistake enough? Or that I got two rows out of place already?

Snow examined the medallion.

You're covered with the Creator, she said, handing it back.

What a relief. Josette put her two fingers up. Me and Gizhe Manidoo. We're like this again.

I've got this question in my mind, said their grandmother. Which husband is Ignatia-iban out two-stepping with in the spirit world?

Why would she pick one of her husbands, said Josette, when she had so many other ladies' husbands to choose from?

Not to mention the unattached ones, either, said Snow.

She had a few, agreed Mrs. Peace.

What about you, Grandma?

Josette and Snow flicked glances at each other.

Oh me, said Mrs. Peace. I stayed faithful to your grandfather all my life.

They were quiet, out of both respect and pity. But still, Josette was curious.

Why did you stay so faithful?

Oh, I wasn't so good—I was just tired of them. Men. They're stressful. You'll see.

We already know that, said Snow, who still kept her disappointing wrestler boyfriend's hoodie on a hook in the back of the closet.

On the way back home Snow and Josette stopped to pick up Maggie. The girls went through the kitchen grabbing carrots and ranch dressing, then into their bedroom with the bowl. Snow drew the flimsy little bolt across the door frame, and they all felt private. She settled on her bed, graceful as a doe, wound her long hair in her fingers, curved herself around her long legs, and chomped a baby carrot.

Mmmmm? Her mouth was full of carrot but her face was serious.

Maggie looked up at the ceiling. Snow and Josette had been odd in the car on the way over, not jokey or at ease. Something was going on with them. Josette cleared her throat, but started coughing and fell over pounding on the bed, laughing until her fit stopped. She was wearing tight jeans. She jumped up, peeled them off, put on sweats. So maybe things were okay? But Josette spoke suddenly.

Hey Maggie, are you doing the thing with Waylon?

Well, yeah, said Maggie, relieved that was all it was.

Having full-on sex, said Snow, to make sure.

Maggie said, Errrrrr.

As your protective older sisters, said Josette.

Right, said Snow.

We want to make sure you are taking precautions. Like, he's using a thingy?

Duh, said Maggie.

For reals, girl.

No, said Maggie.

If he's giving you love, he gotta wear a glove, said Snow.

Above or beneath, he gotta wear a sheath, said Josette.

If he's spoutin' crude, he gotta cap his dude!

If you're gonna rock, make him wear a sock!

Snow and Josette were becoming hysterical.

Oh my god, you guys! Stop!

Maggie put a pillow over her head and rolled away from them. After a moment, Josette stopped laughing and tugged away the pillow.

That's not all either.

Maggie groaned and threw herself on her stomach.

Come on, trust us, said Snow. Do you know what to do?

Course, said Maggie.

Theoretically or in reality?

What do you mean?

I'm talking doctors, methods, ways, you know, contraception and all. Do you know how to get it?

Course not.

Aww, honey.

Snow and Josette held each other's gazes.

First off, said Josette, me and Snow are having a little talk with Waylon.

No!

Just a heart-to-heart. He's got to know we don't let him mess around with our little sister unless he knows what to use. Then he's gotta wait and we'll figure out where to go—I mean, you probably can get in at IHS. There's this one doctor who just lives to fix you up with the right method. She doesn't want this high school momma shit happening. Besides, do you know how risky it is—what did she say—for a young girl to have a baby in a rural health care delivering system? Yeah, that's what she said. We went to her. Well, Snow did when she was with Shane. Not me. I'm not in a mature relationship, right? But this doctor, she's here on and off. We know how to get you in. You've got your future to think about, Maggie. You hear?

He had a whole bunch of sex before you, said Snow. You have to make him get tested, too.

He said only three times!

Okay, well, can you see me rolling my eyes to the heavens?

Maggie turned over and gave up.

Can I get the shot?

If you wanna gain thirty pounds.

How about the yoood?

What are you talking about?

The iiiiyooood.

The iiiiyooodeeee?

Maggie nodded.

Wow, said Josette. We're starting ground level.

Matchless convenience, said Josette. But mostly they give it to grown-up ladies.

How about pills?

Are you good at taking pills?

Yes, said Maggie. But I don't want my mom to find them. What about that cuppy thing?

Technically, a diaphragm. Not a hundred percent. And you want to be batting a thousand against Waylon. His brothers and uncles . . .

No blanks, said Snow. I'm thinking maybe the pill. You can use my prescription for now. Just be sneaky— plus the condom? Always the condom.

That's, like, over a hundred percent coverage.

I'd go with that, said Snow.

HOLLIS SET out chairs, put away random lawn equipment, plastic bats, things that did not belong. He moved along swift and light, doing anything they wanted. The party, for him! He raced around. Taking directions. A graduation party. He still didn't know how to feel. His morose dark vibe was definitely compromised. He caught himself smiling. His party was the weekend before school graduation. Everyone was having their parties then, or the week after, and everyone was also making the rounds. Hollis's party was on Sunday in the late afternoon—just the right time to catch everyone all partied out from the night before, needing hangover soup and more food, but not the kind of crowd that would stay all night. The photos of the graduating seniors had been published in the newspaper. Everybody knew whose houses were having parties. They would have endless guests and guests of guests. You never knew how many people. So far they had borrowed ten Crock-Pots, and Emmaline had scored a case of Famous Dave's BBQ sauce, sell-by date elapsed.

Barbecue sauce never goes bad, right?

Never!

Famous Dave was a cultural hero, a successful barbecue entrepreneur Ojibwe guy with chain outlets.

Emmaline had plugged the slow cookers into every kitchen outlet, laid the big pieces of beef chuck inside, covered them with sauce, and set them on low overnight. On party day everybody woke smelling the overpowering barbecue smell. It wasn't, somehow, a wake-up smell. They opened the windows. Landreaux separated the barbecue meat with two forks and kept the cookers on. By the afternoon, it would be perfect. Emmaline had already made the meatball soup and frozen it. There would be a meat soup, which the old people preferred.

The weeds, constantly mowed, now resembled grass, and there was even grass, quack grass, an unkillable type of grass. The yard was bounded by plastic fold-out tables, borrowed from Emmaline's school. There were lawn chairs, powwow chairs, folding chairs. Over on the side of the yard, they placed a pop-up arbor that Emmaline said was an investment. There would be four more graduation parties, after all, in the coming years. Josette spread Coochy's worn Power Rangers sheet on the food table, then took the sheet off, refolded it.

Not festive.

Emmaline said they could use her flowered queen bedsheet.

Josette was extremely touched.

But Mom. People will spill stuff. Your best sheet will get ruined.

I'll soak it after.

No, I'll use your sheet for the card and gift table.

Josette folded and refolded her parents' bedsheet, smoothed it onto the folding card table. She draped her own plain purple-red sheet on the long rectangular fold-out food table. Barbecue sauce would hardly show. They used the Power Rangers sheet wrong side out for the salad table. Josette stood back, cocked her head to the side. The tables had a gracious effect, standing there, legs hidden. She imagined where the food would go. Crock-Pots on the purple table, extension cords plugged into extension cords, running into the windows of the house, keeping the meats on low. Bread would go beside the meat in the big aluminum bowls, buns still in their plastic bags so they'd stay soft. She'd bought the sesame seeded ones. A little extra. There were also regular salads, macaroni, lettuce, and her own semifamous potato salad.

The day before, she had made Hollis and Coochy peel two twenty-pound sacks of potatoes. She had cut them into bite-size chunks and boiled them, not too soft. Overnight she had let the big dishpans of potatoes cool and marinate in oil, vinegar, salt, pepper, and diced onions. She had left them in the basement, on top of the washing machine, covered with clean dish towels. Now Josette left off planning and brought the cooled-off potatoes upstairs. Carefully, she stirred in mayonnaise cut with enough mustard to give that jazzy goldeny color. But not too much mustard flavor. She diced a couple of jars of pickles, stirred them in too. Snow had hard-boiled a dozen eggs, plunging them into cold water so they didn't grow green fuzz on the yolks. Over the bumpy yellow surface of the big green, orange, and blue plastic bowls of salad, they now laid the sliced eggs, then stippled the eggs with shakes of paprika. Josette plucked up one potato that was sticking out. Ate it. Nodded at the dishpan of salad with a slow, sage frown.

After the boys put out the coolers of pop, covered with coins of bought ice, and the big pot of wild rice and the cardboard box of frybreads, after the choke-cherry jellies were opened, and the knives, spoons, and forks were set out in coffee cups, after the plastic bags of hamburger buns were opened and ready and then the potato salads, the bowls again covered with dish towels, Josette and Snow carried out the sheet cakes. They had turned out so well! The raised lettering was crisp in the sugar icing. The frosting diploma was perfectly curled at either end. The swirled tans in the camouflage icing looked exactly right. Josette had matched the pattern to Hollis's uniform without letting him know. But she had changed the words. She had taken off the *You Go*. The cake had no words because there were no words.

She was keeping track of North Dakota Guard units: the 142nd Engineer Combat Battalion had entered Iraq at midnight on April 27. She was pretty sure that they were in charge of patrolling the roads for I.E.D.s.

Snow and Josette arranged cakes on the end of the two food tables, next to a vase of fresh lilacs. There was a large knife, napkins, paper cake plates. A spatula for each cake. They stepped back, looking at everything. They wouldn't take the plastic covers off the cakes, or cut them, until they had been admired. Until the honor song was sung. Until after everyone had made their speeches, congratulating Hollis.

The guests parked on the dirt drive, then the grass, then the not-grass, then along the main road. The high school kids kept coming because everybody liked Hollis and knew his family would throw a big feast, lots of food. Cases of beer in the trunks of their cars, they came, the girls with graduation cards for Hollis. Mrs. Peace and Malvern arrived, driven by Sam Eagleboy in his low-slung maroon Oldsmobile. Zack came, off duty. Bap drove Ottie, and Landreaux strode out to help unfold Ottie's wheelchair from the trunk and get him settled into it, under the awning in the backyard, with the elders, where they could watch the milling young people.

Don't put Ottie near those pretty young girls, said Bap. They'll try and take my man.

Ottie touched her hand.

The young people's parents were arriving. Their younger brothers and sisters came too, tumbling out of the cars to race toward the snacks. Peter, Nola, and Maggie walked over to the house. Peter quietly shook hands all around. He got Nola a folding lawn chair. They sat together near the arbor, in half-shade at the edge of the yard. Soon the dog ambled up and settled down, leaning incrementally closer to Nola's ankle until he touched and she let him stay. She had decided to come to the party. Strictly speaking, it did not make sense. Yet there was someone here with Nola's body, voice, name. Soon she was eating a plate of barbecue with a dog warm along her ankle. Peter wiped sweat off his temples, giddy with effort. Compartmentalizing on such a high level was a strain. But Landreaux had invited him, not a word about what had happened. Was it some kind of traditional Landreaux thing or did it just mean that now life should go on? Maggie put their graduation card with the twenty-five-dollar check into Hollis's basket. Then she went behind the tables to help her sisters dish out the food. After a while, Nola saw the husky boy who helped them now with farmwork sometimes. Waylon stood next to her daughter.

He bent over, said something. Maggie shot her eyes up to him and put down the spoon.

I see, thought Nola. I know.

She understood herself and, in some ways, she understood her daughter.

Romeo was suddenly at the party now. Maybe he had parked far down the road, or hitched. He sat with the old people. Sam Eagleboy was talking about Mission Accomplished. Romeo said that Bush had looked okay in the jumpsuit, then his voice changed. A Hopi mom had died first—where was acknowledgment of sacrifice? The humility?

The old people stared at him, and nodded.

Hundred-day war, said Romeo.

All of a sudden he felt like he might faint. How odd. He rose and ghost-walked over to the edge of the yard and stood looking off into the deep green woods. That is our home, he thought, where we came from. And now we are living high on the hog. And our young boys are once again fighting for what used to be the enemy flag. Don't have to scramble around for irony, or meat. There's Crock-Pots full, and all that other food. There is Landreaux, whom I nearly got killed, so I must be satisfied with that. And Emmaline who knows I almost killed her man and so, now, will never love me. But Hollis. Hollis, whom it was a far better thing I did to let him go. But here he is, all grown up, and I have swum through my days until recently when I became aware. Too aware. My job making something out of me. And the pain in my body strangely as I move around beginning to subside. As though I've been cranked up wrong ever since Landreaux fell on me and by throwing myself down the church steps, I am starting to get cranked around right.

For he had risen from the church steps, Romeo, risen like one dead and walked alone, without pain, without his old familiar enemy, down the hill. As the days went on the bruises had healed. They hadn't hurt much, well, because he had some prescription left, but then. Nada. He needed less. Then almost nothing. Something shocking—it was as if his bones were slowly shifting, inside of him, back into place. Over thirty years before, Landreaux had crashed off a Minneapolis bridge support; in landing violently he had crushed the right side of Romeo's body. Two weeks ago, Romeo had thrown himself down a wicked series of concrete steps, landing on his left side. Then he'd gotten up and it was a miracle—flat-out. Nobody there to witness, nobody there to pity him, and, sadly, nobody else around to be thoroughly impressed. Somehow the fall had not killed him but fixed him, pushing everything all back

together. That's how it felt. A mysterious inner alignment was occurring. Romeo was increasingly calm
right down the center. He could even balance with his
eyes closed, sign of a healthy mountain climber.

Past him, around the elders, not noticing that the elders or her mother noticed them, intent only on themselves, Maggie slipped with Waylon into the woods.

LaRose was given an eagle feather and an abalone
shell containing a ball of smoking sage. He went
around smudging the food. He brushed the holy
smoke over the electric cookers, casserole dishes,
cakes, the tables, and the basket of cards. He went
around to the elders, who pulled the smoke over their
heads, as did his sisters, and Hollis. Then the sage was
ash. LaRose made a plate with a taste of everything,
even a secret corner of cake, and a pinch of tobacco.
He went down the side of the yard and stepped off
into the trees, put the plate down at the base of a birch
tree. He stood beside the tree, staring through new
leaves, toward the spot he'd fasted, where Dusty and
all of the others had visited him. LaRose didn't know
what to say to them, if they were out there. Oh well,
he'd treat them like regular people.

You're invited, he said in a normal voice.

When he returned, the yard around the house was crowded with people talking, filling plates with food, laughing and laughing, like, well, a bunch of Indians. So many people were eating that all the chairs were taken, then the back steps, the front steps. Towels were laid out on top of the cars so girls wouldn't stain their flouncy skirts with car dirt. People stood talking with plates of food in their hands, eating and eating because the food was top-shelf. Everybody said so. Top-shelf. People brought random offerings, too. Loaves of bread. Packages of chips, salsa, cookies.

When it was time for the cake, Hollis was called forward by Landreaux. Then Hollis went into the crowd, over to the edge of the yard, and stood before Romeo.

Yeah? said Romeo.

Hollis took his arm.

Me?

Come on.

As Hollis walked Romeo up to stand with him at the cakes, Romeo knew, just knew! It had been written in his life that someday he would be walking on air. Now here he was, floating up to the front of the gathering. Everything was passing by him slowly. He could see every detail. The tucked-in shirts. The girls in bright dresses, yellow, pink. And here he was, walking past them beside his son, just regular. No twisted lurch. Before the tables, he stood, aligned from the soles of his feet to the top of his head, beside his son, not hunched over. Did people notice? They must have, but nobody commented. Romeo felt it strongly, though. Rooted, he was rooted right there. He was smiling, maybe, put his hand to his face to feel if that was true.

Ordinarily, at this moment, they would have asked Father Travis to say a prayer. Nobody had thought of asking the new priest. People resented having been assigned a priest named Father Bohner. As if, where else could he go? And you couldn't call him Father Dick. It wasn't right.

Emmaline stood on the other side of Hollis. Her eyes were fixed on Landreaux in a neutral way, not exactly warm, but not with the usual bitter impatience. Josette noticed.

Landreaux sang an Honor Song. His voice was innocent and full. As always, his voice warmed people. Then he asked Romeo to say a few words.

The thing to do at that moment was to speak from the heart. Romeo froze. People always said *speak from the heart.* What would that even mean? Speak from the squashed flask, the dead shoe, cheap cut of meat pulsing in his chest? Speak from the old prune of crapped-on hopes? Well then, be brief. Romeo blinked in panic. He shambled a few steps forward and put his hand on his jaw.

So he . . . Romeo nodded at Landreaux.

So I . . . Romeo nodded at Hollis.

Not much good as a father, said Romeo. Me. Not much good as a mother. Some people don't have an alternative. His voice gathered a little strength.

No alternative to being humble, said Romeo. Because I don't know how to do stuff right. I just grab what I see. That's how I am. So when Emmaline . . .

Romeo ducked his head in Emmaline's direction.

So when Emmaline and my old teacher, my young teacher, haha, Mrs. Peace over there, and so when Landreaux. They took in my baby and they brought him up. And here he is. A graduate here. Romeo's voice box was shutting off. He closed his eyes.

I don't have much to offer, as a person. People say I am a waste and that's being generous. But I was surprised to get a job this year. Even more surprised I kept it. Don't fall down in a fit now, for shock, now, I banked the money.

Romeo reached into his back pocket, took out a brown plastic checkbook. He held the checkbook in both hands, and leaned over with a ceremonial bow.

He offered the checkbook to Hollis, who in surprise accepted it.

There's three thousand in there, he said to Hollis. I live a slight kind of life. So here you can start off to college. Quit the National Guards, my boy.

Hollis stepped forward and put his arms around Romeo, and as the two hugged, Romeo heard people clapping.

Well, fuck me, thought Romeo, after the hug stopped and he stepped back. His faucets were going to burst.

His mom would be so proud, said Romeo all of a sudden, loudly, throwing his arms wide.

Hollis was looking at his father in concentration.

Who was she?

Charisma with a K, Lee with an i. Karisma Li.

Karisma Li? That sounds like a . . . Hollis was about to say name of an exotic dancer, stripper, but he stopped, perturbed.

Yes, said Romeo, I lost her to a Ph.D. program at the University of Michigan.

Let's eat the cake now, said Josette, touching her mother's arm. No more speeches.

Wait!

Sam walked smoothly forward holding out an eagle feather. It was a mature golden eagle tail feather, beaded at the base with leather fringe swooping down.

The most handsome feather I ever seen, hissed Malvern. He sundanced with that there feather, Sam. He dressed that feather up for Hollis.

Sam faced Hollis and said a prayer in Ojibwe. Everybody shushed everybody. The people who understood Ojibwe couldn't hear, but now Sam was talking straight to Hollis. LaRose was listening as hard as he could.

As he listened, the floaty feeling of being with those other people came over LaRose, and he felt them come out of the woods. They wandered up and stood behind him. He felt their sympathy and curiosity. As he felt them move closer, LaRose noticed that the colors of the clothing that the living people wore sharpened and brightened. Yet he heard each word that the other people said distinctly, though all together it was a babble. He watched as they moved together and apart, frowned or laughed, in a dance of ordinary joy that kept moving and vanishing as soon as it happened, and moving again. More of the transparent people came walking out of the trees and stood with the others. Dusty wanted some cake. LaRose told him go ahead, and he walked over and got some cake. Nobody noticed Dusty was there except the dog, and perhaps Dusty's mother, who turned in his direction and smiled in a perplexed way. The old-time woman with the feather in her hat said, *You wait, they are going to get a package and it will be my time-polished bones.* Ignatia walked slowly, but without the oxygen now. Two women he did not remember said, with amused affection, *That Maggie. Watch out for her.* Others spoke about how Hollis and Josette made such a good couple and how Ottie had one night told them to stand by the gate. He would be over there soon. Just look at him. He's on his way. They sat on chairs made of air and fanned their faces with transparent leaves. They spoke in both languages.

We love you, don't cry.

Sorrow eats time.

Be patient.

Time eats sorrow.

Josette served up the first piece of cake.

This is the most beautiful cake ever, said Hollis, his voice scratchy with emotion.

Wait! Wait for the cake song!

Oh no, said Josette. Cake song?

It was Randall, who had come late, but made his way straight to the front to stand with Landreaux. He had a hand drum and a big grin. Randall and Landreaux began to sing a song about how sweet the cake was, all full of sweetness like the life before Hollis, like the love everyone had for Hollis, and the love that Hollis felt for his people. It was a long-winded song and Hollis stood there in front of everyone, feeling a little foolish, holding his piece of cake, nodding, serious but filled with the happiness of the moment, though awkward, the sweetness, smiling along with the song.

Anyway, said Josette, edging around the table, still holding her cake spatula. You can quit the National Guard now, right?

No way, he said, surprised. I signed the papers.

Oh, Hollis.

Josette was staring straight ahead, standing next to him, and her voice was the voice of a woman.

Acknowledgments

Rita Gourneau Erdrich, my mother, mentioned an Ojibwe family who allowed parents enduring the loss of a child to adopt their child—a contemporary act that echoes an old form of justice. Thank you, Mom. Thank you, Dad, Ralph Erdrich, for thirty-five years of National Guard drills. Thank you, Persia, for teaching Ojibwe immersion to a new generation of LaRoses; Pallas, for your close readings and constant cheer; Aza (see below); and Kiizh, Nenaa'ikiizhikok, Sky Woman, for calmly fixing our world. Thank you, Richard Stammelman; Dr. Sandeep Patel; James and Krista Botsford; Brenda Child; David Gizinski; Preston McBride; Jin Auh; Terry Karten, my editor; and Trent Duffy, my copy editor.

My grandfather Patrick Gourneau, Aunishinau-bay, attended Fort Totten Indian Boarding School and Wahpeton Indian School. All his life, he wrote in his trained and beautiful script. Aza Erdrich used his boarding-school handwriting when she designed the cover of this book. In doing this, she connected us all with her great-grandfather and his great-aunt, our ancestor, the original LaRose.

About the Author

LOUISE ERDRICH is the author of fifteen novels as well as volumes of poetry, children's books, short stories, and a memoir of early motherhood. Her novel *The Round House* won the National Book Award for Fiction. *The Plague of Doves* won the Anisfield-Wolf Book Award and was a finalist for the Pulitzer Prize, and her debut novel, *Love Medicine,* was the winner of the National Book Critics Circle Award. Erdrich has received the Library of Congress Prize in American Fiction, the prestigious PEN/Saul Bellow Award for Achievement in American Fiction, and the Dayton Literary Peace Prize. She lives in Minnesota, with her daughters, and is the owner of Birchbark Books, a small independent bookstore.

HARPER LUXE

THE NEW LUXURY IN READING

We hope you enjoyed reading
our new, comfortable print size and found it
an experience you would like to repeat.

Well – you're in luck!

HarperLuxe offers the finest in fiction and
nonfiction books in this same larger print size and
paperback format. Light and easy to read, HarperLuxe
paperbacks are for book lovers who want to see
what they are reading without the strain.

For a full listing of titles and
new releases to come, please visit our website:

www.HarperLuxe.com